# BLOOD KIN

# BLOOD KIN

A Novel

## Marjorie Dorner

WILLIAM MORROW AND COMPANY, INC.
NEW YORK

It is the policy of William Morrow and Company, Inc., and its imprints and affiliates, recognizing the importance of preserving what has been written, to print the books we publish on acid-free paper, and we exert our best efforts to that end.

Library of Congress Cataloging-in-Publication Data

Dorner, Marjorie.
    Blood kin / by Marjorie Dorner.
        p.      cm.
    ISBN 0-688-09531-3
    I. Title.
PS3554.0677B57   1992
813'.54—dc20                                                    91-43482
                                                               CIP

Printed in the United States of America

First Edition

1  2  3  4  5  6  7  8  9  10

BOOK DESIGN BY M & M DESIGNS

For William Jacob Dorner (1943–1963)
This one's for you, Beej.

As usual, I want to thank Judith Weber for her invaluable advice during the draft stages of this book. I also want to thank Mary Borgen for her expertise on Minnesota adoption history and Minnesota adoption law; James Forsyth, J.D., for his legal expertise; Donald Morris, M.D., Winona County Medical Examiner, for his expertise on forensic evidence; and Kathy Mahlke for her skill and speed in preparing the manuscript.

# BLOOD KIN

# Prologue

Kate Lundgren stopped her own car behind the gray Thunderbird, which was parked in the street as it had been the last time she'd seen it. She glanced up at the house; the front windows were dark and the garage was closed. As soon as she stepped from the air-conditioning into the darkened street, she felt the clammy heat close on her like a fist. It had been almost 100 degrees this afternoon, with 85 percent humidity, and now, at ten-thirty, the temperature was still above 80. This street of small, modest houses, which she had seen for the first time only a week ago, was familiar now. The trees, the widely spaced streetlights, the driveways and hedges, all of which looked friendly enough in the daylight, were somehow foreboding, almost sinister, in this oppressive darkness. Many of the nearby houses were dark, too, she noticed—vacation season, national holiday.

Passing her hand over her wide forehead where sweat was already beginning to form, Kate started up the walk, turning her head to look at a car that seemed to be passing much more slowly than the speed limit called for. She watched it as it turned right at the next corner and went out of sight—a black (or maybe dark blue) Mercury Cougar. She'd found herself taking note of passing cars lately, trying to see if there might be one car that kept reappearing. For more than a week, she'd had a creepy feeling of being watched, followed.

On the porch, she rang the bell, waited, rang again. When there was no response, she knocked—pounded, really. After a few minutes, Kate began to feel exposed, vulnerable. She seemed to be the only living creature out of doors, and her position on the raised platform of the porch made her visible from almost every point on the street. She shuddered with distaste at the sensation of a fine trickle of sweat running down her spine.

"Damn you," she said softly to the door. "Damn you for shutting me out."

She left the porch and walked to the side of the house; at the back, a small window facing the driveway glowed with a weak light—no more than a twenty-five-watt bulb. Heading toward the light, she started down the driveway, staying in the center, well away from a tall hedge that separated the drive from the neighboring property.

At the back of the driveway, there was an opening about four feet wide between the end of the hedge and the garage. Here, Kate paused, squinting into the shadows. To get into the backyard, she would have to go through that opening; it seemed somehow like a waiting mouth. The light from the street was dimmer here, throwing shadows in vague patterns across her path. The silence now that she'd stopped made it seem that the night was holding its breath. Kate found she was doing the same thing, and she swallowed, made herself take a few quick gulps of air before she started forward again.

As she approached the opening, the hedge seemed suddenly full of shadows that hadn't been there before, seemed about to erupt toward her in threatening motion. She wasn't the sort of person who was easily spooked, but now she found herself very close to panic. She pinched her eyes shut for a second, took another breath, and then plunged forward. A branch brushed against her forearm, and she spun around, backing up against the side of the garage, her eyes bulging. Before she could move again, there were two sharp, explosive sounds—*crack! crack!*—that pushed the air out of her lungs in a muted scream and made her duck into a crouch. It was only when two more of the sounds reached her, exaggerated across the open expanse of backyards, that she knew what they were—

firecrackers. Somebody in the neighborhood was jumping the gun a little on the holiday—the Fourth of July was tomorrow. Kate knew from her own childhood experience that no amount of legal prohibition could keep fireworks out of the hands of private citizens—midwesterners believed it was their God-given right to blow their fingers off if they wanted to.

By now, sweat was pouring off her face and her heart was slamming. Her impulse was to run, to head straight for light and safety. But she made herself wait, calmed herself—it was only firecrackers, only a hedge, only a backyard. Finally, she stood up straight, pressed her shaking hands against her sides, and walked to the back of the house. A shallow porch led to a door, and next to that was a window glowing with an even fainter version of the light she'd noticed in the side window. When she put her face to this window, she could see that the light source was beyond the kitchen over a door that might lead to the cellar. Beyond that hall space to the right was the living room, most of it hidden from view, but she could see dimly one side of a tweed easy chair.

Someone was sitting in the chair, someone whose left arm was visible along the dark surface of the upholstered chair arm. It was a pale, fat arm with no sleeve in sight. She turned now to the door, raised her right fist, and pounded hard and long; the edge of her hand ached from the impact. Then she put her face to the window again, cupping her hands next to her eyes to prevent distracting shadows. Whoever was in the chair seemed not to have moved. Could anyone be sleeping so soundly that such a racket would go unheeded? Kate straightened and put her hand to the doorknob; it turned easily, a muffled click came up to her ears, and the door swung inward, pulling Kate with it.

The air trapped inside the house was even hotter than the outdoor temperature, and now it poured out past Kate's face, bringing with it a strong, sickly sweet smell. Even as she was beginning to turn her face away, she realized that the smell was familiar. Several summers ago, the freezer in the basement of her home in White Bear Lake had broken down without anyone noticing for more than a week. When her mother finally lifted the lid to take out some of the beef that was kept inside, this was the smell that had filled the house.

# CHAPTER 1

It was on the morning of Tuesday, June 26, that Kate Lundgren got her first good look at the house at 642 Franklin Street. She had sat in her car for two and a half hours, watching the neighborhood come to life: the paper boy flinging his deliveries against porches and doors; women in robes coming outside to pick up the papers; small children with the rumpled look of recent sleep racing toward backyard swings; men with lunch pails climbing into cars and station wagons, leaving for whatever shifts began in Woodard, Minnesota, at 7:30 or 8:00 or 8:30. But the house at 642 Franklin Street remained quiet, nothing moving behind the front windows, which flanked its narrow door like two half-closed eyes.

Kate didn't know what she was supposed to be feeling under the circumstances, wasn't aware of any particular feelings at all. For five days, she'd been just numb—no doubt a reaction from the violent emotions that had swept over her like a series of summer storms during that time. Yet, the moment she had come here to face—the moment she had willed and now meant to force—was one she'd anticipated for more than six years. So why wasn't she more excited? she wondered. Why this dull, formless apprehension? She should have gone to the door long before now, rung the bell, said firmly to the woman who answered the door, "Hello. I'm Katherine Lundgren. I'm your daughter."

She'd imagined the scene thousands of times, considered every possible reaction—stunned surprise, incredulous denial followed by realization; she had even imagined anger or fear. But all of her scenarios ended the same way, with joyous acceptance, an embrace, tears, excited talk. Perhaps, she thought now, it was the possibility that her fantasies could all be wrong, false, illusory, that kept her here in the car and froze her limbs.

Kate couldn't remember a time when she hadn't known she was adopted. Doug and Sheila Lundgren were the enlightened variety of adoptive parents, letting their two children know as soon as they could understand such distinctions that they had been "chosen," were "special gifts," because Mom and Dad had waited so long to get them. Indeed, Kate had spent a charmed childhood, as had her adopted brother, Eric. She'd felt so loved, so secure, that she really believed being adopted had it all over being born into a family in the usual way. She'd felt not offended but merely puzzled when playmates used the word *adopted* in negative ways. Her friend Lynn Grunnert, resentful of her domineering older sister, would jeer in Kate's presence, "You're adopted, Peggy; that's why Mom loves me better." Temperamentally quiet and unassertive, Kate had never challenged these thoughtless slights.

Swept through her childhood in the whirl of school, dance lessons, summer camps, children's concerts, and vacations on Cape Cod, it had never occurred to Kate to think of herself as deprived in any way. In fact, she'd never noticed that, somewhere along the way, her parents had stopped alluding to adoption, had simply begun to speak and behave as if the Lundgren family were just like every other family in the way it had got its children. Yet, in a deep way, Kate had sensed the message in this silence: Reminders of her adoption caused her parents discomfort, even pain. So she, too, affected a surface indifference. Though she never wholly repressed her history in her own mind, she gladly embraced outward behavior that would spare the mommy and daddy she loved.

But adolescence changed all that. What had been reserve and thoughtfulness in the child became brooding in the teenager. And most of her brooding was on the secret issue of her identity. Whenever she found her parents stodgy, overprotective, or "uncool" in any way, she would conjure up in her mind the perfect woman who was her "real" mother. Young, certainly. Doug and Sheila had explained to both children that their birth mothers had been unmarried teenage girls not capable of raising a child, so Kate imagined her birth mother as still quite young, sort of like an older sister. And very "with it," of course. Somebody who would never forbid hair dying or ear piercing or string bikinis. Somebody now established in a career, maybe an actress or a dress designer, who would have a downtown apartment, furnished in funky splendor.

But the growing preoccupation with her birth parents was fueled by something deeper than typical adolescent longing for the ideal parents. More and more, Kate began to *hear* the patter by which most families reinforce and affirm connectedness. "When Jessica was a baby, I thought she looked just like Rob," Aunt Laura would say, "but now that she's growing up, I can see my own sisters in her—Bekka's eyes, for sure, and Patty's chin. She's got Rob's temperament, of course—had it straight from the womb." And Kate would stare at herself in the mirror, thinking, Who do *I* look like? Where does my singing voice come from?

Grandma Larson would talk about how her own grandmother had come to America from Germany in 1860 on a crowded ship, making a mattress during the passage out of the bundle of handmade table linens her mother had given her to start a new household in Wisconsin. And Kate would feel left out, would try to imagine some kinfolk of her own making their way to the New World. But from where? What marks of their own culture did they carry with them, what tokens of their heritage? She knew that, except for her light brown hair, her looks owed little to the Nordic types who peopled the ranks of Olsons and Larsons and Lundgrens. Among them, her dark eyes and raked cheekbones seemed exotic. Who *was* she, then? It became an echo at the back of all her other thoughts—"Who am I?"—sometimes faint, sometimes thundering, but always there. She began to ache from the vibrations of that echo. But she didn't talk about it to anyone. The silence had become an internalized code by this time and she would have felt treacherous voicing her questions even to her best friend at school.

But, by the time she turned seventeen, the internal ques-

tions were deafening and Kate finally worked up the courage
to confront her parents. On the evening of her birthday, she
asked them if she could begin the search for her birth parents.
She'd rehearsed the speech carefully and delivered it calmly
because she didn't want to hurt them, didn't want them to feel
threatened. She tried to explain that her need to find out about
herself had nothing to do with them, with any inadequacy in
them. She loved them and they were her parents—that wouldn't
change. But she *had* to know about her beginnings, *had* to find
out to whom she was connected by blood.

But she could tell from the look on Sheila's face that she'd
miscalculated; the pain in her mother's eyes was clear. Kate
realized that Sheila—in a kind of wishful thinking—had interpreted her daughter's long silence as indifference to the whole
question of her roots. So now this was a real shock. They talked,
all three of them, until two the next morning. Finally, Kate
agreed to the conditions set down by her father: She would wait
two more years, until she was nineteen, the age Minnesota law
said an adoptee could begin a search without the consent of the
adoptive parents. In return, Doug and Sheila would support
her fully at that time in conducting the search—providing both
emotional and financial assistance.

But the next two years had not been easy—for anyone.
Kate was willing to admit now, at twenty-three, that she hadn't
been a very nice person at seventeen or eighteen—moody, re-
bellious, smart-mouthed. Sheila was especially targeted because
Kate had always realized that her adoptive father would say yes
to anything his kids asked him; it was their mother who was
responsible for discipline, for setting limits. Controlled, careful,
overprotective Sheila. By her nineteenth birthday, Kate understood vaguely that the problems she was having with Sheila were
standard issue in the relationships of teenage girls with their
mothers: the daughter trying to break away and find her own
identity, and the mother reluctant to let go—all boringly
normal.

But in Kate's case, it was exaggerated by the issue of adoption, by the continuing obsession with finding her roots. She
would read everything she could find about the successful
searches conducted by other adult adoptees and then leave the
articles lying around where her parents could see them; it never
occurred to her that publishers were interested only in the

happy endings, and so the impressions she was getting from this reading were necessarily skewed. There was some relief from the skirmishing when Kate moved into a dorm at Carleton College in Northfield, but vacations at home always seemed to stir up the tensions again.

Yet Sheila and Doug had kept their promise. During the spring break of Kate's freshman year, a month after her birthday, Sheila had gone with her to the adoption agency. There Kate added her name to the list of adult adoptees seeking their birth parents. The agency immediately cross-referenced her data with the list of parents searching for now-adult children they had given up for adoption. There was no match, so the easy solution Kate had hoped for wasn't available. But the agency counselor agreed at once to try to locate the birth mother to ask if she also wished a reunion. That part hadn't taken long; within two weeks, the agency called Kate in to tell her that they had found her birth mother, but that she had refused contact. To Kate's stunned protests, the counselor had explained that the agency was legally bound to protect the privacy of the birth mother; there was nothing more they could do.

Kate had appealed to her parents, who got their lawyer to file a petition with the court in Minneapolis that had finalized her adoption, a petition filed "pursuant to Minnesota Statute, Section 259.31," which would allow the opening of the original birth records "for good cause." The judge denied the petition, arguing that the agency had been able to provide the nonidentifying information that—"as far as was known at the time of the petitioner's birth"—there were no medical or psychological problems with the birth parents that might "significantly threaten the well-being of the petitioner."

The next three years had been filled with a series of frustrating legal appeals so debilitating that Kate had to put in an extra year of college before she finally got her degree. Affidavits were filed; petitions were resubmitted. Finally another judge agreed to hear the petitions for disclosure, but insisted on another contact with the birth mother first. Kate's hopes soared. Surely the only reason they were still separated was that her birth mother didn't know how eagerly she was looking for her. Less than a month later, the judge convened a brief hearing to tell Kate that her birth mother had filed an "affidavit for nondisclosure": She was formally trying to block the unsealing of the records. Her response, he said, was "unequivocal," and therefore he must deny the petition.

Kate had stumbled through her last year of college, using every chance to pester her father for more help. It was only that her birth mother had never seen her, she argued; once they were face-to-face, she would relent. Would he hire a private detective? There must be clues a detective could follow. But her parents were united on this one: They had done what could be done, and now she should respect the wishes of the other party to the contract. Her schoolwork was put on automatic pilot, but she got through, almost on reflex. When her graduation arrived, she'd fallen short of the honors she might have gained if she'd been able to concentrate, but her records were respectable, nevertheless.

Jason Donnely, her boyfriend of two years, finally despaired of getting her attention and broke off the relationship. "I've tried to be patient," he'd said. "I understand why you would have a real curiosity about your birth parents, but I don't understand why you're so intense about it that you can't pay attention to anything else."

"Curiosity?" Kate had responded, pouncing on the word. "Is that what you think it's all about? Just some idle mental game? Curiosity! You don't understand a goddamned thing about it."

By the time she'd finished, she was screaming at him. Poor Jason. She knew it wasn't his fault. He knew who he was every minute. He had his father's jaw and his mother's eyes and his grandfather's knack with tools, all of which he took for granted like the beating of his heart. At Christmas, he never even heard his pregnant sister's chatter: "I'm not too scared about the birth because Mom always had such an easy time delivering us and the doctor says daughters are pretty much like their mothers in that way." But Kate had heard it, her ears tuned to such talk, and she had wondered, What will it be like for me? What was my own delivery like? No, Jason couldn't understand what it was to have no precedents.

So, college over at last, Kate had come home this summer in a deep depression, had sat around the house like a zombie. She knew she was scaring her family, but she couldn't make herself care enough to alter her behavior. Doug and Sheila finally offered a trip to Europe as a way to cheer up—she could take her college roommate along at their expense. Wouldn't that be fun? How could she make them understand that she and Janet didn't have much in common anymore? Janet had gone on without her into the land of the grown-ups, was engaged to be married. Kate knew, intuited in some profound way, that she herself was held in childhood, her emotional development retarded, almost, by the mystery of her birth. But she was too dispirited to argue. The annual late-June visit to the Lundgren grandparents in Chicago, though, was not something she felt up to. In past years, both Kate and Eric had been expected to stay an extra week so they could socialize with their cousins; Eric still complied with this expectation, but Kate had long since rebelled. And this year, despite Sheila's vigorous objections, she refused to go along at all. Ironically, it was her one effort to snap out of it while her family was in Chicago that precipitated the storm.

She decided to apply for a passport and went to her father's desk to look for her birth certificate. Of course, she'd seen this document, had asked to see it when she was still a little girl, already knew that it contained no information that was useful to her. In Minnesota, "corrected" birth certificates were issued for adopted children, and these certificates named the adoptive parents as the child's only parents. Family papers were kept in the bottom right drawer of the desk; there were brightly colored folders piled inside a steel box that Doug believed would survive fire; she knew that a red folder was labeled "Katherine" and a blue folder was labeled "Eric."

Kate meant to lift the box out of the drawer, but it was so surrounded by papers that she simply pulled out the whole drawer and set it on the desk. She was about to lift the cover on the steel box when she noticed a thin envelope, upside down with the address away from her, between the paper lining and the outer wooden surface of the drawer. It had obviously been deposited there unintentionally with the opening and closing of the drawer. Kate slid the envelope out now and turned it over. Its return address was "Faeger and Dresbach, Attorneys at Law." Louis Faeger, she knew, was her father's lawyer. The postmark was so old that Kate couldn't resist her curiosity about this long-forgotten letter. She pulled a thin sheet of stationery out of the yellowed envelope and opened it.

It was just a short note, addressed to both of her parents.

It said, "I strongly advise against any further contact with or direct payment to the child's mother; these might later be construed as collusion. Let me handle the hospital expenses as we agreed at the outset." The letter was dated March 1, 1968, just three weeks before Kate's birth. She stood with the letter in her hands, staring at the words, trying to absorb the shock of what they meant, what they certainly must mean. When the realization came, it was like a blow to her stomach; she actually bent double, her held breath rushing out of her lungs in a deep moan. Then she stood up and left her father's study, the drawer still on top of the desk, the steel box unopened next to it.

And she waited for Doug and Sheila Lundgren to get back from Chicago. She waited for two days, not eating, hardly sleeping, her shock turning to rage. She stormed around the house, all alone, shouting at her absent parents. But by the time they returned on Sunday night, her rage had calmed into a steadier, quieter fury, and she met them silently in the front hallway. Pale and disheveled, she simply handed the letter to Doug, watched his face as he read it, and then turned it over to Sheila.

"Where did you get this?" Doug asked, pale under his new tan. "I thought I threw all this away long ago."

"Does it really matter where I got it?" Kate said, her voice so tight that she barely recognized it herself. "Is that all you can think of to say?"

The scene that followed was horrible; even after two days, Kate could hardly bear to think about it. Sheila wept; Doug tried in a broken voice to explain. They *had* known her birth mother, had arranged the adoption while the girl was pregnant, had paid the expenses of the prenatal care and the birth.

"We were so desperate to have a child," Doug explained. "We thought the agency would never give us a referral."

"I was thirty-eight," Sheila sobbed, "and your dad was forty-two. We were so afraid that the next time we heard from the agency, it would be to tell us that we were too old to ever get a child. And afterwards, I was so terrified you would be taken away from us, that she would just show up on the porch someday to tell you, 'I'm your real mother.' I didn't want you to have to deal with such a dilemma."

Kate had kept a stony silence through most of this. Now she said in an icy voice, "You were just thinking of me, is that it? Or were you thinking of yourself? Were you scared of who I might choose if I got a choice?"

Her mother looked at her in silence, fright stopping her sobs. Kate felt relentless by now and, almost from habit, she aimed her fury at Sheila.

"You got Daddy to buy you a baby, just like a new set of golf clubs. I've learned enough about the law these past few years to know that what you did wasn't legal twenty-three years ago, so it had to be done with lots of money. And you weren't about to let anyone else lay claim to your property, were you?" She was beginning to shout. "I begged you for help in finding my natural parents, and you just went on lying to me. You even pretended to help me search, paid for all that legal stuff when you knew all along who my mother was. What a farce! You think you can buy anything, don't you? Buy off the truth, buy a human being, buy a child's love."

Doug, ashen and trembling, interrupted. "That's enough, Katherine. You know that isn't fair, and it's just your way of hurting us because you're angry. We did it together, your mother and I, and we did it because we wanted a child to love, because we had so much love to give. Now you apologize to your mother."

"I'd have to find her first." Kate said the words in a flat, venomous voice.

Sheila sat down quickly on the chair behind her, as if driven there by a sudden blow to the stomach. And Kate had felt instant regret, almost panic—the rush of terror that always swept over her when she realized that her sharp tongue had gone too far. But to apologize would be to blunt her anger, and she wasn't ready to do that yet. Into the long silence that followed, she finally said, "The only words I want to hear from either one of you are my mother's name and how to find her." Then she walked out of the living room and went upstairs to her room. For a long time, she sat staring at the wallpaper and curtains that she and Sheila had picked out together four years ago when Kate had decided that the old decor was "too kiddish." Then she got out her suitcase.

The next morning, she walked into the kitchen where her entrance stilled a quiet conversation between her parents; they were in night clothes, but it didn't look as if they'd slept much.

"Well?" Kate said. She'd put her suitcase in the car and was wearing her traveling uniform of jeans, a print blouse, and deck shoes.

Without a word, Sheila stood up from the breakfast nook, reached into the pocket of her robe, and pulled out a piece of paper. She held it toward Kate, who finally looked into her mother's face. Sheila looked ravaged, her eyes puffy and red-rimmed, her usually neat hair awry. The figure that normally looked so fit and lively was now huddled, her shoulders raised under her jawline as if she were preparing to dodge a punch. She looked old.

Kate crossed the kitchen and took the paper from her mother's shaking hand. She was surprised by a sudden impulse to take hold of that hand, to steady it, to give it a squeeze; if Sheila had spoken, said, "I'm sorry," she might have done it, but the moment passed. The paper was folded many times into a tiny square, and Kate fumbled a few seconds in opening it. In the center of the paper, written in Sheila's neat, rounded handwriting, there was a name and address:

> Teresa Cruzan
> 642 Franklin Street
> Woodard, Minnesota

So now, on the morning of June 26, Kate was sitting in her car, staring at a house. Her suitcase was in a room at the Holiday Inn on the other side of Woodard. Her graduation gift money—from Grandma Larson, Grandma and Grandpa Lundgren, Aunt Helen and Uncle Bill, Uncle Charlie—was wadded up inside the canvas bag on the seat next to her. Yesterday, on the two-hour drive to Woodard, she'd thought about the name on that piece of paper. What kind of a name was Cruzan? Teresa was a nice name—"lovely," as Sheila would say. But Cruzan? Slavic? Bohemian? After she had checked into the motel, she found the phone number and tried to work up the courage to dial. When that effort failed, she'd asked directions to Franklin Street and driven past the house several times—no lights on, garage closed.

After an almost sleepless night, she'd driven here again to watch the neighborhood wake up. At this moment, she could think only about the moment that was coming. Face-to-face at last. After six years of planning and hoping—more years than that of fantasizing. So why couldn't she feel anything? And why couldn't she make herself get out of this car?

Now a movement caught her eye—a figure, blurred by sheer curtains, was moving behind the glass in the front door of 642 Franklin. The door swung inward and a woman stepped onto the porch. She was tall, slim, wearing a red silk bathrobe with a Chinese dragon on the left side embroidered in gold thread. When she stooped to pick up the newspaper, the robe gapped slightly, showing a flash of pale, slim legs. Masses of tangled brown hair, worn long like a teenager's, obscured her face. She turned back into the house, revealing an even larger gold dragon on the back of the robe, and closed the door. It had taken six seconds.

Kate sat very still. My mother, she was thinking, trying out the words almost as if she were speaking them. Could that slim, girlish person across the street actually be her mother? Kate's instant impression was that the woman was in her twenties—certainly no older than thirty—but she knew from previous experience that she was not the best judge of other people's ages. Of course, she told herself now, she should just get over to that house, ring the doorbell, and find out up close who the woman in the red bathrobe was.

But she knew, deep down, what had kept her in the car so long, what had pulled her hand back from the phone last night, what was freezing her now: Twice, when approached by officials who said, "The child you gave birth to on March 20, 1968, would like to be reunited with you," Teresa Cruzan had said no—unequivocally.

# CHAPTER 2

$I$t was nine-twenty and Kate had finally made it to the door, had raised a shaking finger to the doorbell—once, twice—before actually pushing it. She clutched her bag against her stomach, resisting the impulse to run. At last the door opened and the woman in the red bathrobe stood before her, no more than three feet away.

Kate stared, wordless, unable even to open her mouth. Up close, the woman no longer looked like a girl; there were fine wrinkles around her eyes, faint frown lines at the top of her nose, extending upward from thick brows. And, this close, there could be no mistake about who this was: almond-shaped, dark brown eyes; raked cheekbones; narrow, tapered nose; full mouth with the bow tips of the upper lip pointed rather than rounded, like adjacent triangles; long, slanting jaw with the hint of a dimple at the point. Completely devoid of makeup, the skin of the face was pale, milky, almost flawless. For Kate, it was like looking into a mirror. The hair was darker, the whole face wider at the temples, shorter in the forehead, but the resemblance was nevertheless striking.

Kate was watching the expression, saw it go from mild curiosity to puzzlement to dawning recognition. The woman in the doorway took a step backward; her mouth had gaped open and her head was moving slowly from side to side, but her remarkable eyes remained fixed on Kate's face.

"Teresa Cruzan?" Kate whispered.

There was no response.

"I'm Katherine. Kate. I'm your daughter."

The woman let go of the door now and stepped backward once more; her slim arm fell to her side and she nodded slowly.

"Yeah," she breathed. "I can see that. I can see it."

"May I come in?" Kate asked, terrified that the next movement from Teresa Cruzan would be the closing of the door.

There was a long pause. Kate saw the woman's confusion, her apparent struggle to absorb what was before her; she had raised one long hand to her throat, and Kate could see that hand rising and falling with the woman's quickened breath.

"Could I please come in?" Kate whispered.

"Sure," the woman said at last. "Come ahead." And she turned her back on Kate to walk away into the house. Was she trying to compose herself? Kate wondered. Decide how to act? Kate followed the receding golden dragon down a narrow foyer into the living room.

"Sit down," Teresa said, swinging around suddenly and pointing at a chair. The stunned expression was gone now, replaced by a guarded look, eyes hooded and even suspicious. Kate sank into the indicated chair, and Teresa lowered herself, without looking around, onto a floral-print sofa. "How did you find me?" she said at last.

"My mother—" Kate started and then broke off, flushing. "Sheila Lundgren gave me your name and address," she finished, sitting forward and looking intently at the disheveled woman opposite her.

"Well, well, well," Teresa said slowly. "Did she really? How did that come about?"

"I found a letter," Kate began again, almost at a loss to explain it all. "Well, let's just say I found out they knew all along about you, about who you were. I made them tell me. I was trying to find you for years and they kept lying to me, but when I found out they knew, they gave me your name."

"I know you were trying to find me. That guy from the adoption agency called a few years ago and then there was that judge last year. I told them I didn't want to be found. Didn't they tell you that?" Her voice had hardened, but her eyes were still wide, dilated, and she kept them fixed on Kate as if she were mesmerized.

"Yes," Kate murmured. "They told me. But I didn't know why. I wanted to ask you why. There's so much I want to ask you."

Teresa Cruzan sprang up from the sofa, a movement so sudden, so full of coiled energy, that Kate jerked back in surprise.

"Look, honey," the older woman said. It was the way a tired waitress might have said "honey" to a young customer who couldn't decide between a chocolate or a strawberry shake. "I got my reasons. I got my own life here."

"I know," Kate said quickly. "I don't expect you to change your life for me. I don't want to be an intrusion." She'd rehearsed this speech, was almost relieved to be able to make it. "And I know this must be a shock for you right now, but I'd just like to find out some things about me, about my roots."

Teresa Cruzan began to pace—lithe, gliding motions like a dancer, with her long arms folded tightly in front of her body, pushing her small breasts up and forward.

"Look," she said, stopping at the farthest end of the room from Kate. "I can't do this. It's too much all at once, you know what I mean?" She wasn't looking at Kate while she spoke.

"Are you asking me to leave?" Kate could hear the horror in her own voice. "Can't I stay and talk to you?"

"Not right now," Teresa said in a strangled voice. Her arms were so rigid that it looked as if she were trying, literally, to hold herself together. "I told you, it's too much for right now."

"Then I'll come back later," Kate said, her desperation making her rush the words. "Can I come back later today, after you've had time to—" And here she faltered, uncertain as to how to characterize what she hoped for. Should she say, "time to calm down," "time to think it over," "time to accept me"?

Teresa Cruzan was looking at her now, the dark eyes luminous. She opened her mouth, closed it again. Finally, she loosened her arms and threw one slim hand up at the ceiling.

"All right," she said. "Later today. Come back about five."

Kate felt a rush of relief, could feel her face breaking into a smile. For just a second, she thought she saw an answering smile in the mirror image opposite her, but then Teresa Cruzan looked away, gave a quick shake of her tangled hair.

"I suppose I could feed you," she said. "Yeah, come for supper." And she moved toward the front door, a clear signal for Kate to rise.

At the door, Kate turned back toward Teresa, who was clearly not expecting the motion because she stepped backward quickly. As if, Kate thought, she's afraid I'll try to touch her.

"I want to thank you," Kate said, stumbling over the words.

"Why?" The woman looked genuinely puzzled.

"For agreeing to see me," Kate answered, stepping out onto the porch. "And for the invitation to supper, too."

"Sure, sure," Teresa said, not looking directly at her. "No problem."

"So I'll see you at five, then—" and Kate broke off with the inflection still in midair.

"What?"

"I don't know what to call you," Kate said, hanging on to the door frame, breathing shallowly.

"Oh, that. You call me Terry, of course." And a trace of a smile played over the wide mouth. "Everybody calls me Terry."

In the car, Kate realized that Terry hadn't asked, "And what should I call you?" Only *one* of the things she hadn't asked. Kate put her head down on the steering wheel, her eyes pinched shut. The counselors at the adoption agency had warned her: "Be prepared for disappointment if and when you find your birth parents; they're usually not what you expected, and their reaction is seldom what you fantasized it would be." Stupid advice! How could anyone prepare for this?

At five minutes before five, Kate was back at 642 Franklin Street. She had got dressed up: The denim skirt was a little wrinkled from being packed, but it was clean and new; the blouse was light blue silk. Her pale hair was freshly washed, and she'd been careful about her makeup—subtle shades of rose and beige, a touch of pink lipstick.

When Teresa answered the doorbell, Kate was stunned by her transformation. Her hair was pulled up into a cluster of curls at the crown of her head. Her face was painted—there was no other word for it—in garish makeup. Hoop earrings dangled almost to her shoulders, and metal bracelets jangled as she closed the door behind Kate. She was wearing a halter top that exposed her midriff, flared shorts, and high-heeled sandals of the variety that, Sheila had often said, "walked toward sailors all on their own." Even while she was thinking the words, feeling ashamed of herself for it, Kate was struck by the irony: She would probably spend the rest of her life thinking in phrases she had picked up from Sheila Lundgren.

At the living room doorway, Kate almost collided with a tall man who was on his way out. She gasped in surprise and stepped back to let him pass.

"This is Max," Terry said from behind her. "He was just leaving."

Kate looked up into a tanned face, dark eyes, brows knitting into a frown under a shock of dirty-looking brown hair. He was wearing a stained T-shirt, low-slung jeans, boots. He looked to Kate to be about forty years old.

"Hello," Kate murmured, averting her eyes as the face above her turned from scowl to penetrating stare. He leaned forward, bringing his face and the smell of garlic alarmingly close.

"Well, who's this?" he said in a low, growling voice. "You been holding out on me, Terry?" He wasn't looking at Terry, though; his menacing face was still pushing toward Kate, as if he were willing her to look him in the eyes.

"Never mind who she is," Terry said calmly, stepping between Kate and Max. "She's not gonna be here long enough for you to care about who she is. Now you run along."

The tall man cuffed Terry on the side of the head as he passed her, a gesture meant to look playful, but Kate could see the earrings jump.

"I'll be in touch, kid," he said and sauntered to the front door. There he turned to take another long look at Kate. This time, she tried to return the gaze, but faltered and looked away. There was something creepy about the man—sinister.

When Terry had closed the door behind him, she led the way through the living room to the kitchen, offering not a word of explanation about the encounter. Kate followed in silence, noticing for the first time the furnishings of the house. Striped draperies, floral-print sofa, tweed chairs—in good condition, comfortable, but not in particularly good taste. The kitchen was papered in a bright print; the table and chairs were high tech, chrome and Formica. The table was set for two. Everything looked clean, as if quite recently polished, dusted, swept.

"You want a drink or something?" Terry said, turning to look at her. Her face wore a challenging expression, as if she were saying, "What do you think of your mother now?"

During the walk through the house, Kate had time to form a horrifying thought: Could Max be her natural father? He was about the right age; if Terry had become pregnant at fifteen by an eighteen-or nineteen-year-old boyfriend, he would now be forty-one or forty-two.

"Is Max your boyfriend?" Kate mumbled, too embarrassed to keep looking at the other woman.

Terry made a snorting sound through her nose, tossed her hair. "Not likely," she said. "No, honey; he's not my boyfriend. And his name isn't even Max. That's just what we call him. He's a business associate of mine." She said "business associate" as if she were reciting a line in a play. "You want something to drink or not?"

"A Coke," Kate said. "Any kind of soda, I guess."

Terry busied herself at the refrigerator, making a lot of noise with ice, glasses, jangling bracelets. When she handed over the Coke, she avoided Kate's eyes. She had poured a beer for herself.

"Well, sit down, sit down," she said, positioning herself against the countertop, leaning back and crossing her ankles.

Kate sat on the edge of the vinyl chair, put the drink down without tasting it. She was staring up at Terry, thinking that the resemblance she'd found so striking this morning was obscured by all that makeup.

"Will you tell me about—" Kate paused. "About my adoption?"

"Sure," Terry said with another toss of her head. "That's easy. I was fifteen years old and pregnant. Not much chance in this town to do anything about it, not in those days. My father had a fit when he found out about it, but then one day he came home and said his boss wanted to adopt a baby. Didn't your folks tell you about this stuff?"

"Some of it," Kate replied. "Not much." She was ashamed to admit that her rage had cut off all but the most cursory explanations from her parents.

"Well," Terry went on, taking a sip of beer, "your dad owned a warehouse here in Woodard in those days, and my old man managed it for him. Pa told me your folks wanted a kid real bad. So I met with them a few times. They seemed nice. I thought Mrs. Lundgren was a real lady. So I agreed to let them have the kid—" She broke off, blushing beneath the heavy makeup. "To have you, I mean, after you were born. That's all there is to tell."

"And they paid your medical expenses, did they?" Kate asked.

"Yeah," Terry answered, looking away again. "The hospital bills and stuff like that."

"That's all?" Kate insisted; she had been brooding about this since Saturday. "No other payments?"

"What does that mean?" Terry flared. "You think they bought you or something? Well, that's crap. I wouldn't have just *sold* you, even if they'd offered to pay, which they didn't. Just the medical stuff."

"But you couldn't have just handed me over," Kate said, leaning forward over the table. "That's not legal. I was placed by the agency and I was six weeks old when my parents—when they got to take me home. That's in my documents. They got me from foster parents."

"Sure, sure," Terry said impatiently, standing up straight and beginning to pace. "I know all that. I gave you to the agency, all right, and they put you with that other family for a while. But your folks were already approved by the agency; they were on a waiting list. I told the agency counselors that I wanted my baby placed with a certain kind of family. Nowadays you get to make all sorts of conditions because there aren't so many babies for adoption, but even then, the counselors would listen to real strong *preferences*." She emphasized the word with her voice. "Your dad's lawyer wrote up that stuff about the family I wanted and I memorized it. I guess there was only one family on that agency's list that fit the description, huh?"

"I guess so," Kate murmured, sitting back at last. "But wasn't that illegal?" She remembered the warning in the note she'd found in Doug's desk.

Terry shrugged elaborately. "Beats me," she said. "I don't know about that stuff." She stopped in her pacing, looked down at Kate. "It worked out great for you, didn't it? Look at you. You're well off, smart, well dressed. They were good to you, weren't they? Well, weren't they?" Her voice was challenging.

"Of course," Kate answered. She couldn't think of any way to make this woman understand that this issue seemed irrelevant to her at the moment. "Of course they were good to me," she repeated, "but I want to know about you. There's so much I want to know about you."

"What for?" Terry said, her long jaw coming forward. "You got nice parents, a good home, a great life ahead of you. What do you want to hang around with somebody like me for? Why do you want to know about me? What's to know?"

Kate ignored the "why" part for the moment. "What's to know?" She repeated Terry's words incredulously. "What do you do for a living? What do you like to do for fun? Did you ever get married? Do I have any brothers or sisters? What are my grandparents like? Are there uncles or aunts? How can you ask me, 'What's to know?' " She was close to tears, and had carefully left out one of the most important questions: Who is my father?

"Okay, honey," Terry sighed, but she still looked exasperated. "You help me get this supper on the table and I'll try to field some of those questions. But you gotta know I'm not the kind of girl who spills her guts so easy. I got my rights to my privacy."

"I know," Kate said softly. "I'll try not to push too hard. But I've wondered about these things so long."

"So long," Terry repeated with a wry, weary smile. "What do you know about 'long'? You're a baby."

They worked together to put the cold meal on the table—shrimp salad, garlic toast, slices of melon. This was obviously something Terry had worked over.

"Eat, eat," Terry said across the table because, after ten minutes, Kate hadn't done much more than push her food around on her plate and take an occasional sip of her Coke.

"I guess I'm too nervous," Kate said. "Too excited. I don't feel very hungry. I'm sorry."

"Cut out that apologizing junk," Terry said, pushing her own plate away from herself. "Okay, listen up. What do I do for a living? This and that. Not much for very long—nothing you could call a career. Right now, I'm on vacation. For fun I like to dance, listen to music, play poker sometimes. You got no brothers or sisters because I never got married and I don't make the same mistake twice." She seemed not to notice Kate flinch at the word *mistake*. "Now, what else did you say? Oh, yeah, grandparents. They're both dead now, the old man in 1972 and Ma in 1980. They were all right, I guess. Old-fashioned, but not mean or nasty. They just couldn't handle kids very well—too old, I guess, when they started having us. My brother, Bob, ran away into the navy when he was eighteen, couldn't wait to get away from here. Oh, yeah, so I suppose he's your uncle, huh? He lives in Arizona someplace and the last time I saw him was at Ma's funeral."

Terry fell silent now, taking a long sip of her beer.

"And that's it?" Kate said finally, looking back at the face opposite her, a face that looked older with all that makeup than it had in the morning, when it was well scrubbed, vulnerable. "There's nobody else to tell me about?"

Terry stood up from the table with another of those sudden motions that made Kate jump—so much tamped-down energy releasing all at once. She turned with the glass in her hand toward the counter. Her back was to Kate when she spoke again. "No, nobody else. That's the whole family. Bob's got no kids either."

"I didn't mean that," Kate said, staring at the narrow back. "What about my father? Who was my father?"

Without turning around, Terry said, "I know what you meant." She was speaking quietly, as if she had prepared carefully for this moment, was concentrating on control. Now she turned to look at Kate.

"I've never told anybody about that," she said evenly. "Not my folks, not the doctors, not *your* folks. Oh, your mother wanted me to tell. 'We'd like to tell the baby someday about its background, just in general,' she said, and I didn't have to give the name, just what nationality, what education—stuff like that. But I never told anything about him at all to anybody. And I'm not gonna start now. So let's just drop it."

"I can't just drop it," Kate responded. "And I'm not just anybody, am I? I've got a right to know because his blood is going around in my veins."

"Where do you get this 'right to know' stuff?" Terry said, stepping forward so fast that the hoops in her ears swung violently. "Other people got rights too, you know." Her voice was losing its controlled quiet, the tone rising in pitch and volume.

"You got a good life, like I said before. Why do you want to go screwing around in other people's lives?"

"I don't want to hurt anybody," Kate replied, setting her own jaw. "But my life can't be really good until it's complete—until I know everything there is to know about who I am."

Terry laughed now, a short bark without much mirth. "And you think knowing who you are is as easy as finding out a name?" she said. "Live a few more years, kid, before you start talking about 'everything there is to know about who I am.' God! How can you know that until just before you get ready to croak?"

"Was he married?" Kate asked; she was starting to get angry. "Is that why you never named him? Because you thought it would wreck his life? Does he even know about me? Does *he* have other kids? You answered only for yourself when I asked if I have brothers and sisters."

Terry faced her for a long moment in silence. Kate didn't know what to make of the series of expressions she saw passing over the older woman's features. There was something especially in the eyes, so like her own, that seemed suddenly hesitant, softened, as if everything that had come before was some sort of an act, and the real Teresa Cruzan was now peeking out. But she finally shook her head slowly back and forth and pressed her lips tightly together.

"Why can't you tell me?" Kate was almost shouting now. "I won't go crashing into his house to confront him in front of his family, if that's what you're afraid of."

"You came crashing in *here*," Terry said, but softly, calmly.

Kate had no answer to that.

"You can't confront him anyway," Terry said now with a toss of her head. "He's dead. There, that's all I'm gonna say about him."

Kate's jaw dropped. "What?"

"You heard me," Terry said, beginning to gather up dishes, not looking at Kate. "He's been dead for a while now, so you couldn't *find* him even if I told you his name. Which I'm not gonna do. So, like I said before, let's drop it."

Kate watched Terry run hot water over plates and glasses. The announcement of her natural father's death struck her as an afterthought. Surely that should have been the *first* thing Terry would say: "It's no use trying to find him because he died." Kate didn't believe it; she felt sure this was a ploy to silence her questions. "Well," she said slowly, "even if he *is* dead, there are still things about him I should know—medical history, what he died of. If your natural parents die young, you should know what to watch out for."

Terry raised her head from the task of stacking dishes; now her eyes were hard again, her full mouth tensed into an angry line. "Look," she said. "You came here and pounced on me. You wanted to see me face-to-face and you did. You wanted to talk and we did. But I've told you all you're gonna hear from me, you got that? You can just get back in your little car and go home now."

Kate couldn't trust herself to speak; she knew she would sob if she tried. She picked up her canvas bag and left the kitchen.

Terry followed her through the house to the front door. "Look, kid," she said to Kate's back. "I don't want us to be mad at each other, okay?"

Kate turned back to face her; she felt she had regained some control now. "I don't want that either," she said. "I guess I'm just not good enough with words to make you understand how much this means to me. It's almost all I ever think about, like a burning in my brain. But I thought you would be able to see it just by looking at me, see how much I need to know."

Teresa Cruzan's face quivered, her remarkable eyes swam for a second, as if the water had welled up there in direct response to the tears in Kate's eyes. But then she gave her head a shake, making the earrings dance, and set her mouth into a thin line again.

"I'm not going back to White Bear Lake," Kate whispered to the averted face. "I'm on vacation, too. So I'm going to get to know Woodard a little. And I'm going to hope we can talk again, soon. I'm at the Holiday Inn, so call me if you want. I'll call you tomorrow."

"I don't think that's such a good idea," Terry said, and her voice was cold. She opened the door and was stepping back to let Kate pass.

"Did you give me my name?" Kate asked softly.

"No, I didn't," Terry said quickly. "That was a job for your folks, and I left it to them."

"Didn't you ever think about me all these years?" Kate asked, and now her voice did break.

Terry made a sound deep in her throat that Kate couldn't interpret. "That's a dumb-ass question, kid," she said, and then she walked away down the hall, leaving Kate to close the door behind herself as she left the house.

# CHAPTER 3

Kate sat in her car in the parking lot of the Holiday Inn, her hands gripping the steering wheel. She'd driven here half blinded by tears and was now trying to get control of herself. She was a young woman who disdained weepiness, and most of the time she could restrain herself from crying, but in the past few days she'd been giving way more than usual, was in real danger of sobbing right now.

For more than ten years, she'd fantasized about the first meeting with her mother, had invested it with an almost fairy-tale quality, so that whenever she reviewed the scenario in her mind—often while falling asleep at night—she was moved to happy tears by the inevitable ending. Never once had she let herself think that she would be dismissed, sent away. Her disappointment was so profound that it was making her physically sick—a pain in the middle of her body that was quite real.

But beneath the disappointment was a deep confusion about Terry's behavior. The woman she'd seen twice today was a study in contradictions. In the morning, she'd seemed emotionally vulnerable, straightforward, on the brink of acceptance. But the woman who had opened the door at five o'clock was hard-edged, defensive. Now that she thought about it, Kate was almost sure there had been playacting going on at that second meeting. It was as if Terry had spent the day not only cooking and cleaning—it was touching that she'd wanted to make a good impression—but planning a role, a manner, that would be so off-putting to her daughter that she would just run back to the Cities. Maybe even the makeup and jewelry, so outlandish as to be almost offensive, had been chosen for the same effect.

Why? What was she covering up? Her own feelings, perhaps? Kate wondered now if this cold, uncommunicative stance wasn't just an extension of a decision Terry had made twenty-three years ago—to give her baby a better life, to give her up for her own good. And she might still believe that a relationship between mother and daughter was "not in the best interests of the child."

That must be it, she told herself now, sitting up straight and wiping under her eyes. She simply refused to accept the alternative possibility—that her long-sought birth mother was a trampy "babe" who didn't want a twenty-three-year-old reminder of a youthful mistake hanging around. No, Terry was just trying to protect *her*, Kate told herself firmly. That was misguided, of course, but perhaps understandable.

What was clearest to Kate at the moment was that she couldn't give up—that would be impossible. She would just have to make Terry realize that her daughter was an adult, not a child who could be harmed by divided loyalties. She set her jaw, climbed out of the car, and walked resolutely into the motel. She would have to plan her campaign.

The next day, Wednesday, Kate held out until noon, and then dialed Teresa Cruzan's number. There was no answer. She counted the rings—eight—and still no answer. She tried again at one and then once more at two-thirty—all with the same result. By three o'clock, she decided to give up on the telephone and drive to Franklin Street. She drove past the house twice, noticing how closed up it looked. On the third pass, she saw someone walking down the driveway away from the garage; it was a man carrying a cardboard box so large that it obscured the lower half of his face. Kate stopped her car in front of a house two doors down and watched in her rearview mirror. The man walked to a black van and stowed the box inside. Kate could see him clearly as he slid the wide door closed with a sharp bang. It was Max, now wearing cotton work gloves and a jean jacket over a costume identical to the one he had been wearing yesterday. Perhaps it *was* the same costume—the jeans were a bit greasier and the boots were the same, surely.

Kate glanced over her shoulder now to look at the garage; the door was sliding downward, making the humming sound of an automatic opener. She caught a glimpse of legs, a flash of bright blue fabric inside the door before it descended to the concrete with a thump. By this time Max was inside the black van; the engine roared into life, making the kind of racket caused by a muffler deliberately customized to produce the opposite effect from the one implied in the word *muffler*. The van pulled away from the curb and thundered away in the opposite direction from the way Kate's car was facing. Terry was home, apparently, and whatever "business" she was in with Max had brought him here two days in a row. What could that be all about? What was in the box? But these were questions that faded quickly for Kate in the face of the one fact that interested her most: Teresa Cruzan was in that house. Hesitating only a moment longer, Kate got out of her car and crossed the street.

She waited almost two minutes after ringing the bell, then rang it again. Yesterday, the bell had worked, but perhaps it wasn't working now. She knocked, using the side of her fist rather than her knuckles. Nothing moved behind the sheer curtains that showed beneath the half-closed shades of the front windows. After standing on the porch for more than three minutes, with the sun beginning to feel uncomfortably warm against her back, she realized that Terry wasn't going to open the door. The wave of hurt, the sense of humiliation, almost overwhelmed her, but she turned at last, stiff-legged, and marched back to her car; her back was straight, her head high, and anyone who cared to notice would have seen that her eyes were dry.

But Kate couldn't stay away. Her hunger to discover herself in someone of her own blood had been growing for too long to be appeased or turned away by hurt pride. Besides, she was beginning to suspect that Terry's odd behavior, her refusal to give her daughter a chance, might be connected somehow to Max. What was his connection to Terry? How long had he been there, in the house, yesterday before her own arrival? Maybe *he* had somehow convinced Terry to be cold and noncommittal—to breeze through some minimal information before sending "the kid" on her way.

That night, Kate drove to Franklin and parked across the street from the little house, determined just to watch for a while. She'd barely switched off the ignition when she saw a red Trans Am, jacked up in the rear over extra-wide tires, come to a stop directly in front of 642 Franklin. A tall, fair young man with an asymmetrical shock of blond hair got out and went to the front door of the house. The door opened about a minute after he rang the bell, and Terry Cruzan stepped out onto the porch, lifted her face to the young man, and gave him a lingering kiss. She was wearing a miniskirted dress and spike heels. Her hair was fluffed out into a fan of dark curls around her face and onto her shoulders. But even at this distance, Kate could see that Terry wasn't as garishly made up as she'd been the previous afternoon. She looked wonderful, like a model, swinging her hips as she and the blond man walked to the car.

When the Trans Am pulled away from the curb, Kate swung her car around and followed at a discreet distance, feeling embarrassed, even furtive. But it was as if the impulse to learn about Terry had a life of its own. The red car led Kate out of town and into the graveled parking lot of a brightly lit building whose neon sign proclaimed that it was WILEY'S GARDENS, though there was no evidence of anything resembling a garden anywhere in sight.

Kate didn't get out of the car. With the windows down, she could hear what kind of place Wiley's was: men shouting in the kind of raucous conviviality that could easily become angry; the higher pitched laughter of women for whom alcohol made everything hilarious; music that could loosely be called country rock. This was what she had once heard Doug call a roadhouse. Too big for just a bar, so there must be a dance floor. Woodard's working class came here to party and dance. Terry had said that she liked to dance—and to play poker. It didn't stretch the imagination too much to picture poker games going on in the smoky haze of Wiley's. It embarrassed Kate to think of Terry in there, with her young boyfriend, joining in that blast of noise. She turned the car around and drove back to the Holiday Inn.

On Thursday, Kate began the day with good intentions. She would let the matter alone for the time being. If Terry had been out late, dancing and drinking, any early morning effort to contact her was bound to produce irritation. Kate had a late breakfast, then took a leisurely stroll through the mall whose backside was presented to her across the parking lot of the motel; there she selected five magazines to help her pass the time. But by the middle of the afternoon, her obsession had pushed itself inexorably to the forefront once again.

By three P.M., she couldn't sit still a moment longer, and went downstairs to her car. The powder-blue Chevy Beretta, a college-graduation gift from her parents, was looking dusty and a bit forlorn. When she took out the keys, the memory came, unbidden, of Doug holding them out to her that first day— "Now this one is for the ignition, and this one is for everything else: doors, trunk, gas cap." For just a second, she couldn't remember being angry with him for any reason, had to shake her head to dislodge the image of his beaming face.

She drove aimlessly for a while, had a notion of trying to find the warehouse her father had once owned, the warehouse managed by Mr. Cruzan—she realized with a twisting sensation in her stomach that she didn't even know his first name—by her grandfather. But she didn't know Woodard well enough to deduce where the warehouses might be and she felt too shy to ask anybody. Finally she found herself in the Franklin Street neighborhood where she stopped her car on the parallel street to the south, and got out to walk. Perhaps if she strolled around in this neighborhood, somebody working on a flower bed or edging a lawn would see her resemblance to Teresa Cruzan, remark on it, strike up a conversation, and then she might learn some details of her mother's life.

When she arrived at Franklin, Kate slowed her steps, peered around the corner. Then she jumped back to hide herself behind a lilac bush; she'd seen the front door of 642 swing inward. Through the thick foliage, she watched Terry come out, glance up at the sky, shrug, and then start down the sidewalk toward the street. She was wearing jeans, a loose-fitting shirt, short boots; her hair was pulled back into a pony tail, and she was carrying a large suede bag with leather fringes hanging down past her knees. She went straight to a gray Thunderbird that was parked along the curb, shaded by a white birch tree, opened the driver's side door, and got in.

As the car pulled away, Kate realized that she'd seen it

there before, that it had always been parked in the same place when she drove by, or parked her own car. It had never occurred to her that the Thunderbird had anything to do with Terry because Terry's house had an attached garage and, of course, she'd assumed that any vehicle Terry owned would be kept there, behind the closed door. Kate's brow wrinkled in concentration. Why would Terry keep her car on the street?

Kate left her hiding place now and walked dejectedly back to her car. The sky was overcast and the thick humidity made her realize for the first time that rain was imminent, perhaps even a storm. No one was outside; there was nobody to talk to. When she pulled her car around the corner to head back to the motel, she saw the black van pulling to a halt in front of Terry's house. As she drove slowly by, she saw Max approach the house, unlock it, and go inside. She stopped her car against the opposite curb and stared, lost in a new thought.

Whose house was it, anyway? She'd assumed that it belonged to Terry, but maybe that was wrong. Every day that Kate had been on Franklin Street, she'd seen Max, either in the house, or just leaving it, or going into it as if it were his own. Maybe it *was* his house. Perhaps *his* car occupied the garage while Terry's had to live on the street. Perhaps Terry's tenancy in the house was related only to the "business" that involved Max and his boxes. Terry was apparently so comfortable with his presence there that she'd given him a key.

And what *did* Terry do for a living? She'd been so vague about that. The house was modest but well maintained, and while the Thunderbird wasn't brand-new, it, too, looked to be in good shape. Because Kate had always taken her own living standard for granted, she seldom questioned how other people maintained their own standard. Now her growing sense of mystery surrounding and blurring this woman she so much wanted to know better was causing her to reexamine every word Terry had said to her. If Max was not her boyfriend now—and the blond man in the Trans Am confirmed that—did that mean that he had *never* been? Might he be the father of Teresa Cruzan's child even if their present relationship wasn't romantic?

Kate considered getting out of the car and going to the house to talk to Max; she still suspected that he might be the key to why Terry was so reluctant to talk about the past. But she remembered the scowling expression she'd seen Tuesday, the sense of barely restrained violence in the way he'd cuffed Terry's head. Kate thought it might not be safe to be in a house alone with Max. As rain began to dot the windshield, she put the car back into gear and drove away. These were questions she should be asking Terry, she told herself firmly.

That night, she waited until eight-thirty and then dialed Terry's number. She listened to the phone ring: six times, seven times, eight times; but she simply set her jaw and let the ringing go on. She was past the nervous fear of making a nuisance of herself; if being a nuisance was what it would take to get another meeting with Teresa Cruzan, then she was willing to let the phone ring a hundred times. But it was after the twenty-first ring that she heard the receiver lifted.

"Well?" The voice was not loud, but irritation saturated the single syllable.

"Terry, this is Kate," she said quickly, dreading the sound of the slammed receiver. "Please let me come for another visit. There's still so much I need to ask you. I won't even talk about who my father is, if you don't want me to. I promise."

"Look, kid," and now the voice was a little louder, "I already told you that's not a good idea. I got my life and there's no place in it for you. So just go home, will you?"

"And I already told you I'm not going home right now," Kate replied, her own voice taking on an angry edge. "I don't want to move in with you or anything, so you don't have to get panicky about it. I think I have a right to know some things about myself—my genetic history, whether there are diseases in my blood family I need to watch out for, stuff like that. You owe me that much, don't you think?"

There was a long pause and Kate held her breath, terrified that she'd gone too far.

"Don't you try to lay that shit on me," Terry said at last. "What I owe you, you already got, and that's your life. Now, you quit calling me, you hear?"

"I won't stop," Kate said, her voice shaking. She'd been prepared to apologize for the "owe me" crack, would have done it instantly if Terry had sounded hurt or sad. "I'll keep calling you and I'll come over there every day. I'll just camp out on Franklin Street if I have to until you agree to see me."

With some part of her mind, she was aware that she

sounded like a petulant child, was appalled at herself for behaving in this way, but she couldn't seem to stop herself. Now she heard the receiver being replaced—not slammed, but carefully set down. She sat there, holding the phone, shoulders rigid, jaw clenched. But still she didn't cry.

# CHAPTER 4

He stood looking past the striped drapes into the darkened street outside. His strong hand opened and closed on the edge of the stiff fabric.

"You did fine," he said tightly. "That should send her packing."

He turned to look at Teresa Cruzan, who stood across the room, her eye makeup smudged from crying, her long hands clasping each other tightly. The sight of the half-frightened face filled him with a sort of low-grade anger. She was still rubbing her wrist from time to time, where his fingers had left red marks like stains on her white flesh. He hadn't meant to touch her at all, but the ringing of the phone had begun to drive him almost mad. If it had stopped after only a few rings, he wouldn't have forced Terry to answer, to say what she'd said.

"I don't know what you're blubbering for," he said. "We agreed that this had to be done."

"I know that," she flared at him. "But that doesn't mean I gotta enjoy talking to her that way."

"You should never have let her come here for a meal on Tuesday," he said, looking out the window again. "That was your first mistake. It only encouraged her to stick around, and you know that can't happen."

46

"And what the hell was I supposed to do?" she said. "She wouldn't have gone away without talking to me. So I see her once and send her home. No problem."

"But she didn't go, did she?" he said bitterly.

"Give it a little time, can't you?" Terry said. "I saw the kid just two days ago and told her it was all she's gonna get. I don't answer the phone when it rings; I only answered it just now because you made me. I don't open the door without looking first to see who it is. She'll get the idea, don't worry. She's not dumb, after all. You know she inherited smarts, don't you, even if she didn't get them from me?"

"Has she been back to the house since Tuesday?" he demanded, turning again to look at the beautiful face carefully—it seemed remarkable to him that she should still be beautiful.

"Yesterday," she conceded, not looking at him. "She rang the bell and stood out there for a while. But I didn't open the door or show myself in a window."

"What about last night?" he asked. "Did she call or come back?"

"I wouldn't know because I wasn't here. I went out dancing and I stayed out late."

"Oh?" And now bitter irony had come into his voice despite his efforts to stay detached. "New boyfriend?"

"Not so new," she answered, looking away from him. "Couple of months. He's nice."

"Once a bitch, always a bitch," he said icily.

"You got no call to talk that way to me!" She was shouting now, her fine pale skin flooding with color. "Just who the hell are you to be making judgments about *me*? You didn't expect me to spend the rest of my life in a convent, did you?"

He laughed—a short, scornful bark. "Now, that *is* a funny notion," he sneered. "They'd have to brick the door shut on your cell."

She didn't speak, but the dark eyes were blazing. He felt surprised by sexual desire, couldn't separate it somehow from the other desire to hurt her, to punish her for causing him such profound anxiety. And he felt ashamed of himself for desiring her—dirtied.

"You're just so damned sure I'm gonna tell," she said at last. "You don't have to worry about that."

"But she's already asked!" He couldn't control his voice.

"You told me just before that she's insisting on knowing. Maybe she won't let up."

"You forget what else I told you," Terry said, pacing again in that nervous way of hers. "I didn't tell her a thing and I'm not gonna tell her. 'He's dead,' I said, and that's all. No other relatives."

"That's not what we agreed on when you called me on Tuesday," he reminded her. "You shouldn't have said anything at all."

"I had to play it by ear," she insisted. "I thought if I said that, it would make her quit asking questions. You didn't have to come around here spying on me, either. I told you I can handle it."

"But I'm worried," he said slowly, starting across the room toward her. "And you should be worrying, too. You should keep in mind what we've been talking about these past few weeks. You want things to go back to the way they were, don't you?"

"Of course I do," she replied, stopping to face him, holding her ground at his approach, trying not to seem afraid—he could see the pathetic bravado. "I hate living the way I've been living lately. And I'm not asking for anything big—just what I'm used to."

"And I've already agreed, haven't I?" His jaw was tense. "But everything depends on your silence, doesn't it? If you open your mouth, the agreement is off."

"Don't you think I know that?" She had taken a half-step backward as he came up to her; he lowered his face toward her and she moved away from him to the side window. "God, I hate it when you treat me like I'm stupid or something," she said with her back to him. "Do I remember our agreement? Of course I remember. I'm not an idiot. That kid is not going to find out from me who her father is. Okay? That's final."

"But it's not good for her to be here at all," he insisted. "You can see, can't you, that she looks just like you?"

Terry turned back toward him and her face had changed—it was softer; she was even smiling a little.

"Yeah, she does, doesn't she?" she said. "She's got lighter hair, of course, but you know she comes by that naturally, too. But her eyes and her mouth—boy, it's almost scary."

He watched Terry's face intently, saw how she went to mush as she talked about Kate, and he knew she couldn't be trusted. Oh, she would pretend as long as he was talking to her, because she had her self-interest to protect. But if she were left to herself, she would see Kate, she would cave in to pressure from Kate, and she would talk. Maybe not a name. She would imagine, because she wasn't very bright, that she could tell other details without revealing identity. But what she didn't understand was that a private detective could take those details and find his way to a name very quickly. "Can't you see why it's dangerous to have her here in Woodard?" he asked, watching her face without much hope.

"No, I can't," she said, her face hardening.

He could feel his anger boiling up again. They had been all through this on Tuesday. Why should he be subjected to this again and again? Why should it be his fate to have the past haunt him in this way? Everything had been fixed, arranged, twenty-three years ago, hadn't it? He respected contracts, was always willing to keep his part of a bargain. The trouble was in trying to make deals with women; they were always willing to trash a contract if their emotions led them in another direction. You're supposed to take care of them, not let bad things happen to them, and then they smash through all your plans because they "love" somebody, or because they think that bargains don't apply to their feelings.

Now he crossed the room in three long steps, pinned Terry in the corner against the window. He took her shoulders in his hands. "If you weren't such a stupid bitch," he growled, "you'd see that she's likely to go poking around all over town. Somebody who remembers might see the resemblance, start asking questions."

"That's just stupid," she said, squirming, trying to free herself. "There's nothing for anybody to remember. I keep telling you that I never told anybody *then*, either. So if nobody knew then, who's gonna know now? It's *me* she looks like."

"I just don't want her here," he said, tightening his grip until he saw her flinch. "You've always put yourself first, haven't you? Now, if you just keep that up, we'll both be all right."

"What about Kate?" she said quietly. "Will *she* be all right?"

"Of course," he said, letting go of her shoulders abruptly

and turning away. "I've told you that from the beginning. It's best for her to go home to the life she's always known. There's plenty in Woodard she's better off not knowing."

"I wonder how much you care about her," she said, and her voice behind him sounded anxious. "I worry about that."

"I told you you've got other things to worry about," he said, turning around to look at her again. "You know my conditions."

"I wonder what you're really worried about," she said, eyeing him shrewdly. "Are you sure there isn't something about business involved here—something about money?"

"You have business of your own to tend to," he answered noncommittally. "And there are one or two things you'd rather not have Kate find out about *you*, aren't there? Like what's in the garage, for instance?"

She just stared at him again.

"Now," he said briskly, aiming at a neutral tone. "That little speech of yours on the phone should do it, I guess. By the way, you paused for a minute before you hung up. Did Kate say anything?"

"No," Terry said quickly, looking away from him as she spoke. "She hung up on me, if you wanna know. That wasn't very pleasant."

"Well, that's the effect we're after, isn't it? But if she's not gone by the weekend, I think you should leave town for a while."

"Leave town?" She looked surprised, even panicky. "To go where?" Her attachment to this place astounded him. She should *want* to get away. Why on earth had she stayed here at all after Kate's birth? Only because she was narrow, stupid. He felt another surge of anger, a deep sense of being aggrieved. She had no idea of what she was meddling in by letting Kate stay in Woodard, by encouraging Kate to ask more questions. If she gave Kate any clues at all about the identity of her natural father, one of those hints might lead her straight to Robert Allan Ford. And if she got that far, the rest would follow—inevitably, inexorably—and then the ruin would be accomplished. Everything would fall apart, and the life he'd planned so carefully for himself for so long would be wrenched out of his grasp. He had no intention of letting that happen.

"You're such a fool," he said bitterly. "It doesn't matter where you go. Check into a hotel for a week, don't tell anybody where you are—not even boyfriends. I'll pay for it, if that's what you're worried about. If you're not here, Kate can't be pestering you to see her."

"And what if that doesn't work in the long run?" she asked. "What if she goes away and comes back? Starts this all over again?"

"We don't have to think about that now, do we?" He felt outraged by her suggestion that his solution might be only temporary. "We deal with it one day at a time, that's all. Give it until the weekend and then you start packing."

He started toward the door now, but he was considering what she'd said. What if she was right and Kate wouldn't give up? What if sending Terry out of town was only going to postpone the problem? Maybe it was necessary to deal with it quickly, after all. Keeping tabs on Terry was going to be a big job; when she went out of the house, it might be with that boyfriend, or to the store, and then he would be wasting his time shadowing her. But Kate had only one goal in Woodard, so it would be more efficient to watch her movements. He valued efficiency. It was risky to start following Kate—more danger of exposure than if he just shadowed Terry. But Kate was the key. In more ways than one. Maybe he could also use her to scare some temporary cooperation out of Terry, just to buy a little time while he thought about what he might have to do in the long run.

He turned back now to fix Terry with a piercing look.

"You just remember that there are all kinds of unpleasant things that can happen to you if I think you're unreliable. And it's not in Kate's best interests, either, to be in the middle of this. You should remember that her well-being is in jeopardy, too."

This had the effect he was looking for—her face went slack, her eyes widened.

"You don't mean—" she started and then fell silent for a second. "You wouldn't hurt Kate," she said then with a nervous little laugh. "She's your blood, too."

"Of course," he said, moving toward the door again. "But you know I've got other things to think of, too. Kate needs both of us to keep her from harm, doesn't she? We don't want to see her hurt in *any* way."

He had packed as much threat into his voice as he could manage. It wasn't that he'd actually thought about any violent solutions, except as some terrible final resort—he didn't really think of himself as a violent man. What he hoped was that the threat would be enough. Terry had followed him to the front door, was staring wordlessly at him while he turned the knob. The fear he saw in those gorgeous eyes gave him a rush of pleasure so intense that it was almost sexual. He could hardly keep the smile off his face.

# CHAPTER 5

By Friday noon, Kate was feeling the effects of exhaustion and hunger. After hearing Terry's brutal words on the phone the night before, she had been unable to sleep, had struggled with all her strength to keep from thinking about anything at all—an instinctive reflex to protect her wounded psyche. Her first impulse—almost overwhelming—had been to pack her suitcase and flee from Woodard. But she was too much a Lundgren to act on first impulses; it was a Lundgren conviction, one she had come to share, that decisions or actions based on raw emotion seldom had happy results. Besides, there was a problem of where to run *to*. Leaving Woodard would give her only one place to go—back to White Bear Lake—and her rage at her parents hadn't faded enough to make that an agreeable prospect.

By morning, her head was buzzing and there was a heavy sensation in her arms and legs. But the thought of food made her feel slightly nauseated, so she skipped breakfast and showered in cool water for twenty minutes in an effort to jolt her consciousness into a fit state for making plans. When she was dressed, she had at least arrived at a decision to go outside. It was warmer now than it had been yesterday, overcast and muggy. As she walked toward the parking lot, her father's regular advice popped into her head: "When you're feeling sorry for yourself, get busy." That sentence typified Douglas Lundgren, a driven businessman who was sometimes angry, but never seemed depressed.

Kate thought now about her father and that positive energy of his; tall, lean, good-looking in the Scandinavian way, he was always "busy." Even on vacation, Doug was the organizer of excursions, the early riser who tumbled his reluctant children out of bed to go to the pool, to the tennis courts, to the golf course. Sheila was by nature more sedentary, but her husband's energy was contagious and she, too, had little patience with what she called brooding. It was not that Kate's parents encouraged their children to talk about their feelings, to work out emotional distress verbally; no, Lundgrens didn't talk about feelings much at all. Their solutions always involved the notion of distraction—get busy and you'll forget what's bothering you.

But Kate had internalized the message, believed in its power; eldest children often accept parental values as their own. Yet the impulse to explore Woodard wasn't a complete distraction from her central obsession because now, in the sticky morning air, it had occurred to her that she might learn more about Terry by examining her environment; Terry had, after all, always lived here. In fact, Kate was beginning to wonder about that: Why had her birth mother never left Woodard? Surely one of the ways to recover from a youthful indiscretion was to leave the town where it was widely known. And from what Terry had said about her own family, Kate couldn't believe that she was held here out of a sense of loyalty to, or responsibility for, her parents. So what else was holding her? Her lover, the father of her child? Did she stay because he was here?

Kate knew it was silly to imagine that nosing around Woodard on her own would provide vital information about her birth mother or magically reveal the identity of her natural father, but she needed to move now, to act, rather than just to wait.

Woodard was the sort of place Kate had almost no experience of—a town of twenty-six thousand people, an old community at the top edge of Pine County. It was the sort of midwestern town that had one of almost everything—one municipal swimming pool, one library, one senior high school, one golf course, one Hardee's. Kate was used to an expensive suburb adjacent to the busy variety of a big city. At home, if somebody said, "I'll meet you at Dayton's," she would have to ask, "Which one?" In Woodard, there was no Dayton's at all, and the only mall was a low-slung series of shops tucked under one roof on the highway outside of town.

She drove around for a while, checking on local landmarks, admiring the houses in the northeast section of town; here the architecture was turn-of-the-century, Victorian and Georgian—elegant old homes with sweeping driveways and mature trees. This was a well-maintained area, obviously a place where the rich of Woodard had decided to remain connected to the first generations who had built the town. Kate's home in White Bear Lake was ultra-modern, a cedar-sided configuration of sharp angles, with solar panels and a tucked-under garage. She found it odd that the antique elegance of this strange town should resonate so strongly with her; there was something in her, obviously, that rebelled against trendiness. She was, she supposed, a closet romantic.

Somehow the driving around had a calming effect on Kate. She felt less desperate, determined to stay in Woodard for a while longer. And she was confident now that she could use whatever resources the town might offer to learn more about her Cruzan relatives; the very smallness of the place seemed reassuring—not like beginning a search in a big city. Terry wasn't the only source of information, after all, and until she came to her senses—this was how Kate had decided to think about her birth mother's behavior, as just a temporary reluctance—there were other places to investigate. Though it was almost noon by this time, Kate didn't look for a place to have lunch; she turned the Beretta around in a Piggly Wiggly parking lot and headed for the public library.

The Woodard Public Library was a turn-of-the-century structure built on the classical model—shallow dome, symmetrical columns. Kate thought it looked like pictures she'd seen of Monticello, except that it was all white. There had been some recent remodeling—the addition of a ramp and a side entrance with an elevator—but it hadn't damaged the lines of the façade. Somebody in Woodard obviously had the good taste to preserve a charming old public building while accommodating the requirements of state codes.

In the ground-floor lobby, the circulation librarian turned on a synthetic smile when Kate asked where back issues of the local newspaper were kept.

"We have the recent ones on microfilm now," she said in a chirrupy voice. "Everything from the present back to 1970."

"I'll look at those later," Kate responded, thinking that she now knew the dates of her grandparents' deaths and could look at their obituaries. "But I'd like to start with the older ones, from the fifties and sixties."

"Those are still up on the mezzanine in the old map room," the librarian said. "It's behind the four-hundred to six-hundred stacks, in the southwest corner. The papers are all stacked by year and they're pretty dusty. Are you sure you want to dig around up there?"

"Yes," Kate said quietly, aware that people were lining up behind her for service. "I'm sure."

"Well, you'll have to put the lights on up there," the librarian said, pointing to a door at the right side of the busy lobby. "Up two flights. The switch is just inside the door to the mezzanine. Then turn right and go to the door in that farthest corner."

Kate left the lobby, made her way up the wide central staircase; at the top, one door opened onto the second floor and another led to one more staircase, narrower than the first, with metal treads. At the top of this staircase was a door leading to the mezzanine, a walled-off story and a half almost under the dome. Here a faint light from the dome's portholes showed Kate the outlines of stacks; she groped for the light switch, felt a grainy layer of dust when she found it. This certainly was not a popular section of the library. The fluorescent bulbs flooded the room with a harsh light, throwing stark shadows of the stacks against walls and floor. When Kate moved forward, she noticed that the room produced strange sound effects. The floor was made of thick glass blocks, and her sandals made clicking noises when she walked, but the heavily laden shelves of books both absorbed sound and deflected it in odd ways. To walk at all was to produce a series of muffled *booms* that seemed to be coming from two or three directions at once.

In the corner of the main room, she came upon a door with a glass panel filling its upper half. Just inside this door, she found another light switch. When Kate turned it on and stepped into the smaller room, she was momentarily daunted by the stacks and stacks of newspapers bundled on top of long tables. Then she took a deep breath and waded in. After about ten minutes of poking around, she began to discern how the tables were arranged and then found 1952 fairly quickly. She wanted to begin there because she calculated that was the year Teresa Cruzan was born. She planned to work her way through the years, looking for references—school sports, plays, class trips— that might include her birth mother. As she began to peel off copies of the yellowed newspaper, she felt grateful for the closed-off privacy of the room, for its quiet. She could hear no sounds at all from the rest of the building.

She was wondering now where she might spread out to begin reading. Was there someplace to sit down in here? As she turned back toward the door, which she'd left slightly ajar, she froze suddenly with a newspaper half open in her hands. The glass upper half of the door was now dark. Someone had turned off the lights in the main room of the mezzanine. Kate could feel the beginning of fear, a prickling at the back of her scalp. But she took a long breath, trying to reassure herself. Perhaps someone on the library staff had noticed the lights and, not seeing anyone in the stacks, had assumed that some library patron had left without turning off the switch. But it was odd, wasn't it, that no one had called out to ask if anyone was using the stacks?

Kate set the paper down on the table in front of her and tiptoed to the door of the little room. For some reason, she felt reluctant to approach the door head-on, felt she didn't want to expose herself so directly to view. She moved up to the side of the door, peered out at an angle. The light from behind her illuminated about an eight-foot rectangle of the room outside. Beyond that, the stacks loomed in the semidarkness for another thirty feet between Kate and the door where the main light switch was located. Her line of vision to this door was blocked by the closely spaced stacks.

She reached out now to ease the door open a little farther, cocked her ear to listen, held her breath in the eerie silence. Was there a sound or had she imagined it? She thought it was like a muffled version of the *boom boom* that her own feet had made on the glass floor; it was coming to her from—from where? The left, where the door was? Or straight ahead behind the stacks that ran parallel with the front wall? Impossible to say in this odd echo chamber.

Kate's breath was now a sort of shallow panting. She tried to tell herself that she couldn't really be in danger. There were people all over this building and they could surely be summoned by a few loud screams. But the rest of the library seemed very far away now, remote from this enclosed space. She dropped into a crouch and slipped her sandals off her feet, moved them into her left hand. Then she picked up her purse from where she'd set it down inside the door and crept through the opening between the door and its frame. A short scramble to her left put her out of the pool of light and behind one of the stacks. Here she stood upright and held her breath again, listening.

Now she could hear only silence. She leaned forward toward the next row of shelves, peeping around into the next aisle, which pointed at right angles to other stacks that ran along the front wall. In the dim light, she could see the dust on the tops of the nearest books, could almost feel it in the air, but she heard no other sounds. She waited for her eyes to adjust to the gloom of the dimly lit room. Maybe she had only imagined the sounds. But still she was reluctant to move.

She crouched again inside the narrow pathway, so that she could see through the spaces between books. Now she heard the sounds again, as if footsteps could whisper. She imagined that the sounds were coming from the left where the outside door was, but the strange deflection of sound made it impossible to be sure. Her eyes strained in the direction of escape. Suddenly, at the far end of the next row of stacks, as if framed by the dusty books on either side of her head, Kate saw a faint shadow thrown forward and elongated against the floor—a shadow shaped like a head and shoulders; it moved, first slowly forward and then quickly backward, as if someone had suddenly noticed the shadow and jerked back to eliminate it.

Kate didn't think who the person might be; she felt profoundly threatened by this sneaking movement and her instant impulse was to escape. Hitching her bag up onto her shoulder, she stood upright and tiptoed to the end of her own aisle, to the place where it intersected with the stacks along the far wall. It wasn't possible to move soundlessly, even in her bare feet, but she hoped that the hum of the floor under her was so slight that the bookshelves nearest her would absorb most of the noise.

Before each new move, Kate would pause, holding her breath, listening. The other stealthy movements were not always apparent, but there were enough of the whispers—*boom boom*—to convince Kate that whoever was in the room with her was now moving faster. She took a right turn into the long aisle against the wall, hoping she might catch a glimpse of her pursuer—she now thought of herself as pursued—in one of the other, right-angle aisles as she passed them. She was moving now in the direction of the main door. But every time she peeked around the edge of a set of stacks, there was nothing there. And now there were no other sounds in the pauses she made as she moved from one stack edge to the next. Perhaps whoever it was had circled the mezzanine on the other side, moving toward the light in the map room, and she would be able to get out without encountering him. She began to hurry now, almost forgetting to be quiet; whenever she stopped, she flattened herself against the metal frame of the stacks, feeling the cold through her thin blouse.

Just as she was considering a quick dash for the door—she would be able to see it if she passed two more aisles—something struck the framework of the row she was leaning against, making a sharp metallic *bang* and sending vibrations straight into her shoulder blades. Kate screamed, a single explosion of terrified sound, and ran back the way she'd come, in a sudden panicked conviction that her pursuer was surely between her and the door. The booming sound of the floor under her feet seemed to her, in her terror, to be almost deafening.

It was perhaps three or four seconds before she realized that her bare feet couldn't be making all that noise; she stopped and heard the exaggerated *boom boom* of other running footsteps, and the crash of a door wrenched open so hard that it collided with the wall. Somebody was running away from *her*. For a few seconds, Kate was stunned by this development. Then she was galvanized into action by the sudden impulse to get a look at whoever had been prowling around in that suspicious way. She sprinted down the aisle between two towering stacks, took a hard left turn just in time to see the last motion of the door swinging shut—it was regulated by a piston mechanism near its base.

Kate ran to the door; even as she was reaching for the knob, she could hear feet pounding down the metal treads of the stairs beyond the door. As she was pulling the door toward herself, she heard the closing of another door below her. She jumped down the metal stairs two at a time, convinced that if she were fast enough, she could catch whoever was running ahead of her. When she reached the door of the main stairwell, she tried to pull inward, not realizing at first that it opened in the other direction. The delay was enough to show her only an empty staircase leading to the ground-floor doorway.

But she ran down anyway and shoved at the door, which opened far more easily than she was expecting; she catapulted herself into the lobby and almost collided with a man who was walking away from her. At the sound of her approach, he dodged to the left and whirled to face her. He was a tall, silver-haired man, very red-faced; he had raised a lean hand to his throat and was breathing in shallow gasps.

"What the hell?" he said, but there wasn't enough breath to make his larynx produce a loud sound.

"Are you following me?" Kate demanded, her own voice ragged from all the exertion.

"Following you?" the man said, recovering enough breath to raise his voice. "You jumped out at *me*! Scared me half to death. Look at this." And the hand he extended in front of him was trembling, indeed.

"You're shaking because you just ran down two flights of stairs," Kate said, deliberately making her voice louder than his. "Why were you creeping around up there in the stacks?"

"I have no idea what you're talking about, young woman," he said, haughty, on his dignity.

"Yes, you do," Kate replied, still almost yelling at him. "You were hiding in the mezzanine stacks and tiptoeing around like a thief."

"You must be out of your mind," he said. "I haven't been out of this lobby."

Kate could feel the silence that had fallen in the room, sensed even before she looked that everyone had turned rapt attention onto the pair at the stairwell door. The young woman from the circulation desk came hurrying up to them, her expression clouded with the disapproval such people always show in the face of a disturbance.

"Is something wrong, Mr. Werner?" she said in a near-whisper.

"This crazy girl is making wild accusations," the tall man said, turning with a patronizing air to the librarian. "I can't make any sense out of what she's saying."

"What's the problem, miss?"

Kate could tell from the tone that the librarian had already made up her mind; this Werner was apparently a Woodard VIP. Before she answered, she looked more carefully at the tall man. He was impeccably dressed—casual but expensive slacks, a silk shirt with a fine gold chain visible at the open collar, crepe-soled summer shoes. He was perhaps sixty or sixty-five—Kate and her friends would have described him as old—but still good-looking; his eyes under silver brows were the sort of crystal blue that made one think of Viking explorers.

"While I was looking at newspapers, someone turned out the lights in the mezzanine," Kate explained, looking now full at the librarian, trying to assume a calm, reasonable air. "And I heard someone sneaking around in the stacks—just moving around in the dark. I saw his shadow once, but he ducked back when he realized his shadow could be seen in the open space between the stacks. Then he threw something against the stacks, or maybe he just stumbled into them. I started to run and then he ran. I chased him down both flights of stairs, and when I came through that door, here he was."

The librarian had a deep frown between her small eyes. "You saw someone on the stairs and you think it was Mr. Werner?"

"Well, no," Kate replied, anxious to be scrupulously accurate. "I didn't ever see him on the stairs—he was just enough ahead of me so that the only thing I saw was doors closing. But I heard him on those metal stairs, and when I came through this last door, I almost ran down this guy, who's all red and breathing hard. You tell me what conclusions I should make."

"I was breathing like that because you scared the hell out of me," Werner said.

"Did it occur to you," the librarian said, "that whoever ran from the mezzanine might have gone onto the second floor?"

Kate's jaw slackened slightly from its belligerent tightness. Of course, that was possible; she might have run straight past that escape hatch and raced down those carpeted main stairs, *assuming* fleeing footsteps ahead of her when she hadn't actually heard them.

"Listen, miss," the librarian said, lowering her voice even more. "We've been having some trouble lately with a flasher who creeps around in the stacks and jumps out at young women. He probably followed you upstairs. But it isn't possible that Mr. Thomas Werner could be that person. Whoever it was escaped onto the second floor and is probably long gone down the side stairs or even the elevator."

Kate didn't ask why the librarian would be so confident of that judgment—it was obvious that she couldn't associate sexual deviance with a respected member of Woodard society. Instead of addressing her skepticism to the other woman, Kate looked up quickly at Werner's face and caught him looking at her. Though he glanced away at once, she was sure that she'd seen for that one brief moment an expression other than outrage. Was it curiosity? Puzzlement? Or was it recognition? But she also noticed that, though Werner's breathing had returned to normal, his forearms were as red as his face. The redness ended abruptly at the elbows, where a band of white skin showed just under the short sleeves of his shirt. The redness Kate had attributed to exertion was actually a recent sunburn. She was beginning to feel foolish.

In turning from her, Werner had focused his attention on the group across the room, all attentively watching the action. "John!" he called in their direction, his voice peremptory. "John Kramer. Come here for a moment, will you?"

A young man detached himself from the group and walked forward, his expression sheepish, as if this sudden shifting of the spotlight were something he would have liked to avoid.

"Now, John," Werner said, putting his lean hand on the young man's shoulder. "There's a misunderstanding you can help to clear up. This young lady has some absurd notion that I've just been upstairs, prowling around after her in the stacks. How long have you been here?"

"Well, I got here about five minutes ago," the young man replied, his voice surprisingly deep for someone so young. "I'm bringing back some of Mother's overdue books during my lunch break."

"Never mind that," Werner said with a gesture of impatience. "Did you see me when you came in? I was walking up and down here."

"Yes, I did see you over here," the young man agreed. Then he turned to Kate, his expression almost apologetic. "I noticed him when I came in. He's been down here for at least as long as I've been here."

"There, you see," the librarian said, her face smug. "I knew you were mistaken about Mr. Werner."

"Now, listen to me, young lady," Werner said, his voice stentorian, hectoring. But Kate noticed that he wasn't looking directly at her while he talked. Was he afraid of what she might see in his eyes—had already seen once? "You should exercise a little more judgment. No doubt you had some sort of frightening experience, but you can't go around accusing innocent bystanders."

Kate had been readying an apology, a murmured "I'm sorry," but Werner's tone made her change her mind. She just glared at his averted face, willing him to look back at her, but he didn't; he turned and walked to the main entrance: graceful, elegant, his silver head held high—playing to the crowd.

"I don't suppose you can give us any details that would help us identify this flasher," the librarian was saying; she seemed more kindly, more human, now that the "great man" had left.

"No," Kate murmured. "I told you; I saw shadows, heard footsteps. I didn't actually eyeball anybody."

"Well," the other woman sighed. "That's too bad. But we're going to get the creep sooner or later. I'm sorry you were scared."

"Thanks," Kate said, but it was just a reflex. She was looking at the entrance, trying to follow the retreating back of Thomas Werner. And trying to avoid the eyes of the curious onlookers.

# CHAPTER 6

It was only when she started to walk that Kate realized she was still barefoot, her sandals clutched in her left hand. She turned from the watching crowd, made her way to a bench near the library entrance, and sat down to put her sandals back on. Bent over, her hair hanging around her face, she was surprised by the sudden convulsion of a sob. Days of holding back gave way to strangled crying; she was ashamed to break down in front of these strangers, kept her sobs as quiet as she could manage. Through the tears, she saw a pair of brown trousers and tan shoes; somebody was standing between her and the other people in the lobby.

"Can I help?" She heard the deep voice above as if it were coming through water.

"No," she gasped. "No, I'm all right." A part of her mind—the observant, detached part—was wondering why people always asserted this lie, and always in these words, whenever they were most miserable.

"Come on," the voice above her said, and she felt a hand cup her right elbow. "You don't want to give the sharks any blood to smell."

Kate found herself deftly escorted through the wide glass doors of the library and onto the street. Only then did she look up at her escort. It was the young man Werner had called John Kramer. He was a little taller than Kate, with light brown hair, freckles, and eyes that, in the sunlight, were the color of caramels. He wore round, wire-rimmed glasses and looked about twenty-five or twenty-six.

"What was that all about?" he asked. "Do you have some beef with old Tom Werner?"

"Oh, I made a mistake, I guess," she answered, wiping under her eyes with the back of her hand. "I *did* hear somebody creeping around on the mezzanine, and that librarian says they've been having some trouble lately with a flasher hiding in the stacks. But you made it plain that it couldn't have been that old man."

The young man beside her threw his head back and laughed, a rich, deep laugh that showed all of his slightly irregular teeth.

"Oh, that's wonderful," he said finally. "Tom Werner as a flasher. I wouldn't put it past him. But he *was* downstairs, I'm afraid."

"You don't like him?" Kate asked. In the library, Werner had turned to this young man with the clear certainty that he was an ally.

"He and his wife are old friends of my parents," he explained; there was something acid in the way he said "parents." "But I'm not too crazy about him, no. 'John, come here!' He can't even remember that I'm called Jack. He's just one of those guys who don't pay much attention to other people, I guess."

"Well, even if he wasn't up in the mezzanine," Kate said, "I'd like to know what he was doing hanging around the lobby. He didn't have any books, did he? And he was looking at me funny."

"What does that mean?" Jack Kramer said, his smooth forehead puckering into a frown.

"I can't explain it," Kate replied, "but once when I glanced at him, he was watching me and he had an expression that seemed to say, 'I know you from someplace,' or maybe even, 'I recognize you.' "

"Maybe he does," Jack responded. "Are you from the north side?"

"No," she said, and now she smiled, remembering her earlier drive through that section of town—Thomas Werner *would* live there. "I've only been in Woodard a few days and I've never been here before."

"Maybe you look like somebody he knows," Jack offered.

"Yes," Kate said, drawing out the syllable. "That's just what I've been thinking. Do I look familiar to *you* in any way?"

Jack Kramer squinted at her now, examining her face carefully and, she could see, appreciatively.

"No, sorry," he said. "And I'd remember if I'd seen you before."

"Does the name Teresa Cruzan mean anything to you? She lives in Woodard." She realized it was the first time she'd said Terry's name out loud to anyone except Terry herself.

He frowned in concentration for a moment.

"No," he said. "That doesn't ring any bells. Is she somebody you look like, some relative or something?"

"Yes," Kate answered. "She's my mother." When she heard herself say the words, she felt a tingly rush of elation followed by a wave of guilt—as if she'd uttered not an affirmation but a denial. For so many years, the phrase "my mother" had been applied to Sheila Lundgren.

"Now I'm confused," he said. "How come you've never been to Woodard before if your mother lives here?"

"It's a long story. And didn't I hear you say you were on your lunch break? You'd better not hang around or your boss'll yell at you."

"Well, actually," he said, "I *am* the boss." He looked a bit sheepish when he said it, as if it surprised even him. "I get to yell at other people if they're late. I love long stories, so why don't you grab a cup of coffee with me at Kelly's—you can see the sign right over there—and you can tell me all about it."

Kate looked at him intently. She felt mildly ashamed of herself for having said so much already. But she also felt drawn to this young man, to those intense eyes behind the plain glasses.

"I don't know that it's a story I'm ready to tell," she said, shrugging slightly.

"Well, just the coffee, then," he said, grinning in a thoroughly disarming way. "I'll tell you *my* life story, which is so dazzlingly entertaining that you'll forget all about library creepers."

Kelly's was the kind of local café where the good people of Woodard could order exactly the same kind of food they would eat at home—meat loaf, fried chicken, mashed potatoes with gravy, powerful coffee, maybe a side dish of creamed corn, and bread pudding for dessert.

"Woodard's idea of haute cuisine," Jack Kramer told Kate across the plastic table, "is when a greasy spoon hangs up plastic ferns and changes the name of its batter-fried shrimp to Braised Prawns."

He also told her that he'd inherited his family's modest real estate development company when his father died almost two years ago. "Curse of the only child, only son. My mother took it hard—it was so sudden. She's not the sort of person who could take charge of a business; she has trouble taking charge of a bridge game. So I got stuck."

"Stuck?" Kate said, wondering if Jack Kramer was talking about his parents because she had so recently made a declaration about her mother, or if people their age just spontaneously related to each other by ragging on their parents. "Wouldn't most guys your age be delighted to have their own business?"

"Probably," he sighed, stirring a second tiny container of half-and-half into his coffee. "But I majored in music at the U. What I wanted to do was go off to Chicago or New York and get into a jazz combo—Chicago has great jazz places, you know. I think I could've got my father to bankroll me for a while— or, rather, I could've got my mother to *persuade* my father to bankroll me."

"Oh, you're musical," Kate exclaimed. "Me, too. Voice lessons for umpty years, college recitals, that sort of thing." She fell silent because Jack Kramer was looking at her with a blank expression, as if he couldn't see any connection between her words and what he had just been saying.

"Of course," she faltered, "I never hoped to make a career out of it the way you did."

"Well, never mind," he sighed. "That little dream is gone now. Gotta watch that bottom line every minute, you know. And I can't leave her now—my mother, I mean. Dad always took care of her, and now it's my job."

"And you don't like Woodard very much, I take it?"

"Oh, Lord," he cried, casting his eyes up at the stained ceiling, "Woodard is proof that hell is full and the dead walk the earth."

Kate laughed in spite of herself. Cynicism of this variety

had always appealed to her because, to some extent, she shared it and equated it with intelligence. And she found it attractive, too; the upbeat cheerfulness of most young men in her acquaintance seemed naïve and boyish by comparison.

"Well, you would know, I guess, because you've always lived here, but I think the place has a certain charm. The only objection I have is that folks in small towns seem more disposed to genuflect in front of people like Werner. I suppose he's some bigwig around here, huh?"

"Well," Jack laughed. "There's an irony there, too. He's not even a native son. Ordinarily, of course, that would make him forever an 'outsider.' But he married right: Elizabeth Proctor, only daughter of Joseph Proctor and only heir to the Proctor millions."

"So, it's only the money they all bow to?" Kate was scornful. "And he didn't even earn any of it?"

"He works for the Proctor interests now, of course," Jack explained, stirring his coffee idly. "Manages the banking stuff. The Proctors made their bucks in lumber and then banking— Elizabeth's grandfather, that is. But Tom Werner came from pretty humble stock."

"So, how come he won the Princess of Woodard?" Kate asked. "Doesn't big money usually marry big money?"

"That, I guess, was a big scandal at the time. My mother told me all about it. The country-club types decided the place needed some big-city class, so they hired a tennis pro. Read for this, a kid who'd played varsity tennis in college. Well, the kid was apparently giving lessons of a different kind to little Liz, who wound up pregnant."

"And that was Werner?"

"That was Werner. Mom says old Joe Proctor did everything he could to stop the marriage. Hired detectives to find dirt on Tom, but all they found was a nice farm family in Iowa and a mediocre college career at Grinnell. And Elizabeth was over twenty-one. After the baby was born, a boy, Joe thawed enough to settle a huge chunk of the estate on the kid, bypassing La Liz because he was still ticked at Tom Werner."

"But he hardly seems penniless now," Kate protested.

"Of course not," Jack laughed. "Elizabeth got a generous share, all tied up in trust conditions so that Tom couldn't lay hands on it if he and Liz split. But she's always been generous, and he made a pretty good money manager for her. My father once told me that Tom might actually have doubled her fortune over the years of the marriage."

"So now everybody in town thinks Werner is God," Kate scoffed. She was still smarting from the tone Thomas Werner had used with her.

"Well, the Werners are sort of 'in the news' right now," Jack replied, "because Elizabeth wants to retire to a warmer climate. She's a few years older than Tom, and Minnesota winters are starting to get to her. That means selling off all the holdings—liquidation. You see, I'm learning the jargon now that I'm a businessman myself." Kate could hear the mocking tone. "The town's not happy about it. In a place like Woodard, change of any kind seems like an earthquake. Rumor has it that Tom isn't too happy about it, either. Once the holdings are just cash, he'll be pretty obviously living off his wife's money."

"And only as long as she's pleased with him?"

"Oh, she seems to have been pretty pleased with him through the years," Jack said. "They give every appearance of being a devoted couple. Their son—Joseph, after the grandpa who made him a millionaire at three—is a successful businessman in California now. Took to it like a champ. In the blood, I guess."

"But not in yours?" Kate was responding to his tone.

He looked straight at her now and she saw a dark wave of bitterness pass over his well-scrubbed features.

"Enough about me and Woodard royalty," he said, shrugging and changing his expression. "It's your turn now. Are you going to tell me what you're doing here? And about the mystery of your mother?"

For just a second, Kate felt again that doubleness in her emotions because she thought almost simultaneously of Teresa Cruzan and Sheila Lundgren when this stranger said "your mother."

"It's not such a big mystery, I guess," she said with a shrug, staring down at the coffee she'd scarcely tasted. "I'm adopted and I came to Woodard to meet my birth mother. I just found out about her."

"Wow," he breathed. "That must be something. And she's the Teresa Cruzan who looks like you?"

"Yes, but it's not going very well. Not what I expected."

"She wasn't glad to see you?"

Kate made the same snorting sound she'd heard Terry make when she had asked if Max was her boyfriend. "To say the least," she replied, glancing away.

"Hurts a lot?" he asked. Kate looked up at him; both the cocky cynicism and the bitterness were gone from his face. A sort of neutral curiosity had replaced them.

"To say the least," she whispered after a pause. "Well, you'd better get back to watching the bottom line. It's getting late for a lunch break." It was her way of letting him know that further talk about Teresa Cruzan would bring on a relapse of crying.

"Can I call you sometime?" he asked, taking her cue and reaching into his pocket for some money. "Maybe tomorrow? Are you staying with her? With your mother, I mean."

"I don't even know how long I'm going to be here," Kate said. "I'm trying to decide if I should just give up."

"Well, if I wanted to call just in case?" His eyebrows lifted above his glasses. Kate felt again the tug of attraction.

"Yes, I suppose you could do that," she said with a little smile. "I'm staying at the Holiday Inn. And my last name is Lundgren." She'd told him the "Kate" part on the walk to Kelly's.

"Better," he said as he stood up. "Kate Cruzan would be too alliterative."

She didn't smile, and he seemed to see at once that she wasn't ready to treat this business lightly. He squeezed her elbow briefly before turning away to pay the check.

Back in her room, Kate turned her mind away from the incident in the library and from Jack Kramer to face at last the issue of what she should do next. She realized that she couldn't make a decision about whether or not to stay in Woodard until she got the answer to a question that had been stealing into her mind every now and then for two days now. When it first occurred to her, she was so horrified by it that she banished it at once, but it kept coming irresistibly back. It began as one question that quickly spawned a few others: Had her adoptive parents *stayed* in touch with Teresa Cruzan all these years? Had they contacted her as soon as Kate was legally able to begin her search and instructed Terry to say no to the request for a reunion? Had they arranged for Terry to file the affidavit of nondisclosure the same way they'd arranged the adoption? As angry as she felt with Doug and Sheila Lundgren for withholding information from her, Kate didn't want to believe them capable of that. Yet they'd baldly deceived her when she tried to enlist their help in the search.

If Terry had said no on her own, Kate might have to accept that her birth mother wanted no part of her. But if she'd said no because somebody had persuaded her in advance that it would be bad for her daughter to be reunited with her, then Kate felt it would explain the sense she'd had on Tuesday of Terry putting on an act. And if Doug and Sheila had persuaded Terry to do that, then Kate meant to stay in Woodard until she could convince her otherwise.

She would begin by asking the question of the people who could answer it. So now Kate lifted the receiver, dialed 1 and then the familiar number of her home in White Bear Lake. The phone rang and rang but there was no answer. Finally Kate slammed the receiver down. She was getting pretty sick of unanswered phones. But partly her irritation was a throwback to her childhood sense of abandonment whenever her parents left home, resenting it even if they went out while she was also out. Once when Sheila said she was going shopping while Kate was at another child's birthday party, she'd responded peevishly, "You're supposed to stay home all the time."

Kate's hand was still on the phone when it rang, startling her so much that she screamed and snatched it away, as if she'd received an electric shock. It was so unexpected. She put a shaking hand back down onto the receiver as the phone rang a second time.

"Hello," she said even before the receiver had reached her face.

"It's Terry," the voice at the other end said without any preliminaries. "Where you been all afternoon?"

"At the library," Kate murmured, her mind numb.

"Well, you don't need that; you're smart enough already." Terry's voice was no longer angry; there was a sort of forced joviality in the tone.

Kate was still too stunned to attempt a response.

"Look, honey," Terry went on. "I'm sorry I yelled last night, but my boyfriend and me were right in the middle of things when you called—you know what I mean—and there's the phone ringing and ringing."

Kate found herself profoundly embarrassed to be told so directly about Terry's sexual activities.

"Are you listening?" Terry said.

"Yes," Kate mumbled. "Of course."

"You still planning to stay in town?"

"Yes," Kate answered, more defiant now.

"What you said on the phone about hanging around on my street." Terry was cajoling now. "That's not a good idea. You just can't do stuff like that anymore. I know you got lots of things you want to know, and I'm gonna see you one more time to help you out."

"Thank you," Kate whispered after another stunned pause.

"We could have lunch on Sunday over there," Terry went on as if she hadn't heard. "They got a nice restaurant there, don't they?"

"I guess so," Kate said, but she'd never eaten at the motel.

"Well, I can come there about twelve-thirty. That be okay?"

"On Sunday?" Kate asked. "Not sooner?"

"Boy, oh boy, kid," Terry said, and now she sounded exasperated. "Can't you take yes for an answer?"

"All right," Kate said hurriedly. "I'm sorry, but I'm so eager. Sunday will be fine."

"And no coming around the house, okay?" Terry's voice was serious now. "You hear me?"

"Okay," Kate said. "No coming around the house."

"And no calling me at all hours? No calling at all?"

"No calling you at all—okay. Sunday, then. Twelve-thirty."

"See ya." And then the receiver was replaced in that quiet way Kate recognized from the night before.

# CHAPTER 7

Kate's elation lasted until the middle of Saturday morning. Her first response to Terry's call had been excessive—a wild joy that drove everything else from her mind. She kept chanting under her breath, "I've won, I've won." She forgot the questions she'd been ready to ask Sheila Lundgren just before Terry called. She began to plan ahead: After Sunday, there would be other meetings; she and Terry would become friends; the magical mother of her fantasies would emerge from the mask Terry had assumed in the mistaken belief that she must drive her daughter away. Because, of course, Kate had selectively forgotten Terry's words: "I'm gonna see you one more time." Sunday's meeting, she was sure, would be only the first of many, each more comfortable, more filled with confidences.

But by Saturday, she had begun to analyze Terry's concession and its conditions. They were to meet for lunch in a public place. This could be an efficient guard against intimacy—no opportunity for raised voices or open pleading. Emotionally safe. And the conditions were, on closer inspection, insulting. Stay away from my house. Don't call me. What did they add up to? I'm embarrassed to let anyone find out about you; I'm ashamed of your existence.

Kate's feelings swung to anger and depression almost as

excessive as her joy had been. This kind of overreaction was part of her temperament; she'd always been moody. A fight with her best friend, an event that would have been forgotten in two hours by any other sixth-grader, had once sent her sobbing into her room, where she'd spent an entire weekend, responding to her mother's frantic questions only with, "I'm never going back to school as long as I live."

And, partly, she hated the waiting. There was just too much time to get through between now and Sunday noon. Waiting had never been easy for Kate. Because she was fairly quiet as a child, people had assumed that she was patient, when nothing could have been further from the truth. Christmas had been the hardest; from about December 6, she was already longing for Christmas to arrive immediately. She wished fiercely that she could be like Samantha on *Bewitched*, that she could just twitch her nose and it would be Christmas morning. She smiled now in spite of herself, remembering how Sheila had stood guard in the hallway on Christmas Eve, saying patiently, "Santa Claus can't come until you're asleep," every time Kate would peek out of her room. The memory filled Kate with a confused longing as sharp as a pain.

After a feeble attempt at breakfast—she was going out to the McDonald's across the highway in an effort to conserve her funds—Kate sat in her room, staring and brooding. When the phone began to ring, she had a momentary and wholly irrational fear that it was Terry calling to cancel the Sunday appointment. Finally, after the fifth ring, Kate picked up the receiver and put it to her ear.

"Hello," she murmured, and she didn't recognize her own voice.

"Is this Kate Lundgren?" a deep voice responded.

"Yes."

"Hi. It's Jack Kramer." The voice was hearty now. "I'm glad you're still here. Are things going better with your mother?"

"Well," Kate sighed, "yes and no."

"Ah," he said, "but enough yes to keep you here for a while longer?"

"Maybe," she said, reluctant now to express any hope; she felt keenly the old superstitious fear that announcing hope would induce the fates to crush it.

"Are you tied up all weekend?" he asked, cheerfully ignoring the taciturn quality of her answers.

"No. In fact, I'm pretty much at loose ends for the moment."

"How would you like to see a play tonight?"

"A play? Here in Woodard?"

"Sure," and he laughed. "Even Woodard has a community theater. They're doing an all-female version of *The Odd Couple*. It definitely isn't the Guthrie, but it might be good for a laugh or two. My mother's one of the patrons and always has extra tickets."

Kate wasn't in the mood for an amateur production, but there were some twenty-four hours to fill until her Sunday lunch date with Terry, and any distraction was welcome.

"Okay," she said, more animated now. "What time and where?"

"I'll come by for you about seven-thirty," he replied. "Believe me, trying to give or follow directions to this place would be like Lawrence of Arabia trying to find his way across the Nefud Desert."

Woodard's Community Theatre was housed in a converted Moravian church; pews had given way to padded seats, altar to stage, and the vaulted ceiling was now crisscrossed with theater lights. In the narrow lobby that had once been the vestibule, Kate stood talking to Jack Kramer. He'd got dressed up in a light beige summer suit, a pale peach-colored shirt, and a tie. Though her anxiety over Terry had made her almost forget Jack since the coffee at Kelly's, his physical presence—the nice clothes, the heady smell of his cologne—reminded her of the almost immediate attraction she'd felt for him. And it also made her aware of how underdressed she herself was, bare-legged in a skirt and silk blouse. But all her good clothes were in White Bear Lake.

On the way to the theater, she had been parrying Jack's questions about Terry, still too confused and tender about her feelings to indulge his natural curiosity. Instead, they had begun to talk about the Lundgrens, a slightly less delicate subject for Kate.

"My younger brother is adopted, too," Kate was saying.

"He's twenty-one and about to become a senior at Hamline—he's already in the law program there."

"Then, you two aren't blood kin to each other, I suppose," Jack asked, leaning toward her so he wouldn't have to shout to be heard above the hubbub of the lobby.

"No," Kate replied, "but we were placed by the same agency. When Eric was nineteen, he contacted the agency about his birth parents—mostly, I think, because I was so preoccupied with the process. He went through the recommended counseling sessions and then gave up the search. He'd never been *very* interested, I think—not like me—and whatever the counselors said convinced him he might be better off not knowing. He's pretty laid back about everything, really."

"Not like you," Jack said, looking down at her with an intense expression that made her blush. There was nothing flirtatious or sexual about it, yet it was profoundly personal.

"Not like me," Kate responded, smiling a little.

"What do your parents do?" he asked.

Again, that odd click—*which* parents? But she could tell that he wasn't aware of the ambiguity in his question.

"My mother stays home and my father owns his own company," she said. "They make chains."

"Chains?"

"Yes, chains." She laughed a little at his puzzled look. "Big chains to haul cargo up ship ramps, little chains to put across the opening of your door. Somebody's got to make chains. They don't just get into the hardware stores by themselves."

"Don't be a smart aleck," he said, but he was grinning.

"The whole operation is in South St. Paul now," Kate explained, "but Dad used to have a warehouse here in Woodard, years ago. Property was cheaper, I think."

"Tell me about it," he said. "Still is, too. Real estate development in Woodard is not, alas, the fastest way to get rich."

A bell sounded and the lobby crowd started to move toward the double doors leading to the inside of the theater. Jack took Kate's elbow and piloted her to the left.

"So you have more than one connection to Woodard, then," he said as they made their way to the side aisle.

"Yes, I guess I do," Kate answered, but she didn't want to explain how the two connections were, in fact, connected to each other. It would have felt somehow disloyal to tell a virtual stranger about her parents' long deception. She made up her mind to forget, at least momentarily, about her obsessions, to just relax and enjoy being with this attractive man.

The play turned out to be very diverting, indeed, not so much from its being a polished performance—it was not—as from Jack's whispered comments about the production and the actresses in it.

"Take a good look at the woman playing Olive," he whispered in the first act. "That's Valerie Gittings, Woodard's answer to Ethel Merman. She gets big roles in every production because she's on the board and contributed most of the furniture in the prop room—her husband, Ted, takes it in on trade at his furniture store and nobody would actually buy it. See that green sofa? It's as overupholstered as Val herself." During the second poker scene, he whispered, "Val *does* sort of resemble Jack Klugman in drag, don't you think?" A middle-aged woman in the row ahead of them turned with a severe glance and said, "Sh-h-h!" Kate and Jack exchanged mocking glances as soon as her back was turned.

But there were quiet moments, too, when the earnestness and the amateur quality of the play reminded Kate inevitably of the school productions she'd been a part of in White Bear Lake—as a mouse in a second-grade pageant, as a computer chip in a fifth-grade production of *Gigo*, and as the eldest daughter in her high school's ambitious version of *The Sound of Music*. But what she remembered most at the moment was her mother devising a way to make the gray mouse ears stand up straight, driving her and her giggling classmates to after-school rehearsal, reading lines with her in a mock German accent. Almost tone-deaf herself, Sheila Lundgren nevertheless fostered and took pride in her daughter's musical and theatrical gifts. And she was always, always in the front row, looking anxious, unconsciously mouthing lines, beaming through the curtain calls.

At intermission, Kate and Jack made their way to the lobby again, where a small woman in an elegant knit dress approached them, a bright smile fixed on her pink and white face.

"Jack," she cried. "Here you are. I didn't see you before the first act."

"Mother," Jack said, and Kate saw his face pull into an expression of worried solicitousness, with perhaps a trace of embarrassment. "This is Kate. Kate, my mother."

"Hello, dear," the little woman said, and Kate could tell that she probably called every female acquaintance "dear."

"Nice to meet you, Mrs. Kramer," Kate said, extending her hand. She saw that Jack's mother was in her sixties, a delicate prettiness still apparent despite the wrinkles on her face and neck. Like Sheila, she had come to motherhood rather later than most women do, but unlike Sheila, she hadn't kept a sprightly athleticism. She was clearly of the "satin pillow" variety of women—pampered, soft. The hand she gave Kate was small, very white, and the clasp was weak.

"Are you enjoying our little production?" she asked.

"Very much," Kate replied, glad that this was not, technically, a lie. She *was* having a good time with Jack.

"Did the Kleins pick you up on time?" Jack asked. "I don't see them." Kate noticed how he bent over slightly to talk to his mother. Even his deep voice seemed lighter, more boyish.

"Oh, yes. They arrived just after you left the house," she replied. "They're still inside, but I needed to stretch my legs."

And get a closer look at me, Kate thought. But she didn't resent this at all; on the contrary, she felt a real warmth toward the little woman who looked up at her son with such open adoration. The expression was comforting—familiar.

"Now, don't you go out drinking and carousing after the play," Jack teased, putting his arm around the thin shoulders. "You're such a bear when you're hung over."

"Oh, you," she said, giving his arm a playful slap and turning to Kate with an expression that clearly said, "Could anyone on earth be more charming?"

And Kate *was* charmed, more by Jack's body language than by his bantering words. This was the same man who had said of his mother on Thursday, "She has trouble taking charge of a bridge game," who had seemed to regard her as a burden. And here he was, so clearly devoted to his mother, so attentive and protective.

Surely, Kate thought, there was no other bond more complicated than the parent-child one, none more knotted and ambivalent; perhaps there were few relationships in life that could even match it for longevity, for sheer intricacy. Lovers came and went; friends who disappointed often enough ceased to be friends; even spouses could be exchanged if the bond weakened and broke down. But parents and children had each other forever, and the relationship was an ocean of shifting tides where dependence and independence changed constantly, where the roles of protected and protector were always being reversed. She liked Jack better now that she had seen him with his mother; the slightly mean-spirited commentary about Woodard's version of *The Odd Couple* had been amusing, but this was a revelation of a more human side.

After the play, Jack drove her back to the motel and they sat in the car for a while, talking. Kate told him she liked his mother; he spoke briefly about how she had only recently started to come out of her grieving.

"I'd like to see you again," Jack said finally—direct, no-nonsense, "but I guess that depends on whether or not your real mother thaws."

Kate felt a pang at the term *real mother*. In her girlhood, she'd often noticed how the phrase hurt Sheila, who never complained of it openly. *Birth mother* was the term the Lundgrens always used, and other relatives had gradually picked it up.

"I guess that's right," she sighed. "Whether or not I stay much longer *does* depend on her." She was still reluctant to talk about the scheduled lunch with Terry. "But you could try next week to see if I'm still around."

"Would you *like* me to try?" he asked.

"Yes," she said, smiling at him in the dark. "I'd like you to try."

They got out of the car and started to cross the darkened parking lot toward the brightly lit doors of the motel. The air felt clammy against Kate's arms. "Boy, I think it's hotter now than it was this afternoon," she said.

"Well, it's July first tomorrow," he offered. "We should expect some insufferable weather pretty soon. I never could figure out how people thought to call this a temperate climate; we go into the deep freeze in the winter and we melt every summer."

They walked on in silence for a moment, Kate trying to formulate some small talk, some way to deflect the notion that they were coming to the end of a first date. She half hoped he would try to kiss her—the sense of his trim body next to her in the gloom made her want to touch him, to take his arm. Suddenly she found herself walking alone because Jack had come to a halt. She turned back to find him poised at attention, looking away from her toward a row of parked cars.

"What is it?" she asked.

"I heard something over there," he said. "Something moving behind those cars." And he lifted his arm to gesture.

"It's probably an animal," she said, but she felt a thrill of fear run up her spine. "We're almost at the edge of the forest out here."

"I'll go take a look," he said, boyishly enthusiastic, actually starting to walk toward the cars.

"No," she called, a little too loud. He stopped to look back at her in surprise. "Don't do that," she went on, more quietly. "What if it's a bear? You don't want your nice suit mauled, do you?"

He laughed, responding to the teasing exaggeration. "You're right," he said, coming up to her now. "And if it's a skunk—much more likely, by the way—that would be worse."

In the lobby, Jack held her hand briefly when she extended it to say good night. Again, his look was searching, intense, but he made no move toward her.

"Good luck with your mother," he said, a little smile playing over his lips.

"Thanks," she told him. "I need the moral support."

In her room, she stood for while at the window, looking down into the parking lot. Every time a car passed on the highway, shadows played along the fence that separated it from the mall parking lot. The moving light created the illusion that the parked cars themselves were moving slightly. What was the noise Jack had heard? Someone had followed her onto the mezzanine at the library, crept closer to her, and then fled when she ran. Was someone following her around Woodard, watching for her to leave the motel, waiting for her to return? Hiding in the parking lot while she said good night to her date? But who? Nobody in Woodard knew her. Except Terry, of course. Would Terry watch her, or send somebody else to watch her? Would Max trail around after her for some reason? Something odd was going on at the house on Franklin Street, and it involved Max, but she couldn't think of any reason for him to follow her around.

She was too exhausted to keep revolving the questions, to ponder the mysteries—she'd done too much of that the night before. Tomorrow would give her a chance to ask some questions. And if she was careful about how she asked them, she might even get some answers.

# CHAPTER 8

Kate sat perched on the bench outside Monahan's, the restaurant inside the Holiday Inn; she was resolutely keeping herself from pacing, from looking at her watch, from any activity that would betray her nervous anxiety. It was twelve-forty on Sunday and Teresa Cruzan was ten minutes late for lunch. The restaurant was serving a buffet-style brunch, and there were people bustling around on all sides. All Kate could think of was, She's not coming. She's changed her mind.

Then a group of people, just arrived from church by the look of their clothes, moved forward past Kate and revealed a solitary figure coming through the glass doors of the motel. It took half a second for Kate to recognize her, but then it seemed as if she had spent her life watching this face coming toward her: the searching glance, the moment of recognition, the little smile—like catching sight of her own moving reflection in a store window. Today Terry looked quite different from the other times Kate had seen her; she had a chameleonlike quality that was beginning to fascinate Kate more and more.

She was wearing her hair back, braided at the sides, caught at the nape of her neck by a silk scarf, and then flowing loose below the scarf. Her makeup was more subdued than it had been on Tuesday, her dark eyes softly emphasized by dusty shades of green eye shadow. She was wearing the same gold hoop earrings she'd worn on Tuesday. Her dress was a simple, sleeveless knit, a creamy beige color, with a wide belt. She was wearing flat sandals without stockings. Only her purse seemed out of place; it was the same fringed suede bag Kate had seen her carry into the gray Thunderbird on Friday. As she came closer, Kate could see fine beads of perspiration on her peaked upper lip and under her eyes.

"Boy, it's a cooker out there today," Terry said without meeting Kate's eyes. "Summer has finally sprung, I guess. You're lucky you got air-conditioning in here. No wonder you look so fresh."

Kate hadn't been outside at all, had showered and dressed carefully in a cotton-knit top and print skirt, had let her hair dry naturally so its curls were more noticeable. She reflected that all the people in the restaurant would be able to see, if they just looked up, the resemblance between the two women now coming through the door, though they might think they were seeing sisters rather than mother and daughter; that's how young Terry was looking today.

As they were shown to their table near the front window, Kate realized that she was feeling very much as she'd felt in the sixth grade when Sheila had appeared for a school tea in a pale-green linen suit, her nails freshly manicured, her blond hair rolled into a French twist. Then, as now, she'd wanted to say to the crowd, "Is this the spiffiest mother in the room, or what?" But she only walked a little taller, glancing furtively at the reactions of those who looked up from their eggs and Belgian waffles. When she looked back at Terry, she saw there for a brief moment the mirror image of her own expression, as if Terry were proud to be walking with her, too.

As the waitress took their drink order—coffee, black, for both of them—and explained the buffet, Kate watched Terry's face, couldn't help noticing that she looked nervous—kept glancing around the restaurant and out the window as if she expected to see someone she knew. No, more than that: as if she were *afraid* she would see someone she knew. They were silent as they made their way through the buffet lines, awkward with each other in this public place. Kate was hardly aware of what she was putting onto her plate, was surprised, after she sat down again, to find six sausages next to her small omelet—she didn't even like sausages, preferred bacon.

"I don't know how I'm going to eat all this," she said as Terry settled into the chair opposite her. "I'll probably gain six pounds."

"Oh, you don't have to worry about that stuff," Terry said, shaking out the big cloth napkin. "I've been eating like a horse all my life and look at me. Skinny is in your genes, kid, so relax."

It was the first spontaneous reference that Terry had made to their biological connection, and it almost brought tears to Kate's eyes. Terry looked straight at her now, saw the expression, and dropped her gaze onto her plate—a faint blush rose in the skin that stretched across the sharply angled cheekbones.

"I been thinking about what you said," Terry said now, as if she were addressing the muffin next to her coffee cup. "About that genetic stuff, I mean. About how you're worried over what might be in the family, or wondering about it, at least."

"That's only one of the things I've been wondering about," Kate said, her fork idle in her hand.

"Yeah, I know," Terry said, glancing up now. "But it's the genetic stuff I came here to talk about, okay?" Beneath the embarrassment, Kate could see the determination in the eyes, in the set of the long jaw.

"Okay," she replied softly.

"You shouldn't worry about that stuff," Terry said, leaning forward, her face earnest. "My folks died from real ordinary kinda stuff and they were pretty old. I been healthy all my life and my brother is a real jock, in all kinda sports out there—we're good peasant stock, my old man used to say. And a lot of that genetic stuff is a crap shoot, anyway. My boyfriend's mother dropped dead from some aneurysm in her brain and she was only forty-eight, never anything like that in the family before. It was just ticking away in there like a little bomb waiting to go off. Now, I figure, either you got something like that or you don't—nothing you can do about it one way or the other. So why make yourself crazy worrying about it?"

"But there *are* some things that can be helped, if we know about them," Kate said, nervous now because she was approaching territory that might provoke anger from Terry. "If it's true that my natural father is dead, I should know what he died of, because early death of a parent is important medical information for a person to have."

"What do you mean, 'if it's true he's dead'?" Terry said, bristling. "I told you, didn't I? You saying I'm a liar?"

"No, of course not," Kate answered, but she *did* think Terry was being unnecessarily defensive. "It's just that you haven't really told me anything about him. I'm not asking for his name, just for you to tell me what he died of."

"Well, it wasn't anything for you to worry about," Terry said, settling down again. "Really it wasn't and he didn't die young, if that's what's bothering you. He was a lot older than me—I mean, a *lot* older—so you don't have to think about pegging out at an early age because of something you inherited from him."

"Older?" Kate said, her mind blank. This didn't square with any fantasy she'd ever had about her birth parents; in her mind's eye, she'd always seen them as kids, young and very much in love, too old to resist temptation, but too young to deal with the consequences. "How much older?"

"Now, I'm not going into details," Terry answered, tearing her muffin in half as if she were angry with it. "You just gotta take my word for it. I'm only telling you this much so you'll stop worrying about inherited diseases."

But she must have seen the skepticism in Kate's face because she blushed again and went on. "In those days—when I was a teenager, I mean—I couldn't stand guys my own age. They all seemed so juvenile, you know what I mean? So this older guy appealed to me. He was so-o-o gorgeous; you don't have any ugly genes on that side either, believe me, so don't worry that your kids will turn out funny-looking. And he was suave, a real gentleman. I guess I was a dumb kid, but I didn't see anything funny about him wanting to spend time with me. Nowadays, people would say there was something kinda creepy about it, but I thought he was dreamy."

Kate put her fork down, clutched for the water glass. Was this true? Had Terry been seduced and impregnated by a dirty old man who lusted after young girls—by a virtual pedophile? Or was this a lie, thought up since Tuesday to cover an earlier lie—the one about her lover being dead? Kate realized with a lurching feeling in her stomach that she didn't trust the woman across from her—the woman with her face. Terry's secretiveness could be explained only if she were trying to protect the identity of a living man—someone for whom a scandal about an illegitimate child could be damaging.

"He was married at the time, I suppose?" Kate said coldly.

"I'm not gonna answer questions like that," Terry said, "so you can just quit asking them." She popped a piece of muffin into her mouth, chewed resolutely, swallowed. "I told you he died, but he was much older than me, so it's nothing to worry about. That's it."

"And nowadays you prefer younger boyfriends," Kate said acidly, angry at this stonewalling. She saw the dark eyes widen, heard the intake of breath.

"How did you know about that?" Terry said, and she looked nervous again, almost frightened.

Kate shrugged. "I was driving by the house the other night, that's all, and I saw you getting in a Trans Am with a guy."

"Spying on me, are you?" Terry said, and the almost-Oriental eyes narrowed into slits. "I told you not to hang around my house. You just got to cut that out, I tell you."

"I saw Max there, too, one day," Kate went on, raising her voice. "Coming out of your garage. What business are you in with Max, anyway?"

Terry had gone pale under the tawny makeup and her face looked less angry than frightened. "My business with Max is just that," she said softly, pausing for effect. "*My* business."

"Is Max my father?" Kate was relentless now, couldn't stop herself. She had spoken loudly enough to make a woman at the next table turn an amazed expression in their direction.

"Oh, what is the matter with you, kid?" Terry was hissing across the table at her, trying to hush her. "Why can't you just give it up? Max and I went to grade school together—the nuns used to take turns beating up on us and that sorta forms a bond, I guess. He's not much, I admit, but we go way back. That's all there is to it."

"You haven't answered my question, though," Kate said, more quietly; the constraints of her own polite upbringing made it almost impossible for her to make a scene in a public place.

Terry stared at her now, her face hardening. "I told you as much as you're gonna get out of me," she said at last.

"But that's nothing," Kate said, her voice shaking with the strain of trying to rein in her emotions. "You've told me nothing, really. And I'm not sure I believe the little you have told me."

Terry sighed, looked around the restaurant, up at the ceiling, as if appealing to invisible onlookers to commiserate with her on having to deal with such a person.

"Look," she said finally, and her voice was almost gentle now, "I made the best deal for you I could think of. Maybe you don't know now how good a deal it was, but you will someday. You're a bright kid, I can tell. Don't be dumb enough to look for a better deal here because you won't find it. I'm not the loving-mother type, believe me, and I'm not gonna start changing now. This is all you're gonna get. Now, go home and have a happy life."

"And you think it's as easy as that?" Kate hissed, rage boiling to the surface. "Well, it's not. You don't know what it's like to have these big gaps in your life—like holes that nothing can fill."

"And you don't know what it's like to be me, either," Terry said. "So I guess we're even. I got some gaps in my life, too, kid. Believe me when I tell you it's best for you to go home."

"I wish you'd stop saying that," Kate responded, setting her own long jaw at Terry. "You can't tell me what to do. I'm getting to like it here in Woodard. I even went to a play last night. I had a date with a nice guy I met at the library."

Terry's face went ashen now, her eyes starting out of her pretty face, whites showing all around the dark irises.

"Are you crazy?" she demanded, pushing her chair back from the table. "Do you think you're just gonna settle down here and start a new life? Get married and make me a grandma? Well, you can just forget it. I don't want you here, do you hear that?" She stood up now, the stiff napkin sliding unnoticed to the floor. "You're screwing up my life. Do you think I want my boyfriend to know I got a kid almost as old as he is? I can't say it any clearer—I don't want you here." She separated each of the monosyllables with a tiny pause. Then she turned away and stalked toward the door of the restaurant. Nearby brunchers were watching with unconcealed fascination now.

Kate lowered her head, tears stinging her eyes. Under her face, the sausages swam out of focus, blurring into the cold omelet next to them. She tried to breathe normally, fought against sobs. Then she felt, rather than saw, a figure next to her, and she jerked upright. It was Terry, her face robbed now of any expression except sadness. The lines around her eyes and mouth were exaggerated by the foreshortened angle, and she finally looked her age.

"I don't want the last words to be mean ones," she whispered, leaning forward so Kate could hear her. "You gotta see that this bashing around in people's lives is just no good. You can do damage you don't even know about, and not just to me, either. You just gotta take my word for this: It's bad for *you* to hang around here."

Kate had blinked away her tears enough to focus on Teresa Cruzan's face bending above her own. The expression she saw clearly for just a moment before Terry again turned and walked away was—what? How could she characterize it? Concern was definitely there, but there was something more; Terry looked frightened, as if she were appealing to Kate to bail her out of some trouble—as if she, Terry, were the daughter, and Kate were the mother.

Kate tried to speak, to call after Terry's receding figure moving with that dancerlike grace Kate had noticed when she'd first seen Terry in the red silk robe. But she couldn't think of what she wanted to say, and when she finally thought of it— "Don't worry. It'll be all right"—it was too late; she had to stay and sign for the meal nobody had eaten, and by the time she got to the lobby, Terry was nowhere to be seen. Outside the glass doors, heat shimmered up off the parking lot, but the gray Thunderbird wasn't there.

Kate was hardly aware of how she got back to her room; she saw a finger push the button on the elevator without recognizing the hand as her own. She found herself sitting on the edge of her bed without any consciousness of having unlocked the door. She sat rocking back and forth, her arms folded tightly across her stomach, her elbows pushing down onto her thighs every time she leaned forward.

Is this the end? she kept wondering, the words echoing over and over in her mind. Is this what ten years of waiting and four years of searching amount to in the end—two brief meetings filled with tension and even hostility? And then nothing? Back to White Bear Lake to try to figure out what to do with the rest of her life? What she felt most of all was a searing anger burning her throat and making her eyes water. It wasn't supposed to be like this! But she hated the anger, felt almost frightened by it: You're not supposed to feel this way about your parents; it's wrong to hate your mother. Better to feel nothing; better just to shut down.

So Kate spent the next thirty hours in a daze, refusing to confront the memory of the conversation she'd had over Sunday brunch. She didn't leave the motel; she sat in front of the lighted television screen in her room without registering what was being depicted there; she didn't eat. Sleep came only in small naps, surprising her with the realization—only when she woke up—that she *had* slept. By Monday night, she came to herself long enough to go downstairs and eat a light supper. Thus fortified, she went back to her room to take stock.

One of the things she considered was that she'd pushed too hard, spoiled her chances by selfishly refusing to consider Terry's feelings. Now she really tried to put herself in the other woman's shoes, to imagine what it might be like to have made a hard choice, constructed a life based on that choice, only to have it all suddenly explode. It might take a while to recover from the shock.

Kate didn't want to think about the long range, was afraid to think that she might *never* get closer to her birth mother than she already had come. The short range was easier to deal with. She needed to get away for a while, to talk to some of her friends, to see Eric—perhaps even to talk to Doug and Sheila, to insist that they tell her everything *they* knew. As soon as she thought of her parents, Kate was almost overcome by the sense of how much she missed their support in this crisis; and it occurred to her that they might have kept the secret of her parentage from her precisely to spare her the pain she was now going through.

Once she'd decided to leave Woodard for a while, Kate fell into a deep sleep, a sleep without dreams. When she woke up again, she was amazed to discover that it was already Tuesday afternoon—the massive exhaustion brought on by days of tension and lack of rest had caused her to sleep fourteen hours. As she'd already missed the checkout time, she decided she might as well stay another night, but she was determined to use the rest of this day wisely. She walked across to the mall long enough to buy some nice stationery at the Hallmark store. Then

she sat down at the table in her room to compose a letter to
Terry.

What she hoped was that she could express herself more
calmly and convincingly on paper than she had been able to do
when she was face-to-face with her birth mother. She wanted
to make clear that she was willing to understand and sympathize
with Terry's feelings, that she was willing to be patient. But she
also wanted to convey her determination to "stay in touch," to
return to Woodard for another visit after "you've had some
time to see that I'm no threat." But she discovered how daunting
the task was almost as soon as she had begun. Even the phrase
about not being a threat sounded negative and a little hostile
when she read it over. She crumpled up the stiff sheet of paper
and started again.

By evening Kate had wasted almost all the stationery, had
gone from merely crumpling failed drafts to tearing the sheets
noisily in half. She took a break for some cold supper and then
went back upstairs to the task. When she finally decided to stop,
she still wasn't satisfied with the version in front of her, but she
sealed it up anyway in one of the envelopes with the floral print
inside the flap. Then it occurred to her that she should deliver
it in person, just hand it to Terry with a short, calm announcement. "I'm leaving Woodard for now, but I'd like you to have
this." If Terry wasn't home, she could leave the letter in her
mailbox.

So it was that on Tuesday night, on the eve of Independence Day, Kate drove through the hot, muggy night to 642
Franklin Street, circled the house on foot, and opened the back
door.

# CHAPTER 9

**K**ate stood on the narrow porch, breathing the hot July air into her lungs, quieting the spasms in her throat. Something was wrong inside the house. It seemed as if the windows hadn't been opened in days. And in this heat! Some food in the kitchen must have spoiled pretty badly to account for that smell. The fat person in the chair was probably unconscious—maybe drunk or drugged. But, then, where was Terry? Her Thunderbird was out front, though that didn't necessarily mean she was home; Kate remembered her getting into the red Trans Am last Wednesday evening.

She stepped just inside the door, holding her breath against the smell, which seemed worse now. She listened intently for any sounds, any sign of movement inside the house, her eyes fixed on that pale arm along the green tweed of the chair arm.

"Terry," she called, a little alarmed at the sound of her own voice, though she hadn't really called very loudly. The arm didn't move.

"Terry!" This time she shouted, then paused, listening. There was no answering sound.

She glanced around the kitchen now, looking for the source of the stench. Everything looked in order, tidy, the countertops clean. She felt a strong impulse to run, to get to a phone and summon those people whose job it was to take care of mysterious silences and bad smells. But what if Terry *was* home, maybe upstairs? Or maybe Terry was responsible for whatever had made that other person pass out. What if Terry was involved in something so bad that she could be arrested for it? Kate decided against phone calls of any kind until she got a look at whoever was in the chair.

She tiptoed across the kitchen. In the short hallway that lay beyond the kitchen, she glanced both ways; on one side was the window she'd seen lit from outside of the house, and on the other was a closed door, a single light bulb glowing above the frame. She swallowed once and went on into the living room, poised for flight if anything should move, but there was no motion, no sound; nothing looked disturbed.

Kate focused now on the chair. She was close enough so that the arm of the person in the chair was visible up to the puffy white shoulder. Why, she wondered, should the smell be getting worse? Maybe that was her imagination. She held her breath, hesitating. Again she was almost overwhelmed by the impulse to flee, but she steeled herself, determined to get one look at this person's face; then she could run for the door and some fresh air. She took three long steps, turned, and looked down.

The light from the hallway was just enough to show her what she wanted to know, and the sight made her hands fall straight to her sides, drove the last of the air from her lungs in a faint whimper. The figure in the chair was only half clothed. Face, torso, and limbs were bloated almost past recognition; but the dark hair, braided into plaits over the ears, was unmistakable. Only the left side was naked, as grotesquely pale as worms long submerged in water; the right side was still clothed in the bright red robe, the arm raised at an awkward angle toward the neck, the elbow pointing down at a small, overturned table. The arm was not supported by the chair, and only by following its line to the hand could Kate tell why it stayed up: Several fingers were caught against the throat by one loop of the red silk cord that had once been a belt, barely visible against the pale flesh which had swollen around it and obscured it. The bones of the face were no longer visible under the bloated, engorged flesh. In the dim light, the whole face looked darker than the shoulder, almost blue, in fact. The puffy eyelids were half open, but so swollen that the skin looked ready to burst. The wide mouth was turned down in a sort of grimace, a thick black mass protruding from one corner—it was the tongue. The whole effect was of some grotesque theater mask—the mask of tragedy. The only other spot of color was a small patch of dried blood on the left earlobe where an earring had apparently been torn through the flesh—the wire was still there, but the golden hoop was gone.

Kate staggered backward, gasping, and the smell of Teresa Cruzan's rotting body filled her nose, her throat, and her lungs. Then she heard someone talking, someone saying softly, "Oh God oh God oh God oh God," in a monotone like that, no pauses. It took almost ten seconds to realize that the voice was her own. She was trying to make her legs move, trying to take her eyes off the horror in the chair, but she couldn't get her body to listen to her brain, couldn't stop the babbling voice, "Oh God oh God oh God." It was the violent upheaval in her stomach that finally galvanized her muscles into action, the reflex to run triggered by an old, old admonition not to throw up on the floor.

She threw up instead over the porch railing, retching until only a dry gagging was left. When she stood upright again, she felt light-headed, the sensation that she would float right up to the roof if she let go of the railing. From across the backyard, she heard the faint *pop-pop* of firecrackers and wondered vaguely if the noise was inside her head. But another part of her brain was functioning normally; it was saying, "Telephone. Find a phone." She looked around at the darkened houses on either side of her and inescapably realized that the closest readily available phone was in the house behind her. She remembered clearly that there was a wall phone just inside the back door—she'd faced it over the table as she picked at her shrimp salad last week—just one week ago today. Without turning toward the house, Kate reached inside the door, groping along the wall until she found the phone. Then she lifted the handset and pulled it around the door frame, so that she was standing outside on the porch as she dialed 911.

Kate sat in the passenger seat of her car with the door open and her feet on the pavement outside. She was bent over, holding her head in her hands, waiting, as she'd been told to.

The 911 call had produced immediate results: sirens, two squad cars, an ambulance—all the noise, lights, and bustle of efficient emergency services. Men in uniforms went in and out of the house at 642 Franklin Street; radios crackled inside the squad cars; the ambulance crew huddled briefly with police and then drove away empty; a small crowd of onlookers gathered on the sidewalk, warned in a matter-of-fact sort of way by one of the policemen to stay back. It struck Kate as an odd warning; these polite midwesterners showed no disposition to crowd closer, were even reluctant to pester the professionals with questions, talking quietly to each other instead.

Three separate uniformed men had asked Kate, "What happened?" and three times she'd answered, "I knocked and rang the bell. When nobody answered, I walked around the house. The back door was open, so I went in and found her in the living room, and I called you. I didn't touch anything. Except the door and the phone. And the porch railing." She had answered calmly. She hadn't cried. As a matter of fact, she was wondering now, with her palms against her forehead, why she hadn't cried. Shock, probably. She would feel something later, something besides this numbness and the sensation of burning in her nose and throat, as if the smell had scorched the soft tissues while passing over them.

"Miss?" The voice was directly above her, and she sat up slowly to look—nothing seemed capable of startling her.

A stocky man, dressed in chinos and a light sports jacket, was standing next to her car. He was about fifty, with iron-gray hair cut close to his head, like a marine. Kate wondered idly when he had arrived—the street was now filled with cars, but she hadn't noticed any since the first ones.

"I'm Lieutenant Erwin Kinowski," the man said. "I'll be investigating this case. Did you know the dead woman?"

"Yes," Kate said, realizing that now she would have to get used to hearing Terry called "the dead woman." "She was my mother."

"Jesus!" Kinowski breathed. "That's tough. I'm real sorry."

"I only just met her last week," Kate said, feeling that she didn't deserve the condolence, that she must explain somehow why she was sitting here dry-eyed. "I was adopted as a baby, and I recently found out that she—Teresa Cruzan—was my birth mother."

"I see," Lieutenant Kinowski said, a frown forming between his eyes. "Well, we're gonna need a full statement from you, Miss—?" When Kate failed to react, he went on, "What is your name, miss?"

"Oh," she said in a voice that sounded as if she'd just been awakened from sleep. "Lundgren. Kate Lundgren."

"Well, Miss Lundgren, like I said, we'll need your statement, but it doesn't have to be tonight. Are you staying here in the house?"

"No," Kate murmured. "At the Holiday Inn."

"Well, just don't leave Woodard for a while, okay?" He kept studying her face. "We got lots of forensic stuff to do here yet tonight, and the MBCA boys are coming in pretty soon."

Kate stared at him as if he were speaking Japanese. She knew he was trying to communicate something to her about what she should do, but her brain wasn't turning over fast enough to get it.

"The Minnesota Bureau of Criminal Apprehension," he explained, as if she'd asked a question. "State crime-lab guys. Tomorrow will be time enough to take your statement."

"Do you mean I should go?" she asked, her voice childlike.

"That would be fine, sure," he said. "You had a bad shock and there's nothing for you to do here now. Probably you don't want to be alone, though. Do you have somebody you can call, some family?"

"Yes. Eric. My brother. I'll call my brother."

"You need somebody to drive you?" He was bending to look at her more closely, and Kate realized that the blocky, square-jawed face above her was wearing a concerned, kindly expression.

"No, no," she said. "I've got my car. This is my car right here. I'll just go to the motel and call Eric."

"And I'll come over there to see you tomorrow morning, okay?"

"Sure. Okay."

He started to walk away from her then, and she remembered what she'd been meaning to ask somebody.

"Lieutenant?" she called after him. He turned to look at her. "Who would do that to her, Lieutenant? Who would do such a thing?"

"That's what we're gonna find out, Miss Lundgren," he

answered. "Don't you worry. These things are usually not very complicated. We'll find out who did it."

"Are you just going to leave her there like that?" She couldn't get the picture out of her mind.

"We have to for now," he said gently. "The crime-lab people have to examine things exactly the way they are. We can't disturb anything."

"I see," she said, but they were just words—polite words.

When Kate got back to her room and dialed, she hoped Sheila would answer the phone. In her shock, she yearned for the familiar, comforting voice, the surest balm she'd ever known for hurt or terror. But it was Eric who answered, on the first ring; she could picture him in his cluttered room, diving for the phone to catch a late call—usually for him, anyway—before it could wake their parents.

"Hiya, Katie," he said when she'd identified herself. "What's up?"

"I need you to come here," she said. "Can you do that? Can you come tonight?"

"What's the matter?" His voice was instantly serious, but calm too. "What happened?"

"Did they tell you about Teresa Cruzan?"

There was a brief pause.

"Yes. Mom told me when I got home Saturday."

"She's dead. I found her dead tonight, and I need to see you."

"God, Katie!" His voice was breathless, young, the way he used to sound at eight or ten.

"I want you here," Kate insisted. "I'm at the Holiday Inn in Woodard."

"Of course, I'll come. We'll all come."

Kate waited a second before responding.

"Just you, Eric," she said finally, making up her mind. "I can't see them just now. I'll wait up for you."

And she hung up before the pleading and arguing could begin.

She knew it would be a mistake to close her eyes, was sure that the image was right there, on the insides of her lids, and she couldn't bear to see it again so soon—that horror in the tweed chair. It occurred to her now that her only response to

Terry's body had been revulsion—there had been no pity, no sorrow, no impulse to touch the poor, ruined face. Even the thought of touching that bloated flesh made her shiver as she sat rigid in the hotel chair, staring down at the parking lot. She reviewed the meetings she'd had with her birth mother, going over every detail with a kind of cold objectivity. And when she was through, she realized that in the week she'd been in Woodard, Teresa Cruzan had never once touched her, had never once called her by her name.

# CHAPTER 10

Erwin Kinowski was an uncomplicated man. In fact, he would sometimes use that phrase to describe himself and was almost proud of his reluctance to "overanalyze." In his judgment, overcautious impulses were ill-suited to a policeman, who should be decisive and direct—sort of like a soldier, which Kinowski had been for six years before he became a cop. Born in Woodard in 1938, he had been too young for the Korean conflict—a fact he always regretted—but too old and already settled into his career as a policeman by the time Vietnam began to heat up.

But police work suited him nicely and he moved up in the ranks steadily despite his lack of a college education—new cops were often products of fancy programs in criminology. Privately, Kinowski was scornful of such formal preparation. No school could teach him about crime in Woodard; what there was to see, he had seen—repeatedly. Vandalism, domestic violence, breaking and entering, armed robbery, and—yes—even murder. And lately, the curse of drug traffic had invaded even this small, isolated community, bringing with it the attendant violence and theft which were hallmarks of the trade.

But, in Kinowski's experience, crime was seldom complicated. If someone was floating bad checks, he knew exactly

98

which crook to lock up. If a downtown store was burgled in the middle of the night, he could tell by examining the jimmied door which of five or six locals had probably done the job. In some ways, murder was the least complicated crime of all. Had a woman been beaten to death? Find her husband or her boyfriend, whose bruised knuckles would give him away at first sight—unless, of course, he'd already shot himself to death in a fit of remorse or terror or despair. Was some guy found shot to death in a field? Look for the brother-in-law (or best friend, or ex-girlfriend) who had been seen openly quarreling with the deceased and who had not even bothered to get rid of the gun or remove fingerprints from the victim's car. Ninety, ninety-five percent of the time, murder was easy.

The murder of Teresa Cruzan didn't strike Kinowski as anything special. The fact that the body had remained undiscovered for several days made it slightly more difficult since that meant the killer had time to calm down, to fabricate an alibi, to cover his tracks. It also meant that the work of the BCA crew was more important—the gathering of on-site evidence. Kinowski didn't like to turn over his cases to the BCA, who struck him as "snooty," not like real cops at all. But he also had a passion for what he called concrete evidence—stuff you could hold in your hand or photograph through a microscope or make plaster casts of to take into a courtroom. It was so satisfying to be able to say on the witness stand, "Wherever Mr. Jones claims to have been on the evening of February fifteenth, his left forefinger and thumb were in Bell's Bar holding this shot glass, because we know all the glasses were washed before four P.M. that day and not used again until the bar reopened at seven o'clock." People lied and manipulated, but hard evidence could be counted on to point straight at the truth. Juries loved it, too.

So he'd welcomed the crew from Minneapolis to Franklin Street, being careful to allow no disturbance of the crime scene before they could get to work on it. But he'd also done some careful poking around in the rest of the house on his own. And in the garage. It had taken him less than ten minutes and only one blade of his pocketknife to find out what was in Teresa Cruzan's garage. Once he knew, he left it for the state lab boys to deal with.

On Wednesday, July 4, Kinowski cheerfully worked holiday hours on the case. Family had long ago been sacrificed to the job, and his ex-wife and grown children were probably picnicking together somewhere in Illinois, where they all lived now. Kinowski occasionally got letters from his son, who was a stockbroker, God help him, and he saw the boy about once a year. But Jenny, his twenty-five-year-old daughter, seemed to share her mother's view of Erwin Kinowski and only rarely sought contact—he got neutral, unenthusiastic cards from her at Christmas time and on Father's Day. Holidays always made Kinowski remember his kids the way they looked in grade school, and that usually depressed the hell out of him.

So, on the morning of July 4, he'd been glad to go over to the Holiday Inn to see the girl, the poor kid who had found the body. She still looked like a zombie on Wednesday morning, eyes sunken and staring, skin deathly pale. Her brother was with her, and she sat next to him while she talked. Kinowski was struck by the contrast in the two kids, and not just a physical contrast, either. The girl was slim, tall, with dark eyes and high cheekbones—a real beauty—and even her present shocked state couldn't completely mute a kind of coiled energy, a throbbing intensity that Kinowski could sense just below the surface.

The boy was shorter than his sister, a compact, wiry kid with curly blond hair and blue-green eyes—a kind of homely cute face with a slight gap between his front teeth, a self-depre-cating smile, a few freckles. But what was most noticeable about him was his manner, his presence; what he projected was a deep calm, a steadiness and maturity that contradicted his youthful appearance. If he hadn't been looking at the pair, only listening to them, Kinowski would have guessed that the girl was younger than the boy. It was as if a wise old man had been magically transported into the body of a high-schooler—Kinowski had been told that Eric Lundgren was about to become a college senior, but the kid looked about sixteen. The contrast in the pair made more sense after Kinowski learned that they were both adopted, but he reminded himself that his own two kids were temperamentally quite different even though they both had the same set of parents—or, at least, he believed they did.

The girl told her story haltingly, with lots of backtracking for suddenly remembered details, and when she'd finished, Kinowski thought he had what he needed. Teresa Cruzan had no husband, but there was a boyfriend. And there was Max. As soon as Katherine Lundgren had described the man her mother had called a business associate, the man she'd seen carrying a box out of the garage at 642 Franklin Street, Kinowski knew who he was. Bruce Maxwell, lifelong resident of Woodard, school dropout, sometime auto mechanic, was well known to the police. Kinowski was ready to put money on Max as the killer.

Kinowski left the Lundgren girl and her brother without revealing how much he already knew—time enough later, when the kid was over some of her shock, to let her know that the mother she'd come to find was tied up in some pretty bad stuff. That afternoon, the lieutenant had sent some officers to try to discover who the boyfriend was—questioning the neighbors, that sort of thing. He also used the evidence of victim's involvement in criminal activity to get a court order for Teresa Cruzan's bank records, credit-card information, employment and tax history.

Kinowski himself went looking for Bruce Maxwell.

# CHAPTER 11

$K$ate felt intimidated by the Woodard Law Enforcement Center. She had never been inside a police station before, and if Eric hadn't been with her, she might have turned back from the squat dark-brick building that also served as a jail. Its ugliness seemed deliberate, a sort of architectural deterrent to crime, as if the builders had tried to scare people with a modern version of a dungeon. The face of the officer who showed them where to wait for Lieutenant Kinowski looked like it was made of crudely chipped stone, and every sound the man made produced a metallic echo.

It was late Friday afternoon, and Kate had finally tired of waiting for the police to let her know what was going on. The newspapers were no help at all, repeating details Kate already knew. She had grumbled to Eric that the police would certainly have been more forthcoming if she were Terry's legal daughter, and had finally persuaded him to call for her, to ask for an appointment with the investigating officer. And now Kinowski wasn't even there: "He'll be here any minute," the other officer had said, not offering any explanation of where he might be.

"Did we come here just for information, or do you have something else on your mind?" Eric asked her now, shifting on the narrow plastic chair to look directly at his sister. "You could have asked that other guy about the case. Why do you want to see Kinowski in person?"

"Okay," Kate sighed, uncomfortable under his knowing gaze; she had never been any good at fooling her little brother. "I need to tell him something. Something I didn't say on Wednesday."

"What's that?" Eric said, his smooth brow wrinkling with sudden worry.

"The last time I saw her"—they had developed this shorthand, seldom referring to Terry by name—"alive, I mean, on Sunday, she was scared of something. She kept looking around as if she was afraid she might get caught with me or something. And she warned me to leave, to go away. She said I could do damage I didn't even know about, and her eyes were so scared when she said it."

"So what do you think she meant? Obviously you've been brooding about it."

"We'd been talking about who my father was," Kate said, tapping her car keys absently against her purse. "I think she was scared about what my questions would lead to. Like she'd been warned to get me away from that topic, to get me *away*, period."

"And you think somebody killed her when she didn't get rid of you?" Eric sounded exasperated.

"Maybe somebody killed her before she could give in and start answering my questions." She didn't look at Eric when she said it, held her breath now, waiting for his response. Speaking out loud the suspicion that had been growing inside her since Wednesday had scared her, and she longed for her sensible brother to tell her that the fear was nonsense.

"It's just like you, Katie," he said quietly, "to turn it all into something to do with your own obsessions."

She swung her head to look at him, anger flaring up in her. "What the hell does that mean?"

"You don't know anything about this woman's life," he said, calm in the face of her challenge. "You have no idea what she might have been into, who her friends were, what was going on with this Max guy you saw at her house, who was not even the same guy as the boyfriend. There could be any number of reasons for somebody to want her dead. Maybe whoever did it didn't even mean to kill her—just got mad and couldn't stop himself. Why does it have to be connected to your arrival in her life, to your questions about your parentage?"

"I didn't say it *had* to be," she responded, calming down in the soothing wake of his gentle tone. "I'm only saying it's one thing the police should consider and they can't consider it if I don't tell them about it."

"Fine. Then, that's just what you should do," Eric said, and then he grinned. "We seem to be in the right place for that."

They waited in silence until Kinowski came in, looking hurried, a little flushed. He ushered them into his tiny office, then listened without interruption or change in facial expression to what Kate had to say about her suspicions regarding Terry's mood the last time she'd seen her alive.

"I know you'd like to help," he said gently after she'd finished, "and I *did* tell you to let me know if you remembered anything else. But I don't think it's very likely that your mother's death was connected at all with you being here in Woodard."

"Why?" Kate said, deliberately not looking at Eric's response to hearing Teresa Cruzan referred to so casually as "your mother." "What have you found out that makes you so sure? I expected to hear from you before now, you know. About the investigation, I mean." She tried to keep petulance out of her voice, to sound calm. "The newspaper doesn't say much."

"We don't let the newspapers in on everything," Kinowski said, but then a flicker of compassion passed over his blocky features. "I thought it would be better to have a more complete picture to give you before I got back in touch. We're still looking into some details."

"Was there an autopsy?" Kate asked, and then drew a quick breath—even the sound of the word scared her.

"Yes," Kinowski answered. "No surprises there." He stood up from behind the small metal desk, which, like everything else in his office, seemed wrong for him. The cramped quarters seemed to constrain an energy that might have found better expression in some outdoor setting—Kate could see him at a construction site or an oil rig, any activity that would use the power of those bulging forearms. "She died of asphyxiation. We think sometime on Sunday afternoon or evening. But that time-of-death stuff is tricky. People think you can be accurate to the minute or something, but it doesn't work that way. We know you saw her alive at lunchtime and that she still had her hair fixed the same way when you found her on Tuesday night, so we can guess Sunday. That and the amount of decomposition, of course. Except for her throat, there was very little other injury, not many bruises. She wasn't sexually assaulted."

Kate was wincing with horror over the clinical details, beginning to feel sick to her stomach. Kinowski had been talking in a detached voice, looking at papers on his desk, but now he glanced at Kate's face, and he looked suddenly stricken. When he perched on the edge of his desk in front of her, his voice was kind. "It was probably pretty quick. There wasn't much struggle—just that one table turned over. I don't think she suffered for very long."

"Thank you," Kate whispered. "Thank you for telling me that."

"No evidence of a break-in," Kinowski went on. "Looks like it was somebody she knew. Somebody she let into the house."

"But you seemed sure it wasn't somebody who wanted her to stop talking to me," Kate said. "How can you be so sure? Do you think you know who it was?"

Kinowski got up again, his urge to pace obvious, his frustration over being confined to such a tiny space clear in the way he jammed his hands into the pockets of his chinos.

"Look," he said from behind the desk chair. "Teresa Cruzan was into some bad stuff and I think that's what got her killed. I don't think there's much of a mystery here."

"What bad stuff?" Eric had to ask the question because Kate was frozen in surprise.

"Her garage was full of stolen goods," Kinowski explained. "Mostly electronic equipment. We've traced some of it to a Radio Shack over in Willow River, and some of it came from a break-in at the Best Buy right here in Woodard. We think this has been going on for some time now."

Kate could feel the blood draining from her face. She tried to speak, tried to make her mouth move, but all she could manage was a shuddering sigh.

"That's what you almost saw, Miss Lundgren," Kinowski went on, "when you spotted Maxwell carrying a box to his van that day. Bruce Maxwell is bad news. Has been all his life. Petty theft when he was a kid, lots of bar fights. He's got a regular gang now and they're all pretty tough characters. They steal mostly electronic appliances and ship the stuff out of town to fences in the Cities and Duluth. He was using Terry's premises for storage and to repackage the goods—we found lots of boxes and tape."

"So, is he in jail now?" Eric was still speaking for Kate, sitting forward on the narrow folding chair. "Have you arrested him for the murder?"

"He's not in jail right *now*." Kinowski sounded irritated by this fact. "We had him here for forty-eight hours of questioning, but we had to either release him or charge him. And I don't have enough to charge him yet. What we know and what we can prove are two different things."

"But if he's a thief—" Eric began.

"We can't nail him for that either," Kinowski said, lifting his fists from his pockets in a sudden gesture. "Nobody's caught him in the act so far, and he never has any stuff at his own place. We dusted every inch of that garage for prints and it's clean."

"He was wearing gloves." Kate was finally able to speak, though even she could hear how stunned and unnatural her voice sounded. "I forgot to tell you that on Wednesday. You know, those cotton work gloves? That's what he was wearing when he was carrying the box to his van."

"What did he say about that?" Eric chimed in. "About what Kate saw him carrying?"

"Oh, he's a cool one." Kinowski shook his close-cropped head. "He claims he didn't know anything about what his old school friend might have been keeping in those other boxes. He was just storing his new microwave at her place until he finished building a rack for it in his kitchen. He was only picking it up when you saw him. It's not his fault if Terry was dealing in stolen goods. By the way, he *does* have a new microwave and the sales slip to show where he bought it. We checked."

"But he was there, at Terry's, three times," Kate insisted. "How does he try to explain what he was doing there so often? I even thought he might own the house."

"He says he and Terry were old friends and he likes to visit his friends. No law against that, is there?" Here Kinowski was imitating Max's sinister purr. "And we can't prove otherwise because none of the neighbors ever saw Max himself take things into the garage. They've noticed some of the activity over there, vans backed up to the garage, but they can't positively identify any of the photos we showed them of Max's cronies."

"*Did* Terry own the house?" Kate asked.

"Oh, yeah," Kinowski replied. "Lived there twenty years and the mortgage is almost paid up. The neighbors say she always took good care of the place. Lawn always looked just so and the walks always shoveled in the winter. Had that nice flower garden out back. She did it all herself, too. No hired help." He said all of this with an exaggerated enthusiasm, as if he were offering the information to Kate as a compensation for the unsavory things he was also passing along about Terry.

But Kate didn't respond; she was thinking how odd it was that she'd never noticed the lawn or the flower garden.

Now Kinowski pulled in a ragged breath to forge ahead. "But it doesn't look like she could have been making those mortgage payments out of her own earnings." He looked quickly at Kate and then away again.

"What do you mean?" she asked sharply.

"Well, we checked her employment record back to when she was a teenager, and there isn't much there. She had part-time jobs every now and then—was an Avon lady for a while last year, did some waitressing from time to time. But mostly, she was unemployed."

"I don't believe that!" Kate felt outraged, as if she herself had been accused of something.

Kinowski looked at her in surprise for a second. Then he reached over onto his cluttered desk and picked up a piece of paper. "Here's the list," he said blandly. "It's arranged chrono-logically."

Kate looked down at the piece of paper. There were per-haps twelve items on the list: "Jackson Street Cafe, waitress, June 9–August 2, 1983" was followed by "K mart, part-time checker, Sept. 5, 1986–Nov. 20, 1986." Similar gaps, many of them even longer, were evident throughout the list. Just before she handed the list back to Kinowski, she focused on the first item: "Country Club, busing tables, May 6, 1967–August 2, 1967." Terry's first job and, it suddenly occurred to Kate, span-ning the time when she got pregnant.

"What does it mean?" Eric was saying. "What's your point, Lieutenant?"

"Teresa Cruzan always paid her bills on time," Kinowski went on in a patient voice. "Even had a few credit cards. She drove a nice car, had pretty nice furniture, spiffy clothes. And we know she didn't inherit money from her parents. Somebody else was providing the money."

"And you think it was Max?" Kate asked. "In exchange for letting him keep stolen goods in her garage?"

"Not exclusively," Kinowski answered, and his voice was even more guarded. "We don't think Max has been into this big-time stealing for very long. The neighbors didn't notice the activity around Terry's garage until about a year and a half ago. But they say she's had boyfriends all along, for twenty years."

Kate could feel the blood rushing to her face, a constriction around her heart. "Are you saying she was a prostitute?" she gasped.

"No, no!" Kinowski looked genuinely startled by the word. "The neighbors would see one guy coming around for a year, sometimes less, then nobody for a while, then another guy. That kind of thing. They say none of them ever actually lived in the house."

"Were they all young?" Kate asked, still preoccupied with Terry's association with at least one man old enough to be the father of a twenty-three-year-old.

A faint smile passed over Kinowski's square face. "One lady across the street said the men stayed the same age while the rest of the neighborhood got older. So I'd say they were mostly in their twenties, yeah."

"And you think they paid her bills?" Kate wanted to be clear about this. "That she was a kept woman with a string of sugar daddies?" It was a term she'd heard once in a play and she used it because she was afraid that if she didn't try to sound tough, she might begin to cry.

"I don't know for sure," Kinowski replied. "So far I've talked to only one of them, the latest. A guy named Duane Nelson. I don't think he qualifies as a sugar daddy, though. He's a mechanic at Eddie's Standard Station and I don't think they pay him enough to maintain two households."

"Is he blond?" Kate asked. "Does he drive a red Trans Am?"

"That's the one," Kinowski said. "He's the one you saw, I guess."

"Could *he* have killed her?" Eric asked. "A lover's quarrel or something?"

"We've been on that possibility from the start." Kinowski sighed as if he were growing slightly tired of answering obvious questions. "I grilled this kid myself. He doesn't have much of an alibi—says he was in his apartment watching baseball all Sunday afternoon. But he hasn't made any noises like a guilty man so far. We still don't rule him out, you understand, but my money is on Bruce Maxwell. I figure maybe she told him he had to quit using her place, maybe even threatened to turn him in if he didn't get out. He wouldn't take very kindly to that."

Kate sat up straight, a new possibility having just occurred to her. "But *that* might have been because of me," she said. "Because she didn't want me to find out she was involved in something criminal. She was so fierce about me keeping away from the house." Now she turned to Eric, her mouth twitching. "And I thought she just didn't want anybody to know about me, that she was ashamed of me. If I hadn't shown up, if I hadn't kept pestering her, she might not be dead."

"You are just determined to take the rap for this, aren't you?" Eric said, taking her trembling shoulders in his hands and giving her a gentle shake. "Just cut it out."

"Now, Miss Lundgren," Kinowski said firmly. "Your brother is right. There's no reason to blame yourself. Maxwell is a bad egg and everybody involved in his doings is at risk for any number of reasons. I was just suggesting one possibility. Maybe they argued over how much he was paying her. He's got a temper and a history of knocking women around."

Kate felt a sudden impulse to flee, to get out of the cramped office. She had come seeking information, but now she felt she'd heard too much, couldn't take in one more sordid detail. She pulled away from Eric and stood up, locking her knees to prevent her legs from shaking. "Thank you, Lieutenant," she murmured. "I hope you'll let me know if you make an arrest. I may not have known her for very long, but she was my mother." She made the last assertion almost defiantly.

"Of course," Kinowski said soothingly, but he could scarcely hide his relief that the interview was over, that he was going to be able to escape from his office. "I suppose you'll be staying until after the funeral."

"Funeral?" Kate said, staring at him as if he'd switched to a foreign language. "What funeral?"

"Her funeral," Kinowski faltered. "Monday. I just assumed they would tell you."

"Who is 'they'?" Eric asked, his usually calm voice tight with anger. "Nobody has told Kate anything at all."

Kate felt a rush of anger so powerful that she was unable to speak. Her birth mother was murdered, snatched from her just at the moment she'd found her, and no one seemed to understand that she had an interest in this event. The police treated her as if she were some stranger who just happened to stumble over the body, and now this. A funeral was planned without anybody even bothering to tell her about it.

"I thought you might have made the arrangements yourself," Kinowski was saying, his blush spreading farther up his face.

"No, we didn't," Eric answered for his sister. "What details can you give us?"

"It's at one o'clock," Kinowski answered, gratefully reassuming his "official" voice. "Fawley's Funeral Parlor. That's all I know."

Kate was finally able to find her voice, to swallow her anger enough to speak in a quiet voice. "Do you know who made the arrangements? Has her brother come from Arizona?"

"No," Kinowski replied, frowning. "We called him, of course, but he said they haven't been close for years, so he wouldn't be coming. But maybe he made the arrangements from there. You'd have to ask them at Fawley's."

"Let's go, Eric," Kate said to her brother, looking away from Kinowski. She'd had enough—too much, actually—and needed to get away from this place, needed some time and space to think.

"Fine with me," Eric murmured. Then he again took on the role of official family spokesperson. "Thank you for your time, Lieutenant."

"Sure thing," Kinowski responded. He then put a clumsy hand on Kate's shoulder. "Don't you worry, Miss Lundgren," he said. "We're gonna nail this guy. Maxwell can't get away with murder in my town. It's just a matter of time."

Kate shrugged his hand off her shoulder and left without

a word. She knew that it was mean-spirited, that it was unfair to be angry with the messenger just because she didn't want to hear the message he had to give her. But she couldn't help herself. She was terribly shocked by what he'd told her, yet she recognized the ring of truth in all of it. It was that truth that she couldn't face.

When Kate and Eric got back to the Holiday Inn, she ran ahead of him into the lobby. Just before making the turn toward the elevator, she saw Jack Kramer sitting in one of the lobby's overstuffed chairs, a newspaper half open on his knees. The sight of him sent a wave of strong memory over her, brought the whole of last weekend flashing before her. Since Eric's arrival, she'd almost lulled herself into forgetting that she was in Woodard—having her brother around *felt* like home. Now she started over to Jack, not realizing that Eric wouldn't know why she was approaching a stranger when she'd spent the past few days ducking reporters. Jack did a small double-take, his face changing as he recognized her, and then he stood up, tumbling the newspaper to the carpet.

"Hello," he said, straightening his jacket in a self-conscious gesture. "I'm on my way home after work, so I thought I'd take a chance that you might be here. I was going to wait another five minutes."

"Hi," Kate responded. "Thanks for calling on Wednesday. I'm sorry I was such a zombie on the phone."

"No, no," he said, waving off the apology. "I should have waited for a while. It was too soon after—" And he faltered to a stop for a second. "When I read the paper, when I realized who she was, I just reached for the phone—didn't think about it."

By this time Eric had come up behind her, and Kate made the introductions, watching the two young men eye each other coolly, sizing each other up. She'd seen this before, the way newly met men openly assess each other, gauging status, position in the present environment. Women did this too, she knew, but much more covertly, being early trained to mask competitiveness, to "make nice."

"Have the police found out who did it?" Jack asked, directing the question to both the sister and the brother.

"They have some theories," Kate said numbly, reluctant to go into detail about anything Kinowski had told her today. "But they won't say much until they're sure, of course."

"Well, you should be told," Jack said. "You're the next of kin, after all, and you have a right to know."

Jack's assertion, despite its clichés—perhaps even *because* of its easy assumptions about "next of kin" and "right to know"—had a soothing effect on Kate, and she smiled gratefully at him. And he'd come here at the end of a long day's work just to see her. She was beginning to remember how much she liked him.

"Is there anything I can do for you?" Jack asked now. "Is this place comfortable? You could stay at my house. Both of you, I mean. Mother would be glad to have you—she was so upset about the news, so sorry for you."

"No," Kate said softly. "We're fine where we are, thanks. It's really nice of you to offer to take us in, but, really, we're fine. Eric is settled into his room now, and it's just down the hall from mine. We'll be leaving, probably, in a few days."

"I wish," Jack began, faltered, looked at Eric, and then back at Kate again. "I wish your association with Woodard could be a happier one all around, that you didn't just want to forget all about it."

Kate looked at him carefully now, saw the concern and kindness on his face. She felt sudden regret, a sense that she was letting go of something she should consider more carefully before giving up. "Maybe there is something you could do for me," she mused.

"Just name it," he said eagerly.

"Could you play hooky from work on Monday? I'd like it if you could go to my—to Terry's funeral with us. It's at one o'clock at a place called Fawley's. I don't know anybody else in Woodard, so I won't know anybody who might turn up there. Maybe you could help with that—tell me who people are."

"Sure," he said, a sudden smile transforming his face. "I'll be there. Glad to help."

"Thanks," Kate said, an answering smile on her own lips.

"I'd better get cracking," Jack said, glancing at his watch. "Mother will have dinner waiting."

When the glass doors had closed behind Jack, Kate looked

back at Eric, whose sandy eyebrows were raised in a bemused expression.

"What do you think the chances are," he said, "of that guy knowing *any* of the same people she knew?"

"Never mind," Kate said peevishly, sinking down onto the chair Jack had been occupying. "Why the hell should you care, anyway?"

Eric sighed and sat in the chair facing her. "I'm sorry," he whispered. "I know you've had a tough day."

Kate looked at the far wall, blinking away the tears his sympathy had brought to her eyes. "I don't know what's the matter with me, Eric," she said after a long pause.

"What does that mean?"

She could feel him leaning forward to look at her, and she turned back to meet his gaze. "I don't feel sad." She was whispering now too. "I feel angry. Boy, do I feel angry. I spent so much of my life waiting to find her. And all I got was two short meetings, and then we were fighting most of the time. And now there'll never, never be another chance. I'm just furious with whoever took her away from me so that there'll never be another chance. And I'm furious with her, too, for not giving me more of herself when I *did* see her. Is this making any sense to you?"

"Of course," he said soothingly. "And now you've had to find out those unpleasant things about her from Kinowski. That has to be pretty hard."

"But why don't I feel sad?" Kate demanded, searching his face as if she might read an answer there. "It was so awful, and I still feel the horror of it. I'm not sleeping much because I'm afraid to close my eyes, afraid of seeing it again—what she looked like in that chair. And food doesn't taste right. It's like that smell has ruined my taste buds or something. But I don't cry. I can't grieve. I looked for her for such a long time—in my dreams, I mean—and now that she's dead and gone from me forever, I don't feel any big grief."

Eric reached over to close his left hand over her right hand. "You didn't know her," he said simply. "I guess it's hard to grieve over somebody you just met. It's not like if Mom or Dad died, is it?"

Kate stared at him for a moment, held the steady gaze of

his blue eyes. "Maybe that's it," she said finally. "I didn't know her at all."

Now she stood up, a motion so quick that Eric jumped a little in surprise. "But I'm going to find out about her," Kate said firmly. "And I don't care if some of it is 'unpleasant,' as you put it. I still have another parent to find out about, too. Don't forget that."

Before Eric could speak, Kate strode away from him toward the elevator, determination stiffening her back and lifting her chin.

# CHAPTER 12

He couldn't meet his own eyes in the mirror. When he shaved or brushed his teeth, he paid careful attention to the details of the task itself—the razor moving over his jaw, the brush working the paste up into the gum above his teeth—but he didn't glance up at the reflection of his eyes. And he was so jumpy, so hypersensitive to any loud sound—on Tuesday morning, he had sliced open the skin under his left ear when a tap had sounded on the bathroom door. He was watching the bright trickle make its way toward his chin while the familiar voice was saying through the closed door, "Hurry, darling. Breakfast is getting cold. Paper's here."

The newspaper had been an ordeal, too, on Monday and Tuesday. He had scanned the headlines, bracing himself for the expected item, forcing his face to remain unconcerned under the loving eyes across the table. Once already in the past week he'd fielded questions: "What is it, dear? I know things have been bad lately, but is there something new you're not telling me?" When Wednesday's paper finally showed him the headline he'd been dreading, he didn't react at all, but felt only numb and dissociated, as if he were reading about some *other* murder. Only when he read that Teresa Cruzan's body had been discovered by Katherine Lundgren, "the natural child

Cruzan gave up for adoption twenty-three years ago," did he feel some of the expected anguish—he would have given a lot if only someone else could have found the body.

Whenever he thought about Sunday—and often he couldn't stop himself—waves of nausea swept over him, a wrenching in his stomach that sometimes made him bend forward on his chair or at the wheel of the car. The memory of the violence itself revolted him more than the result—slumped in the chair afterward, Terry had looked rather peaceful, almost as if she might be asleep. But the struggle, the way the muscles of his arms felt as he tightened the cord, the feel of her thrashing body against his chest and thighs, the terrible sounds she made, deep in her throat, gurgling and inhuman—these memories would come full upon him without warning, and a taste like ashes would fill his mouth.

But he felt anger, too—a dull, smoldering sense of being aggrieved. Hadn't he warned her? Hadn't he been perfectly clear about his conditions? Don't see Kate, don't talk to Kate, don't open the door to Kate, don't answer the phone. *Why* did the stupid bitch have to fly in the face of everything he had said to her? And then to imagine that she could sneak behind his back like that. He'd made the mistake of telling her once that he needed to be home on weekends, so she thought he wouldn't be watching her on a Sunday. Imagined she could get away with it and he would be none the wiser. It made him shake with fury whenever he went over it in his mind.

He had been at the Holiday Inn—actually, in the mall parking lot across the way, sitting where he could see Kate's car. He'd made his excuses at home for the whole weekend—wasn't expected there until late Sunday evening. What he was hoping to witness was Kate's departure from Woodard. For two hours he half expected to see her emerge with her suitcases, put them into the Beretta, and head toward the on-ramp of I-35 South. In his imagination, he was already savoring the relief he would feel. But instead he'd seen the gray Thunderbird pull in with that reckless abandon that always marked Terry's style of driving. As he watched Terry go into the motel, he pounded the steering wheel of his own car in helpless rage.

Later, when he followed the Thunderbird back to Franklin Street, he parked around the corner as he always did, slipped through the alley, and went to the back door of the house.

When Terry came to the door, she was already in her bathrobe. It was one of the things that drove him crazy about her—that slatternly tendency to lounge around in the middle of the day in what he always thought of as bedclothes. Now her face paled at the sight of him, her eyes widening in fear as he pushed his way past her into the kitchen. She made no effort to deny being at the Holiday Inn.

He made her repeat every word she'd said to Kate. "Were those the *exact* words?" he said, barely keeping his voice under control.

"How the hell should I know?" she flared. "I ain't a tape recorder. I'm telling you I didn't give her any real information. She don't know one thing that could lead her to you."

"But you told her about the age difference. That's another clue she might be able to follow up on. Why can't I make you understand that giving her any information at all is dangerous?" And he came straight up to her, lowering his face until his nose was almost touching hers. "You can't be trusted around her. Now she's encouraged to believe that if she just keeps pestering you long enough, you'll eventually tell her everything she wants to know. And *I* think you will, too. I think I'm going to have to stop you from talking to her ever again."

Even then, he might not have done more than slap her around if she hadn't reacted the way she did. Instead of cowering away from him, she leaned against him and grinned up into his face. He could feel her breasts through the thin silk.

"I know what you really want," she purred in that rich, husky voice of hers. "You can't fool me. I know how you look at me when you think I don't notice."

And her hands brushed against the front of his pants as she began to undo the cord of her robe.

"Cut it out," he said, but he knew he didn't sound as if he meant it. It appalled him that she could fluster him so easily. So he tried harder, working himself up into a rage. "You make me sick, that's what you make me. You think taking your clothes off is the answer to everything. Well, that doesn't always work, you stupid bitch. Not always."

By this time, she had the cord in her hands and was lifting one of the tassled ends to his face, aiming for his nose. He twitched away as if the red fabric were a branding iron, and then he ripped the cord from her yielding hands. The robe fell from one of her shoulders as she tried to spin away from him, but he flung a loop of the cord over her head. It caught first across the bridge of her nose and jerked her head back. She said, "Ow!" in an annoyed and surprised voice, the way she might have reacted had she accidentally bumped her elbow. Before she could react further, the loop caught next under her chin.

He wasn't a killer, he told himself now—had been telling himself repeatedly since Sunday. He wouldn't accept this as a characteristic act. He'd been driven to it, pushed past endurance. The crazy woman had no idea what her blabbing would mean, what a catastrophe it could bring on him, but she should have followed his instructions anyway. She had no right to imperil him the way she had. Hadn't she brought him enough grief already? She would have ruined his life if he hadn't stopped her.

And now he could only hope in a frantic and half-despairing way that it was over, that no one would start to make connections. The police would conclude that Terry's death was connected to the stuff in the garage. Kate would leave Woodard. He would be safe. And, in time, the memories would fade, the nausea would go away. Surely it wouldn't always feel like this. He would once again be able to look into his own eyes in the mirror without the terror that he might see a monster looking back.

# CHAPTER 13

The sound of a compression hose made Kate jump as if she'd heard a gunshot at close range. The garage was crowded and busy—Saturday morning was obviously a good time for people with Monday-through-Friday jobs to have their cars serviced.

"He's in the break room," the man behind the counter was saying; his face was pulled into a disapproving scowl. "And he's gotta be back at work in five, six minutes. He knows the rules about having friends visit him on the job."

"We won't keep him long," Kate said, already looking toward the door the man had indicated with a gesture of his head. Eric stood next to her, his face almost as disapproving as the service manager's. He'd come along only because Kate had insistd she would otherwise go alone.

"Why do you think you need to see this guy?" he'd asked her, no longer bothering to hide his exasperation.

"He knew Terry," Kate had replied stubbornly. "And *I* want to know Terry better. It's as simple as that."

Now she began to cross the grease-slicked floor of the garage without even looking to see if her brother was following her.

"Hey!" the manager snapped. "You can't cross the work

119

floor. We ain't insured for that. Go around the building. There's an outside door to the break room. And tell Nelson he better be back out here by—" and he paused to look up at the round clock above his head. "By ten-fifteen."

When Kate led Eric into the break room, squinting to adjust from the bright sunlight to the smoke-filled gloom inside, she didn't think that either of the two men watching television there could be Duane Nelson. Both were dressed in grease-stained coveralls that had once been blue, and both had their hair stuffed up under grimy caps. Both turned blank faces to stare up at the new arrivals.

Then one of the men stood, his hand lifted to his forehead as he leaned forward from the waist toward Kate. His eyes widened, the whites showing clearly against his grime-darkened face. Then he stepped backward, backed right into his own chair, making it scrape across the floor. "Jesus," he breathed. "Jesus Christ."

"You're Duane, aren't you?" Kate said, for now she could see wisps of blond hair sticking out from under the cap. "I'm Kate Lundgren and this is my brother, Eric. Terry Cruzan was my mother."

"Yeah," he said. "You look just like her. I thought for a second I must be seeing a ghost."

The other man stood now and reached over to turn down the sound on the professional wrestling show they'd been watching. He was shorter than Duane, older, and his face was now suffused with undisguised curiosity.

"I'm sorry to interrupt your break," Kate said, "but I'm trying to find out something about Terry. I'd just met her, you know."

"Sure," Duane said. "I read that in the paper—that you found her—found the body, I mean."

Kate looked at the other man and then back at Nelson, who got the message surprisingly quickly.

"You gotta get back on the floor, don't you, Pete?" he said to his companion. "I got a few minutes left on my break, but your fifteen is just about up."

The other man shrugged, his face clearly showing his disappointment at missing this new show, but he left through the doorway into the garage without a word of protest.

"Sit down?" Duane said it as a question. He couldn't seem to stop staring at Kate's face.

"No, thanks," she said. "This won't take too long."

Eric leaned against the door frame behind him, his thin arms folded across his chest. All his body language said that, while he was here in the role of protector to his sister, he wanted no further involvment in what was going on.

"You were dating Terry for a while?" Kate felt embarrassment now, could feel herself blushing. She hadn't thought about what she might ask, had just wanted to meet him, to talk about Terry with someone who had known her.

"About four months," Duane answered. "I met her at a dance."

"She told me she liked to dance. When did you see her last?"

"A week ago Wednesday. We went out to Wiley's Gardens to party."

Kate frowned, remembering what Terry had said about Kate's allowing the phone to ring twenty-one times: "My boyfriend and me were right in the middle of things when you called."

"Not after that?" she asked now. "You weren't at her house two days later, on Friday evening?"

"No, I wasn't," he said, his voice suddenly defensive. "We usually spent weekends together, but not that one. At Wiley's she told me she had some personal stuff to work out, and I should just wait for her to call me. That's what I did, but she never called. I already told all this stuff to the police."

"I'm sorry," Kate said softly. "I'm sure you have, but I didn't know that. I guess I must be the personal stuff she was talking about. It must have been quite a shock for you to read about me in the newspaper—to find out she had a daughter."

"No, I knew about you," he said simply.

"You knew?" Kate's frown deepened. "She told you I was in Woodard?"

"No, not that. But I knew she had a kid when she was young. She was real honest about stuff like that. She told me the first time I met her how old she was and she said, 'I got a kid almost as old as you are.' Like she was daring me to keep on being interested in her."

"What did she say about me?" Kate asked eagerly. "How much did she tell you?"

"Not much," he shrugged. "She said she had a kid out of wedlock, a girl, and that she gave it up for adoption. That she was just a kid at the time herself."

"Nothing else?"

"No. I didn't push her about it because it seemed to make her sad. She was usually so much fun, and I didn't want to stir up bad memories for her."

"I see," Kate murmured, trying to hide her disappointment. "Did she seem scared about something last week when she told you she had personal stuff to take care of?"

"Scared? Naw. Nothing scared Terry." His face took on a dreamy look for a second. "She was something else, you know? Not just a looker. I admit I was only interested in that at the beginning. But she was funny and smart and sort of classy. I mean, she wouldn't take nothing off of nobody. She was, like, *proud* of herself. She took care of herself and of her house. She loved that place. She said, 'My folks always lived in dumps. I betcha they'd fall over if they could see this.' "

He fell silent, embarrassed at having said so much.

"Do you know if she had other—" Kate began and then stammered in embarrassment herself, "other boyfriends?"

"I never asked her about other guys," Duane answered, drawing himself up. "When she was with me, she made me feel like I was the king of the world. That was enough for me."

"Did she ever ask you to help with her expenses?" Kate struggled over forming the sentence in a way that would cause the least offense. "Or did you ever offer her financial help?"

"No!" Duane sounded indignant. "I never thought she needed anything like that from me. I'da offered if I thought she needed something, but she always gave me the impression she could handle everything in her life by herself."

"Thank you," Kate said, glancing down at her watch. "I see that you have to go back to work and I don't want to keep you." She began to turn away toward Eric and the outside door.

"Look, miss," Duane said behind her, and she turned back toward him. "I know that cop thinks I mighta killed Terry, but you gotta believe me—I wouldn'ta touched a hair on her head. And I got no idea who mighta done it. She was the greatest thing that ever happened to me. A really good person, you know? I'm gonna miss her a lot."

Kate could see that tears had filled the grime-circled eyes. Behind him the silent television screen showed a close-up of a simian face contorted with mock rage—one of the wrestlers posturing for the fans. By contrast, Duane Nelson looked even younger than his years, like a sad schoolboy.

Outside, Kate walked ahead of Eric to her car. Only when they were inside did she turn to him to speak. "I don't think he could have killed her, do you?"

"Maybe it's an act," Eric said, always a skeptic.

"No," Kate said, shaking her head. "He loved her. You can see that. But I did learn something interesting in there. Terry told me on Sunday that I had to leave Woodard because she didn't want her boyfriend to find out that she had a kid almost as old as he is. But he knew all about me, knew how old she was. Why would she lie to me about that?"

"Maybe he's the one who's lying," Eric offered.

"No way," Kate said emphatically. "There would be no reason for him to make up a thing like that. But *she* would make up a lie if she didn't want me to know the real reason she was trying to get me out of town. And she was fast about it, too. Just a few minutes earlier, I'd let her know that I saw her with Duane—I even made a crack about how young he was for her. So she played off that. She was smart. Duane was right about that."

"So you think you know the real reason she wanted you to leave Woodard?" Eric was looking at her with troubled eyes.

"Because I was asking about my natural father." Kate said it as if it were now an established fact. "She didn't want me getting close to that particular secret. And there'd be no reason for her to worry about it if he was dead. I think she lied about that, too. He's alive and probably somewhere in this town. And that's why she was scared."

"But isn't it much more likely that she didn't want you hanging around a garage full of stolen goods and that it was Max who told her to get rid of you?" Eric insisted. "Think in terms of probability, Katie. She was involved with crooks. Maybe Max wasn't the only one. For years and years somebody was giving her money for something, long before Max was putting stolen stuff in the garage."

Kate had looked away sharply during this speech and was now blushing violently.

"What's the matter?" Eric asked, quick as always to read her moods.

"I've been thinking about that since yesterday," Kate said quietly, looking out over the steering wheel. "About how she paid her bills, I mean. I didn't sleep much last night from thinking about it. You heard Duane say she never asked him for money. I don't think she asked any of the other boyfriends, either. I don't think she had to. But I don't think she was getting money all those years from crooks. How many crooks could a place like Woodard have, anyway? We don't even know Max was *paying* her to keep that stuff for him. They *were* old friends from school and maybe she was just doing him a favor."

"So where do you think she got it, then?" His voice sounded irritated. "Stop being melodramatic and tell me."

"I can think of only two possibilities," Kate answered, still not looking at her brother. "She might have got it from my natural father, a sort of on-going compensation for her silence. If he's a local man, married and afraid of scandal, he might have persuaded her right from the start to keep his identity a secret in exchange for a modest livelihood. She could have been worried that my questioning would make all of that stop."

"Or?" Eric said, lifting his eyebrows. "You said *two* possibilities. What's the other one?"

Now Kate looked away from him again, feeling the reluctance to speak that had made her blush a moment ago. "Maybe Mom and Dad were paying her all along to stay out of my life," she said, her voice barely above a whisper.

There was a stunned silence from the other side of the car and then the expected explosion. "You're nuts! What a rotten thing to say!"

Outbursts of anger from her brother were so rare that Kate had to grip the steering wheel to hold up against this one.

"Why is it nuts?" she asked at last. "They all knew about each other from the start, so Mom and Dad would always have to be afraid she might look them up—'just show up on the porch someday' is how Mom put it two weeks ago. They *arranged* the adoption, so maybe they also *arranged* for her to stay away.

And when I was making the legal search, they could have contacted her again and told her to file that affidavit of nondisclosure." She looked at Eric now, saw the expression of horror on his face.

"How can you believe they would do that?" he demanded. "You've lived with these people all your life. How can you know them so little?"

"I thought I knew them," she said, her jaw coming forward in defiance. "But I just found out they've been *lying* to me all my life."

"That's different," he said, but he faltered slightly. "They were trying to protect you from knowing too much too early."

"Too early?" she snorted. "Were they going to wait until I turned fifty? Maybe they've been lying to you, too. Maybe they know who your parents are. Did you ever think of that?"

"No, I never thought of that," Eric said quietly. "And I'm not going to think of it now. I know they've been wonderful parents—the only parents I've ever known, and the only ones I *want* to know."

Kate felt dangerously close to tears, looked away from him again.

After a long silence, Eric spoke again in a small voice. "You don't really think Mom and Dad were doing that, do you?"

"I don't know," Kate sighed. He seemed to need reassurance, and this was so unusual that she didn't know quite how to act. "You could ask them."

"You could ask them yourself," he said quickly, "if you were speaking to them."

"I'm not ready for that yet," Kate murmured. "I don't know when I will be."

"Let's let it go for a while," Eric said finally. "Look, you're not the only one having a bad time, you know. They're just sick about what's happened. And worried about you. I haven't said much about it to you because you seemed so upset by the murder. But Mom cries all the time and Dad just looks like death. It's like he got old overnight. We always take him for granted—he'll take care of everything. But you should know that he's been carrying around a couple of extra burdens lately. The business is on shaky ground. That strike last year hurt, and there's been trouble at the plant all spring—slowdowns, some sabotage. Production is way off. Dad's been down in St. Paul much more than usual lately. He spent the whole weekend there trying to find out what the problem is on the night shifts, holing up to watch things without anybody knowing he was around."

"Why are you telling me all this, Eric?" Kate asked, feeling reluctant to have her sympathy aroused. The remark about Douglas Lundgren getting old overnight had frightened her—she didn't want to know this on top of everything else.

"To make you think of somebody besides yourself," Eric said simply. "You're quick to blame Mom and Dad, to think they would bribe Terry to give you up permanently, but you don't seem to see what that makes *her*. What kind of a woman would blackmail people like Mom and Dad where the welfare of her own child was concerned?"

"I never said blackmail," Kate cried, stung to tears at last. "I said they might have had a long-standing arrangement that everybody just got used to. Let's drop it. I don't want to tell you things if you're going to be like this."

"All right, Katie," he said more kindly. "We'll drop it. Don't be like that yourself."

She started the car, made the tires squeal a little as she drove out of the side lot at Eddie's Standard Station. At the stop sign, she spoke without looking over at her brother. "You never told me, Eric. Why did you abandon your search for your birth parents when you were nineteen? You started and then you just dropped it."

"The counselor told me what people find sometimes," he said softly. "Some find out they're the product of incest, or that their birth mothers tried to kill them. Or they just find parents who are bound to be a major disappointment—they have only blood in common. I didn't figure it was worth it."

"Do you think you might have sensed that Mom and Dad didn't *want* you to be interested in your first parents?" Kate ventured. "Maybe that factored into your decision, too."

"Maybe," Eric said after a short pause. "But I don't think it makes them bad people to have those feelings, either."

"Did I say anything about them being bad people?" Kate said, pulling the car out into traffic.

"You're treating them as if they are."

They drove in silence for a while.

"Look, Kate," Eric said finally. "Different people have different needs. I know the genetic information that's important to me, the stuff about nationality. And that's enough for me. I've *got* parents. I've got a family. Why mess with that when looking for another family might lead to a load of grief like the one you found?"

"Because some of us need to know," Kate said without looking at him. "No matter what the grief, we need to know."

Eric reached over to pat her shoulder and made the familiar chuckling noise in his throat. "Maybe it's genetic," he said.

Kate glanced at him and smiled, the first really amused smile since she'd found Teresa Cruzan's body.

# CHAPTER 14

Kate stood to one side of the gleaming casket, her hand resting lightly on the brass rail. What she'd been trying for five minutes to do was to imagine Terry's body inside this cold, expensive box. When she tried to picture the lean, graceful woman she'd seen coming to meet her outside Monahan's, she found herself helpless to fend off the memory of the bloated body in the chair, unable to turn her mind from questions of how a body, after an autopsy, is prepared for burial. All she could seem to feel was a shivering revulsion.

They had come early, she and Eric, claiming the rights of family. Mr. Fawley, the funeral director, had agreed to keep all press people outside. It was to this person that Kate gave the letter she'd written to Terry on the day she found the body. She'd kept it in her purse all along, sealed, and had never reopened it.

"Could you put this in my mother's coffin?" she asked quietly.

Fawley raised his impressive eyebrows. "The casket is already sealed," he said, as if that were the end of the conversation.

"Still, I'd like this letter put inside," Kate answered, surprised at her own determination.

"As you wish," Fawley said stiffly. "We can do it en route to the cemetery."

Kate had bought a simple black cotton dress, uncertain if this social convention was expected, but feeling a need to follow some ceremony, some traditional mark of mourning. Eric, as usual, looked uncomfortable in a tie, but had agreed without fuss to buy one—he'd brought no suits or even sports jackets from White Bear Lake, but the tie dressed up the white short-sleeved shirt. On a small table near the head of the casket was the crystal vase and single white rose that Kate had brought with her. There were no other flowers in the room.

At a quarter to one, Jack appeared, dressed in a simple summer suit and looking serious, concerned. When other people began to arrive, Jack and Eric positioned themselves on either side of Kate, like sentinels. The first four arrivals were women, complete strangers to Kate; each identified herself as "one of Terry's neighbors," but none of them had anything of a personal nature to say about the deceased. All of them showed an undisguised fascination with Kate, and not only because she was the long-lost child whose existence they all claimed was unknown to them until they read the papers after the murder. They kept asking her about finding the body—"Was it horrible?" "Did she look bad?"—and all of them hung on her answers, almost as if she were a celebrity—as if her proximity to violent death had conferred on her some sort of glamour.

Duane Nelson appeared, shiny clean, dressed in a sports jacket and pale slacks. With him were two young couples whom he introduced to Kate as "some of our friends," and Kate realized that these were Terry's most recent dancing and partying acquaintances. They, too, gaped at Kate. Duane himself seemed stiff and embarrassed, as if Kate were some former lover he had inadvertently encountered at a public gathering.

A few minutes after one, just as an usher was whispering to people to take their seats, a small sensation was triggered by a loud voice coming from the hallway—funeral parlors were places of discreet murmurs, of hushed exchanges, so even a normal speaking voice would have seemed shocking.

"This one?" the voice said. "The one on the left?"

And then Bruce Maxwell came through the French doors, piloting a woman ahead of him by holding her right elbow. He was dressed in a red shirt, open at the neck, and shiny black trousers. His brown hair seemed no cleaner than it did when Kate had last seen him. The woman in front of him had auburn hair done in a seventies-style flip and was wearing a tight-fitting green dress. Her face was hard, her thin mouth set in a firm line across a narrow jaw.

"It's Max," Kate whispered to Eric and Jack.

The pair crossed directly to Kate, moving with a speed that seemed almost menacing; Kate cringed away from the onslaught. Maxwell came to a stop within two feet of her, as if he had calculated the private space she was used to and had deliberately encroached on it. The red-haired woman was right at his side, leaning into him a bit. Now that he'd come this close, Max spoke in a quiet purr. "Hello again. Too bad we don't see each other under happier circumstances."

When Kate didn't respond, Max looked slowly from side to side, first at Eric, then at Jack; a dismissive smile flitted across his face. Then he leaned even closer to Kate. Jack made a quick step forward and Eric reached out to take Kate's arm, but Max didn't bother to look at either one of them again. "This here's Elaine," he said, fixing his eyes on Kate but pushing the other woman forward a little. "We're both real sorry about Terry."

"Thank you," Kate murmured, a polite reflex she couldn't stop.

"You know," Max went on, "Terry and me was close. Old pals." And he put the crossed fingers of his right hand in front of Kate's eyes.

"She told me," Kate said coldly, recovering her equilibrium. "But it wasn't very friendly of you to drag her in on your thieving."

A slow smile spread across Max's face, a smile more alarming than a snarl would have been. "There you go again," he said softly. "You already been slandering me to the cops, ain't you? I don't know what you think you seen, and I don't know what Terry told you about it. But it ain't nothing to do with me if your old lady stacks up hot properties in her garage. You understand?"

"She might have needed money enough to let you use the garage," Kate said, raising her own voice deliberately, "but you'll never get anyone to believe she was responsible for stealing that stuff. That's *your* work."

"Slander, slander, slander," he said, and his voice was sing-song. "You should be more careful, little girl. Spreading slander could get you in a lot of trouble. Didn't your mama ever tell you that?" The threat in his voice was unmistakable.

Jack stepped forward now and spoke quietly in his deep voice. "Back off, mister. This isn't a helpless person you can push around, and she is not alone here. She has friends."

Max looked Jack over again, his thick eyebrows going up in mock surprise. "And who might you be, little man?" he purred. "Should I be scared of you?"

"Be scared of both of us," Eric said, pulling Kate against his side. "The two of us and that cop over there should be enough to make you think twice."

Kate turned along with Max in the direction Eric had indicated with his head. Lieutenant Kinowski stood just inside the French doors, eyeing the tableau at the front of the room with interest.

Max swung his gaze back to Kate for a moment and his expression remained the same—sneering, unflappable. "You just be careful, honey," he said, and the meanness in his flat gray eyes was terrifying. "Will you do that for me? Will you be real careful?" And then he piloted the redhead to the second row of padded chairs.

Mr. Fawley, the funeral director, had been hovering nearby and now asked Kate if they should begin the service. When she nodded, he pointed to a row of three chairs just at the head of the casket.

"I didn't know Kinowski was coming," Eric said as they moved toward the chairs.

"Maybe he was following Max," Kate offered.

"Or maybe he believes that old legend about the killer showing up at the funeral," Jack chimed in as he took the chair to Kate's left. "Actually, Kinowski and Mr. Fawley are the only people here I recognize at all. I guess I just don't get out much to the places these other folks go. I'm afraid I haven't been much help for you today."

"It's a help just to have you here," Kate said, giving him a wan smile. She looked over the room now, counted heads—an even dozen, counting the officer investigating the murder. How sad that the passing of a life was being noted by such a pathetically small number of people, and only *she* was, literally, family.

For the first time, Kate felt a wave of pity for Terry, a sense of outrage that her existence had apparently meant so little in the world.

Mr. Fawley approached the lectern now, cleared his throat. He was a peculiar-looking man of indeterminate age, so thin and so sharply angled forward at the shoulders that he looked like a bent drinking straw. His voice was nasal, grating. Of course, he had never met Teresa Cruzan, so he spoke in very general terms—and only briefly—of loss and sorrow, of the comfort of prayer. When he finished, he turned his gaze out over the room.

"Would anyone else like to say a few words?" he said.

Kate followed his gaze, noted the slight, embarrassed shifting in the small gathering. Duane Nelson caught her glance for a second, then focused on his own folded hands. Max stared at her with his insolent smirk. No one was going to speak, she realized. A twisting sensation in her stomach almost made her gag. She would have to stand up, she told herself; she would have to say something. It was too horrible that only silence would follow Teresa Cruzan to her grave.

"I would." A voice from the doorway made everyone jump as if they had heard an explosion. Heads swung in unison toward the wide opening. A woman in a floral-printed dress was halfway into the room now. Her hair was that shade of platinum blond that could best be described as white, poofed out into a bouffant halo around a deeply tanned, heavily made up face. If her skin had been smoother, she might have passed for thirty, but the tanning had done its damage, and she was surely nearer forty. "I'm sorry I'm so late," she said, coming forward. "I couldn't find this place. There was only Minty's Funeral Parlor when I lived in Woodard. All this development out here is new to me."

Mr. Fawley cleared his throat again, his narrow face struggling to cover his outrage at this apparition. Before he could find something to say, the woman had reached the front of the room and turned her back to him.

"I'm Tammy Travers," she said. "The only face I recognize here is you, Bruce"—Maxwell cringed at this use of his proper Christian name—"but I knew Terry since we was kids together. I haven't seen her much in the past few years, but I called her every New Year's Day—that was our deal—to sort of compare notes on the whole year. I couldn't believe my eyes when I read in the papers about what happened to her."

Here she paused to shake her head, and her earrings bounced from side to side. "Terry was a pal," she went on. "She was the funniest kid I knew when we was in grade school, always up to some shenanigans that would make Sister Zora crazy. But she was never mean, never really bad—just a little wild, like a colt or something. She wanted so much out of life. She had dreams and plans. But she wouldn't have forgot her old friends, even if she *had* seen those plans come true. She was a real *person*, sorta like—" And here she groped for a second. "Sorta like Cher, you know what I mean? Honest and straight from the shoulder like that."

Now tears were making the mascara run in dark streams down Tammy's face. "I don't know what else to say," she finished in a shaky voice, "except I hope the son of a bitch who killed her rots in a hell deeper than regular sinners go to."

A stunned silence followed the woman to a chair in the first row, and Mr. Fawley was finally able to squeak, "Burial will be in St. Mary's Cemetery. Mourners are invited to a graveside ceremony in about fifteen minutes. Cars will have to remain on the street, but it's just a short walk to the left inside the gates on Seventh Street."

Kate felt a tremendous rush of gratitude toward Tammy Travers, a deep satisfaction over the phrase "the son of a bitch who killed her" that she would never have been able to explain to her brother or her parents and their polite friends. While Mr. Fawley pulled curtains around the casket—presumably so that no one's sensibilities would be offended by seeing it taken through service doors to a waiting hearse—Kate stood and walked directly up to Tammy, who was dabbing under her eyes with a tissue.

"Thank you," she whispered, leaning down toward the cotton-candy hair. "Thank you for coming."

The woman looked up at her, blinked, and then gaped. Fresh tears sprang from her eyes. "Oh, you're the kid," she sobbed. "You're Terry's kid. You look just like her, just a regular copy of her. Not the hair, but everything else. I saw you when you were just born, you know."

Kate sank into the empty chair next to Tammy. "You did?" she said eagerly. "I'd like you to tell me about that."

"Oh, sure, honey," Tammy said, mopping under her nose and sniffling a little. "We were both just kids ourselves, Terry and me—I just turned sixteen, I remember."

Eric had come up to stand next to Kate. "That Fawley guy says we have to leave for the cemetery," he said, eyeing Tammy with a mixture of awe and mild disapproval.

"Would you like to ride with us?" Kate said earnestly to Tammy. "My friend, Jack, is going to drive us, and he'll bring us back to our own cars later." She looked at Jack pleadingly, saw him nod.

"Sure, honey," Tammy sniffled. "I'd like that."

In the back of Jack's Pontiac, Tammy Travers had recovered enough to chat openly about herself in a cheerful voice. "I work in Minneapolis now," she said. "I'm a dancer in a club. That's the closest to show biz I ever got. Terry was gonna be a great lady and I was gonna be a movie star. We used to laugh about that on the phone in later years, I can tell you."

"A great lady?" Kate interrupted. "In what way?"

"She used to say she was gonna marry one of those European princes she was always reading about—like Grace Kelly did. Or else she was gonna own her own chain of fashion stores and live in the south of France. She read a whole book once about the south of France, where it's always warm and you can hire maids real cheap."

"You said you saw me after I was born," Kate interrupted again, conscious that the car was moving them toward at least a temporary end to this conversation.

"Oh, yeah. It was right here in St. Francis Hospital. Terry wasn't supposed to have visitors except her folks, but I snuck in. She was holding you—that was supposed to be against the rules, too—and just crying and crying. No offense, but you looked all red and wrinkly to me, but Terry just kept on saying, 'Isn't she cute?' "

"Did she talk about giving me up?" Kate was barely able to talk above a whisper.

"Oh, sure. I told her to just keep you if she wanted to, but she said, 'I have to give her away. I signed all the papers.' And she told me everybody kept telling her it would be the best thing for the baby. She said she guessed that was probably right. Then one of those snooty nurses came in and booted me out of there."

"Did she ever tell you anything about my father?" Kate asked now. "About who got her pregnant?"

"Not much," Tammy said, craning her neck to see where the car was going. "Never a name. I tried to guess, of course, just as soon as I found out she was preggers. But she just said, 'No, no,' or 'Get serious,' whenever I guessed a guy at school. Finally she just said, 'It isn't any kid from school. It isn't a kid at all. And it isn't anybody you know.' She wouldn't give in to my begging and pestering, either. I'd never be able to keep a secret like that, I can tell you."

"Nothing else?" Kate couldn't keep the disappointment out of her voice. "She never gave you any hints or clues?"

"Not a one," Tammy said, looking back at Kate now. Then her frown lifted slightly. "Oh, once, early on, when I first found out she was gonna have a kid, I asked her why the guy didn't just marry her or at least support the kid, but she said, 'He can't marry me, that's all. And I don't want him to support the kid. I don't think I want him to *know* the kid.' You know, like she was mad at him. But that was before she decided to give you up for adoption. Later she just said, 'It's all fixed now. I didn't want it to be like this, but it's for the best, I guess.'"

"We're here," Eric said, and, indeed, Jack was pulling the car to a stop next to a high wrought-iron fence.

"Just a minute, honey," Tammy said as Kate reached for the door handle. "I want to give you my card. I gotta drive right back to the Cities afterwards because that asshole boss of mine won't give me tonight off. But maybe sometime you might wanna call me, just to talk about Terry."

"Of course," Kate said, putting her hand out to take the card Tammy had fished out of her large purse.

"It seems silly," Tammy said, "but these days everybody's got a card. Best to call after lunch. In the mornings, I sleep in."

Kate glanced down at the card. It said in tiny print, "Tammy Travers, Exotic Dancer," with the phone number underneath. Most of the card was filled with a photograph of Tammy posed against a tropical backdrop; she was wearing only a G-string and pasties. It was also clear that it was not a recent photo.

"Thank you," Kate said, and she gave Tammy's hand a squeeze. "I *will* want to talk to you more about Terry, find out what she was like as a girl. Do you have any pictures?"

"Oh, sure," Tammy said, opening the car door on her side. "I got my old yearbooks around someplace, and my ma still has those pictures from St. Casimir's where we went to grade school."

Waiting for them in the cemetery was the casket—suspended above a newly dug grave—Mr. Fawley, Duane Nelson, and two of the women from the Franklin Street neighborhood. Lieutenant Kinowski stood off to one side against the inside of the iron gates. Max and his girlfriend were nowhere to be seen. A priest, dressed in black with a white stole around his neck, joined them at graveside, having appeared like a ghost out of a small grove of trees. Mr. Fawley introduced him as Father Gregg, and Kate had no idea if this was his first name or his last.

"I'm sorry there was no funeral mass," the priest said to Kate, "but your mother was a fallen-away Catholic, hasn't been to church for fifteen years at least. She's being buried here because her parents are here." And he gestured at a headstone next to Terry's grave.

Kate looked down at a simple red-granite slab that told her the names of her grandparents: Peter and Lorraine Cruzan.

"Let's gather for the prayer," Father Gregg was saying, and the small group formed a ragged semicircle.

Kate stood between Eric and Jack in the warm July sunshine, only half listening to the prayer, whose formal diction and rolling rhythms had a sense of "rightness" about them, even though Kate had no more experience of this religion than she had of Buddhism. Tammy sniffled loudly from time to time. Kate was thinking of the scene in the hospital twenty-three years ago, Terry holding her infant and weeping over it. It was an image she now had to put beside the memory of Terry saying, "I'm not the loving-mother type." What she felt most strongly, looking at the casket winking in the sunlight, was the impulse to comfort Terry, to say, "It'll be all right," as she'd wanted to comfort her in the restaurant when Terry had looked so frightened. Why, Kate suddenly thought, hadn't she been nicer to Terry when she was alive? Why *hadn't* she offered comfort, understanding? Because her own neediness had blinded her to the other woman's needs. And now it was too late.

"Forever and ever, amen," the priest was saying, and the familiar coda brought Kate back to attention. She murmured her thanks to Father Gregg and led the group of mourners toward the gate.

Lieutenant Kinowski pulled himself erect from where he'd been leaning on the iron fence. "Could I talk to you for a few minutes, Miss Lundgren?" he said as she came within earshot.

"Yes, certainly," Kate answered.

"Look, honey," Tammy said from behind Kate's left shoulder. "I hate to be a pest, but I really gotta get back. My boss is not an understanding guy."

"I'll take her back to her car," Jack said quickly, having noticed Kate's confusion. "Probably the lieutenant could give you and Eric a lift."

Kinowski nodded and Kate gave Jack a grateful smile before turning to Tammy Travers. "I want to thank you for coming," Kate whispered. "I don't think I can say how much it meant to me."

"Well, gosh," Tammy said, still red-eyed and looking rather disheveled. "Terry was my oldest pal. How could I not come?"

Kate was not normally a demonstrative person, but she moved spontaneously forward to fold this blowsy, overly made up woman in a tight hug. It made Tammy start to cry again.

"Should I call you tonight?" Jack asked as he stepped back to let Tammy start toward his car.

"I wish you would," Kate said. "And thank you so much for everything."

He shrugged in a self-deprecating gesture and followed Tammy Travers out of the cemetery.

"What did Maxwell say to you back at Fawley's?" Kinowski asked just as soon as the others were out of earshot.

"He threatened her," Eric said, suddenly fierce. "Can't you arrest him for that?"

"How did he threaten you?" Kinowski addressed himself to Kate, a frown closing his thick eyebrows almost against each other.

"The *words* weren't threatening," Kate said, squinting to

remember. "It was the manner. He was scary even when he was telling me to be careful. *Especially* when he was telling me to be careful."

"Yeah," Kinowski sighed. "He knows how to be cautious about stuff like that. You can't arrest people for looking mean. Anything else? Did he talk about the stolen goods?"

"Just to deny knowing anything about them," Kate responded as they moved out onto the sidewalk. "But he *did* seem worried about what Terry might have told me about the stuff. 'I don't know what Terry told you,' is what he said."

"Ah," Kinowski nodded. "I can see why that might worry him. What you saw might not be enough by itself, but if you could testify that your mother implicated him in conversation with you—well, that would be a different thing. So he's trying to scare you off. That's one more nail in *his* coffin."

"We aren't worried," Eric said. "We'll be gone from Woodard in just a few hours, so Kate won't have to look over her shoulder for that stupid thug."

Kate looked sharply at her brother; they hadn't discussed the timing of a departure at all.

"He's not so stupid," Kinowski was saying. "He's a dangerous man, and you'd be well advised to steer clear of him."

"Have you learned anything else?" Kate asked. "About Terry's murder, I mean?"

"Yes," Kinowski answered. "That's also what I want to discuss with you. I think we might have found out how she paid her bills over the years."

Kate just stared at him, so he went on, looking away from her eyes. Kate was beginning to see that this was how he dealt with the problem of telling people bad news or potentially embarrassing information.

"Her credit-card records turned up a pattern we thought was interesting. A gas station in Duluth where she bought gas over the years—always the same station, always on weekends. Starting in 1970, then three or four times a year until about two years ago. Neighbors have said she sometimes went out of town for weekends."

"And that adds up to what?" Kate asked, watching his rugged profile.

"I sent an officer to look into it," he said, staring at the fender of his own car. "That gas station is right next to a Ramada Inn, so we checked that out, showed pictures of the deceased. Sure enough. That's where she stayed. Made the reservations in her own name and always paid in cash. She was seen there in the company of an older gentleman—gray hair, tall and thin. But he stayed mostly out of sight. She always took care of the bill, tipped the room-service guy. So nobody there could ID this gentleman, but they had the impression he had money. I was wondering if your mother ever mentioned to you her relationship with a man in Duluth."

"No," Kate said, her face and mouth numb. "I told you that already. She didn't tell me anything about her personal life." After a pause, she went on. "You think he might be the sugar daddy?"

"Something like that," Kinowski said, looking back at her briefly. "It looks like he provided the cash for the weekends, but gave it to her to pay the bills because he didn't want to be recognized. Maybe he was generous enough to keep the wolf from the door here in Woodard, too."

"She told me that my natural father was much older than she was," Kate said quickly, putting it together now. "I didn't believe her because I thought she was just trying to distract me from the truth. But she told Tammy the same thing—'It isn't a kid at all. And it isn't anybody you know,' is what she said. And it fits, doesn't it? For all these years, she kept up her relationship with him, and he was paying her conscience money. That's what it is."

"Maybe," Kinowski said. "Or it could just be some other boyfriend she wanted to keep a secret from her local boyfriends. It stopped two years ago, so I suppose we can assume somebody broke it off."

"And then she needed money," Kate said, the light dawning, "so she got mixed up with Max, let him keep that stuff in her garage."

"Could be," Kinowski said, nodding. "So then the Duluth man wouldn't be related to the murder. That's what I suspected."

"Why do you assume the man is *from* Duluth?" Kate felt exasperated. "They might have gone separately to that motel from here. It wouldn't do to meet locally if the man was afraid he'd be recognized, that it would get back to somebody he didn't want to know about it."

Kinowski mused for a second, then shook his head. "No," he said. "Seems more likely she would go there to meet the man because she had more leisure time to travel than he did. Some businessman, probably. If this man *is* your natural father, why do you think he stopped supporting her two years ago? If that's what happened."

"I don't know," Kate said, looking back and forth between Kinowski and Eric. "Two years ago is just about the time Terry filed the affidavit of nondisclosure—the document saying she didn't want to be reunited with me. Maybe one—or both—of them just saw that as the end of it."

"Or it was just some other guy she broke up with," Eric said, and it was clear from his tone that he was exasperated at her return to her usual themes. "And maybe they didn't break up at all, but just changed motels."

"Think it over, Eric," Kate said irritably. "She bought the house a few years after I was born, and she was going off on weekends with this guy ever since. Tammy said Terry was mad at my father at first, like she didn't want anything to do with him. But she could have reconciled with him later. He could have been sorry, wanted to make it right with her by then."

"Or she could have found *another* charming older man by that time," Eric insisted. "Didn't she tell you she preferred older men when she was a teenager? We don't even know it was always the *same* guy in that Ramada Inn in Duluth."

"Listen," Kinowski interrupted, heading off an angry retort from Kate, who was glowering at her brother. "I gotta get back to work. I think the Duluth thing is a dead end."

"Not for me," Kate said shortly. "Not if this man might be my father."

Kinowski lifted his eyebrows briefly, a sort of facial shrug.

"Is there anything else?" Kate asked. "What about those leads you mentioned on Friday?"

"Just some stuff the BCA is working on." Kinowski was obviously not going to be very forthcoming. "Fiber analysis, that sort of thing. It takes them a while."

"What fibers?" Kate demanded.

"Whatever they find that doesn't belong in the house," he sighed. "There were some fibers on a gold wire in her earlobe, for instance."

"Oh, yes," Kate murmured, remembering with startling

clarity the spot of dried blood where the wire had been pulled through the flesh.

"I'll take you back to Fawley's now," Kinowski said, and Eric stepped immediately into the backseat of the plain car.

As Kate turned to open the passenger-side front door, she noticed a maroon car pulling away from the curb on the opposite side of the street at the end of the block. Her recognition was instant, that certain identification of familiar objects even when they appear in unexpected contexts. When the car made a left turn, she caught a glimpse of the driver—the only occupant of the car—and her first impression was confirmed. The car was her family's Oldsmobile and the driver was Douglas Lundgren.

# CHAPTER 15

When Lieutenant Kinowski had dropped Kate and Eric at Fawley's parking lot, Kate realized that she must deal with having seen her adoptive father at the cemetery. She was still unable to account to herself for her feelings when she'd recognized the car and Douglas Lundgren driving it. Her instant reaction had been a glad one, a sense that emotional relief was at hand: "Daddy's here" was the way it presented itself in words inside her mind. In fact, she very nearly said those words out loud to Eric. But that first impulse was overtaken by a sudden compunction about letting Lieutenant Kinowski know that her father was in Woodard; his sudden appearance seemed mysterious, and Kate was reluctant to expose her family mysteries to a professional detective. What had triggered that protective impulse? she wondered now. At first, she hadn't even felt she wanted Eric to know.

But she told him now, watching his face intently for any indication that he might have been in contact with their parents, might have known that Doug meant to come to Woodard.

"He must have read about the funeral in the Minneapolis papers," Eric said. "And he thought you might need him."

"Why didn't he come forward, then?" Kate demanded.

"I don't know," Eric replied, his boyish face open, sincere. "Maybe he was afraid of how you'd react. You've made it clear you don't want to have any contact with Mom and Dad right now."

"Then, why come at all?"

"Maybe he thought there would be a chance to see you, but he sort of chickened out when he got here."

Kate mused for a second, then turned from the car to walk toward the funeral parlor. "I forgot to ask Mr. Fawley something," she said in answer to her brother's puzzled expression.

Eric trailed after her, and when they found Mr. Fawley, Kate saw by the look on his face that their unexpected return was an annoying surprise to this professionally polite man. But he recovered quickly, even attempted a discreet smile.

"How can I help you?" he said smoothly.

"Who arranged my mother's funeral?" Kate asked bluntly. "Who paid for it?"

"Well, uh—I don't know that I ought to say." Mr. Fawley was clearly shocked by such a direct reference to money. His reluctance to answer was, no doubt, part of a habitual sense of business decorum.

Kate changed tactics, softening her voice to a cajoling tone. "I naturally assumed that her brother must have made the provisions for her funeral because her parents are dead and she had no other relatives living here. If Robert Cruzan was responsible for the arrangements, I should write him and thank him."

Mr. Fawley smiled, grateful to have a legitimate way to resolve the awkwardness: A thank you was required, so Miss Lundgren would need to have a name.

"No, no," he said. "It was not Mr. Robert Cruzan who made the arrangements. It was Mr. Douglas Lundgren of White Bear Lake. A relative of yours?"

"Yes," Kate murmured. "Yes, that's right. Thank you, Mr. Fawley."

Outside in the parking lot again, Kate was building up a head of steam as she and Eric reached the car.

"Did you know about this?" she said, wheeling to face her brother. "Did you and Dad have a series of secret phone conversations after I was asleep at night?"

"No!" Eric was emphatic. "I swear to you, Katie. I didn't

know. But I don't see what you're so mad about. I think it was pretty darn nice of Dad to do this, to take it off your hands."

"Take it off my hands?" Kate asked, genuinely puzzled. "What does that mean?"

"What would you have done if the police had come to you and said, 'Her brother isn't paying for a funeral, so what should we do with the body?' How would you have kept her from a pauper's grave?"

"I didn't think—" Kate began and then faltered to a halt. She knew this was true. She was so accustomed to having things taken care of for her—tuition, medical insurance, even dental appointments that Sheila scheduled to coincide with school vacations—that she didn't think about how these things were done.

"And you know Dad as well as I do," Eric said. "He *does* think of that kind of stuff. He's used to taking care of things for everybody else. So he took this burden off of you before you knew it was your burden. Just so automatic for him."

Kate stood for a moment with her hand on the recessed door handle of her Beretta.

"But it seems too automatic," she said at last. "Almost as if he was used to making arrangements for Teresa Cruzan, and this was just the last one he had to think of."

Eric snorted in disgust. "So, you're back on that again. Why are you so determined to believe that Mom and Dad were paying that woman to stay away from you?"

"Don't call her 'that woman'!" Kate flared, her emotions—raw from the events of the day—finding expression in anger. "She was my mother."

Eric calmed himself for a moment before he spoke again.

"Okay, Katie. I guess the only way to settle this business is for you to ask Mom and Dad about it directly. We'll go check out of the motel right now and we can be home before dinner."

"I'm not going," Kate said flatly. She'd been waiting for this confrontation ever since she'd heard Eric so confidently tell Lieutenant Kinowski that they were leaving Woodard in a few hours.

"What does that mean?" Eric said. His voice got more quiet when he was angry—sometimes the only symptom of this emotion in him.

"It means I'm not finished with business here in Woodard,"

Kate answered. "Terry was murdered and nobody's in jail. I don't know anything about her, really, and I still don't know who my father is."

"Let me get this straight," Eric said slowly. "You're going to try to play detective on your own in a town where a known thug is afraid you'll get him sent to prison for grand theft? Is that about it?"

"I'm not afraid of Max," Kate lied, pushing her long jaw forward. "And if all I'm doing is asking around about Terry and who impregnated her, I'm no threat to him. So why should he bother me?"

"You think you can locate your natural father on your own, is that it?"

"I don't know," Kate said in exasperation, "but I've got to try. Somebody's got to try."

Eric was silent for a moment.

"Well, I'm going home, Kate," he said at last, quietly and firmly. "I've got a job that won't wait for me forever. I took the bus here; I'll take it back."

She was stunned for a moment. She'd expected that she could bully Eric into extending his stay, felt a wave of panic at the thought of being alone in Woodard again. But she knew he was right about his job. He'd been the head lifeguard at one of the municipal pools for three summers now, but that wouldn't save his job if he didn't get back soon. So she swallowed her fear, opened the car door to cover the slight tremor in her voice when she spoke. "Okay, if that's what you have to do. But I have to stay."

"And what do you want me to say to Mom and Dad?" he asked, relentless.

"You can tell them what I just told you," Kate answered. But she could hear how cold it sounded. "Try to minimize that danger stuff, too. Don't let them worry about me. I'm not going to do anything dangerous."

"You don't think I should tell them about this Max character, then?" he asked, his eyes narrowing slightly.

"Think about it, Eric," she said, lowering herself into the car. "Why worry them about something they can't do anything about?"

"All right" he said grudgingly. "I won't tell them about Max."

Later, after she'd driven Eric to the bus depot, she sat in
her room wondering how she should begin. What leads could
she follow? She was just thinking that perhaps it was best to go
back to the beginning, to the summer Terry got pregnant, when
the phone rang, startling her as it always did in this small room
where she didn't expect phone calls.

"Hello, Kate." She recognized Jack Kramer's deep voice at
once. "I know I told you I'd call tonight, but I just realized I
might miss you if you guys are going back to White Bear Lake
today."

"Eric went back," Kate said. "I'm staying on for a while. I
don't think I could stand being down there, wondering what
was going on here, wondering whether the police had made an
arrest."

"I see," Jack said. "But Eric had to go back?"

"Well," Kate said with a sigh, "he doesn't exactly approve
of my staying on. So when I insisted, he went back without me.
It's kind of a long story."

"Well, you're still here," Jack said heartily, "so I can pass
along my mother's invitation. She was worried about you being
at loose ends after the funeral—she's sure there should always
be a meal somewhere after a funeral. That's the tradition
around here. So she told me to ask you and your brother to our
house for dinner tonight. I'm sure she would be even more
insistent if she knew you were on your own now."

"Thanks, Jack, but I really don't feel up to it tonight," Kate
said. "I need to be by myself right now. I'm just done in."

"Tomorrow night?" Jack said eagerly.

"Are you sure your mother's invitation is that open-
ended?" Kate asked with a rueful little chuckle.

"Sure," he replied. "Believe me, she'll be delighted to have
you whenever you say you'll come."

"Okay, then, tomorrow night. Thank you for today, Jack,
and for taking Tammy back to her car."

"She's quite a character, isn't she?" Jack laughed.

"I think she's wonderful," Kate said quickly, responding to
a hint of mockery she thought she'd heard in Jack's voice.

"I agree, absolutely," he responded, and he sounded
sincere.

"I'll see you tomorrow night," she said, mollified.

* * *

On Tuesday afternoon at three-fifteen, Kate was sitting in a sunny but empty dining room at the Woodard Country Club, waiting to see one of the cooks. She had driven there, propelled by a powerful impulse to reconstruct the year of Teresa Cruzan's pregnancy. Terry's long involvement with an older, possibly married man might have begun during that first summer job. The membership of the club, then as now, must have included large numbers of older, well-to-do men. One of them, Kate deduced, was probably her biological father.

When she'd arrived at the club, uncertain as to how to begin asking questions, the first person she'd encountered was an overweight man in a garish golfing costume coming out of the door she was about to open.

"Well, hi," the man said, smiling broadly. "Are you looking for me, I hope?"

Kate had laughed at the good-natured joke, and had then explained briefly that she was looking for anyone who had been a club member or employee long enough to answer questions about the summer of 1967. The golfer identified himself as Ted Gittings and said he'd been a member for only nine years. Kate remembered *The Odd Couple*, with Valerie Gittings as Olive, and felt shocked by the realization that she'd seen that play only ten days ago—it seemed like months.

"But there's lots of guys who've been members longer than me," Gittings volunteered. "And old Cy Walters in the kitchen has cooked here since before the Flood. He's back there now, I bet, getting ready for this evening. Come on in, and I'll dig him out of there for you."

And now, as she sat waiting in the sunny room, Kate was wondering why she'd postponed dinner at Jack's house. As exhausted as she felt yesterday afternoon when she begged off, she hadn't been able to get to sleep, but had lain awake, staring at the ceiling, where the lights of passing cars chased each other from the corner above her head to the top of the bathroom door across the room—wave after wave of ghostly light moving restlessly overhead like lost souls looking for a peace they couldn't find.

"You looking for me?" The voice made Kate jump and turn around to face a huge man who had come up behind her silently on thick crepe-soled shoes. The stained apron over T-shirt and jeans made it apparent that this must be the Cy

Walters who had cooked for the country club since before the Flood.

"Yes," Kate said, standing up. "I understand you were already employed here in 1967."

"Been here since fifty-nine," the man said, passing one hand from his forehead all the way to the back of his head in a gesture that seemed habitual, as if he were checking for any hairs that might have reappeared on the shiny, bald surface.

"Then you must have known Teresa Cruzan when she worked here in the summer of 1967," Kate said. "She was fifteen then, busing tables."

Cy Walters gaped at her for a second.

"That's it!" he cried in a voice so loud that Kate staggered back from him in a half-step. "I told the missus I heard that name before when I read it in the paper last week. 'Where do I know that name from?' I says to her, and she says, 'You always think you know everybody.' But I was right. Sure, sure. I remember now. Pretty thing, dark eyes—sort of Chinese-looking."

Now Walters furrowed his brow, thrust his alarming face toward Kate. "Sort of like you," he said. "She looked a lot like you, as I remember her."

"She was my mother," Kate said, holding her ground now. "Yes, I do look quite a bit like her. I'd like to know what you remember about her, Mr. Walters."

"Call me Cy," the big man said, subsiding now into a manner that seemed almost kindly. "You're the poor kid who found the body, ain't you?"

"Yes," Kate murmured. "I did. You understand that I didn't know Terry very well. I just met her a few days before she was killed. So I'm trying to put together some things about her life. I know she worked here that whole summer before I was born, so I'm hoping you'll remember something to tell me."

Unconsciously, Kate had formed the sentence out of her own preoccupations, and Cy Walters responded with surprising quickness to the spirit of her inquiry. "You wonder if I seen her with anybody," he said, and Kate could feel herself blushing. "Any boyfriend?"

"Well, something like that," Kate stammered.

Walters frowned in concentration. Through the wide windows behind him, Kate could see golfers making their way back to the clubhouse.

"Naw," he said at last. "I don't think there was any boy coming around here to be with her, and as I recall she didn't want much to do with the other kids working here. Yeah, it's coming back to me. She was pretty uppity with the caddies who was always trying to get her attention between rounds—she was a looker, all right, and those guys all buzzed around her like bees around a flower."

"What about members of the club?" Kate asked now. "Did any of them seem interested in her?"

Again Walters frowned, trying to remember. "She wasn't a waitress, you know," he said. "Some of the waitresses flirt with customers, but the kids who clear tables don't usually have much contact with the club members. But I don't know what she did in her off hours. You know, back there in the kitchen, I don't see much of what goes on out here, anyway."

"Do you remember anything special about her at all?" Kate was beginning to realize what it would be like trying to investigate something that had happened so long ago.

"I found her crying once," Walters said, nodding in sudden recall. "Just huddled up next to the big cooler, crying her heart out. I remember how surprised I was because she was usually so cocky, so sure of herself—she was full of ginger, that one. But she wouldn't tell me what it was about. Just straightened herself up and marched away without a word."

"Do you remember when that was?" Kate asked eagerly. "What time of the summer?"

"I don't remember any date," Walters said. "But it must have been later in the summer because I kind of felt I knew her by then—I mean, I thought she shoulda been able to tell me why she was bawling, and I wouldn'ta thought that if she was just new on the job."

"How many members does this club have?" Kate asked, taking a new tack.

"Oh, I don't know," Walters shrugged. "Coupla hundred, I guess."

"Are many of the present members longtime members? Long enough to have been members in 1967, I mean."

"Oh, sure," Walters answered quickly. "We got lotsa old-

timers. Some of 'em been members forty years. Woodard don't
have a lot of turnover, you know."

Kate sighed noisily. Obstacles everywhere. Television private eyes always made this sort of thing look so easy. "Well,
thank you, Mr. Walters," she said vaguely.

"Cy," he corrected her again. "And I don't know what
you're thanking me for. I ain't been much help." Then, after a
pause, he added, "I liked Terry. She was a good worker, never
lazed around on the job. And she had spirit. Some kids are just
a mush, you know, but she had gumption. Shame about her
being killed."

"Thank you, Cy," Kate whispered. "Thank you for telling me."

When Cy Walters had returned to the kitchen, Kate sat for
a while in a patch of sunshine coming through the windows.
She wondered if she should ask someone for a list of club
members. Would they give her such a thing? Were there open
records of such membership anywhere in Woodard? The problems for a private citizen in conducting any investigation were
becoming steadily clearer to her. She sighed, stood up, and
turned to leave the dining room.

A man was standing in the doorway of the room, watching
her; from his stillness, Kate guessed at once that he must have
been standing there for some time. It took her a beat to go from
a sense of vague recognition to a positive identification. The
man was Thomas Werner.

"I thought that was you," he said in his officious voice. "I
saw you through the windows when I was coming in off the
course."

Kate stood speechless, staring at him. His sunburn had
faded into the beginnings of a tan and his clothes were impecca-
ble, beautifully tailored and obviously expensive. The silver
thatch of hair glinted a little in the artificial light of the hallway—hairspray, Kate thought, to hold the leonine mane in
perfect place.

"What are you doing here?" Werner said, stepping forward
into the room. "Are you applying for a job in the kitchen? I saw
Cy Walters in here with you."

"No," Kate said, finding her voice. "I was discussing my
mother with Mr. Walters. She used to work here."

"Really," Werner said, his handsome face impassive. "Have you had any trouble lately with men following you around?"

Kate knew she was blushing, was angry at herself for being so intimidated in this man's presence. Terry's murder had shoved the incident in the library to the back of her mind, and this reminder of it was somehow disconcerting. "Not that I'm aware of," she said, more assertive now, "but that wouldn't be impossible. Did you know that the murdered woman you've been reading about was my mother?"

She watched the face intently, focused on the blue eyes. There was a slight widening of the pupils and she heard a quick intake of breath, but whether this was surprise at new information or alarm at having this subject introduced at all, Kate couldn't tell.

"Really," he said again, his voice controlled. "Yes, I have read about it. And so you are the daughter who found her. How awful for you."

"I wonder if you might remember my mother," Kate said guardedly.

"Remember her?" Werner said, the silver eyebrows lifting.

"Well, I understand you've had a long association with this country club, first as the golf pro and then as a member."

"Have you been asking questions about me?" And for the first time, a frown creased the high forehead.

"Just a few," Kate said, feeling unaccountably happy at having got a rise out of him. "Teresa Cruzan worked here during the summer of 1967. I thought you might remember her."

"Well, that was a long time ago, my dear," he said, recovering his smooth manner. "I can't remember every girl who goes in and out of this place."

"I thought you might remember this one," Kate insisted, "because, at the library, you looked at me as if you thought you recognized me. I look very much like Teresa Cruzan."

"I don't know what you mean," Werner huffed slightly. "I do wish you wouldn't go on about that nonsense at the library. I thought that was all cleared up." Just as if he weren't the one who'd brought it up in the first place.

Kate's heart was racing because she had made a lightning-fast series of connections: older man, married, plenty of money, but only as long as his wealthy wife was "pleased" with him— a man who fit the description given by the Duluth motel clerk.

"Terry told me she had no use for boys her own age when she was a teenager," Kate said carefully, trying to control her own breathing. "And Cy Walters told me she wouldn't have anything to do with the young caddies who were after her when she worked here. She was fifteen that summer and I was born the next March."

"Why are you telling me this?" Werner asked, the frown returning. He actually took a step backward.

"Because I think the man she was seeing that summer was an older man," Kate said, leaning toward him slightly. "And it occurs to me that she might have met him here. One of the members, perhaps."

She paused to let this sink in, watched the pale eyes carefully.

"So, if you could remember her," she went on, "maybe you could remember whether she spent time with one of the older men here."

Werner was silent for a moment, but his face was a study in rapidly changing emotions. Kate had trouble trying to characterize these emotions. Had she seen surprise? Fear? Horror? Outrage? Certainly outrage was the emotion he ended with, the one he gave voice to when he finally spoke.

"You have an incredibly vivid imagination, young lady. You seem not to care one whit that your wild accusations might damage people's lives. I do not remember the woman you speak of, so it would be impossible for me to speculate about who might have been her lover and, presumably, your father. I recommend that you stop speculating about members of this country club."

"I'm not going to give up," Kate said stubbornly. "I intend to find my natural father. Just remember that."

Werner drew himself up to his full and impressive height. His eyes were like ice now, his face flinty.

"This is private property, young woman," he said. "Only members and their guests are permitted on these premises. I don't believe that you are either one."

"I'm going," Kate said hotly. "But I'm not going far."

And she stalked out of the dining room, shoved vigorously at the outside door, and marched across the parking lot to her car. It was only when she was behind the wheel that she started to shake, putting her forehead down against the steering wheel. Could it be possible? Could that pompous man be her father? Would Terry once have considered him "dreamy"? If it was true, she realized with a shudder, it put her encounter with him at the library in a whole new light. She had accepted the notion that she'd been stalked on the darkened mezzanine by an anonymous flasher. But maybe Werner had been following her around for several days before the murder. Maybe he had been hiding among the parked cars the night Jack brought her back from the play. And maybe *he* was the reason Terry had seemed so scared the next day.

Now Kate sat up straight, her eyes widening with a new and terrible thought. Since her visit to the law-enforcement center when Kinowski had made that series of shocking revelations about Terry, Kate had accepted the policeman's assumption that Max or one of his gang had killed Terry over some aspect of their criminal activity. But what if that wasn't true? What if her earliest feeling about the killing had some basis, after all, and Terry had actually been killed to keep her quiet about a much more personal matter? That man inside the country club could be both her father *and* Terry's killer. And she had just confronted him!

What should she do? She felt suddenly very alone, very unprotected. She steadied her hands by gripping the wheel. Lieutenant Kinowski, she thought. She should tell all of this to him. Why, she wondered now, hadn't she told him in the first place about the creeper in the library, about the noises in the parking lot? The shock of Terry's murder had simply driven everything else out of her head.

She glanced down at her watch. There was plenty of time to go to the law-enforcement center before she had to get ready for dinner at the Kramers'. She started her car and drove resolutely out of the lot, past the rows of BMWs, Volvos, and Chrysler New Yorkers, deliberately racing the four cylinders of her own car in defiance of Thomas Werner's arrogance.

# CHAPTER 16

"It's nice to see a girl with an appetite," Mrs. Kramer was saying as she cleared dishes from the table. "Too many young people these days think they have to starve themselves. Of course, there's no need for you to watch your figure."

"I don't think anyone could have resisted this meal, Mrs. Kramer," Kate said, rising to help with the clearing. What she didn't say was that she hadn't eaten since breakfast, so her appetite wasn't solely a tribute to the lemon chicken, good as it had been. "That homemade sherbet was especially nice. It tastes different from the kind you buy in the stores."

"Mother is famous for her desserts," Jack offered from the sink, where he was running hot water over the plates before arranging them in the dishwasher. "Woodard's only gourmet club is always threatening to give her awards."

"Oh, it's not a gourmet club at all," Mrs. Kramer laughed, but she was blushing a little, too. "Jack is always teasing. It's just a few of us who get together for potluck dinners." When she looked at Kate again, her beaming face became serious. "Now you just sit back down, dear," she said solicitously. "There's no need for you to help. You're the guest and you've had some bad shocks lately."

This oblique reference was only the second time during

the evening that Mrs. Kramer had alluded to Kate's recent experience. The other had been made when she first greeted Kate at the door. "You poor, poor dear," she'd said, taking Kate's hands. "What you've been through! Sit down and rest." It was clear that this small, frail-looking woman treated all emotional distress as if it were a physical ailment, but an ailment of a delicate nature whose details well-bred people would never discuss.

Kate sat down, unwilling to argue with this odd logic, and watched the mother and son at the kitchen counter. Mrs. Kramer was wearing a cotton knit dress of a pale lavender color and a short string of pearls that Kate guessed must be genuine. Her gray hair was stiffly coiffed, her makeup discreet. Kate wondered if she'd done this because a guest was coming to dinner, or if she always looked like this. She leaned toward her son as she spoke to him, touched him frequently—a pat on his forearm, a quick smoothing gesture against his shirt collar. Kate had noticed this behavior throughout the meal, too, almost as if Mrs. Kramer felt compelled to confirm with her fingers that her son was still there. For his part, Jack took this attention with good grace, though he sometimes made an embarrassed grimace at Kate when his mother wasn't looking at his face.

"Who's up for a postprandial stroll?" Jack asked when the dishwasher was loaded.

"I never know what you're talking about when you get into these moods," his mother said, her expression half reproving, half mildly amused.

"An after dinner walk, Mother," he said with a chuckle. "It's not so hot out there now, so I think you could manage it."

"Oh, you young people go along without me. I'm not dressed for walking. When you get back, you can play something for our guest."

"I'm not going to play anything, Mother," Jack said, a flash of irritation apparent in his voice.

"Of course you will," Mrs. Kramer said in her mild voice, and Kate intuited a whole lifetime of Jack's objections being flattened by this smiling steamroller. "Music after dinner is so pleasant, don't you think so, dear?"—this to Kate who couldn't even begin to formulate a reply before the older woman went on—"And Jack plays so beautifully, several instruments, you know."

At the front door, the mother stood leaning against the door frame as Kate and Jack started down the porch steps. "It's a pity the neighborhood is so spotty," Mrs. Kramer said with a noisy sigh, speaking to Kate as if Jack were not there. "There haven't been many sales lately, I'm afraid. We just can't understand why people aren't moving out here. We love it so much ourselves, and Jack is working so hard."

"You'd better close the door, Mother," Jack said. "We can't afford to air-condition east-central Minnesota."

Kate and Jack walked in silence for a while, so she had a chance to take a more leisurely look at the development she'd glimpsed from Jack's car as he drove them here. Kramer Valley was an almost brand-new housing development at the southeast edge of Woodard. Its terrain was scenic, hilly, with stands of mature pine, deep ravines separating the lots, so that it didn't look like the squared-off grids of most midwestern towns. The few houses that had been built on the landscaped lots near the entrance were relatively modest. The Kramer house was slightly more upscale, as befitted the home of the developer—a three-bedroom Cape Cod with a low fieldstone wall separating its wide lawn from the street. It was at the back of the development and only two other houses were near it. Many of the lots were empty, their stakes-and-twine outlines almost obscured by high weeds. The new streets had no sidewalks yet, so Kate and Jack had to walk along the pavement. He took her hand as they walked, casually, as if he'd done it many times before. When they came upon a narrow footpath that led sharply downhill, Jack left the road without a word and Kate followed him, sure-footed in her flat sandals.

"It just makes me crazy when she does that," Jack said suddenly, as if there had been a conversation already in progress in his head and he were simply continuing it aloud.

"Asks you to entertain?" Kate asked, watching the side of his face as they walked.

"Oh, that too," Jack said with a shrug. "But what I meant is the way she talks about this development as if its failure was my fault. Not that she blames me, of course. Oh, no, I'm just a poor baby, too sensitive to be expected to succeed in business."

"Come on, Jack," Kate said briskly. "She didn't say anything like that."

"No, but it's what she means," Jack said, looking at her now. "She can't face the idea that the development was a bad idea in the first place, so it must be my inexperience that explains why we can't sell any other houses here. The truth is that the housing market was already depressed around here when Dad got the idea, and this recession is only making things worse. Why should people plunk down ninety-five thousand for a house out here when they can get something bigger in town for a lot less and not have assessments to worry about, either?"

"Well, I'm sure your mother knows that," Kate said, not sure how to respond to the combination of sadness and anger she could hear in his tone.

They had to negotiate a sharp descent in the path, and Jack took Kate's hand again to help her down. When he spoke next, his voice sounded more resigned. "It's just that I don't feel ready yet for all this," he said, gesturing at the landscape. "I don't even think of myself as a grown-up a lot of the time. Do you ever feel like a kid still?"

"Sure," Kate said with a rueful smile. "In some ways I *am* still a kid. I mean, I don't have a job. I don't have my own money. I don't even have any solid plans for what I want to do with my life. I guess it's partly because I've got such a sense of unfinished business. As if I can't think about where I'm going until I'm sure where I've come from."

Jack was silent for a moment as they made their way down toward a steep ravine where both the landscape and the sound effects indicated that they were approaching a stream. Kate wondered if part of her attraction to Jack Kramer might not be based on an early intuition that, like herself, he was enmeshed with family troubles that were holding him back from an adult identity. She glanced again at his clouded face and then gave his hand a sympathetic squeeze. He responded with a pause and a quick smile.

"I don't know why you want more parents," he said at last, almost as if he'd read her thoughts. "Aren't two enough for anybody?"

"It's hard to explain," Kate sighed as they came to a halt at the ravine's edge, where they could finally look down at the rushing water. "It isn't parents I'm looking for; I'm looking for me. But nobody understands that."

"Well, let's drop it," Jack said with a slow smile. "I'm sorry to lay my own troubles on you. Tell me what's new with you. You were awfully quiet in the car on the way over here."

"Well, it's been pretty hectic." Kate sighed, swatting idly at mosquitoes, which were rising from the grass around the edge of the ravine. "I guess I'd better start from the last time I saw you." And she told him about what Kinowski had revealed of Terry's trips to Duluth to meet an older man, of seeing Douglas Lundgren at the cemetery and her subsequent suspicions about continuing payoffs to Terry from her adoptive parents. And she told him about her visit to the country club and her encounter with Thomas Werner.

"It all fits, don't you think?" she asked him finally. "You told me Werner's financial well-being depends on his wife, and if she ever found out he had a longtime mistress who'd given birth to his child, she'd divorce him like a shot and then he'd be penniless. And I never did think he had any real business at the library that day. I think he's been following me around since right after I got to Woodard. At the country club, he said he'd seen me accidentally through the window, but I wonder. Maybe he followed me there and got scared when he saw me talking to that cook who knew Terry."

"Don't you think you're going a little fast?" Jack said now, but he had looked thoughtful the entire time he'd been listening to her suspicions about Werner. "What you're saying is that you think Tom Werner might have killed your mother."

"Yes, I suppose I am," she faltered. "Aren't you going to say the obvious, that you can't believe him capable of such a thing?"

"No, no," Jack answered. "I'm not so sure I know *what* people are capable of. But did the motel clerk in Duluth give a very detailed description?"

"He wasn't very specific," Kate said defensively. "He says he didn't see the man very often. But maybe he could identify him from a picture. You know, if the police showed him a bunch of photographs and put Werner's picture in with them."

"And that's what you were suggesting to Kinowski this afternoon, I take it," Jack said, indicating a stump where she could sit down. "What does he think?"

"He thinks I'm crazy," Kate sighed, sinking onto the rough surface. "He didn't say that, of course, but it's what he thinks.

He's so sure Max killed Terry, and he's clearly horrified at the suggestion that one of Woodard's leading lights might be guilty of anything. He thinks Terry had an older lover who lives in Duluth, but that they broke up long ago. So Kinowski can't see any connection between this man and Terry's murder."

"He's probably right," Jack said, squatting down on his haunches next to her. "He's an experienced investigator, and if he doesn't see a connection, why should you?"

"I know, I know," Kate murmured. "After I talked to Kinowski, I began to think it was all pretty melodramatic myself. But what I know for sure is that Terry spent a lot of time in Duluth with an older man. And I want to find out who he is, even if it isn't connected to her murder. Kinowski doesn't care if that man is my father or not, but I care. I'm going up to Duluth to see what I can find out. Do you think I could get pictures of Werner from old newspapers? Nothing too recent, because this clerk would have seen him several years ago."

"I think this is a bad idea, Kate," Jack said, standing up straight again and beginning to pace in front of her. "Maybe your brother is right. Maybe you're just too emotionally in-volved to be rational about all of this."

"Maybe you're too close to it," Kate flared. "The Werners are friends of your parents, and you just can't believe they'd be involved in anything sordid."

"That's not fair," he said, stopping to look down at her, his eyes wounded behind the glasses. "I've already told you how I feel about Tom Werner. I'm just concerned about you. You seem so obsessed."

Kate looked away from him now, scuffed her toes in the dusty grass. "If you were in my shoes for even five minutes, you'd know why I'm obsessed," she said finally.

"All right, I'm sorry," he said. "When do you think you want to go to Duluth?"

"Tomorrow," she answered instantly. "If I get pictures in the morning, I'll go up in the afternoon. Kinowski gave me the address of the motel. It's only about an hour's drive."

"Can't you wait till the weekend?" Jack asked, his brow wrinkling again. "I could go with you on Saturday."

Kate smiled up at him in the gathering gloom. "And I'd appreciate the company, but I can't wait that long," she said.

"My money is running out and I don't think I can ask my parents for more."

"I could lend you a little," Jack offered. She couldn't figure out his tone. Was it embarrassed? Reluctant?

"No," she said firmly. "I may have to go home soon because I'll be broke, but at least I'll be chasing my obsessions with my own money."

"Don't be like that," Jack said. "I'm sorry I used that word, okay?"

"I'm not mad at you," she said softly. "I really need to do this on my own. I am *trying* to grow up, you know."

Jack reached down to help her get up, closing his surprisingly warm hands over her wrists. When she stood, she placed her hands against his shirt front, leaned in toward him. He bent forward and kissed her lightly on the mouth.

"It's almost dark," he said. "And the mosquitoes are getting mean. I suppose we'd better get back to the house so Mother can force me to 'play something' for you. I haven't played for so long now that it'll probably sound like amateur night."

"What instruments do you play?" Kate asked, falling in with the sudden swing to casual conversation.

"Clarinet, saxophone, and piano," he said with a low chuckle. "I'm a versatile guy. I'll probably treat you to the piano tonight."

"Good," she said. "I like the piano."

Kate knew enough about jazz music to recognize that Jack Kramer was an accomplished musician. This love of music, she reflected, was another bond between them. He sat hunched over the piano, his boyish face serious, almost dreamy. He didn't look at his fingers and there was no sheet music on the piano. Kate guessed that the music he was playing was at least in part improvised—a nervous, almost discordant piece that had the cumulative effect of deep sadness. As Jack played, Kate glanced at his mother, who sat erect on a low chair, as if she were in a concert hall; she never took her eyes off her son, and her face had an expression almost identical to his—dreamy, abstracted. Kate had already noted that Jack resembled his mother—this comparison of parents and children was an old reflex of hers—and now she was even more struck by the similarity.

Again, Kate felt a strong connection to Jack Kramer. His ambivalent relationship with his mother seemed like an echo of her own present turmoil. He was chafing against his responsibility toward this soft, dependent woman—was sometimes openly bitter when he talked about her—and yet he so clearly loved her, craved her approval. And while Mrs. Kramer's devotion to her son was transparent, it was tinged by her own needs, too—as a widow, she clung to Jack and made demands on him. It struck Kate, looking at the mother and son, that she was able to see this more clearly as an outsider in this house than she could see it in her relationship with her own parents. Your parents might love you both selfishly and unselfishly at the same time, it seemed, and your momentary anger with your parents didn't change how you felt about them in the deepest part of yourself. This family stuff was a complicated business, Kate thought—perhaps for everyone. And as the music washed over her, she felt a sudden pang of homesickness.

It was almost eleven-thirty when Jack got Kate back to the Holiday Inn. They sat in the car without speaking for a moment, though they'd chatted easily enough on the drive over.

"I like your mother," Kate said finally. "She's a very gracious lady."

"I know she is," Jack replied. "Sometimes I need to be reminded of it, I guess. But didn't you find it odd that she never once referred directly to your mother's death? Like it was some unpleasant disease you're not supposed to talk about. That's one of the things I'm still trying to get over—that refusal to deal openly with negative feelings."

"Actually, I found it rather refreshing," Kate laughed, "after those ghouls at the funeral. All that prurient interest masquerading as niceness. It gives me the creeps."

"I know what you mean," he said, turning to look at her with a surprised expression he seemed to wear every time he discovered that they thought alike about something. "I've always said there's something sinister about people who are forever commanding you to have a nice day, when they couldn't care less whether or not you fall under a bus."

"Well, I suppose it's better than being around people who would think nothing of pushing you under the bus," Kate sighed. Then after a pause, "Of course, the truth is that even among these 'nice' people, there are always a few who *do* push people under buses—or strangle them."

Jack sighed but offered no comment for a moment. "See?" he said finally. "I'm enough like my mother that I can't think of an appropriate response to that, except to say that of course you're right."

"Do you want to come in for a while?" Kate asked, watching his profile. "We could have a nightcap in the bar."

He turned to look at her, his expression thoughtful as he registered this invitation and all of the things it might mean.

"I'd better not," he said. "Looks like we've both got a working day tomorrow. Will you call me when you get back from Duluth? Let me know what you find out?"

"Sure," Kate said, opening the door on her side. "You do look a little tired and I didn't get much sleep myself last night."

Jack reached over quickly, caught her left hand, and brought it briefly to his lips.

Back in her room alone, Kate assessed the evening and her feelings about Jack Kramer. She'd channeled so much of her emotional energy into locating and wooing Teresa Cruzan—it had really been a strange kind of courtship, she now realized—that she hadn't left herself much room for other emotional attachments. And since her breakup with Jason six months ago, she had led a celibate life. But the depression that had followed her through graduation and into the summer had been so overwhelming that she'd scarcely noticed her deprivation.

Now Jack had begun to establish himself in her perception as a distinct personality—not just a nice, good-looking young man but *this* particular person who loved his mother and was exasperated by her, a man who played nervous-sad music on the piano but was shelving his dreams of a jazz career because family responsibility had suddenly intervened. A man who seemed ready to serve her like some medieval knight without asking or expecting anything in return. In short he was becoming almost irresistible.

Why, she wondered now, had he responded the way he did tonight? She could tell that he understood the significance of her invitation, had considered it with interest before saying no. Then that impulsive kiss on her hand, as if to say, "Please don't think the idea doesn't appeal to me immensely, because it does."

And he was the one pursuing her, wasn't he? Calling her, asking her over for dinner. So what did he have in mind? Was it possible that he could read her more clearly that she'd suspected? That he measured her sense of abandonment, her need for comfort, and refused to take advantage? Perhaps he had an ambition to be something more than a "quick fix" to her and was willing to wait on that account, but his delicacy prevented him from talking about such things openly—his mother's son. Or, she suddenly realized, it could be that he had a girlfriend somewhere whose existence he'd simply failed to mention.

She shook her head to dislodge the exasperation and got ready for bed. The preparations ended with putting on the sleep mask she'd bought that afternoon before going to the country club. Tonight there would be no sleepless tracking of the ghostly lights across the ceiling.

# CHAPTER 17

The Ramada Inn was just off the highway, its sign reaching up into the sky to snag the attention of passing motorists. Kate had spent part of the morning at the Woodard Public Library, this time in the ground-floor room where the newspaper files were kept on microfilm. In a two-hour search, she found several photographs of Thomas Werner: one from 1979 when he'd been named the Jaycee's Man of the Year, one from 1986 showing him in a golfing foursome for the local tournament, and one from a 1988 charity ball to benefit St. Francis Hospital. In this last one, Werner looked especially handsome in a tuxedo and was pictured with his wife, who was identified as Elizabeth Proctor Werner in the caption—the local newspaper was apparently also in the business of kowtowing to Woodard royalty. She was a large woman with obviously dyed hair and a rather ostentatious display of jewely; in the photo, she looked older than her athletic husband. Kate spent her dimes and nickels making Xerox copies of the three photos and then folded them in half to slip them into her purse.

The woman behind the desk in the lobby of the Ramada Inn was no more than twenty-five and had worked there, she told Kate, for less than a year. When Kate indicated that she was looking for the same clerk who'd already spoken to the police about the murder victim in Woodard, the young woman perked up. Oh, yes, she'd heard all about that. But Barry—he was the clerk the cops had talked to—wasn't working today. Wouldn't be back on duty until Friday.

Kate stood there trying to swallow her disappointment. Why hadn't she called ahead? "Can you give me his home address?" she said finally.

The young woman frowned, her uncertainty looking like anger. "I don't know," she said slowly. "Are you a cop or something?"

Kate decided that honesty was the course likeliest to get results here. "I'm the dead woman's daughter," she said, feeling a twinge that now she, too, was referring to Terry as "the dead woman."

"Oh," the clerk said, her eyes widening. "Oh, I see. Well, Barry lives over on Snyder. The house number is here somewhere." And she began to scan the bulletin board behind her. "Here it is," she said, pointing a long fingernail at a tattered sheet. "It's 1563 Snyder. Maybe you should call first."

Kate thanked the woman for her suggestion, dialed the number the clerk read to her, and secured Barry Hinton's enthusiastic permission to visit him, along with instructions about how to find the house.

It turned out to be a rather seedy-looking place in a run-down area of the city. The man who answered Kate's knock was about fifty, his thin hair plastered tight to a large head, his middle bulging slightly into a bright red knit shirt. He led her into a sparsely furnished living room whose walls were covered in posters depicting heavily muscled young men leaning against motorcycles or lying on tables while lifting weights with their feet.

"I told the police what I remember about your mother," he said after waving Kate into a chair. "Did you ask them about it?"

"I did," Kate answered carefully, "but they didn't go into much detail. I'm most curious about the man, the one she came here to meet."

Hinton stared at her for a moment from watery blue eyes. "You didn't know about him, I suppose," he said with a little shake of his head, a sort of "tut tut" expression on his wide pudding of a face.

Kate sighed and explained that she hadn't known about her mother, either, until a few weeks ago, so it would be all right to talk about this freely—he wouldn't be embarrassing her. Hinton looked relieved, leaned forward in his eagerness to tell what he knew, now that his one compunction had been removed.

"Well, as I told your police officer, I didn't see much of the man and, even though the records show your mother was coming here since 1970, I've only been at the motel for the past ten years, so I can't speak for anything earlier."

"I understand," Kate murmured.

"Okay, then," he said, sliding closer to the end of his own chair as he readied himself for disclosure. "She always arrived first, checked in, got the key. That would be on a Friday, usually. I think he would come later that day—I say 'I think' because I never saw him come in the front doors. I expect he just parked in the side lot and went in by the entrance on that side. But the next morning there would be room service for two. We talked about it sometimes hanging around in the lobby. She'd pay for it in cash—with a big tip—but he was usually in the bathroom. And he always left before she did, too. We know because she would sleep in on Sunday morning and order breakfast for one."

"How many times would you say you actually saw him?" Kate interrupted him.

"Oh, three or four times, I guess," Hinton answered, his florid face thoughtful for a moment. "Once Yolanda—she's one of the maids—saw him leaving the building and told me about it, so I ran out the front and saw him in the parking lot. Another time, I almost ran him down in the lobby when I was rushing back to the desk from the john. He must've come out for a newspaper—it was early in the morning, as I remember."

"So you saw his face clearly?" Kate asked eagerly.

"Well, I don't know about clearly," he said, sitting back a little. "It was so fast and I was embarrassed, too. Some of the maids saw him from time to time—I don't believe any of them are with us anymore. We all talked about them, of course, about how she was too young for him—we don't get many regulars, you know. The maids said he was handsome, but I don't know about that. He wore really nice clothes, I remember—expensive-looking. He was tall and lean—you know, the kind who look good in clothes, any clothes. And he had a springy walk, you know, like an athlete or something. Pretty spry for a man his age. Yolanda said he had a wedding ring—she was shocked that he didn't even bother to take it off."

"Did anybody have the impression that he was a local man? From Duluth, I mean."

"Well," Hinton shrugged, "we didn't recognize him at all, if that's what you mean. But, of course, we don't know everybody in Duluth. People with lots of money don't usually stay at a Ramada Inn, do they? Unless they're trying to avoid seeing their rich friends."

"Do you think it was always the same man?" Kate was thinking of what Eric had said.

"Oh, sure," Hinton said emphatically. Then he frowned. "Of course, I can't be positive, but nobody ever said anything about there being more than one."

"If you saw a picture of him," Kate ventured now, "do you think you could recognize him?"

"I might," Hinton said. "Sure, I might recognize him."

Kate took out the folded Xerox sheets, selected the one with the golf foursome in it, and handed it over to Hinton.

"Could he be one of these men?" she asked.

Hinton examined the picture with the sheet held close to his pale eyes. "This is pretty bad quality," he said, sounding personally aggrieved somehow. "Only one of these men is tall enough to qualify, anyway." And he turned the sheet toward Kate with his finger pointing down at Thomas Werner's likeness.

Kate felt sheepish now about not having brought photos of other men—she hadn't created a very fair lineup. There was nothing else to do now except to show him the other two pictures, so she handed over the papers.

"Well, I don't know," Hinton said, squinting and moving the pages back and forth in front of his face. "It could be, I suppose. He looks the right age. I'm sorry, but I can't be sure one way or the other." And he handed over the pictures.

Kate sat back, at a loss. She'd imagined all the way to Duluth that she would get a positive identification, and then she would know for sure that Thomas Werner was her biological father. She stood up now and moved toward the door. Hinton struggled to his feet and followed her.

On the shallow porch, she turned back to him. "Did you ever see his car?" she asked. "Could you remember the make and model?"

"I suppose I saw it that day in the parking lot," Hinton said, "but I honestly can't remember anything about it, not even the color. But Yolanda saw him getting into his car one day—it must've been in the early eighties sometime—and she reported to us the way she did about everything. She said it was one of those boxy foreign cars—a Volvo, maybe. She thought it was a Volvo."

Kate stood on the porch, gaping at him for a second.

"Did she say what color?" she was finally able to say, but her voice was choked.

Again, Hinton scrunched up his wide face to concentrate. "I don't remember if she said a color or not," he said finally. "But she said it was 'one of those boxy foreign jobs with the funny snouts.' I remember that part, about the snouts, because that's what she called the grille on a car."

"Thank you," Kate murmured, and then she trotted down the steps and half ran to her car.

Inside, she sat for a long time, staring out at the shabby street without seeing it and without starting the car. Her mind was in high gear, racing over a new and horrible possibility. From 1978 until 1985, the Lundgrens had been a two-car family: Sheila hauled her children around in a small Ford station wagon, and Doug drove a forest-green Volvo sedan. In 1985 he had traded the Volvo away for the first of the two Oldsmobiles he'd owned since then.

Douglas Lundgren was a tall, good-looking, athletic man with gray hair; once blond, he'd been gray almost as long as Kate could remember. He always prided himself on dressing nicely—"important in business," he often said—and his business, Kate now remembered, sometimes took him out of town on weekends. It was Doug who had "found" a baby for the Lundgrens to adopt; his warehouse in Woodard must have brought him there on many occasions in the years Teresa Cruzan was growing up.

Kate's thoughts were going so fast that they seemed to tumble over each other. She was breathing in shallow gasps, and her eyes were beginning to sting from her long stare without blinking. Suddenly she fixed on a single clear memory: Sheila, always the more confiding of her parents, saying to her when she was about thirteen, "The infertility problem was mine, you know. If Daddy had got a different wife, he could have had natural children."

Kate gave her head a sudden shake. No! It was impossible. It was just a coincidence about the car. That maid wasn't even sure it was a Volvo—just a boxy foreign car. It wasn't possible that her father could have seduced a fifteen-year-old and then kept her as a part-time mistress for twenty years. He couldn't have "bought" his own child and then lied about it to Sheila. The man Kate knew wouldn't be capable of such a complicated and prolonged deception. But he *had* been capable of the prolonged deception of his adopted daughter, hadn't he? Hadn't he joined in a conspiracy to keep from her the identity of her birth mother, even when he knew she was almost desperate to locate her? A month ago, she wouldn't have believed he could do that, either. Now Kate remembered what Jack Kramer had said last night: "I'm not so sure I know *what* people are capable of."

Under the crumpled Xerox sheets in her purse, she found her car keys and brought them out with trembling fingers. Then she started the car and pulled slowly away from the curb. She'd driven several blocks before she let the next thought into her mind: If Douglas Lundgren had been the one who fathered Teresa Cruzan's child, he might also be her murderer.

She could hear the phone ringing as she was unlocking the door to her motel room. She fumbled for a second, turned the key the wrong way, finally got the door open. When she snatched up the phone, she blurted a breathless "Yes?" without any greeting.

There was a pause, the sound of indrawn breath on the other end of the line. "Katherine?" Just her name, but enough for Kate to recognize the voice. "It's Mom."

"Yes?" Kate said again, as if she couldn't think of any other syllable. Yet the sound of Sheila Lundgren's voice had brought her almost instantly to the brink of tears.

"Will you talk to me for a moment?" Sheila's voice sounded breathless, as if she were really afraid Kate would hang up.

"Of course," Kate managed to say, holding herself in.

"How are you, darling?"

"I'm all right," Kate lied. "I'm coping." It was the word Sheila herself always used when she was at her most harried.

"Are you coming home soon?" Kate could hear the nervous apprehension, the fear behind the seemingly casual question.

"I don't know," she answered, and this time she was telling the truth. "There's still a lot of unfinished business here."

"That's what Eric said you were feeling. That you felt you needed to stay there until the investigation was over. But that might take such a long time. Do you have enough money? Do you need anything?"

"Don't worry about me," Kate said, her voice neutral now.

"Of course I'm going to worry about you, Katie," Sheila said, and now her voice had the slightly exasperated ring of an unappreciated mother. "Eric hasn't said much about what the police know. But the papers suggest that she—" And here she faltered to a stop, at a loss, apparently, about how to refer to Teresa Cruzan.

"That Terry was involved in something illegal," Kate finished for her. "It's nothing for you to worry about."

There was a silence now and Kate could almost see her mother's face pursing, the outward sign of a mental caution so typical of Sheila Lundgren.

"Eric told me something else," she said at last. "He said Daddy paid for the funeral and that—"

"You didn't know about that?" Kate interrupted, eager for information now.

"No, I didn't," Sheila answered. "After Eric mentioned it, Dad and I discussed it. He didn't want to upset me but, of course, I told him it was just what I would have done if I'd thought of it. He knew you would want her to have a decent burial. You know how he is."

Kate made no response, and there was another uncomfortable pause.

"Eric told me you suspect us of bribing Teresa all these years to stay away from you," Sheila said at last in a single rush of breath.

"Did he say that to Daddy, too?" Kate asked.

"No, just to me. Your father has been hit so hard by all this—he's so upset by your anger. And Eric can sense that. But he confided it to me when I couldn't understand why you hadn't come home along with him."

"And Dad is upset about the business, too, isn't he?" Kate interrupted again, half ashamed of herself for using Sheila to inadvertently inform against Doug. "Eric said he spent last weekend at the plant to see what's going wrong down there." On the drive back from Duluth, Kate had remembered that Doug had been in St. Paul at the time Terry was murdered, or at least that's where he'd told his wife and son he was going to be. But he had also said he was going to "hole up" so that he could check on things without anyone knowing he was around.

"Yes, that's true," Sheila responded, but she sounded confused at this turn in the conversation. "And he got back so late on the Sunday that I didn't even wake up when he came in. Just today he had to fly off to Chicago to meet with some nervous stockholders, and I don't expect him back until late tonight. You know how he tries to keep from worrying me about anything, but it's very hard on him to have extra troubles right now." And Kate thought she heard an accusatory tone.

"Well, I wish things were better for him, of course," Kate said, but her voice was cool again.

"Katie, I don't know how you can believe that we would bribe your birth mother," Sheila said firmly, and it was clear that she had come at last to the reason for the phone call. "We paid her hospital expenses twenty-three years ago and that was the end of it. We had no contact with her whatsoever after that."

"Don't you know how I could believe it?" Kate said, her anger flaring again. "Don't you really know? You tried to prevent me from finding out who she was even after I was legally an adult, so why shouldn't it occur to me that you might have tried to keep her away from me when I was a kid?"

There was another silence.

"You've got to believe me, Katie," Sheila said finally, "when I tell you how sorry I am about deceiving you. You were only seventeen when you suddenly began saying you wanted to find her, and I was terrified of losing you to her. I tried to tell you when you turned nineteen—I meant to tell you. Then I thought I would leave it up to her. If she agreed to see you, I would tell you about it before you met her. But when she refused, I thought it was an omen—like a sign—that you weren't meant to find out. I realize now that it was just a rationalization on my part. It was a mistake not to tell you, a mistake I'll always be sorry for. But you musn't believe that I got Daddy to *buy* you, like you said, as if you were some toy. That's too cruel of you, darling."

Kate could hear that her mother was crying, and it occurred to her for the first time that the "arrangement" of her adoption might have been the work of only one of her adoptive parents—that Sheila might have no knowledge about the depth and length of that arrangement.

"I said some pretty mean things before I left home," Kate said now. "I was angry. I guess I'm still angry, but I know a lot of that stuff wasn't fair to you. You should know by now that I've got a short fuse and that I say more than I mean when I blow up like that."

"Once you said I was just like the Wicked Witch in *The Wizard of Oz* because I wouldn't let you have a dog." Sheila sounded eager to accept Kate's words as a sort of apology. "I cried all afternoon about that one, but the next day you said you didn't remember saying it."

"I remembered," Kate said softly. "But I was ashamed of myself, so I lied."

"Can I send you anything?" Sheila said after another pause.

"No, Mom, really," Kate said, swallowing the lump in her throat. "I'll be fine."

"Will you keep in touch?" Again the fearful tone, the half-shy expectation of rejection.

"I will," Kate answered. "I'll call you."

Kate had just put the receiver down when the phone rang again, vibrating under her hand.

"There's a letter down here for you, Miss Lundgren," the voice of the desk clerk said in answer to her hello. "You went past me so fast a few minutes ago, I didn't get to mention it."

Kate brought the envelope back up to the room before opening it. Inside was a single piece of notepaper, torn from a spiral-bound pad, and it said simply, without a salutation, "Thought you might like to have this snap. I dug it out as soon as I got home. It's from the third grade." The note was signed, "Tammy," and it was wrapped around a color photograph of two little girls—one fair-haired, short, and plump; the other taller, skinny, and dark-haired. Kate turned it over and read, "Class clowns. School picnic, 1961," in a round, tidy handwriting—probably Tammy Travers's mother.

Kate carried the photo to the chair next to the lamp and

sank down. The two nine-year-olds in the picture were leaning their shoulders against each other, their hips and legs as far from each other as they could manage without falling over. They were grinning at the camera in the phony and exaggerated way that children do on such occasions. Behind them, an out-of-focus game of softball was under way, its umpire a nun in a modified habit, her short veil making a dark wedge above the blond child's shoulder.

Kate stared into the face of the dark-haired child. The front teeth looked too large for the narrow face, the cheekbones hadn't yet achieved the raked angle of the adult woman, and the eyes were crinkled up by the exaggerated smile, but this was unmistakably Teresa Cruzan. There was a vitality, an energy, in the cast of her body, in the lean arm thrown over the shoulders of the smaller child. In the tilt of the head there was a jaunty carelessness, an overall presence that overshadowed the blond Tammy, who was actually prettier in a conventional way.

Here, Kate thought, was a child at the magical stage, Terry before she could even imagine the life-shaping event that waited for her only six years into the future. For the first time, Kate saw Teresa Cruzan as a person separate from her own illusions, a person apart from Katherine Lundgren's fantasies and emotional demands. And someone had cruelly strangled this person.

Kate bent forward in the chair, held the photograph against her breast, and began to cry. Her sobs began quietly enough, but their very sound seemed to make her cry harder. Perhaps it was more than grief over Terry's death finally released in her; perhaps it was partly her fear about Doug, partly the need for mothering triggered by the sound of Sheila's voice on the phone. But whatever the reasons, she sobbed like a child, desolate and almost wailing, shaking and rocking at the same time, bent double in the rigid motel chair.

# CHAPTER 18

He paced in a short, circular path in front of the closed door, and on each pass, the discreet lettering in the glass insert skittered by his peripheral vision. The lettering was backward, of course, facing the hallway beyond the door, but he knew what the words were: ROBERT ALLAN FORD, ATTORNEY AT LAW. He was pacing partly to keep himself between the other man and the door, though the old man sunk in the leather chair before him looked too frail to rise. But he also needed the movement to keep the panic from overwhelming him. He could feel the queasiness deep in his gut, a sick clenching of his innards that got worse whenever he sat down. It had been getting worse ever since the phone call this morning, almost twelve hours ago now. All day he had told himself, "He wants to see me about something else, some other business," but deep inside, where the sickness was growing, he knew.

"I'm sorry we have to be here so late," the old man was saying. "It would have been more convenient if you could have come in the afternoon."

"I told you on the phone that I can't just take off in the middle of the day." He was struggling to control his voice. "And today, especially. I had to work late."

"Well, it doesn't make much difference to me," Ford

sighed. "Since my illness forced me into this partial retirement, the days and the nights seem almost the same. And maybe this is better. We have more privacy here without the partners being around."

He took a few more pacing steps, realized how ridiculous it had been to entertain a wild hope that the old man would die before ten o'clock could arrive. He'd been waiting patiently for Robert Allan Ford to die for some time now. Liver cancer was the diagnosis—hopeless was the prognosis. And if this old man could pass quietly into his grave, too distracted by the process of dying to reopen a certain matter, he would be almost entirely safe. But, apparently, he'd counted overmuch on the dimming of alertness he thought must be part of the business of dying.

"Why couldn't you tell me on the phone what you needed to see me about?" he asked now, pausing near the door.

"I think you know what it's about," the old man sighed, leaning back in the chair, which seemed to have grown too big for him now that his disease had shriveled him in this terrible way. "Do you think I've stopped reading the papers?"

"I tell you, I don't know what you mean," he snapped, his hands jammed into his pockets. "What's in the papers?"

"I figured out who that Lundgren girl must be." Ford sounded tired, more sad than angry. "To think that I let you talk me into leaving it all to you." And he shook his pale, hairless head from side to side on the thin, ropy neck. "I believed you when you told me you were looking for the child yourself."

"I *am* looking for her!" He was trying not to shout, but he couldn't control his voice. "This is a different case altogether. It's just a coincidence."

"Please, don't insult my intelligence." The old man's voice was so quiet, it hardly carried across the small room. "Of course, I was never told the mother's identity—only you had that information—but the document in my possession contains the date of the child's birth, as you well know. The newspapers have given Katherine Lundgren's age. One reporter was even enterprising enough to get the records of Teresa Cruzan's hospital stay at St. Francis—those dates were in Monday's paper. But, I'm sure you know that. You must be following this story very closely."

Now the old man had to pause to breathe; the speech was a long one and it seemed to have exhausted him.

"I suppose it's more than just the scandal?" Ford spoke again, and he said it as a question. "The provision made for the girl involves more than you originally thought, doesn't it?"

"Don't be absurd," he snapped, but he'd stopped in his pacing to stare at the old lawyer. Sharp, sharp; much sharper than he'd ever given him credit for being. He saw the shrewdness in the faded eyes.

"I've got some contacts in the police department," Ford went on. "I called in to ask some questions about the case."

"Kinowski?" he demanded, as if the name were itself a whole question. Then, after drawing a ragged breath, "Did you talk to Kinowski?"

"No," Ford sighed. "I don't know him. Just some of the guys I used to know when I did some criminal law. They tell me they might be close to making an arrest, though they won't say who. I realized that once the case is solved, the girl will go away. And then I also realized that you must be hoping for that—that she would just leave. Then you won't have to have it come out who she is to you. But you must know that I can't let that happen."

He'd stepped forward to stare down at the old man. A flood of relief washed over him. Ford didn't realize there was any connection between what he knew and Terry's murder. Perhaps the old man's perceptions were fading after all. And if he hadn't made the connection, then he couldn't have told anyone about it.

He leaned over the old man now, bringing his face close to Ford's. "Why can't you let it alone?" he asked, pitching his voice at a softer, more cajoling tone. "Think of the pain it's bound to cause if it becomes known who fathered that girl. It will cause heartache and trouble for everyone. Believe me."

A skeptical look passed over the frail features, and Ford shifted in the leather chair as if something hurt him. "You've used that argument to delay things in the past," he sighed. "But I don't believe you mean to let the girl have what's rightfully hers, and I can't be a party to fraud."

Rage flooded him, making the blood beat up behind his eyes, and starting him in his pacing again. The pathetic old fool was going to bring him down one way or the other. Some old-fashioned idea of professional ethics made it impossible to keep his sick mouth shut. And the police wouldn't be so slow to make the connection between that damned piece of paper and Terry's murder.

He stopped in front of the chair, bent forward over the old man, and said quietly, "I want you to open the safe."

Now Ford sat forward a little, a look of alarm on his shrunken features. "I can't do that. The safe is in Jerry's office now because he's the senior partner. And even if I did, even if I could give it to you, what would you do with it? You can't destroy it because lots of people besides me know it exists, even if they don't know the contents. And if you tamper with it, destroy only the part that's dangerous to you, the rest of it will be invalid, and you'll be caught anyway."

"That's right, that's right," he murmured, panic churning in his stomach again. Thwarted, blocked on every side.

Ford was looking up at him out of his ashen face, the old eyes filled with something like disappointment, as if he'd actually hoped he might be wrong. When he spoke again, it was in his lawyer's voice, cold and official-sounding. "I'll have to go to the police if you persist in this stonewalling. Or to the girl herself. That would take care of it, too."

He stood looking down at Ford as if from a great height; everything inside of him had gone still, the violence in his stomach pausing as if it, too, were listening, waiting for the next word. "Why haven't you done that already?" he asked at last. "Why are we here?"

"I wanted to give you the chance to do it," Ford said quietly. "I think you must know that."

"You're such an idiot," he snarled. "Such a fucking idiot."

He watched the pale face register shock and then distaste. Then he stepped quickly forward, reaching past Ford's frail body to snatch up a piece of notepaper from the neat stack on the corner of the desk. The old man cringed away from him and gasped in alarm. Odd, he thought, that a dying man could still be so afraid. He glanced down at Ford's averted face. Maybe it was *because* he was dying that he was so afraid, so jealous to preserve every remaining minute, so alarmed that another physical insult might be added to the ones he already carried inside his narrow body. And that pathetic gesture of looking away from an imagined threat, as if the old man were saying, "You can't hit me if I'm not looking—it wouldn't be sporting."

He moved with a deliberate care now, turning Ford's chair

toward the desk, placing the blank notepaper in the exact center of the blotter, lifting the mahogany pen out of its engraved stand. "Just put your signature at the bottom of this paper," he said softly.

"Why?" Ford asked, but even the single syllable betrayed a quaver.

"Never mind. Just do what I ask." Again, he didn't raise his voice, didn't glower.

"If you're planning to fill this sheet with something you can then hold against me, that won't work. I'm hardly going to be bothered by threats of blackmail."

Ford was beginning to regain his equilibrium, and that would have to be stopped. He spun sharply around—he'd been facing the desk, pointing at the paper—and grabbed Ford's left wrist, half lifting the old man out of the chair. At the same time, he thrust his own face down toward the pale face below him.

The old man gave a strangling gasp and began to cough. It was a horrible sound, hoarse and deep, racking the man's whole body; each cough ended in a gurgling sound that seemed to be coming more toward the front of his mouth with each onslaught. The pale skin was becoming flushed until the cheeks looked almost engorged. Tears leaked out of the corners of tightly pinched eyelids. Finally, the coughing subsided, and he fell back until he hung like a limp doll from the wrist that was still caught in a tight grasp.

Holding the wrist was just a convulsive reflex now, because he was almost overcome with nausea at the spectacle of this sick old man, so terrorized that he might die right in front of him; maybe he *was* dead. He held his breath, listening, until he could detect the old man's shallow breathing. Finally he saw the flesh around the jaw relaxing, the eyes opening.

"Sign it," he said, and his anxiety translated into something that sounded almost like a growl.

The old man looked up at him now and the pale eyes were filled with terror. It took only one little twist on the frail arm— it felt like a bundle of dry twigs—to make him reach for the pen. His right hand shook as he wrote.

"Thank you," he said, releasing the wrist and carefully lifting the piece of notepaper from the blotter. "It's warm in here, isn't it? The air-conditioning must be turned off at night. I'll just get us some fresh air. We could use some air, couldn't we?"

He walked across the small room, willing his legs to move, pausing to put the piece of notepaper down on top of a file cabinet. It was a struggle to open the window. At first, it seemed immovable, its white painted frame apparently glued to the wide sash. He jerked on the handles, trying to move the window from side to side, finally pounded on the frame with the heels of his hands. Then he squatted slightly, using the muscles of his legs to reinforce his arms and back. The window made a slight groaning sound and then flew upward with a sudden force that almost threw him off balance. He drew a ragged breath and glanced out—five stories below was a brick court-yard whose fountain provided the view for three office build-ings. At ten-thirty P.M., this part of downtown was virtually deserted; no sounds of traffic came up to the open window—only the humid night air.

When he turned from the window, he caught Ford on his way to the door. The old man froze now under his glance, like a deer in headlights, and the expression on his face made it clear that he knew what the struggle to open the window was really about. For a long moment, neither of them moved.

"You killed that woman," the old man whispered, his voice dry as old leaves. "You killed her." His eyes were wide in shocked realization.

He leaped at the old man, grabbing his shoulders, dragging him easily across the shining hardwood floor. There was almost no resistance. At the window, he reached down, scooping Ford up into his arms as one might pick up a child or a woman one meant to carry across the threshold. But the old man kicked his thin legs away, shoved with all his feeble strength against the arm that was holding him at the shoulders. It took a hip smash, pinning the old man against the wall, to squash the resistance, to immobilize him so that he could be lifted.

One thin hand, the right hand, swung at his face so that he had to dodge away—the color of the skin, the liver spots, even the fine dusting of white hair above the knuckles, passed under his eyes with a kind of slow-motion clarity. Ford was gasping; there was a little grunt of expelled breath as he launched that pathetic punch. He turned his face to avoid blows or fingernails—but mostly so that he wouldn't have to see the face with its panicked eyes—and forced the old man's buttocks onto the windowsill. With one more push he folded the frail body in the middle and shoved the fold out into the night air. One leg kicked convulsively outward, the shoe scraping along the windowsill. Then, in a gesture a man might make to heave a hay bale onto a stack, he propelled the burden of Robert Allan Ford's body away from himself. There was a tug at the sleeve of his sports jacket where the thin hand made one last effort to hold on.

The scream wasn't loud—just a thin wail, fading below him before a muffled thump and silence. He waited without looking down, waited for any other sounds. When several minutes had passed without any audible hint of movement below, he turned from the window and walked back to the file cabinet where he'd left the sheet of notepaper. When he picked it up, he noticed that his hands were shaking. He would have to wipe everything down before he left, he told himself—the doorknob, the window and frame, even this paper. Mustn't leave fingerprints.

Now he steadied himself against the file cabinet, swallowed his nausea, and carried the paper in both hands to a small table where an old Underwood upright sat on a foam-rubber pad. He rolled the paper into the carriage, centered it, and began to type, moving with elaborate care so that his fingertips, still trembling slightly, wouldn't strike two keys at the same time.

# CHAPTER 19

"Just because Hinton can't identify Werner from the pictures doesn't mean it *wasn't* Werner," Kate was saying to Jack Kramer across a table at Flo's Diner, where they'd agreed to meet for lunch. "Nobody there got a very sustained look at Terry's 'friend.' Just enough to give a general description."

In her distress the night before, Kate had forgotten her promise to call Jack when she got back from Duluth, had telephoned him at his office this morning to apologize.

"Well, you wouldn't have found me home anyway," he said. "I had to show some property in Wrightstown, a possible industrial park. Nobody ever wants to look at land during business hours. As it turns out, they aren't really serious about the land, anyway. Another of Dad's speculations that isn't working out. Meet me at Flo's for a burger? They're the best in Woodard—nice and greasy. Guaranteed to make your cholesterol count spike before the day is over."

Now he sat, munching a tuna sandwich and listening to Kate tell about her visit with Barry Hinton.

"I'll tell you, Kate," he said at last. "A Ramada Inn just doesn't sound like Tom Werner."

"Well, isn't that just the point?" Kate insisted. "Would he take a woman to a hotel where his own social class was likely to hang out? Even in Duluth, where there must be businessmen he knows?"

"Maybe you're right," Jack sighed. "And remember, I don't hold any special brief for Werner. I wouldn't put anything past him, really. But it could be somebody else, too. Somebody who lives in Duluth, like Kinowski said. Terry could have had a boyfriend up there, too." She noted that he'd adopted her own habit of calling Teresa Cruzan "Terry," had stopped referring to her as "your mother."

"I know that," Kate said slowly. "And Hinton told me one thing that's got me worried. He said Terry's mystery man might have driven a Volvo in the early eighties. My father—Douglas Lundgren, I mean—drove a green Volvo until 1985."

Jack stopped halfway into his next bite, lowered the sandwich, and stared at her. "I don't get it," he said stupidly. "What's that got to do with anything?"

"I haven't given you all the gory details about my adoption," Kate said, feeling herself blush. "I only just found out about them myself. But my adoptive parents knew the Cruzans—at least my dad did, because Terry's father managed his warehouse for him here in Woodard. When Dad found out about Terry's pregnancy, he arranged for the adoption. They'd been trying to adopt a baby for a while—my present parents, I mean—and this looked like a good chance."

"I'm not following" Jack said, sitting back in his chair with a frown. "What does this have to do with your dad's Volvo?"

"I know I'm not telling this right," Kate murmured, looking away from Jack's intent stare. "This is hard for me. I've been thinking that maybe Dad knew about the pregnancy because *he* caused it. Maybe he was Terry's 'gorgeous' older man. Then he saw a chance to give my mother—Sheila, I mean—what she wanted, and also to have his own child with him."

"I see," Jack said when she fell silent. "And your dad is a tall, slim, gray-haired man, I suppose."

"Yes, he is." Kate was almost whispering.

"Then, you think he kept up the affair with Terry all these years? Supported her? Met her in motels?"

"I didn't say that I think that," Kate flared, looking back at him. "I said the possibility occurred to me when I heard about the car. But Werner is also a strong possibility. I wish I could find out what kind of car *he* drove back then. But the man at the hotel only said it was a boxy foreign car, like a Volvo, so we can't even be sure what we're trying to identify."

"Are you going to tell Kinowski what you learned on your trip up north?" Jack asked, lifting his coffee cup and wrapping both hands around it.

"No!" She spoke quickly, vehemently. "He doesn't think my parentage has anything to do with the murder."

"But *you* do," Jack said quietly. "All along, you've been worried, haven't you, that your natural father might have killed her? So, if your adoptive father is your *real* father, he might be the killer."

"There's no motive," she said quickly. "He wouldn't have killed her just to keep her quiet about my parentage."

"So you *have* been thinking about it," he said, and now he reached over to cover her hand with his own. "Couldn't such a revelation end your parents' marriage? Maybe that's motive enough."

"I don't think Mom would divorce him for that," Kate responded, drawing her hand away, refusing to accept comfort because she couldn't help feeling that such acceptance would mean there was truth in her fears. "They love each other very much. Oh, they don't take out billboards about it, but anybody who knows them knows it's there. Mom would be devastated, for a while I suppose, but she'd get over it. They would stay together, I think."

"Well, maybe there are things you don't know about," Jack said, putting both hands back around his coffee cup. "But it should be easy to put your mind at rest. Just ask your brother where your dad was on the night of the murder."

"Eric already told me," Kate murmured. "He said Dad was at the St. Paul factory on the weekend Terry was killed. I've been thinking that ought to be pretty easy to check, but I'm not sure how to start. I don't know any of the people at the plant, so I don't even know who I might ask. It's funny, isn't it, that I've lived my whole life with Dad and I can't name one person he works with?"

"Not so funny," Jack said with a shrug. "Until my father died, I hardly knew any of the people in his business, either. We take all of that stuff for granted, I guess. It supports us, but it isn't our business to know about it."

"Maybe you could help me with some of the stuff I'd like

to find out here in Woodard," Kate said, pushing a french fry around on her plate with her fork.

"Me?" Jack said, sitting forward again. "How could I do that?"

"Well, for one thing," Kate said with a little smile, "you could find out what kind of cars Thomas Werner drives. That shouldn't be too hard, since your mother pals around with him—or at least used to."

"Well, I suppose I wouldn't have to be Columbo for that," Jack laughed. "What else?"

"You know people in the business community now," Kate went on, nervously tapping the fork against the plate. "People who might have known my father when he used to come over here on business. You could ask around about him."

Jack was silent for a moment, his brow furrowed again.

"I suppose I could," he said finally. "Do you know when your dad sold the warehouse?"

"No," Kate sighed. "Another symptom of my ignorance. In the late seventies, I think. It became a storage place for grain, Dad said."

"Oh, that would be Branhart's Milling, I guess," Jack said. "It must have been Ev Branhart who bought it from your dad. But it's empty now. That whole area on River Drive is getting pretty rundown."

"Do you know this Branhart guy?" Kate asked eagerly. "Would he have kept on any of the people who worked for my father?"

"I don't know the answer to that one, but I do know Ev slightly. I'll see what I can find out. What, exactly, should I be asking?"

Kate thought for a moment, letting her eyes range, unseeing, over the other lunch customers.

"You should try to find out how often Dad came to Woodard in the days he owned the warehouse. Did he spend more than a few hours here when he came? Who did he know? Who did he spend time with?"

Jack made a little snorting sound. "You should go to work for the FBI," he said.

"Well, I've had some time to think about this since yesterday," she said with a sheepish smile.

"I don't suppose you're sleeping much," Jack said, and the deep voice was soothing to her.

"Not last night," Kate admitted. "I was thinking just now that you look a little bushed yourself." After a little pause, she added, "I thought it might be your mad social life."

Jack gave a short, mirthless chuckle. "No, I don't have much of a social life these days," he said. "What you see is probably just discouragement. Showing properties to people who never buy, stuffed shirts in seven-hundred-dollar suits, can wear you out."

"I suppose," Kate said. "So there's no girlfriend?" She was aiming at a casual tone, but she could hear the tightening of her voice.

He looked at her shrewdly across the table until she could feel the blush moving up her face. "Not since about six months ago," he said at last. "She was—and still is—part of the music scene in Minneapolis. When I was playing, I was always down there. But, you know how it is. Different roads now. We drifted apart."

"Yes, I know how that is," Kate said, finding the rim of her Coke glass interesting for a second. "That's something like what happened to me and my college boyfriend."

"So," he said, his eyes opaque in the harsh restaurant lights, "we're both free agents."

"That's a funny term, isn't it?" Kate said, looking at him now. "I don't feel so free."

"Me, either," he said, looking away from her now. "There are all kinds of entanglements, aren't there?"

"There sure are," she said, feeling an undercurrent in his remarks, wondering what it was. Could his consistent withdrawal every time she wanted to move closer be connected to some sense he had that he couldn't make any commitments to a woman while he was so enmeshed with his mother, with the struggling business he'd inherited?

"Are you going to give up the hunt for your father for a while and get some rest?" he said now, a gentle scolding tone coming into his voice.

"Maybe," she sighed. "I feel I should be doing something all the time, but I don't know where I should turn now."

"You should wait for me to get back to you," Jack said,

mock stern now. "Give it a rest until I see what I can unearth. Okay?"

"Okay," she said, and smiled at him over her Coke.

Back in her Beretta again after lunch, Kate drove around for a while, thinking. The sky, already cloudy when she got up, was darker now, ominous banks of thunderheads rolling upward in the west. Ever since yesterday in Duluth, she couldn't seem to stop thinking about the father who'd raised her—energetic, positive, no-nonsense Douglas Lundgren. Born on a farm in northern Illinois, dragged from rural serenity at the age of nine to live in a raucous neighborhood in Chicago, he'd seen his standard of living plummet steadily as the Depression took its toll on his father. As soon as he turned eighteen, he'd enlisted in the army to spend the last year of the war stateside. It was the connections he'd made during his hitch that started him on the bootstraps regimen that eventually led to owning his own business. But it was the force of his own will that had built the business into the one that now not only provided his family with a very comfortable life but also supplemented the pension of his aged parents.

Kate couldn't remember ever seeing her father in a down mood—his strongest expletive was "dammit," said as one word and usually under his breath—yet, she now realized, there must have been struggles along the way, worries and stresses accompanying the management of a company that employed some two hundred workers. But he kept all of that hidden from his family, masked by the cheerful face, the hearty laugh. What did it say about the character of a man that he could so thoroughly repress the negative aspects of his life? Was such repression a virtue? Or was it dangerous?

Kate remembered with sudden clarity an incident from her childhood, during a vacation at Yellowstone when the camping trailer was brand-new. She must have been six or seven. After an early morning hike, the family had come back to the campsite to find two teenage boys ransacking the trailer. Alerted by the noise, Doug had warned his wife and children to stay back and had then waded in. One of the boys escaped immediately, scampering away into the nearby woods, but Doug came out of the trailer dragging the other one, a scrawny kid with dirty hair, maybe sixteen years old. The kid was cowering and beginning to blubber, but Doug shook him hard, bunching the dirty T-shirt up into his fists.

"You rotten little son of a bitch," he snarled. "You never worked for anything in your stinking life. Where are your parents? Huh?" And after every phrase, he gave the boy another shake. The kid's silence seemed to inflame Doug more than a smart-aleck answer would have. "Do you know anything about what it takes to earn nice things?" He was almost bellowing now. "You and your mongrel kind just grab, don't you? Let other people work for things you can run off with. Fucking degenerates, all of you." And he threw the kid against the side of the trailer, which made a hollow, echoing sound, like an empty oil barrel.

"Douglas!" Sheila cried, stepping forward now. "Stop it. You're going to hurt him. Let him go. Just let him go and be done with it." Kate had looked up in wonder at her mother's face, gone pale and frightened, almost as if the anger and violence were being directed at her.

Doug had stood there a moment, looking from the ragged boy to his wife and then to his children, huddled together near the burned-out campfire. Then he turned and stalked away into the trees. The boy scrambled up from where he'd slid down into a crouch and ran away in the opposite direction. For the rest of the day, even after Doug had come back in a calmer mood, Sheila and Eric and Kate had tiptoed around, speaking in hushed voices, recovering slowly from this rare display of physical and verbal violence.

The sudden splashing of raindrops against the windshield brought Kate back from her reverie. She was aware all at once of how much time she'd been spending in her car lately, almost as if the Beretta had become her home. Here she was, driving around aimlessly, oblivious to weather or even to traffic, looking for—for what? Why was she so consumed by this impulse to keep moving, to keep searching, even when she had no idea of where she was going? She pulled over to the curb now and waited for the rain squall to pass.

When the rain had slowed to intermittent drops, Kate formed a resolution. She couldn't just sit around. Jack might be working for her, but she had to work for herself, too. Maybe there were people still working in the warehouse district who remembered Douglas Lundgren and Peter Cruzan. If she could find somebody who did, she might get closer to solving the mystery of who had fathered her. She opened the glove compartment and dug out her map of Woodard—the one she'd got for two quarters from a machine in the lobby of the motel. It took her only a few minutes to find River Drive, a narrow red line at the southwest edge of the town.

A man stepping into a pickup truck outside a building labeled MILT'S LAWN AND GARDEN FERTILIZER pointed and said, "Last building on the right," when Kate asked if he knew where Branhart's Milling Warehouse was located. To get here, she'd driven past grain elevators, lots with rows of gleaming International Harvester machines—reminders of how closely towns like Woodard were still tied to the farm economy. Yet, Jack was right about the seedy condition of the warehouse district— many of the buildings looked shabby, and several seemed completely abandoned, the glass in the windows shattered.

She spent almost two hours going from building to building in the near-vicinity of Branhart's. But she learned only that there must be a brisk turnover in the few remaining warehouse employees: Of the five men she spoke to, the longest employed had been on the job only six years. No one knew Peter Cruzan at all, and no one had ever heard of Douglas Lundgren.

Discouraged and tired, Kate started to drive away, but then changed her mind and turned the car back toward the two-story gray building that had once been the Lundgren warehouse. A battered FOR SALE sign listed toward the north in the waist-high weeds at the front. The air was clammy and still as she stepped out of the car. The rain squall was apparently not the only turbulent weather Woodard could expect today, for the sky was still leaden and the western horizon an even darker gray. Kate's knit shirt stuck to her shoulder blades as she started toward the building. Crates were piled against the outside walls, heaps of burlap bags were moldering in the damp air next to a set of wide doors held in place by a long iron bar. The glass in the door's high windows was broken, jagged pieces still clinging to the edges of the frames.

Kate stood for a moment, wondering what she was doing here. There was no one around to talk to, no one to answer her questions. But her grandfather had walked this ground, had gone in and out of these doors. And the only father she'd ever known had been here often, had perhaps met Teresa Cruzan here. She felt a vague need to stand where the confluence of her family had begun. Besides, to leave would mean going back to the stark motel room, to wait and to brood.

She began to circle the building now, watching where she put her sandaled feet, for the ground was soggy, with bare spots marring the grass. On the north side, she came upon a door, ornately framed to indicate that it had once been considered the office entrance. The door was flanked by narrow vertical windows, three on each side; these windows were made of glass bricks. The door was barred, a chain and padlock holding the bar to a large iron ring embedded in the frame. But Kate noticed that the padlock was hanging to one side and there was a space between its curved upper bar and the heavier mechanism at the bottom: It wasn't locked. She stepped closer, pulled the padlock from the chain, and swung the long bar outward. The door itself was not locked. Kate stepped carefully over the high threshold into the gloomy interior.

The room she entered was indeed an office, small and empty except for a rusted file cabinet. There was a door—directly opposite the outside door—standing wide open to reveal the dim interior of the building. A musty smell, like flour, filled the air. Kate walked over to this door, peered inside the huge storage room that loomed beyond it. The gray light coming through the high windows revealed more heaps of burlap, a scattering of twine, a large wheelbarrow. The smell in here was heavier, oppressive like the silence.

A rumble of thunder shook the building, rattling the walls and sending a bird flying straight up from in front of Kate's feet. She gasped, leaped backward toward the door behind her. As the rumble died away, rustling noises made themselves heard above the sound of the thunder. Rats? Other birds? Kate's search for the confluence of her family suddenly lost all of its charm. She turned and ran back to the outside door. What met her was a wall of rain, a sudden cloudburst so intense that she could scarcely see ten feet into the gloom outside. It was a long way to her car, and she knew she would be completely soaked before she got there; the clothes would dry, but her purse and shoes would be ruined.

She sighed and retreated into the office to wait for the rain to let up. As long as she didn't go into the warehouse proper, she reasoned, she wouldn't have much to fear from creepy critters. The old file cabinet caught her eye again. It was probably empty, abandoned like the building, but it *might* have records in it still. Maybe there were some references inside it to the days when this building was owned by Lundgren Chain. There might even be something put there by Peter Cruzan. Lightning lit up the room and answering thunder followed. Kate crossed the room to the file cabinet; at least looking inside would distract her from waiting for the next crash.

She pulled on the handle of the top drawer and, for a moment, thought it was locked. But another tug moved it and the drawer slid slowly out, making a sharp grating noise as it did so. Empty. Kate pushed it shut again, jumping as a flash of lightning lit up the small room. The second and third drawers revealed the same dusty emptiness as the first, spotlighted by the brilliance of the lightning flashes. Each time she closed a drawer, its rusty noises seemed to be accompanied by celestial sound effects as the claps of thunder came closer and closer together.

As Kate stooped into a crouch to open the last drawer, she heard another noise, closer, more intimate than the crashing noises of the storm: a grating of metal and then a muffled rattle like someone shaking a box of bolts.

Kate sprang upright and whirled toward the door behind her. She'd left it wide open, and now it was closed; the sound she had heard was the sound of the chain being pulled back into place. Panic closed her throat and suspended her reason. She flew at the door and threw herself into it. It opened about an inch before it came in contact with the iron bar now locked firmly in place across it, and Kate bounced back with such force that she almost fell. When she recovered, she stood in numb shock for a few seconds. Why would somebody lock her in? Follow her here, spy on her, and wait for her to make covering noises with the squeaking file drawers before quietly closing the door. Somebody standing out there in this driving rain.

She was trapped in here! There was no way to break that heavy door. Another crack of thunder made her scream and bolt across the small room to the door opening into the warehouse interior. Here she paused to get her breathing under control. Again thunder shook the building, but the lightning that preceded it had been enough to show Kate that the wide doors across the room were boarded up. Could she reach the windows? She calculated their height quickly. Maybe, maybe. If she stood in the wheelbarrow, she might be able to reach the lower sills and pull herself up. The next clap of thunder was a resounding *cra-a-a-ck*, like an explosion over her head. There was a lifting sensation in her scalp, and the hairs along her arms stood on end—there was electricity in the room, no doubt about it.

She ran for the wheelbarrow, oblivious to the squishing sensation of the bags under her feet. The handles were bare metal, cold and damp to her touch. It was unwieldy, its front tire flat and wobbly, but she got it moving as the rolling aftershocks of the thunder faded away. She muscled the wheelbarrow into place under a window, and began to climb into it. One of those eerie silences that sometimes follows an electrical explosion had fallen, and in it, Kate heard an unmistakable sound: a car's engine coughing into life. Before the next roll of thunder she heard the grinding of tires on gravel, a sudden burst of spitting stones as the tires accelerated too fast. She stood up in the wheelbarrow, trying to see out the window, but its lower edge was just at the level of her nose and all she could see was the sky, slashed now by the falling rain. She grasped the window and tried to pull herself up. But the windowsill had a downward slant; her hands slipped off, and she almost lost her balance.

She climbed out of the wheelbarrow and looked around the room again. Maybe she could loosen some of the boards over those big double doors, get into the other half of the building and out one of the lower windows at the front. She made her way across to the doors, listening to the thunder as it moved toward the east—a fast-moving storm—and became less terrifying. She tugged at the boards, leaning back and crouching so that her body weight was dragging against her arms. Nothing moved. Somebody had done a good job with plenty of long nails. She stood up straight again, kicked against the boarded-up doors. Then she turned her back and leaned against the wall, trying to think.

Behind her and from somewhere near the floor she heard a strange sound, faint at first and then a little louder. She sprang away from the wall and wheeled to face it. The noise was coming from the room beyond the wall—the other ground-floor room accessible by the wide double doors she'd first seen when she got out of the car. It sounded like somebody shaking potato chips in a half-empty bag. Kate stood frowning in concentration. Where had she heard this before? Why was it familiar? And then she remembered—even before she began to notice the smell, she knew. It was the sound of a fire just beginning to get a good start, the crackling of dried wood being consumed by leaping flames.

# CHAPTER 20

Lieutenant Kinowski was having a long day. The excitement had begun almost as soon as his shift got under way at eight-thirty A.M. Sergeant Johnson was waiting for him, holding a piece of paper. Some downtown businessman going to work early had found a body in the courtyard behind the Coburn Building. Quite a mess. Looked like a jumper.

Of course, the body had been moved by the time he got there. The first impulse was to call for an ambulance. People did that even when it was clear that the person was dead, that an ambulance couldn't help. Human nature, he supposed—that refusal to accept the fact of death. He'd once gone in the middle of the morning to a suicide by hanging only to find the father still trying to administer CPR, when it was apparent that the kid had hanged himself the night before. Today, the jumper had been taken to the hospital morgue, the only morgue in Woodard.

Quick questioning among the bystanders—quite a crowd had gathered by nine-fifteen—revealed that the dead man was Robert Ford. Kinowski gave a short whistle of surprise. A very big cheese, this Ford guy. A pale man in an expensive suit identified himself as Gerald Rettig, Ford's law partner. He pointed up toward the Coburn Building to where a fifth-floor window was standing open. That, he explained, was the dead man's office.

"Do you have a key?" Kinowski asked.

"Yes, in my office," Rettig responded. "I'll take you up."

Ford's office was, indeed, locked, but it was apparent that it was the sort of lock that remained engaged as soon as the door was closed—the door would open from the inside, but not from the outside. The office had a dusty smell as if it weren't cleaned often enough. The furniture was fancy, expensive-looking. Everything seemed neat and in place. Rettig moved across the room behind him and was the first to notice the note lying in the center of the big mahogany desk. He started to reach for the note.

"Don't touch anything," Kinowski said sharply. "We'll have somebody going over the room pretty carefully later on today."

Kinowski bent forward slightly, finding the correct distance to read the note—he knew he should put his glasses on, but he hated his glasses, felt diminished whenever he wore them. The note was neatly typed, short: "It's better this way. Forgive me." The signature was shaky-looking, but readable: "Robert Allan Ford." He looked around the office, saw that the old Underwood was the only typewriter in the room.

"Did he use that typewriter exclusively?" he asked Rettig, who now seemed self-consciously careful not to brush against anything.

"I don't think he used it in fifteen years," Rettig replied. "It's sort of an antique—for show. Our secretaries do all the typing on PCs now."

"Well, it looks like he used it last night," Kinowski said as he moved over to the window. There was no breeze and the sky looked somber, as if nature itself were marking the passing of the great man.

He looked at the window frame, then at the sill, where he noticed a scrape with a trace of dark stain along its edges. The lab boys would look at that, no doubt. Personally, Kinowski thought it was a waste of taxpayers' money to lavish so much attention on such a simple case—like ordering a full autopsy when somebody had a stab wound to the heart. As if there could be some mystery as to the cause of death. But it was procedure, mandated by powers higher than himself. "Any family?" he asked without turning around.

"Evelyn," Rettig sighed. "His wife. There are two married children, and grandchildren. They all knew he was dying, of course. But, still, this—" and he faltered into silence.

"Will you tell the widow, or should I?"

"I suppose I should do it." Rettig sounded reluctant. "It would be appropriate. How do you ever get used to doing something like that?"

"You don't," Kinowski growled. "Tell the widow I'll need to talk to her early this afternoon."

Kinowski hated interviewing the bereaved—it was the one job in police work he would have cheerfully delegated to somebody else, but he'd learned over the years that, when it came to evaluating information, nothing substituted for the direct interview; secondhand reports always placed a layer of somebody else's judgment between him and what he wanted to find out.

Mrs. Ford was remarkably composed, a woman of great dignity, in command of the social graces. No need to fear hysteria here, Kinowski could see, and he felt immensely relieved.

"He said he needed to go to his office on business," she said, her blue-veined hands folded around a handkerchief in her lap. "When I asked him *what* business, he wouldn't tell me— just that it was something important he had to take care of. I thought it was odd, because he hasn't been on the job for over eight months now. Not since he began the first round of chemotherapy."

"Had he seemed depressed lately?" Kinowski knew the list of questions well—in Woodard, he'd investigated far more suicides than murders.

Mrs. Ford considered the question carefully, her blue eyes squinting a little in concentration.

"Well, Lieutenant," she said finally. "It's pretty depressing, just in general, to be dying of cancer. But, no, I didn't notice any worsening of that in the past few days."

"You've seen the note, I understand," Kinowski said, "before the police took it away to the lab. Is it your husband's signature?"

"Oh, yes," she said. "It's awfully shaky, as if he were trembling when he wrote it—" And now her voice broke; she raised the handkerchief to her mouth in a gesture Kinowski had seen before—as if to catch the grief, to hold it in the hand. Her narrow breast heaved once, twice, and then she lowered the handkerchief again. "It seems so odd to me," she went on, "that he would sign his whole name like that—so formal. If the note was meant for me, why didn't he just sign 'Bob'?"

"It's hard to tell what goes through the mind at a time like that, Mrs. Ford. Maybe because it's the last thing they'll leave, they want to give the whole name—to make it sort of official."

She walked with him to the door, took his hand before he left. "My children are on the way," she said, though he hadn't asked. "We—Bob and I—talked about calling them here just before the end, so I wouldn't be alone when he went. Why would he do this, without warning? He knows how much I hate surprises."

Kinowski covered her thin hand, still inside his grasp, with his free hand. "Maybe because he thought this would be easier for everybody," he said gently. "Like he said in the note."

"Well, if he thought that, he was wrong," she said, looking up at Kinowski with the pain so raw in her eyes that he felt pounded by it. "I wanted every minute I could get with him, and I thought he wanted that, too. I don't know how I could have been so wrong about that." Tears slid from the corners of her eyes, but she didn't seem to notice them.

Kinowski was barely back in his office when the call came in from the fire department. He'd started to say impatiently to Johnson—who was once again standing with a piece of paper in his hand—that he couldn't understand why a warehouse fire was any concern of his. But Johnson silenced him with a single sentence: "The Lundgren girl was in the building."

So now he was sitting in a squad car behind a smoking warehouse, looking out at a virtual lake of water—some of it from the recent downpour, most of it from the fire hoses, which were still at the ready in case any flames started up again.

"So how did you get out, then?" he said, turning back to the girl who sat next to him, huddled inside a blanket one of the firemen had given her.

"The file cabinet," she said, shivering again. He knew it couldn't be from cold, because the afternoon was still warm—fright, that's what it was. "There was an old file cabinet in the office part. It was empty, not very heavy. I moved it into the big room—the one with the windows—and then I just climbed onto it to get out. The windows were all broken on that side. It was a drop to the ground, but I didn't get hurt jumping."

"So you came out here looking for somebody who might have known your grandfather and went inside the warehouse for some idiotic reason that you can't explain to me," he said, recapping what she'd already told him. "And somebody followed you here and then locked you in."

"And then tried to fry me," she said, sitting upright, suddenly fierce. Her dark eyes flashed and that pretty jaw came forward. "Somebody tried to murder me, and you seem pretty calm about it."

"No, no," he said, reaching out to pat her arm. "Nobody tried to kill you. I've talked to the fire marshal—he's that man in the suit over there—and he says the fire was started by a lightning strike. Says you can see on the inside where it came right down the side of the chimney and hit a pile of bags inside that biggest room. There's a regular scar, he says—unmistakable."

She turned inside the blanket to peer at him more closely with troubled eyes, a frown pulling the shapely eyebrows together.

"I felt it," she said finally. "The strike, I mean. It was a great big crack, and then I felt it in the air, like static electricity everywhere."

"Yeah, I've been told before that's what it feels like when a strike is near you."

She was silent for a moment, looking past him toward the building.

"I think it was somebody trying to scare you," he went on. "Trying to get you to give up on Woodard and go home."

He saw the extraordinary eyes widen. She looked for a second as if she might want to tell him something. Then she frowned again, sank back against the seat.

"Looks like Maxwell told one of his buddies to throw a scare into you," Kinowski explained patiently. "He sure doesn't want you to testify about seeing him toting stuff outa that garage. Remember, I'm still working on a case against him. I got something else cooking on the grand-theft charge and he knows it, so he's getting antsy."

She'd turned to look at him again and the exasperated

expression was back. "Why are you so certain that this was Maxwell?"

"I know for a fact it wasn't Max himself this time," he said, smiling at her, "because one of my officers reported him at a gas station on the other side of town when this stuff out here was going on. But he's probably behind it. I got one of my boys taking imprints of the tire tracks we found in the mud over there"—and he pointed to the place where Kate guessed her pursuer's car had been parked. "We'll keep looking among Maxwell's buddies until we find a match on one of their vehicles."

"Maybe you'll be looking in the wrong place," she said softly.

"What does that mean?" he said, feeling irritated again. Why couldn't this kid just go home and stay out of his hair? "You're not still on that business about Mr. Werner, are you?"

"Max is 'Maxwell,' but he's 'Mr. Werner,' isn't he?" she said peevishly. "We wouldn't want anybody to get the idea that we're investigating Mr. Megabucks, would we?"

He felt his face growing hot. Impartiality in doing his duty was something he prided himself on. "You listen here, young lady," he said, trying to control his voice. "I don't have to take that kinda crap. I do my job, by the book, no matter who's involved. Now, you just give me some good reason to start on Werner, and I'll do it. But it can't just be because he looked at you funny, you hear me?"

"I'm sorry," she said, looking away from him, but he could see her chin trembling.

"Look," he said, more kindly. "I know you think I should be spending every minute, twenty-four hours a day, working on your mother's case, but that's not how police work goes in a small town. We don't have specialists, teams of homicide detectives like you see on television. Everybody does a little bit of everything. Today, for instance, I got a suicide case to work on—top priority, the chief tells me—and I got no choice but to take it."

"I didn't read anything about that in the paper," she said, "and I'm looking at the paper every day now."

"It won't hit until tomorrow," he explained patiently. "But it'll be front-page stuff then, you can bet. This guy was one of the biggest lawyers in town. Ford, Thiele, and Rettig."

"Which one killed himself?" she asked, looking back at him

now; she seemed calmer. Maybe it was best to distract her for a bit.

"Robert Ford," he explained. "Threw himself out of his office window last night. Old guy. Dying of cancer and getting pretty frail. But in his day, the waves parted for him. He was the chief attorney for old man Proctor, managed all the legal stuff for the Proctors for forty-five years."

The girl had stiffened and sat upright again. "Proctor?" she said. "That means he was probably Elizabeth Proctor's lawyer too. Elizabeth Proctor Werner. So, he might have been Thomas Werner's lawyer."

"So?" he said. "What does that mean? This is a small town and the old guy probably had lots of bigwig clients. You're not going to try to connect this to Teresa Cruzan's murder, are you?"

"Look," she said, and that intensity he'd noticed at his first interview with her was filling the squad car. "You said it yourself. This is a small town. How often do people die violently here? And now two inside of two weeks. Maybe it's not just coincidence."

"I don't follow," he said. "Do you think Ford killed your mother and then offed himself about it?"

She looked thoughtful for a few seconds, as if she was considering the possibility.

"Was he tall?" she asked at last. "Good looking?"

"Oh, no," Kinowski said with a snorting laugh. "Short. And he looked a little like Edward G. Robinson."

He could tell from her blank stare that she didn't recognize the name, and it made him feel depressed somehow.

"Look," he sighed. "Not everybody in the world is tied up in your life, you know. That's what you think, I suppose."

"No, no," she said, shaking her head sharply. "But my natural father has been very careful to hide the fact that he had a child with Terry. Maybe this lawyer knew something about it, knew one of his clients had made an arrangement with her to keep this secret. Maybe there's even something in writing, and so Ford had to be silenced."

"You don't just mean one of his clients. You mean Werner." He felt uncomfortably aware that he'd dropped the "Mr." in speaking to her about this man. It made him cranky that this fierce girl could intimidate him in this way.

"I suppose I do," she said. "But it fits, doesn't it? Somebody regularly paid Terry's bills. She had nice cars, nice clothes. Maybe it was more than just personal conscience. Maybe it was a business agreement."

"Look, Miss Lundgren," he said in his best patient public-servant voice. "Ford was dying of cancer. He told his wife he had some business at his office. Nobody was around. He typed and signed a suicide note, saying 'It's better this way,' and then he bailed out of a big window. That's all there is to it."

She was silent for a moment, her face sullen.

"People can be forced to sign notes," she said suddenly. "If nobody saw him jump, how can you be sure he wasn't pushed?"

He thought now that it would be best to give standard, professional answers. There was no point in arguing with this stubborn girl. "The case is under investigation," he said tightly. "There will be a coroner's inquest, of course."

The Lundgren girl eyed him for a moment, and it struck Kinowski that her expression was familiar. He'd seen it before on the faces of other women—his wife and Jenny, for sure. What did it mean? It was half exasperated and half pitying, as if the woman wearing it were just barely stopping herself from saying, "You blockhead!" But it also looked expectant, as if the wearer were waiting for him to make some response she craved, hoped for without much belief that he could give it.

Finally, the Lundgren girl just opened the door of the squad car and got out.

"Where are you going?" Kinowski asked, hoping to hear her say, "Home."

"Back to my room," she said. "I need a shower. I need to think. Will you thank those firemen for me? They were very nice."

But she didn't wait for him to answer. She jumped out onto the soggy ground and half ran toward her little blue car. What a girl, he thought. Half the time, she seemed like a needy child, and he felt an almost paternal urge to comfort and shield her. And half the time, he wanted to tell her to get lost, to take her anxious face away from his sight so he wouldn't have to puzzle over what she wanted from him.

# CHAPTER 21

Kate stood in the shower for a long time, the drumming water keeping pace with her tumbling thoughts. When she'd escaped from the warehouse and got over her terror enough to consider what had just happened, she'd felt an odd rush of elation. Somebody had tried to kill her, perhaps because she was circling too close to the answer to Terry's killing. Maybe somebody had found out about her trip to Duluth. But that somebody couldn't be Douglas Lundgren. Whatever else she might be led to suspect about him, she couldn't believe he would seriously harm *her*. He had been a loving father to her for twenty-three years.

His parenting style had been traditional, a little aloof. And, of course, his hectic business life kept him from being an on-the-spot father, though he'd always tried hard to save weekends for his family. During her adolescence, she'd noticed a kind of puzzled nervousness in his attitude toward her, as if he half expected her to rear and stomp him like a skittish horse. But she'd noticed that look in the fathers of some of her friends, too, so she guessed it must be pretty normal. Yet he'd never raised his hand to her, was always—if anything—overindulgent to her, and to Eric, too.

It would be, she realized, an exaggeration to say she'd al-

ways been close to her father. He had never made any sign that
he would welcome emotional intimacy; on the contrary, he had
made it clear that such things embarrassed him. But she'd never
had any doubt that he loved her; that was one of the great
givens of her life, as was Sheila's devotion. So, of course, it was
impossible that he would lock her in a building and then set it
on fire—to send her to the most painful kind of death it was
possible to imagine—even if he *had* killed Teresa Cruzan.

But then she'd learned that the fire was an unforeseen
accident, and Kinowski had said those words: "somebody trying
to scare you, trying to get you to give up on Woodard and go
home." Maybe Douglas Lundgren would do that. If he had
killed Terry to silence her about her daughter's father, he might
now want that daughter out of Woodard, out of the snooping
business. The scare was relatively harmless—he could easily
have got her out again with an anonymous tip to a neighboring
warehouse. But it might be enough to send her running back
to White Bear Lake, and then the police here would just be
content to pin the rap on Bruce Maxwell.

When she got out of the shower, she considered calling
Sheila to ask where her father had been today. Yesterday, he'd
gone to Chicago to soothe the stockholders, Sheila had said,
and he didn't get back until late last night. She paused in the
vigorous rubbing of her hair with the stiff motel towel. At least,
that's what he'd *told* Sheila. It might have been a cover to spend
time in Woodard, following his nosy daughter around. She
realized how easy it would be for Douglas Lundgren to cover
his trail. He could tell Sheila he was at his office in Minneapolis
and yet tell his secretary he was going down to the St. Paul
factory. Or the other way around. And his claim of the need
for sudden out-of-town trips would never be questioned—this
was an old story, part of the job description for a man building
and maintaining a company with international accounts.

No, no, no, she told herself, tossing the towel onto the
bathroom floor. It wasn't possible. Douglas Lundgren was much
more likely to use direct tactics, to phone her and demand that
she come home. He wouldn't sneak around, she told herself,
shaking her damp head to dislodge the sudden memory of the
Oldsmobile moving quietly off after Terry's funeral.

No, no. Thomas Werner was a much more likely candidate.

He was, after all, on the spot here in Woodard all the time, and his duties for the Proctor interests were probably pretty flexible—no need for such a man to punch a time clock or explain why he was leaving his office. And this supposed suicide was very interesting. No matter what Kinowski said, it just seemed too much of a coincidence that the Proctors' lawyer should die under suspicious circumstances less then two weeks after Terry's murder. If she hadn't been so angry with Kinowski when she'd left him, she might have asked him nicely just to check out whether Werner had been one of Ford's clients. That shouldn't be so hard to do, should it?

She stood in front of the mirror for a moment, looking at her naked body. Her ribs, normally only slightly visible, were sticking out rather noticeably. She wasn't eating. The meal at the Kramers' on Tuesday was the only really decent meal she'd had in almost three weeks. And the broken sleep was beginning to take its toll, too. She leaned into the mirror to confirm that the dark patches under her eyes weren't just shadows from the harsh overhead light. She padded out of the bathroom and dug out fresh underwear and a short-sleeved shirt. She dressed hurriedly and was just snapping her jeans at the waistband when she heard a faint sound, a kind of muffled scratching. It was coming from the door. She stared first at the door itself, then at the floor at its base. The light from the hall always showed faintly under the door—it didn't quite meet the flat pile carpet—but now that narrow band of light was broken in two places by dark shadows, each about four inches wide. Someone was standing just outside with feet very near the door—just standing there, not moving, not knocking. It couldn't be the maid; she always came in the morning and the room was already made up.

Kate was afraid to move, couldn't take her eyes off those two shadows. What had made that sound? Had someone leaned against the door to listen? She wanted to fly across the room and fling the door open, but she was too scared of what she might find on the other side. Should she tiptoe to the phone and call down to the desk? But surely whoever it was would hear her voice and run. She knew from experience how sounds carried through the walls of this building. She was beginning to feel a little faint from holding her breath, made herself push the air out and then drew new air into her lungs—but quietly, quietly.

Now there was another sound coming from the base of the door, a rustle of paper, and then a white rectangle appeared under the door, made its way into the room as if it were a living thing. It was an envelope, a business-size envelope, and even from across the room, Kate could see that it had no writing on the outside. As she stared, the two shadows moved and then withdrew, leaving only the faint bar of light.

Kate sprang forward now, put her hand on the knob, but she couldn't seem to make her wrist turn. Maybe it was a trick. Somebody could simply have pulled back to the other side of the hallway to see if she would respond to the envelope by opening the door. Then he would be able to pounce. She let go of the knob, stooped to pick up the envelope, turned it over several times in her hand. It was sealed and there was nothing at all on the outside, but she could feel that there was something inside. She ran her thumb under the flap, startled by how loud the sound of ripping paper suddenly seemed to be. Inside the envelope were four fifty-dollar bills. No note, nothing else at all.

Kate stood for a moment, staring at the money, and then she opened the door. The hallway was empty as far as she could see in either direction. The distance to the corner where she turned to get to the elevator was only about ten feet—easy enough for someone to be very quickly out of sight, especially if he had kept the elevator waiting by pulling out the stop button. But the elevator was slow, she knew.

She sprinted in the opposite direction, her bare feet pounding against the hallway carpet. At the long end of the hall was the stairway exit and those stairs ended at a side door that opened into the parking lot. The fire door felt heavy against her hands as she shoved it open and started down. Her room was on the third floor—the top floor, in fact. She pounded down the stairs as fast as she could without risking a fall. At the ground floor she saw the outside door swinging shut toward her.

Kate froze now. It had never occurred to her that whoever had been outside her room would have used this exit, might be only a few steps ahead of her. She approached the door carefully, stood to one side of it so that she wouldn't be exposed as she eased it open. When it was open about six inches, she peered around it into the parking lot. A man was opening the driver's side door of a car parked less than a dozen feet from the building. He had his back to her, but there was no mistaking that silver mane, that erect carriage. It was Thomas Werner, getting into a black BMW.

# CHAPTER 22

**K**ate had to get the desk clerk to let her back into her room—she had run out without her key—but she didn't even bother to make up an excuse for why she was in the hallway without her shoes, her hair still damp and mussed. She was simply dumbfounded at this latest turn of events. Part of her mind was relieved—the presence of Thomas Werner skulking around her motel room seemed to be confirmation that her suspicions about him were true, and that left Douglas Lundgren off the hook. But what on earth was she to make of Werner slipping two hundred dollars under her door and then running off down the side stairs? She slumped onto her bed, trying to puzzle it out.

If Werner had followed her to the warehouse and locked her inside, he certainly drove away before the fire started. But maybe he heard about the fire on the radio—it would be on the local news almost at once—and then drove back to check on her because he hadn't meant to kill her. Maybe he saw her drive away after talking to Kinowski, followed her back here. Was the two hundred dollars conscience money? Maybe even Thomas Werner was appalled that he had almost burned his own daughter alive. It would be like him, she thought, to imagine he could make up for it by giving her money like this.

Should she call Lieutenant Kinowski and tell him about it? He'd reacted with disdain to her suggestion that the lawyer's supposed suicide could be connected to Werner and to Terry's murder. Probably he would find nothing significant in her having seen Werner in the parking lot outside the motel. Maybe, she thought with sudden horror, Kinowski would even think she was making it up just to get him to focus on Werner. When she thought about it objectively, it *did* seem pretty fantastic—a rich man slipping money under her door and then sneaking off.

Kate sat up and held her damp head in her hands. Tears pricked at the corners of her eyes and she wiped them away fearfully. She was beginning to feel like a nonperson, a sort of marginal being unconnected to anything solid. She had a sudden insight into how quickly people could deteriorate when they were suddenly cut off from the familiar routine, a home base, the economic and social buttressing of a middle-class family to support them, to tell them in thousands of little ways that they were important. And if worry produces a pattern of skipping meals, of sleeplessness, the deterioration must happen much faster. In two weeks, a once-confident, assertive person could be reduced to blubbering in a motel room, afraid to call for the help she needed.

Kate stood up now, gave her tangled hair a determined shake, and walked to the phone. She *wouldn't* just feel sorry for herself! But once she'd put her hand down onto the receiver, she paused, glanced at her watch. It was almost five o'clock. She opened the phone book to find the place where she'd already circled the number for Kramer Development.

"Can you come over here after work for a little while?" she asked after she and Jack had exchanged greetings. "I've got a few things I'd like to run by you."

"Sure," he answered. "I haven't found out much yet, but there's some news."

"News?" Kate said blankly.

"What you asked me to find out about your father," he explained, and she could hear the puzzlement in his voice.

"Oh, that," she said quickly. So much had happened since lunch that she'd almost forgotten about her plea for Jack's help. "Good. About the news, I mean. I'll meet you in the lobby, okay?"

* * *

Jack arrived at 5:35 and they found a quiet corner of the lobby to talk, facing each other across a small faux-marble table. While Kate filled him in on the warehouse and the fire, he sat with his jaw agape, his caramel-colored eyes as round as his glasses.

"What the hell were you doing out there?" he said at last, his deep voice throbbing with suppressed outrage. "It's an empty warehouse, for God's sake. What did you think you could find?"

"I don't know," she said, irritated at being scolded on top of everything else. "My grandfather worked there. I just wanted to see it."

"You promised me you'd wait until you got some word from me," he went on in the same hectoring tone. "We agreed that you'd try to get some rest."

"I didn't promise," she said peevishly.

"Are we going to quibble about semantics now?" he said, raising his arms in a gesture of exasperation.

"Well, I can't just sit around doing nothing at all," Kate explained, trying to adopt a patient tone. "Especially if I have to sit around here." And she made a gesture that took in the lobby, the desk, the elevator doors.

"I'm just so worried about you," he said, his own voice more mollified now. "Were you hurt?"

"Just a little scrape from climbing out the window," she answered, pointing down to her shin. "The fire people called Kinowski, but he's got a one-track mind. He thinks Max is behind it somehow, trying to get me out of Woodard by having somebody follow me around, looking for chances to scare me."

"Well, it makes sense to me," Jack said. "Max seemed like a pretty scary guy when I met him. But you don't agree with the lieutenant?"

"No, I don't. I think it was Thomas Werner."

"Why?" He leaned forward, his brow wrinkled in genuine curiosity.

"Because later, after I got back here, I caught him sneaking out of the side door of this building after putting this under my door."

She handed the envelope to Jack, who glanced inside, ran his thumb over the bills before handing it back to her. Now his frown was one of bewilderment.

"Why on earth would he give you money?"

She explained her conscience-money theory and then said, "I think he knows I went to Duluth. Maybe he even followed me there. I wasn't thinking about being followed, so I wouldn't have noticed."

"He's driving that black Beemer now," Jack said absently. "One of those sporty ones."

"Yes, I saw it today," Kate replied. "He was getting into it when I spotted him in the parking lot."

"One of the things I found out today," Jack went on in the same musing tone, "is that he also owns two classic Beemers—sedans. Pampers them like kids. If he owned and drove one in the early eighties, that could be the car the motel people spotted in Duluth."

"Of course," Kate exclaimed. "That's a boxy foreign car with a funny grille, I suppose. Or at least Yolanda might think it looked funny."

"What does Kinowski think of this theory?" Jack asked.

"I haven't told him about all of it," Kate admitted sheepishly, and when Jack raised his eyebrows, she rushed on with an explanation. "I wanted to hear what you thought about this business of Werner giving me money before I called Kinowski. He always sounds so mocking when I say anything about Werner, as if he's verbally patting me on the head. And today, he's all involved in that lawyer's suicide."

"I know," Jack murmured. "It's awful. All of downtown has been buzzing about it all afternoon."

"He was the Proctors' lawyer, Kinowski says." She was watching his face for a reaction. "Maybe he was Werner's lawyer too. Don't you think it's odd that he would kill himself just now? So soon after Terry's murder?"

"Why odd?" he asked, the frown deepening. "He was very ill—dying. I guess he just wanted to end it before it got worse. There was a suicide note. At least, that's what people are saying downtown."

"But what if Werner is my natural father?" Kate said. "Just go along with me on this for a minute. And what if there was some legal agreement for Werner to keep supporting Terry? In exchange for her keeping it a secret that he was the father, I mean. Wouldn't Werner's lawyer know about such a document? And then, after killing Terry, Werner might have to silence him—maybe get the document back first, and then shove him out a window so he couldn't talk."

Jack's jaw had gone slack again, his eyes popping. "I swear, Kate," he said finally, "you have the most vivid imagination I've ever run into. You think that just because two things happen at or near the same time, they must be connected to each other. That's just absurd. There *is* such a thing as random occurrence, you know."

Kate sat back in the low chair, anger smoldering in the pit of her stomach.

"Fine, then," she said. "I'm just a crazy person. Making mountains out of mole hills."

"Don't pout now," he said, trying to assume a lighter tone. "You're a bright woman. You must realize how this sounds."

"Yes, I suppose I do," she grumbled. "But it can't hurt to ask the questions, can it? Why will no one even dare to ask questions about somebody like Werner—not even consider that behind the protective crust of money there might be a criminal?"

"This bashing of the rich is pretty funny, coming from you," he said gently. "I believe you are a child of privilege yourself."

"Well, we didn't worship money," she grumbled.

"No, of course not," he laughed. "When you *have* money, you don't have to worship it. Now, don't scowl at me like that. I'm the same way. These business setbacks are pretty recent for me. When I was growing up, we had everything we wanted, so we never thought about it at all. Took it for granted."

He was quiet for a moment, watching her.

"But you know what I think amazes me most?" he said now, leaning forward to peer at her intently. "It amazes me that you're so defensive about your birth mother, so quick to take offense when anybody suggests that she might have been into shady dealings, might have had a weak sense of ethics. But you think Werner is your natural father, and you're so eager to nail him."

Kate sat for a second, her breath caught, holding back an angry retort while her mind absorbed what he was saying.

"You're right," she sighed finally. "I guess I never invested as much fantasizing in him as I did in her. I could always *see* her so fully in my imagination, and he was just a shadowy figure.

I don't mean that I could see her the way she really was—the way she turned out to be. Of course, I idealized her. So now I feel defensive about that picture I had of her. But it's more than that. The real Terry was not a bad person, and she didn't deserve to be killed in that awful way. And if my father did that to her, he deserves to be nailed."

Jack looked away from the fiery gaze, but he reached out to take her hand.

"I guess you're right about that," he said softly. "But I also notice that you might not be so quick to nail your natural father if you thought he might be Douglas Lundgren."

Kate looked away from Jack just in time to catch a knowing look on the face of a man who was passing them on his way to the elevator. She realized with a little mental shock that he must think they were lovers, huddled here in a corner of the lobby of a motel with their heads together in intense conversation. No surprise in that, she realized. Lovers in public always looked like co-conspirators, whispering about secrets no one else must be allowed to share.

"I would just like to start by getting the answer to one question," Kate said now, sitting up straight. "Was Thomas Werner one of this lawyer's clients? Do you think his law firm would give me a list of his clients?"

"No, I don't," Jack answered, recovering his businesslike tone. "That's all part of the privilege code. Sort of like psychiatrists can't reveal the names of their patients."

"But the police could get the list if they wanted it, I bet."

"I suppose, but I can't think of a reason for them to do that when they think they're dealing with a suicide."

"Back to square one." And she blew out her breath in a short, explosive sound of irritation. "I don't even know if I should tell Kinowski about this money when I have nothing else to go on."

Jack stared out into the middle of the lobby for a moment, his eyes thoughtful. "Yes, that's the one concrete thing you've got," he said slowly. "And it seems so odd, so disconnected from the other things that have been going on. Look, why don't you sit on this until tomorrow after I get a chance to do some poking around? I know one of the secretaries in Ford's firm—well, I know her slightly. She's the mother of one of my high school buddies. I'll try to pump her for some information about clients.

If Werner *was* a client, maybe she knows some dirt. If we can put that together with this business about his coming here to leave you money, maybe you'll have enough to get Kinowski to listen."

"Thank you," Kate breathed, almost overwhelmed at the prospect of having an ally at last.

"This time, I want you to promise me you'll sit tight until you hear from me," he said, thrusting his face at her for emphasis. "No more sneaking around in dangerous parts of town."

"All right," she said, laughing a little. "This time I promise."

"I've got to run," he said, standing up now. "Mother starts to get worried if I'm not home by six-fifteen or so."

"I think I might be able to rest now," Kate responded, standing up next to him. "It's been one hell of a day."

"There *is* something else I have to report," he said now, as they began to move toward the doors. "If you're still interested. It's about your father—your adoptive father, I mean."

"What?" Kate stopped in midstride to look up at him.

"I called Ev Branhart right after lunch and he told me he didn't know your dad at all—just bought the warehouse through an agent. But he did name an employee who worked at the warehouse under both Peter Cruzan and the new man when it was being used by the milling company—a guy named Ben Lubinsky. I looked him up and gave him a call. He's retired now."

"What did he tell you?" Kate asked, her stomach knotting in anxiety.

"He remembers Doug Lundgren very well. Says he came here often in the days when he owned the business. Thought of him as a 'nice, friendly gentleman,' he said. 'Always good to us regular folks.' And old Ben *did* remember a time when Mr. Lundgren had some visits with the Cruzans—with 'old Pete Cruzan' in the office and with 'little Terry,' too. For a while, he said, Terry seemed to hang around the place whenever Mr. Lundgren was there. He remembers seeing them in deep conversation on several occasions."

"Did he say when this all happened?" Kate asked, her voice tense.

"He said some of it—the office conversations—happened the summer Terry was working at the country club. He said he remembered because it was the only time he ever saw the kid in the summer without a tan, and wasn't that funny because you think of tans when you think of country clubs. In fact, he remembers, she looked 'sickly.'"

"Well, that was probably because she was having morning sickness," Kate said emphatically, "and what he saw was the negotiations for my adoption. I already know this stuff."

"But he remembers earlier visits, too," Jack said slowly, in a tone that suggested that he was reluctant to go on. "For more than a year, he says. Terry hung around the warehouse and Mr. Lundgren was 'real friendly' to her. 'Took a special interest in the child.' It's pretty clear that Lubinsky sees nothing suspicious in it."

"Well, maybe that's because there *is* nothing suspicious in it," Kate flared. "Just an employer being nice to his foreman's daughter."

"I'm just reporting what he told me," Jack said, raising his hands as if she were holding a gun on him. "Don't kill the messenger."

"I'm sorry," Kate murmured. "I know I told you to find out about it for me. But I don't think it's relevant. The car Yolanda saw probably wasn't a Volvo at all, but a BMW sedan. I was just overreacting to the mention of the car, that's all. Werner is the guy we're interested in."

"Okay," Jack smiled. "Whatever you say. I'll call you tomorrow. About noon. Take care of yourself." And he folded her in a quick hug, so quick she didn't have time to respond before he let go again.

"Bye," she murmured as he hurried to the entrance.

She stood for a moment, lost in thought. It was such a relief to have Jack's help. She could still feel the warmth of his body against hers, the slight rasp of his jaw against the side of her face. She realized how easy it would be to get used to that, how much she was looking forward to more. His interest in her was clear, his concern palpable. Maybe he just needed time to lose his apparent shyness—she wasn't used to small-town shyness. His intelligent response to her theories was a nice balance to her own impulsiveness; they would make a good team. Yes, Jack Kramer was definitely a "keeper."

She turned now to look around herself, to consider what she should do next. Jack's parting words had been an admonition to take care of herself. She thought of her jutting ribs, made a resolution to begin by having a good meal. The envelope felt heavy in her hand. Two hundred dollars. Well, at least now she could afford a steak at Monahan's. If Thomas Werner wanted to leave her money anonymously, she might as well use it to make herself ready to keep up her pursuit of him.

# CHAPTER 23

Kate was awakened on Friday morning by the ringing of the telephone. She swam up out of sleep, then snatched at the sleep mask to free her eyes. The phone was on its fourth ring by the time she reached for it; she'd been sleeping very soundly. "Hullo," she mumbled, her voice thick with sleep.

"Kate?" The voice was peremptory. "This is your father."

He always identified himself like that on the phone, as if he were calling the power company—"This is your customer at four-seventy-two Hickory Lane"—his voice businesslike and crisp.

"Hi, Daddy," she said, still so close to a dream state that she hadn't yet remembered that she was supposed to be angry with him, even fearful of him. "What time is it?"

"It's eight-thirty," he answered, his voice softer now. "Did I wake you?"

"It's okay," she said, her brain beginning to turn over now, to register her surroundings, to remember recent events. "What is it?"

"We've read the morning paper," he answered after a short pause. "About the warehouse and the fire. It said you were in the building. Are you all right?"

Kate hadn't realized that, since Terry's murder, any news

215

item connected to that event, even the separate activities of the daughter who'd found the body, would be "news" in the Twin Cities. If she'd known her parents would read about her this morning, she would have called them last night to say she was unharmed.

"Yes, I'm fine," she said, sitting up now. "I got out before the fire got near me."

"But the paper says you escaped through a window. Why was that necessary?"

Kate was fully awake now, realized that Kinowski must have withheld from the newspapers the fact that she'd been deliberately locked inside the building; if the papers had said that, her mother would be here at this moment. "I was in a locked part and I couldn't get out any other way," she said vaguely. "I had to jump, but I'm okay. Just a little scrape. It's nothing."

"What were you doing there?" And now she heard a familiar tone—disapproving father demanding an explanation.

"I wanted to see where my grandfather worked," she answered, her voice tight. "He's dead now, by the way. Did you know that? He died in 1972."

There was a silence on the other end of the line now, and she could almost feel him deciding how to handle this tack.

"Of course I knew," he said finally. "I went to his funeral."

"But I didn't go," she said, remembering now why she was angry with him. "He was my grandfather, but I didn't get to go to his funeral."

"For Christ's sake, Katie! You were four years old. What would that have meant to you?"

"But when my grandmother died in 1980, I was twelve." She felt relentless now. "What's your excuse for keeping me away from *her* funeral?"

"I don't want to fight about this on the phone," he said. "I don't want to fight at all."

"Okay," she said noncommittally. "We won't fight at all." This was the typical Lundgren response to conflict, she realized—don't confront it, and maybe it'll go away.

"We want you home," Doug said now, and it sounded like a command. "If you won't come on your own, I'll come there and bring you home myself."

"Get real, Dad," she said hotly. "I'm not a baby anymore.

You can't make me do anything." One part of her mind was amazed at how this conversation was going, when she had begun it longing for reconciliation with her parents.

"Then I'll come to stay there for a while," he said stubbornly.

"It won't do any good," Kate snapped. She was determined, for reasons of her own, to keep him away from Woodard. "I won't see you, and I won't leave here."

Doug didn't speak for a long time. She could hear him breathing.

"Your mother is very upset," he said, so quietly that she knew he didn't want Sheila to hear him.

"I'm sorry about that," she said, and she was. "But I'm not going to run away from Woodard until I find some answers. That's all there is to it."

"Will you talk to her?" he asked softly.

She was torn now. She really *did* want to hear her mother's voice, hear her fuss, reassure her, because in that way, she could reassure herself. But she knew Sheila's weapons of persuasion, feared she might give in to them. "Not today, Dad," she said softly. "I'll call on Sunday. Okay?"

"All right, then," he said. "When on Sunday?"

"In the afternoon."

She heard an excited cry in the background and then a muffled conversation. Puzzled at first, she suddenly realized that Sheila, hearing only half the conversation, might have interpreted "When on Sunday?" to mean that Kate was coming home on that day.

"I've got to go talk to your mother," Doug said now, his voice ragged, tense. "Here's Eric." And then the phone was simply handed over.

"Just a minute," Eric said without any preliminaries. After about ten seconds, he spoke again. "They're upstairs now, so maybe you'll tell *me* why you're being such a brat."

"Get off my back, creep," she said peevishly. "Why is everything *my* fault? If you keep that up, I'm going to hang up on you."

"Calm down," he said now in that wise-old-man voice of his. "I just don't like to see Mom in such a state. She's been like that ever since she got back from Woodard yesterday."

"From Woodard?" Kate said stupidly.

"She was there yesterday, in your motel," he explained. "She drove up to see if she could help in some way, but she came back without even trying to talk to you. Cried about it for a while when she told us."

Kate sat among the rumpled bed sheets, her jaw slack, her brain trying to process this new information.

"Oh," she said finally, the light dawning. "It was Mom who left the money."

"Who did you think it was, the tooth fairy?"

"Never mind," she said vaguely. "She came up here to give me money. Sure, I see it now. When I was talking to her on the phone Wednesday, she asked if I needed money."

"She said pretty much the same thing to me," Eric said after a short pause. "You know how she goes on: 'Do you think she's eating right? Maybe she'll cut corners by starving herself.' That sort of stuff. And when she found out about the fire this morning, she was almost hysterical. To think that she'd been there, probably when it happened, and left without knowing. Well, it was pretty bad."

"What is *with* those two?" Kate said irritably. "Daddy pays for Terry's funeral and even comes to the funeral, but hides out in his car and drives off without talking to us. And now Mom comes to see me, lurks outside my door like a thief, and then runs off without letting me know she's here." She knew it was ludicrous for her to feel so abandoned when it was *she* who had run away from home, she who refused contact with her parents after Terry's murder. But she couldn't control her emotions right now.

"Did it ever occur to you," Eric said in his deliberate way, "that they're very hurt? And that they're afraid of your anger?"

"Afraid of me!" Kate said scornfully. "Why should they be afraid of me?"

"You can be pretty fierce, you know," Eric responded. "And they're so afraid you'll reject them, that you don't want them to be your parents."

"That's rubbish," Kate snorted, but tears had sprung to her eyes. What she wanted to say was, "I've never wanted parenting more than I do right now," but that would have been a speech impossible for her to make. Was it, she suddenly wondered, her Lundgren upbringing that made her so reticent about her feelings, or had she *inherited* this proud inability to say what she meant? Terry, she remembered, had also denied with her lips the emotions that were in her eyes. "Tell them I'm sorry," she said now, her voice almost gentle. "And I'll call on Sunday. About one."

"Okay," he said. "I gotta run to the pool now—sunny day here."

"Eric?" Kate said suddenly. "Where was Dad yesterday afternoon?"

"At work, of course," he said. "Where *would* he be? He got home about six-thirty. Beat Mom home for a change."

"I see," she said slowly. "What about Wednesday night? Was Daddy home on Wednesday evening?"

"Wednesday, Wednesday," he said musingly. "Let's see. He's been so tied up lately, it's hard to keep it all straight. But Wednesday. Oh, I know. He went to Chicago to talk to stockholders. He didn't get back till way after midnight. He's just wearing himself out."

"I see," Kate said quietly.

"What's this all about, Kate?" Eric sounded suspicious now. "Why are you asking about Dad's whereabouts?"

"Nothing," she said quickly. "I was just wondering if he's around much to take care of Mom. She's so upset, you said."

"Well, no, he isn't around much," Eric said. "But I try to listen, to let her worry at me."

"Of course you do," Kate said, smiling in spite of herself. "You're a world-class listener, little bro. Now get going. Don't be late for work."

Kate spent the rest of the morning in a state of nervous concentration. She intended to keep her promise to Jack, but the inactivity was hard on her. She went for a walk, just in the neighborhood of the motel. The sign at the mall entrance reminded her that it was Friday the thirteenth, and she did that reflexive business of being extra careful about traffic and other hazards, even though she didn't consciously believe herself to be superstitious in any way.

So, Werner hadn't crept into the hotel to leave her some money. The shadows under the door had been made by Sheila Lundgren's feet. Whenever Kate thought of Sheila putting her ear to the door, listening, and then slipping off without knocking, it brought tears to her eyes. So she put it determinedly out of her mind. The one solid clue she was left with was the presence of Thomas Werner at this motel yesterday afternoon. He may not have been skulking around outside her door, but he'd been here—at least in the parking lot—and there was no other explanation she could think of for that, unless he was the one who'd been following her around. Had he been watching her room? Been scared off by Sheila's arrival? That would explain why he'd used the side stairs.

It didn't matter what had made him leave, she decided. Thomas Werner wouldn't be able to claim any longer that he had no connection to her. The Holiday Inn was hardly the style of a man as wealthy as he was, not a place where he would be hanging around on a Thursday afternoon. It wasn't like the public library, where everyone would go, where he could claim their encounter was pure chance. At a minimum, it must mean that he was concerned about her search for her biological father. Even if he hadn't killed Terry—and she was still willing to admit that the murder might be a separate thing connected to Max and his gang—he was pretty anxious about something.

Kate went inside the mall for a while; yesterday's storm had pushed the hot weather east and the breeze was a little too cool for her taste. But she found herself listening to a conversation between two elderly men who were sitting on a low bench outside the drugstore. They were comparing lists of acquaintances who had died recently and graphically discussing the causes of death—"No, that was bowel cancer. They did that surgery first and he had to wear one of them bags, but it killed him anyway in the long run." It made Kate remember that Robert Allan Ford had been dying of cancer. She'd read the newspaper carefully this morning and, just as Jack had said, Ford's death dominated the front page, where it was described as a probable suicide. And thinking about Ford made her remember that Doug Lundgren's whereabouts on the night the old man died weren't easily verifiable. Finally, she walked back to the motel to wait for Jack's call.

When the phone still hadn't rung by twelve-twenty, she started to call Jack's office, but was interrupted by a soft tap at the door. She crossed the room to find Jack standing in the hall.

"Hi," he said. "I thought it would be nicer to see you in person, so I'm taking an early lunch hour."

"Come on in," she said. "I've got some news for you."

"Please," he said. "No more surprises. You haven't been playing detective again, have you?"

"No," she laughed, showing him to a chair as she sat down on the bed. "But my family called this morning, and I found out it was my mother who left the money yesterday."

"Well," he breathed. "I guess that's one mystery solved at least."

"Only half the mystery," she corrected him. "Thomas Werner *was* here yesterday and he was sneaking out the side door. There's still no explanation for that. I'm thinking he could have followed me here and been scared off by my mother's arrival. Can you think of any other reason he'd be here in the middle of the day?"

"No, I can't," he sighed, "but I don't pretend to be able to figure out old Tom."

"Do you have any news?" Kate asked eagerly, leaning toward him. Their knees were almost touching in the small space.

"A little," he said slowly. "I popped over to Ford's building this morning and chatted with Mrs. Jensen—that's the secretary I told you about, Eddie's mom. She was still jumpy about the whole business, of course. Didn't want to tell me anything at all about Ford's client list. I blew some smoke about some land deals I was working on that might be held up if the buyers' legal affairs were tied up over this death. Charmed her."

"I'll bet you're good at that," Kate said, laughing a little, deliberately flirting. But he remained serious, all business.

"She remembers me as a sweet little boy, so she didn't get suspicious. But, still, no dice. I suggested that I could just say a few names and she could nod her head if any of them were Ford's clients. She agreed to that. I made up a short list from guys I know in business around town. Most of them got no response from her. Then I said, 'Thomas Werner,' and she nodded. That seemed to open the door just a crack because then she said, 'In fact, he was in here already this morning to see about having his files moved.'"

"I knew it," Kate said triumphantly. "There's something that lawyer knew about him and Terry, so Werner had to silence him. Now he's trying to get his hands on whatever written proof there might be."

"Not so fast," Jack said, holding up his right hand as if he were trying to stop traffic. "A lawyer like Ford has lots of important clients and just being on the client list doesn't connect Werner to Terry. And he probably wants his files transferred fast because La Liz is eager to get the Proctor holdings turned into cash so they can go off to Monte Carlo."

"Okay, I agree that it's just the first question," Kate said, more subdued. "But it's a beginning. Do you think it's enough to get Kinowski to take a look at whatever legal dealings Werner had with this lawyer?"

"No, I don't," Jack said firmly. "And I tried to pump Mrs. Jensen for some details, but she clammed right up. 'I've said enough already,' she said."

"But if I tell Kinowski that Werner was lurking around here after the fire," Kate went on, "wouldn't that get him going?"

"Probably not," Jack replied. "He'd probably just say it was Werner's own business what he was doing here just as long as he didn't approach you or threaten you in any way."

Kate was silent now. She knew Jack was right—she could almost hear Kinowski saying the words.

"But there's more," Jack said now, and his voice was careful, tentative. "I said one other name to Mrs. Jensen. I said Douglas Lundgren's name."

Kate stared at him, her breath caught, the question in her eyes rather than on her lips.

"She nodded," Jack went on. "And then she said one sentence. She said, 'Not recently, but years ago when Mr. Lundgren owned property in Woodard.' "

Kate sprang up from the bed, brushed past Jack to stand at the window. Her face was burning and she was breathing as if she'd been running. "It doesn't mean anything," she said finally. "Of course he would have had a local lawyer when he owned the warehouse. But Ford had nothing to do with my adoption. I saw the letter, and it was handled by my father's present lawyer."

"Maybe your father had legal dealings he didn't want his hometown lawyer to know about," Jack suggested quietly. "Legal dealings he didn't want your mother to know about, for instance."

Kate looked back at him, trying to formulate a response, but she found that her mouth wouldn't work. She walked back to the bed, sank down. "Eric told me Daddy got home very late Wednesday night," she whispered. "He was supposed to be in

Chicago, but they have only his word for that. Just like they have only his word that he was in St. Paul the day Terry was killed."

"Kate, listen to me," Jack said, reaching over to take her hand. "This is making you crazy, I can see that. Just let it be. Let the police do their jobs. There's no reason for you to take this all on yourself. It's all just speculation, anyway. Maybe your dad *was* in Chicago and in St. Paul. Maybe Tom Werner had some meeting in one of the conference rooms on the first floor here. And probably Kinowski is absolutely right when he believes Max or one of his goons killed Terry. Why do you want to torture yourself like this?"

Kate looked into the concerned face opposite hers, saw the new freckles that the sun was bringing out on the bridge of Jack's nose and on his cheeks. She leaned forward until her forehead touched his. "You don't know how much I want all of that to be true," she whispered. "How much I'd like it all to just disappear." Then she sat up straight again, smiled at him. "But I just can't let it go," she sighed. "I can't forget Terry's face the last time I talked to her. She was afraid of something. I know that. What I can't forget is that she might be alive if I hadn't pressed her to tell me about my father. I can't just quit on her now. And I can't just reconcile myself to never knowing, never finding out who my parents are."

She saw an exasperated look pass over Jack's handsome features.

"So what do you want to do next?" he asked.

"I guess I should talk to Kinowski," she answered. "At least tell him about Werner being here at the motel on the same afternoon somebody locked me in that warehouse."

"Not about Ford's client list?" he prodded.

"Maybe that, too," Kate sighed. "What do you think?"

"Well, if you're determined to tell him about that, at least wait until I can go with you. I can tell him about my interview with Mrs. Jensen."

"Can you do it this afternoon?" Kate asked, though she wasn't eager to pronounce Douglas Lundgren's name to Lieutenant Kinowski.

"No, I can't," he sighed. "As a matter of fact, one of the reasons I came over here in person was to tell you I have to run over to St. Cloud this afternoon—stay over until tomorrow afternoon, too. My father bought some land over there on spec in the seventies—just farmland then, but now the city is getting close to it. I think I might be able to unload it to a development company over there. We could use a little profit right now."

Kate was surprised by the little rush of panic she felt at the prospect of being in Woodard without Jack. As usual, she translated the fear into irritation.

"Am I just supposed to wait around?" she said. "I hate not having anything to do."

"I've thought of that," he said with a soothing grin. "You'll go out to stay with my mother. She was just beside herself when I told her about the fire, and when she read about it in this morning's paper, she said, 'Just bring that poor child out here where we can take care of her.' "

"Well, I suppose you're right about Kinowski," Kate said, standing up again. "He's more likely to be persuaded to take me seriously if I have a local businessman with me. But, I'll take a raincheck on your mother's invitation. I'm settled in here, and this will give me time to think of just how I can present this stuff to the police."

"You're sure?" he asked. "Mother will be disappointed. She'll fuss."

"I'm sure." Kate turned to smile at him. "I'd feel funny being there without you. Besides, maybe I'll call my mom a little later. I think she's having a bad time of it."

"Okay," he sighed, standing up now, too. "Whatever you say. I'll give you a buzz as soon as I get back. And will you please stay out of trouble?"

"I'll be good," she said, following him to the door and opening it for him. "I've had enough of being stalked, enough to last me for a few days at least."

"That's very sensible," he laughed, putting his arm around her lightly.

Almost by reflex, Kate put her face up to be kissed. At first, Jack pulled back, almost in surprise. Then his arms tightened and he pulled her hard against his chest. His full, soft mouth met hers in a lingering kiss.

"Bye," he murmured in a thick voice. "Tomorrow."

"Tomorrow," she whispered, and gave his chin a quick kiss. "Make a bundle in St. Cloud and hurry back."

"I'll try," he said, recovering his normal voice. "You take care."

She leaned against the closed door, a faint smile on her face. This was more like it, she thought. Much more like it.

Kate tried to stay put after Jack had left. She went out to McDonald's for a quick lunch and then sat in her room trying to read. Twice she started to call Sheila, but each time she put the receiver back down, guilt and shame overwhelming her. How could she say, "I'm sorry I've been giving you such a hard time," when what she was thinking of doing here in Woodard— talking to Kinowski about the client list—might give Sheila Lundgren the hardest time of all?

She was having a difficult time sorting through her feelings about her father—always, in the past, the parent she would have said she got along with best. Her present terror that he might be somebody quite different from the man she thought she knew had pushed into the background her initial rage about the deception practiced on her by Sheila in the search for her birth mother. By comparison, Sheila's sin of omission seemed slight, almost normal—the understandable reluctance of a loving mother to hand over her daughter to a competing mother. In trying not to think too much about Douglas Lundgren, Kate found herself dwelling on Sheila Lundgren. And she longed to see her, to look into those quiet, hazel eyes, to feel that cloak of acceptance and concern wrapping around her shoulders as it always did when she was in her mother's presence. No words would be necessary.

Kate remembered suddenly a scene from the summer when she had learned to ride her new bike—the pink-and-white two-wheeler with the white basket and the bell. Doug had removed the training wheels after the first month, and then Sheila had assigned herself the job of running alongside, holding the back of the seat, while Kate pedaled up and down in front of the house, gaining speed all the time. This added exercise for Sheila had been going on for some days when, one evening, Doug came outside to watch.

"You've got to let go of the seat," he said when they'd stopped near him so that Sheila could catch her breath. "At least for a few seconds at a time."

"But she might fall," Sheila protested, fanning herself with her hand. "She could hurt herself."

"Well, she's never going to ride on her own this way," Doug snorted. "Come on, Mommy. All kids get a few scrapes when they're learning to ride a bike. It's normal, for God's sake."

"She could hit her head," Sheila protested hotly. "Or poke an eye out."

"That's a lovely thing to say in front of her," Doug grumbled, getting angry now. "Do you want her to be afraid to try anything new?"

Eventually, Kate reacted against Sheila's overprotectiveness enough to ask Doug to run beside her while she practiced. And she *did* fall—several times—when he let go of the seat. Once she scraped her elbow, and that brought a flood of tender ministrations from her mother, who looked daggers at Doug. But she was soon riding without help, racing cheerfully away from Sheila's worried frown.

Now she found herself wondering if Douglas Lundgren was still willing to let her suffer a few scrapes, a scare or two, if it meant she would give up searching and questioning into something he didn't want her to uncover. She knew he could have been in Woodard in the early afternoon and still have had time enough to get back to White Bear Lake by six-thirty, the time Eric had said he got home. Had *both* her parents been here yesterday, one to hover over her anonymously like a nervous angel and the other to administer harsh medicine? She held her head in her hands, trying to squeeze the questioning voice into silence.

Finally, Kate became too restless to stay in the motel room. She opened the phone book and found Thomas Werner's address. A cross-check with her town map showed her where to find it. By three-thirty, she was parked across the street from the sprawling Tudor-style house on Crocus Circle—in the same northside neighborhood she'd driven through when she was first exploring Woodard. Ages ago, it seemed now—in that other life before Teresa Cruzan had died.

The house was old—turn of the century, probably—and surrounded by a high, spiked fence made of black wrought iron. Through the fence and its wide gate, Kate could see the manicured lawn, the jewel-bright flower beds. Probably there was a gardener—the couple she'd seen in the news photo didn't have the look of people who liked to putter in the yard. Of course, this must be the Proctor house, inherited by Elizabeth from her powerful father. Thomas Werner had wealth and power only because he married into it. Still, Kate could see how easy it would be to become enamored of all this, how hard it might be to think of its being snatched away. Maybe the fear of losing it all—and the golf afternoons, the barely veiled adulation of waitresses and librarians—was enough to drive an Iowa farmboy to murder.

There was no movement in or around the house that Kate could see. The double garage doors were closed, and there was no car in the drive. In the still-cool summer afternoon, the whole place gave the impression of a fortress: closed up, defensive, turning a blank face to the world of ordinary people. What had she imagined she could learn by coming here? The idea seemed foolish now. Kate started her car and made a U-turn on the shaded street. As she passed the house, she thought she saw a movement to her right. She turned quickly, but the face of the Proctor estate seemed impassive. Her impression was that it had been something pale moving against a dark background. Had it been a breeze turning the leaves of the silver maple tree that shaded the front walk? Or had it been the movement of the white curtains in the window next to the door?

# CHAPTER 24

She was dreaming about school, about Lincoln Elementary School and its familiar playground. Children were crowded at the west gates, some of them running and playing, but most of them looking out at the street. Cars were pulling up and kids were running out to climb inside and be driven off. One child, whose blond hair and plump-pretty face looked familiar, though Kate couldn't think of a name for her, was saying, "Is your mom coming for you? Or your daddy? My mom is driving today. We're going on a picnic."

Kate was trying to answer, but other children were making so much noise that she couldn't be heard. They seemed almost desperate to reach the fence, to get into the cars, which were coming and going much faster now. In a twinkling, there were no children left and Kate could see the empty expanse of the playground—the swings, the four-square court, the sand pits under the slides. She was trying to run toward the fence, but her legs wouldn't move; her shoes seemed rooted to the pavement. A car swept slowly past the entrance, pausing without actually coming to a stop, and then driving on. It was the station wagon, her mother's car, and it was going away without waiting for her. She tried to shout—"I'm here! I'm right here!"—but nothing came out of her mouth. The back of the car was receding down the shady street. Kate could smell the exhaust, a sharp fuel smell, like a bus—like diesel fuel.

And then she was choking, fighting herself up out of sleep, her consciousness sharpening with panic, her muscles finally able to move. Something was pressing against her face, against her mouth and nose—something that smelled like petroleum. She knew she was awake now, but she couldn't see—something was pressing on her eyes—and though the muscles of her arms were engaged, her hands were struggling to rise to her face, to tear away the suffocating pressure there, but she couldn't move her arms. Something was pressing them to her side and there was a weight against her stomach, too.

She jerked her head from side to side and the thing pressing against her mouth slipped, a burst of air was sucked into her lungs, but then the reeking pressure came over her face again. Adrenaline had reached her brain now and her mind was functioning separate from the panicked struggle of her body. Why couldn't she see? Was she blind? Then the thing on her face moved upward, brushed against the strings going over her ears—the sleep mask! She couldn't see because she had worn the sleep mask to bed because there was too much light in the room and this was the Holiday Inn and she was in Woodard and someone was attacking her in her sleep. The thoughts were lightning fast, tumbling over each other.

Only her legs seemed unfettered—she could feel them thrashing around. Now she concentrated, pulled her legs up at the knees and thrust them out as hard as she could, arching her back so that the burden on her stomach was shifted forward, thrown off balance. The pressure on her face slipped, loosened, and she was able to turn her mouth away. She gulped air, pushed it back out in a scream, but there wasn't enough force behind it for a loud sound—in her ears it sounded more like a squeak. And now the smelly object fumbled for her nose and lower face again. But Kate had drawn her legs up once more, using the long muscles like pile drivers to carry the rest of her body lower on the bed, shifting the weight above her onto her chest. And finally she got an arm free, could use the muscles of her hips to turn. She was reaching up to tear at the mask when the blow fell, a stunning jolt to the left side of her face.

There was a sudden, stabbing pain in her ribs as something sharp was pressed into her side—a knee probably. But she pulled in another breath and, this time, managed a lusty scream. It was cut short as the slippery thing that smelled like a bus came over her mouth again. She could hear breathing now, a labored gasping punctuated by grunts, and she guessed that the other face must be just above her ear. She got her free hand up there, came in contact with fabric, something coarse, but there was a head under the fabric. She ran her hand over this surface until she felt hair, closed her fingers, and pulled with all the strength that panic could propel. There was a yelp of pain now and then another blow landed on Kate's jaw, a glancing one that ended up against her throat, triggering the gag reflex.

She whipped her head to the side, the reflex to prevent drowning in one's own vomit, and the next punch fell on her right temple. She yelled again—once, twice—forcing as much of her breath as she could into producing a loud sound. She was drawing her knees up again against the rib-bruising pain when a blow connected with her jaw and lights burst inside her head and then began to fade. Sudden torpor deadened her limbs, made her unable to move her head as the suffocating pressure descended again on her mouth and nose.

But she could hear something. Above and behind the buzzing sensation inside her head she could hear pounding and then a voice shouting. It was saying, "Hey! Hey!" And then, just before she began to lose consciousness, there was a sudden lifting of the pressure against her body, a sensation of intense relief as she dragged air into her lungs. Then she rolled over and began to vomit, the terrible spasms rising upward in her throat, stinging her mouth with the harsh acid. For a moment, her body could attend to nothing else. Only when the spasms had subsided into painful coughing could she reach up to snatch away the mask; only then could she register the sounds of a grunting struggle, an occasional cry of pain.

She sat upright, turned toward the sounds. Light from the hallway made a long, bright rectangle on the dark carpet, but it stopped short of the moving shapes on the floor next to the bed. Then one shape loomed upward, cutting off the light, moving away from her. It was a human figure, crouched over, running for the door. All of the figure was dark, black—there was no flash of bright clothing, of flesh. Kate sat frozen even after the bright rectangle had reappeared on the carpet.

Then she heard a groan from somewhere on the floor, and

Eric's face swam into focus as it was raised past the edge of the bed.

"Katie," he mumbled. "Katie, it's me."

She tried to say, "Eric," but her voice wouldn't work—her throat ached at the effort to speak.

By this time, he'd scrambled up to sit on the bed beside her, to throw an arm over her shaking shoulders. "Are you all right?" He was whispering close to her ear. "Should I get you an ambulance?"

All she could do was nod.

Two policemen arrived at the same time as the ambulance crew, and Kinowski showed up about a half hour after that—in time to hear Kate's refusal to go to the hospital.

"You said there's nothing broken," she was saying to one of the medics. "And I don't seem to have a concussion or anything. So why should I go to the hospital?" Her voice was still hoarse, but she could speak now without pain.

"For observation," the young woman replied. "And maybe for some pain medication. That's going to be a nasty shiner, and your jaw is swollen, too."

"I don't need to be observed," Kate said stubbornly. "My brother is here now and he'll look after me. I hate hospitals. And I can't afford it, either."

"Well, we can't force you to go," the young woman sighed. "We can leave you some mild pain relievers and I suppose the motel has an ice machine so you can apply cold compresses to that eye. We'll leave a plastic bag for it."

"Thanks," Kate murmured, feeling sorry now that she'd sounded so cranky.

It was almost four in the morning now. Eric, who had received some attention from the medics himself for a bump on his head, had already explained his miraculous apparition. When he'd got home from work late on Friday afternoon, his mother had sat him down for a long talk. Since Kate had refused to come home and wouldn't have either of her parents near her right now, he must go back to Woodard to take care of her—at least for a few days—to keep her from prowling around in abandoned buildings. He had protested at first, but finally agreed, spending the next few hours arranging for staff to cover him at the pool until Monday.

By the time he got to Woodard and secured the room next to Kate's, she was already asleep—he'd tapped at her door a few times—so he just packed it in himself, tired from a long day in the sun and from the drive. But he had been awakened by Kate's screams and raced to her room. The door was not locked. They knew now that it had been jimmied and then closed again once the assailant was inside. Eric had pounced on Kate's attacker and struggled briefly with him in the dark. When his head was slammed into the leg of the bed, he'd lost his grip and the other man had escaped before he could make another grab at him.

Now Kinowski took over, sending the uniformed police-men out to investigate the grounds around the motel. He looked unkempt, frazzled, his shirt wrinkled and the wrong color for the khaki slacks. He explained that he'd been roused from sleep to come here, having left instructions that any big development in his major case was reason enough to wake him. He'd been examining the door and now he turned to Kate.

"You didn't have this door double-locked, did you?" he said, and his tone was both concerned and accusatory.

"No, I didn't," Kate flared; she always seemed to be angry with this cop. "And don't worry. The other officers have already scolded me about it."

"How much can you tell me about your attacker?" Kinowski asked after fixing her with a long glance.

"Almost nothing," Kate sighed. "I've already told all of this. I was wearing that damned mask"—and she gestured at the bed table where the sleep mask was lying—"and by the time I could get it off, he was already fighting with Eric. I saw him run, but only from the back and he was all hunched over."

"And what about you?" Kinowski said, turning to Eric.

"I didn't see much more," Eric said, shaking his rumpled curls. "I just jumped on him from behind and dragged him off Katie. He was dressed in dark clothes and I think he must have been wearing some sort of cap, because I didn't get any impression of hair color."

"I yanked on his hair pretty hard at one point," Kate inter-rupted. "But I felt some sort of cap, too. Maybe I pulled some of his hair out." And she looked over at the tangled bedclothes.

"Don't worry about that," Kinowski said, following her

gaze. "We'll get somebody in here to pick up every scrap of evidence there is to find. Do either of you have an impression of general size—height, weight?"

Kate and Eric looked at each other for a second.

"Not me," Kate shrugged. "He was kneeling on me, so of course he felt heavy, but when I saw him running, he didn't look so big."

"I couldn't say for sure, either," Eric said. "I had the impression he was tall, but when you're only five feet six, you think everybody's tall."

"Is there anything you can think of that you didn't tell the other officers?" Kinowski asked, his frustration beginning to show just a little.

"I think it was Thomas Werner," Kate said suddenly.

Kinowski did a slow take, staring at her for a second or two.

"What makes you say that?" he asked finally.

"Well, there've been a few developments since the fire that I didn't tell you about," Kate said shamefacedly.

"Such as?" Kinowski looked more irritated than curious.

"Yesterday," Kate began. "Well, I suppose I should say Thursday because it's Saturday now, isn't it? On Thursday, after I got back here from the warehouse, I saw Werner getting into his car just outside the parking-lot entrance of this motel. I thought I heard something in the hall outside my room, so I ran down the stairs. I saw the door on the ground floor just closing. When I looked out, there was Werner getting into his car."

"I see," Kinowski said, his square face thoughtful now. "And you think he was sort of 'casing' your room?"

Kate could feel herself blushing, yet she was reluctant to tell him that the hallway noise she'd heard was really her mother slipping her some money anonymously.

"Maybe," she said defiantly. "Why else would he be hanging around this place?" Kinowski's idea that Werner had been checking on her room for a later attack made good sense to her.

The lieutenant was silent now, obviously considering her question.

"And I went out to his place yesterday," Kate hurried on. "Just to see it, to get some impression of how he lives. When I was leaving, I thought I saw a curtain move. Maybe he saw me there, and it was just the last straw for him."

"The last straw?" Kinowski asked.

"Well, what if he's been following me around?" Kate explained, her voice growing excited again. "He sees me doing stuff that could be an investigation into my parentage. He tries to scare me by locking me in the warehouse. But I don't go away. Worse, I drive out to his house. Maybe he finally decided that he just had to stop me permanently."

"Do you have anything concrete to identify your attacker here tonight as Thomas Werner?" Kinowski asked.

"No, nothing concrete," Kate shrugged.

"And you think that could have been a sixty-five-year-old man?" Kinowski was relentless. "Attacking you, fighting off your brother here?"

"Werner is an athlete," Kate insisted. "He's strong and he's bigger than Eric. There's no reason to think of him as feeble just because he's that old." She felt angry with Kinowski for minimizing her theory.

"But you didn't see or hear anything tonight that could positively identify Mr. Thomas Werner as your assailant." Kinowski said it with a grim finality.

Kate was silent for a moment, thinking.

"Eric," she said. "Could you go down to the ice machine and fill the bucket for me? I guess I'm going to need it for my eye."

"Oh, sure," he said, jumping up from his chair, eager to help. He showed no suspicion that Kate might be trying to get him out of the room for a moment.

"Lieutenant," she said after Eric had gone out, "I think you ought to consider pretty carefully a connection between Werner and that lawyer you think killed himself. Yesterday I found out that Werner was one of his clients. Never mind how I know, just take my word for it. Now, I know you'll say, 'So what?'— that Ford had lots of clients, and that's true."

Now she paused, took a breath, and made the decision to reveal the information she didn't want Eric to hear.

"My adoptive father, Douglas Lundgren, was also one of his clients once—when Dad owned that warehouse here, I mean." If Kinowski did investigate Ford's client list, Kate didn't want Doug's name to come as a surprise to him. "But it might be a good idea to find out exactly *what* legal business Werner had with Ford. I still think there's a link between his so-called suicide and Terry's murder."

"How did you learn about Ford's client list?" Kinowski asked, ignoring her other comments.

"That's not important," Kate insisted, reluctant to say anything that might get Jack into trouble. "What matters is that you should at least consider the possibility that it wasn't suicide. Is there anything new in the case at all?"

"Nothing for public announcement," Kinowski said, but his eyes looked suddenly furtive, not meeting her gaze. "That investigation has just begun."

"But there *is* something," Kate said, leaning eagerly toward him. "I can tell by the way you're acting. What did you find out?"

"It's just the preliminary stuff from the medical examiner," he said, shrugging as if to dismiss the issue.

"Found something besides the disease, huh?" Kate insisted.

"It's nothing to get excited about," Kinowski replied. "Some fiber traces under his fingernails—linen, the lab boys say—that don't match what he was wearing or anything else in the office. And yes, I *did* cross-check the fiber content with the fiber we found on your mother's earlobe. Not the same. That was light wool. We'll probably find the match for the linen when we go through the stuff in Ford's house."

"But under his fingernails?" Kate said slowly. "Doesn't that suggest that he scratched at something—maybe at the clothing of somebody trying to push him out a window?"

"We don't jump to hasty conclusions, Miss Lundgren," Kinowski said peevishly. "We wait until all the evidence is in."

"Anything else?" Kate asked, glancing at the door, anticipating Eric's return.

"Some bruises," he sighed. "Of course, a fall like that will cause lots of bruises, but these are on his left wrist and the ME doesn't think they were caused by the fall. He calls them wrap bruises, from something encircling the wrist."

"Maybe somebody holding on tight," Kate said eagerly. "Dragging him to the window. That's possible, isn't it?"

"Look," Kinowski said, standing up now and beginning to pace. "We are being very thorough in our study of this case.

When we report for the coroner's hearing, we will have all the information that's available to us, and then it's for somebody else to decide if the death was suicide or foul play."

"But you're not so sure anymore, are you?" Kate said triumphantly.

"I wait for evidence before I decide what I'm sure about," Kinowski said, closing his mouth in the sharp way that Kate hated. She just stared at him, trying to think of a way to get him to *see*.

"And why are you looking at me that way?" Kinowski said now, his face reddening.

"What way?" Kate asked. "How am I looking at you?"

Eric came back with the ice before Kinowski could answer.

"You won't be able to stay in this room until we have somebody go over it with an evidence kit," Kinowski said. "Where will you sleep?"

"Next door," Eric answered for her. "In my room. There are two beds."

"I'm going to post an officer outside," Kinowski said. "For your protection, just until we find out who's trying to harm you."

"Thanks," Kate said softly. "That'll make me feel much better."

Now one of the young police officers came back into the room; he was holding something in his hands. "Found this stuff in the parking lot," he said to Kinowski. "This was just inside the chain-link fence that separates the motel lot from the mall lot." And he held up a black glove—heavy leather with wide cuffs, like the kind worn by motorcyclists. "And this was caught in the chain links right above the glove, at the top. Looks like somebody got snagged trying to scale the fence." Now he handed over a scrap of black fabric—shiny, probably nylon.

Kinowski took the glove, turned it over, felt inside it. "Damp," he said. "Somebody was sweating inside this pretty recently." Then he turned to Kate. "Could your assailant have been wearing gloves like these?"

"Let me smell it," Kate said, feeling a little wave of nausea as Kinowski brought the glove close to her face. The smell of petroleum, of oil and gas combined, almost made her gag. "That's it," she said, swallowing. "That's what he put over my face."

"Well," Kinowski said, and his square face looked suddenly happy. "This gives us something to go on. If we can trace this glove, this scrap of fabric, we'll have the guy who was in here tonight. I'm going to get right on this. You try to get some rest, Miss Lundgren."

When Kinowski had left and one of the uniformed cops had been given a chair to set up his watch in the hall, Kate and Eric sat on the beds in his room, both too jangled to even try to sleep.

"Do you think you're going to be ready to go home tomorrow?" Eric asked tentatively.

"Probably not," she answered. "Oh, I'm scared as hell, you can believe that. But I'm not running away from this. Now that I've got police protection, I'll be all right, I suppose."

"I was thinking of Mom and Dad, too," Eric said, stretching out on his bed, grimacing a little as the back of his head came in contact with the pillow. "Mom is so distraught. Not just because of the business about the fire, but because she's afraid you'll never trust her again. That's what she said. And Dad is almost as upset. His skin is just gray now, and he looks haggard. I don't think he's slept six hours in the past five days."

"I'm sorry," Kate said lamely, leaning back gingerly against the pillows Eric had propped behind her back. "I didn't plan for any of this to happen."

"You know, Katie," Eric said now, "we always think our parents will stay strong forever. But most people Dad's age are retired already, enjoying their golden years. I know it's hard to think of him that way, because he always seems so vigorous. But I'm worried about him. I don't know how much more of this he can take."

Kate was silent now, for she'd thought of something that it might be useful to find out. "Was Daddy home when you left last night?" she asked softly.

"Not yet, but Mom was expecting him any minute," he answered. And then he yawned, a big contagious yawn that made Kate yawn, too.

"And he didn't plan to go out again?" she asked after she'd got her mouth back under control.

"No," Eric answered, "not that he told us, anyway. Why?"

"Oh, nothing," Kate replied. "I just didn't want to think of

Mom being alone, that's all." And she was thinking that at least it would be easy to check, this time. To find out once and for all that Douglas Lundgren had nothing to do with the series of hideous events that had been occurring in Woodard. All she would have to do was to call Sheila in the morning to confirm that Doug had been home all night.

"I'm glad you're thinking of them," Eric said, innocently oblivious to her dark thoughts. "It's the Katie I like best."

Kate was quiet for a long time now, pretending to fuss with the ice pack she'd been holding against her face. She felt ashamed for using Eric in this way, ashamed of herself for ever thinking their father could be a killer. She glanced at the window, where the edge of the drapes already showed a weak light. The sun would be up soon.

"Eric?" she said finally, turning back to look at her brother.

"What?" he said, and his eyelids looked heavy.

"Thank you."

"For what?" And he yawned again.

"For lots of things," Kate answered, and she didn't yawn this time. "I think you saved my life tonight."

"Aw, shucks," he said, using the Deputy Dawg accent he'd learned as a kid. "T'weren't nothin'."

"Yes, it was," she said. "You're a remarkable person. And a tough little cookie."

"Shut up and go to sleep," he said, turning over to hide his pleasure at being praised.

# CHAPTER 25

It was 11:35 on Saturday and Kate was examining her face in the bathroom mirror. Her left eye was swollen almost shut and had already turned a reddish-purple. The right side of her jaw was swollen and there was a red blotch on her throat. The neck edge of her nightshirt was stained with the blood that had come out of her mouth and nose. Her body ached all over, a dull throbbing that signaled every overstrained muscle. When she took the nightshirt off to get into the shower, she saw a bruise the size of a baseball on her lower rib cage, on the left side.

After she got dressed—Eric had brought her clothes from her room and reported that there was now a different cop on guard in the hall—she asked her brother if he thought she looked better after cleaning up.

"You look cleaner," he said, laughing a little. "I'm glad you got some sleep finally."

"I don't even remember when I passed out," she said. "After you, because I could hear you snoring."

"I do not snore," he said, mock-angry. "I just breathe loud."

"Well, I think I slept pretty soundly once I got to sleep, though. Maybe about five hours in all."

The phone rang then and the brother and sister exchanged glances before Eric went to pick it up.

239

"Yes, she is," he said after the greeting and brief moment of listening. "I'll get her."

He put the receiver against his stomach and said, "It's Jack."

Kate took the phone, started to say, "Hello, Jack," but he interrupted after the first syllable.

"My God, Kate, what's going on there? Somebody just came in for lunch and said he heard on the radio that there was almost another murder in Woodard, that this time it was the daughter who'd found the first body."

"I'm all right," Kate said soothingly. "Bruised a little. And I've got a black eye, but nothing broken or anything."

"But what happened?"

"Somebody broke into my room last night and tried to smother me. But Eric was here and stopped him. We didn't get a clear look at who it was, I'm afraid, so we can't make an identification. I've got a cop guarding me now and, of course, Eric is here. I'm all right, really."

"I'm coming back anyway," he said vehemently. "This business here can keep."

"Oh, no," Kate said quickly. "Finish your business there first. I'm really fine." But she *did* want him to come straight back, was surprised at how much she wanted him here.

"I don't think these jokers are serious about buying anyway," he said, the deep voice firm. "I'll leave now and I should be there in about three hours. Will you be at the motel?"

"I'll make sure I am," Kate said. "Thanks, Jack." She felt relieved, glad to think that three men would soon be near her to prevent any further trouble. At least that was the reason she gave herself for being glad that Jack was coming back immediately.

"He found out from some guy who heard it on the radio," Kate said to Eric as she hung up the phone.

"Then we better call Mom and Dad right away," he said. "I thought we might be safe because it wasn't in the morning papers, but if it's on the radio, they might hear about it. It might even be on television by now. Terry's murder was all over the Minneapolis stations, so they're bound to pick up on somebody attacking the first victim's daughter."

"I'll do it," Kate said, lifting the receiver again.

It was Sheila who answered. Kate briefly explained the

events of the night before, minimizing her injuries, emphasizing that a large policeman was now protecting her. But, of course, none of her strategies prevented her mother's near-hysterical reaction.

"This is too much, Kate," she said, and Kate could hear the half-sob that was just behind the words. "Pack up and come home right now. Both of you. I want you both home today."

"Not just yet, Mom," Kate said calmly. "The police have a solid lead now and I'm going to wait until they follow it up. Once they find out who broke into my room last night, they'll have the person who killed Terry."

There was a long pause on the other end of the line.

"Then we're coming there," Sheila said finally, her voice determined now. "Daddy and I will come to you until this is all over."

Kate was almost overwhelmed by the urge to say yes, surprised by the force of her desire to see her mother, to crawl into her lap. But the mention of her father reminded her once again of her deepest fears, made her hesitate. "Is Daddy home right now?" she asked.

"He just stepped out to get some fresh fruit for lunch," Sheila answered. "He slept in pretty late this morning, even later than I did. Why? Do you want to talk to Daddy about this?"

"No, that's all right," Kate said quickly. "So he was home last night? With you the whole time?" She was already breathing fast in relief.

Again there was a pause, as if Sheila were puzzled by the turn in the conversation.

"Yes, of course," she answered. "He got home late from work—about nine—and I told him about sending Eric to you. We talked about coming ourselves then. He could see how upset I was, how much I wanted to see you. But we were just exhausted, both of us. He's been working so hard lately, you know. He finally decided it was best to stay home if you didn't want us there. I couldn't get to sleep, though, so Daddy made me take a sleeping pill. You know I don't like to do that—they really knock me out and then I'm groggy half the next day. But I finally agreed it was the only way."

Kate could feel her throat going dry. "So you must have slept pretty soundly for the rest of the night," she said softly.

Sheila, typically, interpreted this as concern. "For more than ten hours," she responded. "But I don't feel as rested as I would if I'd slept naturally. I'll feel better when I see you."

"Look, Mom," Kate said now, forcing her brain into high gear. "It's not worth the trip for you. I've got police protection. Eric is here with me. And this will probably be all over in a few days. I'd rather sort through this stuff on my own right now. Try to understand."

"Let me talk to Eric," Sheila said, and now she sounded angry.

Kate handed over the phone to her brother, whispering, "Back me up, please," as she did so. Then she listened to his side of the conversation, his gentle reassurance, his soothing repetition of, "I know, I know." When he began to say the words that indicated the conversation was coming to an end, Kate signaled that she wanted to speak to Sheila again.

"Mom," she said when she got the phone in her hand. "I want you to know that it's not because I'm mad at you. I'm not—not anymore."

"I hope that's true, Katie," Sheila said, and her voice sounded teary again.

"And, Mom," Kate said, "thanks for the money. It will really come in handy."

Over lunch, ordered in from a pizza place, Eric and Kate talked about the phone conversation with their mother.

"I'd like you to go home and keep them there," Kate said. She'd scarcely touched her lunch because her jaw hurt too much to chew and the cuts on the inside of her mouth smarted from the tomato sauce.

"I'm not leaving you here alone," he said, reaching for another slice of pizza.

"But I won't be alone at all," Kate insisted. "There's a well-armed cop in the hallway, and Jack will be back in just a little while. I think Mom and Dad will feel better if they have you home."

She couldn't tell him that the real reason she wanted him in White Bear Lake was to keep an eye on Douglas Lundgren, to make sure *he* was staying at home. If her father had used the opportunity of his wife's deep sleep to make a trip to Woodard last night, she wasn't sure she wanted to know about it. But she *was* sure that she didn't want him here now, under the eyes of the police. Under her own eyes. She was half ashamed of herself for suspecting him, afraid to look at his face for fear of what she might see there.

"Mom told me to stay with you," Eric said, chewing calmly.

"Well, you can make up your own mind about what's best," Kate said, her voice softly cajoling. "You know what a calming effect you always have on her—on both of them, really. Tell them to call if they like, but please, for now, just keep them at home. I've got too much to deal with at the moment without having to deal with the stuff that's between me and them."

It took the rest of the pizza, but Kate finally convinced her brother that she could not possibly come to any more harm in Woodard and that he would serve her best now by leaving her. But after he was gone, she felt the fear closing on her again. Perhaps this was a normal reaction for someone who'd just suffered through an assault—this numbing dread, this strong conviction that she could never go outside again. And, oddly, she felt ashamed, as if her battered face would signal the world that she had somehow invited such awful violence. Irrational, she told herself—just the sort of victim-blaming she was always inveighing against when it was directed at other people. But the feeling persisted.

At two o'clock, there was a tap on the door, which was now double-locked with the night chain in place. She knew it wouldn't be Jack—he would still be on the road from St. Cloud. In answer to her timid inquiry, Lieutenant Kinowski's voice came through the door, sounding unusually cheerful.

"I've made an arrest," he said after she'd let him in. He looked triumphant, beaming at her as if he'd come to give her some prize she'd won in the lottery.

"Who?" she gasped.

"Bruce Maxwell," he answered. "And this time, we're gonna nail him good. We got the evidence we need and the warrants we need to get more evidence."

"Start at the beginning," Kate said, sinking down into a chair and staring up at him. She could feel nothing except a vague sense of disappointment that she'd been wrong about everything.

"I had to dig up a judge to get a warrant this morning," he said, settling into the chair opposite her. "Judges don't work on weekends, you know. But I had a hunch about that glove when I first saw it—just Maxwell's style. We took a peek in his car and we found what we were looking for on the floor in the back-seat—the other glove stuffed into the pocket of a black jacket. And that scrap of torn cloth is a perfect match for a tear in the sleeve."

"And you arrested him?" Kate said. "On the spot? Has he confessed?"

"We've got him downtown," Kinowski answered, leaning back a little. "He's a tough nut. So far, all he will say is that he was in his girlfriend's bed all night, and he has no idea how that stuff got into his car. Of course, he knows she'll alibi him for anything. But now we can go looking in his place for other stuff—for fibers, for instance, that might match the ones on the dead woman's ear. We got him this time, but he just doesn't know it yet."

"Does he deny that the glove and jacket are his?"

"Oh, no," Kinowski exclaimed. "He's too smart for that. Other people could ID those things. He says it's all just old stuff he keeps in his garage for when he's working on his motorcycle. Right out in the open, he claims, where anybody could find it and walk off with it."

"Maybe that *is* what happened," Kate said, sitting forward now. "Maybe somebody's trying to frame Max because he's the likeliest suspect."

"Naw," Kinowski said, shaking his blocky head from side to side. "When we first confronted him, he claimed he'd left his car locked up outside the girlfriend's place. And it was locked when we found it, too. No broken locks or glass. So whatever was in there, he must have put there."

"But why would he do something so stupid?" Kate asked. "You told me that he's an experienced criminal. Why would he run away from here, leave that incriminating stuff in his car, and then just wait around for you to show up?"

"Panic can make people do some odd things. You have to put yourself in his mind when he left here. He's failed to do what he came to do. He doesn't know if you or your brother got a good look at him or not. He doesn't even know if he's being chased. He runs like hell, pulls off the gloves, and tries to stuff them in his pockets—doesn't even realize he's dropped one. Panics still more when he gets caught in the fence and hears a rip. But he can't stop to look. He knows somebody is calling the cops, so he runs inside his girl's apartment to set up his alibi, so he can be in his little jammies if we come calling right away. Then he can't go back outside, because maybe we're watching the house. You see what I mean?"

"I don't know," Kate sighed. "Maybe you're right. But it sounds too easy, too much like a setup."

"The average citizen tends to overcomplicate the solution to crimes," Kinowski said, and now he sounded pompous again. "It's usually much simpler than you would think. Especially you." And here he paused for emphasis. "You seem determined to tie your mother's death into some mystery about your father, so you ignore the obvious. Max is it, you can take my word for it. I got concrete evidence now and I'm on my way to get more."

"But why would Max try to kill me now?" Kate asked stubbornly. "You said on Thursday that he didn't want to kill me at the warehouse because you would be all over him if he did. You said he was just trying to scare me. So, why would he change his mind in one day?"

"Well, for one thing, you wouldn't scare," Kinowski said smugly—clearly he was not going to be detoured from his conviction. "And for another, he knows I'm working hard on one of his former pals. If I can get that guy to tell what he knows about Maxwell's fences in the Cities, I can put it together with what you saw and get charges brought. He can't get at this new witness because I've got him stashed, but he figures he can get at you."

"You've got an answer for everything," Kate said, feeling again the wave of disappointment.

"I just stopped by on my way to Maxwell's house to give you a preliminary report," Kinowski said, standing. "And to collect Officer Carter. We need him on another assignment. You and your brother will be fine as long as Maxwell is in custody."

"My brother's gone home," Kate said, feeling a flash of alarm at the prospect of losing her police protection.

"Oh," Kinowski said, frowning. "Do you feel you need somebody here with you?"

"No," Kate sighed. "I've got a friend on the way. He'll be here very soon, as a matter of fact. I'll be all right."

"I'll let you know as soon as we get Maxwell's confession,"

Kinowski said, starting for the door. "It's only a matter of time now."

When he'd gone, Kate carefully secured all the locks—the motel people had said it was all right for her to stay in the room Eric had rented for last night. Then she huddled down in her chair again, feeling all the aches and bruises on her body with an exaggerated intensity, as if being alone caused a direct aggravation to her injuries.

Jack arrived at 2:45, a little earlier than he promised—"I drove a little over the speed limit," he admitted sheepishly—and was as solicitous as she could have hoped, wincing at the sight of her injured face. He was especially relieved to hear about Bruce Maxwell's arrest.

"Well, that's the end of it, then, thank God," he said.

"I hope it is," Kate told him, though she was aware that this was, in fact, a lie, "but it doesn't feel right to me. It's too easy. What if somebody else planned in advance to frame Max? Snitched the gloves and jacket out of his garage, deliberately left clues here for the police to find, and then found some way to get the other glove and the torn jacket inside Max's locked car? I would be out of the way and Max would take the rap for both murders. Then the real killer's secret would be safe forever."

"Here we go again," Jack said, and he looked really disgusted this time. "You won't give up on this oddball theory of yours about your natural father, will you? Is it just that you can't face the fact that your birth mother died at the hands of a sordid crook? Is that why you need this fantasy?"

"What I don't need is you lecturing me and judging me," Kate said hotly, crossing the room in an angry rush of energy. "I get enough of that from everybody else."

"I'm sorry," Jack said soothingly. "I know it must be hard for you to give up on something you've invested so much emotional stuff in. You've had a bad time of it. I won't say anything else about it."

She turned to look back at him. "Okay," she said. "I'm sure I *do* come off like some kind of a flake. But I need a friend right now."

"You've got one," he said, smiling and thumping himself on the chest. "Right here. And one thing's for sure. You're not staying in this motel tonight. You're going to take my mother up on her standing invitation and stay in our guest room."

"Did she say it would be all right?" Kate asked gratefully. She certainly hadn't been looking forward to the night with no policeman in the hall.

"Well, I came straight here," he said, "so I didn't stop at home. But I know what she'd say."

"Maybe you should call her," Kate said dubiously.

"She's probably not back yet," he said, glancing at his watch. "She was going to be out most of the day with the community theater board. They're selecting the program for next season and they usually spend the morning doing the work and then have a posh lunch somewhere—a long lunch. But I know my mother, and I can hear her right now—'You just bring that lovely young lady here this minute.' "

Kate smiled at this imitation; she'd been in Mrs. Kramer's presence only twice, but she could easily imagine her making that very speech.

"Come on," Jack said, standing up. "Get your stuff together and we'll get you checked out."

"Checked out?" Kate asked. "I'm not sure I should do that."

"Of course," he insisted. "Why should you pay for a room you're not using?"

When she still hesitated, he went on. "If you get sick of staying with us, you can always check back in again."

"Okay," she said, smiling happily. "I *will* feel better if I don't have to stay here. This place is starting to give me the creeps."

# CHAPTER 26

Lieutenant Kinowski was practically staggering from exhaustion. It was after five, and he'd been up since three A.M. Double shifts had been easier twenty years ago—hell, even ten years ago. It hadn't been an "easy duty" day either. Running around to secure search warrants had made the morning hectic, and Kinowski hated that kind of red tape. If he had his way, cops would jump on the evidence first and worry about warrants later. And questioning Bruce Maxwell was a very tiring job. This was a tough son of a bitch, arrogant and confident. He hadn't budged an inch in six hours of grilling. He just kept repeating that it was a frame—he had never put the jacket and glove in the car; he had never been near the Holiday Inn; and how could they think he would be this stupid? For the past half hour, he'd been saying over and over, "Charge me or let me go." His pals were probably working on scaring up some dirtbag of a lawyer, and pretty soon there would be no choice but to quit the questioning. Kinowski had decided to take a break because he'd found himself wondering how much punching in the face Maxwell would take before he started to sing. Peterson had taken over.

Now Kinowski was slumped in his tiny office, wondering if he should just knock off for the day; it was no longer a question of his shift—that had been over hours ago. But he hated leaving things undone. Once lawyers got involved, he knew, things started to slip away. And this one was so obvious—the felon had screwed up, left behind the sort of concrete stuff that juries love.

There was a tap on the open door of his office and he looked up to see Sergeant Johnson peering in at him, wearing the sort of expression a dog gets when it has just shit on the carpet.

"What is it, Johnson," Kinowski growled. "Something I'm not gonna like, I bet."

"Right," Johnson said, coming into the room a little way. "I just heard from the guys who were going over Maxwell's car. They found fresh scratch marks all along the vinyl on the inside of the passenger side door—concentration is near the lock. Looks like somebody used one of those wires to get that door open."

Kinowski stared at him, his jaw tightening.

"And they can tell for sure that this just happened?" he asked finally.

"That's what they say," Johnson replied. "Nobody touched them or rubbed over them—that sort of thing."

Kinowski blew the air out of his lungs, forcing it through clenched teeth.

"That's not all," Johnson said, more confident now that there had been no loud explosion from his superior officer. "Boys downstairs tried to do a hair match with the ones we found in the Lundgren girl's bed. Sorted out the ones that are hers for sure, and compared the rest with the ones they got from Maxwell's car. Nothing doing. Whoever the kid grabbed, it wasn't Max."

"Jesus Christ!" Kinowski said, banging his fist against the top of his desk. "Can't we get a break on anything? We're gonna have to let the bastard go, I suppose. And get me the Lundgren girl on the phone, will you? We'll have to put a man back on guard duty. Looks like somebody else is mad at her."

"Okay," Johnson said, backing out of the office. "We're going to nail Max one of these days, count on it."

"Yeah, right," Kinowski said, tamping his frustrations down to a low grumble. "I just hope it's before I die."

Now he stood up wearily and wandered out into the receiving area, feeling the need of activity just to keep awake. Probably he should go home and crawl into bed—about fourteen hours of sleep, and he'd feel like a new man. The "action" of Saturday night wouldn't start for hours yet, so the receiving area was quiet—only one officer standing around chatting with the dispatcher, another on the phone at the booking desk. That one hung up now and looked up at Kinowski.

"Oh, good," he said. "You're here. Save me a trip."

"Was that about the report I'm waiting for on Ford's office?" Kinowski asked. "Somebody finally in gear over there?"

"Krause says you'll get it in writing on Monday," the officer said, "but here's the gist. The only fingerprints on the pen and the suicide note belong to the deceased. Couple of latents on the typewriter—also his. But here's where it gets funny. No prints at all on the window—not on the handles or the frame or the glass. And that scrape on the windowsill you thought came from a shoe? You know, where you thought he might have pushed off? Krause says the dark stuff came from the heel on Ford's shoe, but the scrape was inward—came from the outside in. So, unless the guy took a back dive, that doesn't make much sense."

Kinowski was frowning now, deep in thought. "Any match yet on the fiber traces?" he asked.

"Not started," the young officer answered. "Mrs. Ford says the crew can come to the house Monday. There's something else funny about the window, though."

"Well, don't keep me in suspense," Kinowski snapped.

"You remember the secretary said that window had a tendency to stick? Well, after they were done dusting for prints, Krause's boys closed it and tried to open it again. No go. They had to wrestle with it for quite a while before they got it open."

"Maybe the wood swelled because of the rain," Kinowski offered.

"Naw, the rain was coming from the opposite direction. The people in the office say the window was always like that, so nobody ever opens it. Krause says his guys don't believe a sick old man could've got it open on Wednesday night."

"Well, well, well," Kinowski said, and then he whistled softly. "So the kid might be right, after all. Monday, first thing, I gotta get a court order to look at the old guy's files, find out what he might have known that would be worth somebody dropping him off a building to hide. Good thing we told that partner—Rettig, that's his name—to put a lock on all Ford's stuff. This is getting interesting."

Kinowski felt more awake now, alert. There was nothing like a break in a case to liven things up. It wasn't enough to make up for having to let Maxwell out, but it was certainly something. Woodard hadn't seen this much action in so short a time in all his years on the force.

Sergeant Johnson came looking for Kinowski now, emerging from the cavernlike hallway that led to the back offices. "Just got off the phone to the Holiday Inn," he said, then went on because Kinowski was giving him a blank look. "About the Lundgren girl?"

"Oh, that," Kinowski said. "Is she on the line?"

"No," Johnson responded. "She's gone. The brother, too. Checked out, all paid up."

"Well, that's a relief," Kinowski sighed. "They must've gone home to Mommy and Daddy at last. That means I don't have to spend a man on guard duty. I'll set him onto Maxwell instead— follow that son of a bitch until he does *something* we can nail him for."

Still, he felt a vague sense of regret that the girl was gone. He would have liked to tell her that he was beginning to take her suspicions seriously—to see her face when he told her.

"You gonna get some rest now, or what?" Johnson said, careful to express concern nonchalantly.

"Naw, I don't think so," Kinowski answered. In fact, he didn't feel tired anymore. "I'd like to make some stops on the way home. You know, Johnson, I'm plenty glad to get that Lundgren girl out of my hair, but it's funny to think she might have been right about a connection between Terry Cruzan and that old lawyer."

"Yeah," Johnson said noncommittally. "Weird."

The cop who'd been chatting with the dispatcher had been listening in on this talk and now he came forward, cleared his throat until Kinowski looked at him. It was Harrigan, a man who'd been on the force almost as long as Kinowski, yet had never risen above patrolman—slow on the uptake, Kinowski remembered. "I heard you mention that Cruzan woman," he said now, bobbing his head in a gesture of deference—just the sort of thing that always annoyed Kinowski about him. Of course, he wouldn't go on without a prompt.

"Well?" Kinowski snapped.

"I heard you say just now there might be some connection between her and Ford," Harrigan went on.

"So?" Kinowski sighed, resigning himself to playing straight man.

"Well, last week, I got a call from Ford," Harrigan said. "I used to know him in the old days, helped him on some cases."

"Really?" Kinowski was interested now. "What did he want?"

"He asked about the Cruzan case, about the girl," Harrigan went on. "The Lundgren girl, I mean. Thought he might know her parents—the ones who adopted her, I mean. Expressed concern about her, about how she was getting along. That sort of thing. Just trying to be nice, I thought. I didn't think at the time that it could mean anything."

"Well, well, well," Kinowski said, looking back at Johnson. "This is getting thicker by the minute. Too bad it's Saturday. I'd love to get at those files right away."

"Well, Monday will be time enough, I suppose," Johnson answered.

"I suppose," Kinowski sighed. "But at least I can pay a little call on Mr. Thomas Werner today."

"And then get some sleep?" Johnson said it as a question.

"Are you my mother or something?" Kinowski growled, but he smiled at Johnson just before he turned to leave.

# CHAPTER 27

Kate was holed up in the Kramers' guest room, a sparsely furnished place with a small window. She was feeling nervous and acutely embarrassed. Jack had been right when he said his mother wouldn't mind if Kate stayed over at the house, but his failure to check in with her had meant that Kate had arrived without knowing that Mrs. Kramer was expecting guests for dinner.

Jack's mother had spent the first ten minutes after their arrival exclaiming over Kate's bruised and swollen face. It was all Jack could do to get her calmed down enough to hear the explanation. After that, she was as firm as Jack had been about Kate's not remaining at the motel alone.

"Of course, you'll stay with us," she breathed. "As long as you like. I hope that wretched man is sent to prison for years and years. We don't need his kind here. What must you think of Woodard? You've had nothing but trouble since you came here."

Even before Kate could start to say that *some* of Woodard's citizens had been very kind to her, Mrs. Kramer began talking to Jack.

"You know that the country-club dance is tonight, don't you? I'm sure I told you I was planning to go."

"No," Jack said slowly. "I'd forgotten about that. Maybe I blotted it because you kept trying so hard to get me to go."

"I gave up on you weeks ago," she laughed. "But, of course, I can cancel the dance now." And she looked sympathetically at Kate.

"Oh, please don't do that," Kate said, feeling her face begin to beam. "I don't need to be cared for, really I don't. I'll feel awful if you change your plans because of me."

"Well, if you're sure, dear," the older woman said, patting Kate's arm in a solicitous gesture. "I'd planned to go with some friends and even to stay over at their house until tomorrow. They live near the club and, this way, they wouldn't have to drive back across town to bring me home. I don't drive anymore. I even sold the car. But I could arrange to be brought back if it would make you uncomfortable to be here without me. I mean, just by yourself with—" And then she fell silent, her own face red with confusion and embarrassment.

Jack was the first to interpret his mother's words. "For God's sake, Mother," he said, and his laugh was half amused, half irritated. "This is not the Dark Ages!"

Then Kate understood that Mrs. Kramer was concerned about the propriety of leaving her son and a young lady in the house all night unchaperoned, and her own blush deepened. "Please don't change any of your plans on my account, Mrs. Kramer," Kate said. "All I need is a quiet place to get some sleep. I didn't get much of that last night."

"Of course you didn't," Mrs. Kramer exclaimed, her soft face once again creased with concern. "And you look as if you could use a good meal, too. Happily, I'm planning a rather nice dinner—one of my specialties. The friends I mentioned are eating here before we go on to the club for the dance, but we won't be having dinner until about seven-thirty. Could I fix you something now?"

"No, no," Kate protested, more conscious than ever of being an intruder into this poor woman's weekend plans. "I probably won't even have dinner with you." She was thinking of her wrinkled clothes, her battered face; she didn't relish the idea of sitting across from strangers dressed in party clothes and trying to make polite conversation.

"Of course you will," Jack's mother insisted. "It's nothing elaborate, just an Indian curry that's easy to stretch, and you'll be fine just as you are. I think you'll like the Werners. They're really old friends of ours."

Kate and Jack gaped at each other for a second, and then he spread his hands and lifted his shoulders in a gesture that seemed to say, "Who knew?"

"You should get some rest for a few hours," Mrs. Kramer was saying, oblivious to the pantomime between Kate and her son, "and Jack can help me. You'll see. It'll be just fine. My friends and Jack's friends are bound to get along." And she took Kate's arm, piloting her toward the stairs. "Bring those bags, dear," she said to Jack without even looking at him.

Kate made her legs move to mount the stairs, but her brain wasn't turning over fast enough to formulate a response. Since the mention of Werner's name, she hadn't been able to think of a syllable to say, and so she was propelled into the guest room without being able to protest.

Jack had stayed behind after his mother went back downstairs. "I swear, I'm as stunned as you are, Kate," he said when she looked at him accusingly. "They haven't been here since way before Dad died. I didn't even know Mother was still seeing them."

"Do you think you can make excuses for me?" Kate asked. Now that she'd sorted through some of her tumbling emotions, she found that what she felt most strongly was fear—a deep aversion to encountering Thomas Werner so soon after the attack in the motel room. "I don't want to see him at all. Not today, at least. I'm a little scared, if you want to know the truth."

"Well, I don't think Mother will take no for an answer," Jack responded, helping her to unpack some of her clothes. "You've seen her in action, so you know how hard it is to resist her. But there's nothing for you to be scared of. You're safe here and I won't budge from your side."

"I'll see how I feel about it later," Kate sighed, holding up a skirt that looked pretty sorry from repeated packing and unpacking. "They'll be all spiffed up for a country-club dance, and I have only this stuff to wear. Talk about being at a disadvantage. And this face of mine."

"Does it occur to you," Jack said, taking her by the shoulders, "that if what you suspect about old Tom is true, it might be very interesting to see how he reacts to finding you here? Then the disadvantage would be all on his side."

"Yes," Kate said slowly. "I suppose that's true."

"You need something ironed or something?" Jack said, gesturing at the clothes Kate had laid out on the single bed. "I'll do it for you."

"You iron clothes?" Kate said, and grinned at him in spite of the pain it caused to the inside of her mouth.

"Well, of course," he snorted. "Don't tell me you're one of those sexists who think ironing is only woman's work."

Now Kate laughed out loud. "Just bring the iron and ironing board to me," she said. "You need to help your mother get enough food ready for an unexpected guest."

"Two unexpected guests," he replied with a grin of his own. "She wasn't expecting me, either. Remember? But she always makes too much food anyway, and then we're eating leftovers for a week."

He brought her the iron and board, and she had time to plan strategy while she worked on a skirt and her blue silk blouse. But as seven o'clock approached, she began to lose confidence again, and now she was sitting, fully dressed, without a light on, wondering if she should just beg off after all—ask Jack to bring something up on a plate.

There was a soft tap at the door. Kate glanced down at her watch before answering; it was six-fifty. "Yes?" she said. "Come in."

Jack stuck his head into the room. "You want to be downstairs waiting when they get here?" he asked. "Or make an entrance later? I put your car in the garage with mine, so he'll have no warning that way, but I can't guarantee that mother won't spill the beans the minute they arrive."

"I'm still feeling funny about this," Kate answered.

Now Jack came all the way into the room. "I promise you, I'll see to it you never have to be alone with him," he said, bending to look into her face. "Nothing can happen. After dinner they go off to the club and he can't get away from La Liz for the rest of the evening. Come on." And he held out his hand.

She looked up at him a second, then took his hand and stood up.

They could hear the doorbell ringing as they started down the stairs, and Jack held her arm to slow their pace until Mrs. Kramer could cross from the kitchen to open the front door.

They listened to the greetings, paused on the landing for the usual amenities to be over, and then started down the last eight steps.

Kate took in the group gathered below her in the front hall: Mrs. Kramer in a soft, rose-colored gown with a scattering of sequins at the neckline; the other woman—larger, more imposing—in a black-and-white ensemble with a long, straight skirt; Thomas Werner in a tuxedo, the pleated shirt front gleaming white under his tanned face. The three lifted their faces at the sound of people on the stairs, and the reaction on the man's face was all Kate could have hoped for: from mild curiosity, his features widened into a look of stunned surprise and then—yes, she was sure of it—fear. He actually looked behind himself at the door in a gesture clearly indicative of an impulse to flee. Kate squeezed Jack's arm, and he reached over to cover her hand with his own—an exchange that meant, "Did you see?" and, "I sure did."

Mrs. Kramer began to make introductions in her breathy, enthusiastic voice, but Kate kept her eyes fixed on Werner. He was recovering, but only slowly. He'd turned back to look at Mrs. Kramer, avoiding eye contact with the young people on the stairs. His tan had reddened visibly, but the color was now draining and he was swallowing repeatedly. He lifted his right hand to his bow tie, lowered it again.

"Hello," he finally said, when it was clear that it was his turn to speak, but he still didn't look at Kate, only at Jack. "Nice to see you again, John." And then he coughed, a nervous sound, and looked back at Jack's mother.

The dinner was an odd business—longer, it seemed to Kate, than any meal she'd ever eaten. Mrs. Kramer chatted in that airy voice of hers, with no apparent consciousness of the tension in the air. Elizabeth Proctor Werner made polite responses, but was clearly uninterested in, or perhaps just unskilled at, dinner-party repartee. After her initial surprise at learning of Kate's connection to recent horrific events in Woodard—Mrs. Kramer had "explained" in her usual combination of euphemisms and half-finished sentences—Mrs. Werner virtually ignored Kate. The only significant detail, for Kate, was that Mrs. Werner seemed genuinely indifferent to who Kate Lundgren might be—a clear indication that her husband had not told her about his conversation with this young woman at the country club or about his encounter with her at the library.

What Kate could not help noticing was the way Elizabeth Werner directed most of her attention toward her husband. She spoke to him and for him and about him; she watched his plate and his glass as if she were solely responsible for seeing to it that he was well provided with food and drink; she reached out to touch his sleeve whenever she mentioned his name: "Tom says—"; "If we go to Barbados, Tom would like to—"; "Of course, the board will defer to Tom on that."

At one point, she leaned across the table toward Mrs. Kramer, who'd been talking about the proper fertilizer for roses, and said, "I've been telling Tom he's looking so tired lately. Don't you think he's looking tired, Margaret?"

"For God's sake, Elizabeth," Werner said, almost hissing the words through his teeth, and his wife turned a surprised glance at him.

Mrs. Kramer saw trouble, headed it off smoothly. "I've been telling Jack the same thing," she said, smiling at her son and including Kate in the glance. "He's just been working too hard. They all work too hard, the men. Don't you think?"

Kate left her meal largely untouched and said very little, for she was busy watching and listening. Now that she saw Elizabeth Proctor in person, she could tell that the expensive ministrations of makeup experts and hairdressers and jewelry consultants and wardrobe planners could just barely disguise the fact that this was an essentially plain woman—large-boned, physically awkward, her dark eyes set too deeply in a rather shapeless face. Her one social coup, Kate suspected, was winning and holding the handsome man at her side, and as long as she was sure of him, she would defer to him, pamper him, flatter him. But something about the set of her thick jaw, the hard lines around her mouth, suggested what she might become if she wasn't so sure of him.

And Kate kept stealing glances at Thomas Werner himself, so close to her there across the table. Could this be her father? She could see nothing of herself in him, in his essentially Aryan beauty. Could those long, tapering hands have strangled Teresa Cruzan, attacked her while she slept last night? Once, when he reached for his wineglass, she saw that his hand was shaking, and when she looked quickly up at his face, she caught him just looking away from her. Perhaps he was sneaking glances at her, too, she thought, and wondering, Why don't I see myself in her? Was that why it wasn't so hard for him to attack her? Because he was able to fool himself into believing she was no part of him?

Jack and his mother cleared the table before dessert, and an awkward silence fell at the table. Kate didn't expect Thomas Werner to make small talk with her, but it surprised her a little that Mrs. Werner should be so socially inept as soon as her hostess left the room. Perhaps it was just that someone of her station felt it was unnecessary to be polite to a plainly dressed girl with a bruised face.

On the last pass gathering up salad plates and used silverware, Mrs. Kramer said blithely, "Jack is helping me construct the dessert, but I know you'll entertain each other nicely." When she disappeared into the kitchen again, a leaden silence fell over the table.

"Do excuse me," Mrs. Werner said, standing slowly. "I'm going upstairs to powder my nose. Tell Margaret for me, won't you, darling? I won't be long." And then she swept out of the dining room before either her husband or Kate could react.

Kate turned back slowly to look at the man across the table, her breathing suddenly fast and shallow. She didn't know what to expect, felt a terrible impulse to run into the kitchen. When she finally focused on Werner's face, she was surprised to find him leaning toward her with an earnest look.

"I'm glad for a chance to speak to you alone," he said, his voice low, barely above a whisper.

"Oh?" Kate said. "I wonder why."

"I'm amazed that you keep turning up wherever I go," he said, speaking very fast. "And more than a little appalled. I don't know what your problem is, but you've got to stop implicating me in it. A policeman came to see me this afternoon, for God's sake."

"Really?" Kate said, genuinely surprised. "Which policeman?"

"Some person named Kinowski," he answered. "He asked me what I was doing at the Holiday Inn, said you'd reported me lurking outside your door."

"And what did you tell him?" Kate found herself speaking

in the low, secretive voice, too—almost as if Werner's urgency were contagious.

"Of course I told him it was complete nonsense. I was nowhere near your room."

"I saw you in the parking lot," Kate interrupted, angry that he would try to lie even now.

"I suppose you did," he said, shushing her with a gesture of his hand. "But I didn't even know you were staying there. I was leaving after a meeting."

"What kind of a meeting?" Kate asked, incredulous.

"Please keep your voice down," Werner said, glancing nervously at the door to the kitchen and then toward the stairs, which were visible through the archway leading to the front hall. "All right, then. It was a lady friend. I see her every week, on Thursday or Friday. In fact, when you accosted me at the library that day, I was waiting for her to meet me there. We had a late lunch planned for out of town."

Kate just stared at him; she knew her face must betray her skepticism because she saw Werner make an impatient twitch of his impressive eyebrows.

"It's the truth," he hissed at her. "If you persist in this insane delusion that I'm somehow connected to that—to your unfortunate mother—you'll ruin my life. My wife is unlikely to understand about this friendship of mine. She won't see that it's unimportant as far as she and I are concerned. Do you want to be responsible for wrecking my marriage?" He was red-faced again, a desperate look in his blue eyes.

"And did you tell this part to Kinowski?" Kate asked, her own face rigid, cold.

"Yes, I did. He seems to understand. He's a man of the world, after all."

Kate snorted at this cliché applied to Erwin Kinowski, someone who'd always struck her as provincial in the strictest sense of the term. "Well, you can't expect *me* to believe you," she said, leaning toward him now, her face blazing. "Are *you* going to persist in the fiction that you didn't look at me as if you already knew me when I first saw you in the library? In the fiction that you don't remember Teresa Cruzan?"

"All right, all right," he said now, his whole body twitching in his nervous fear that he wouldn't be able to finish this without interruption. "I *do* remember your mother from when she worked at the club and that's why I thought I recognized you at the library, but that's all there is to it. You seem to have some crazy idea that I'm your natural father, but it just isn't true. Give this up before you wreck innocent lives."

"Innocent?" she cried, and was startled by how loud her voice sounded after all the near-whispering.

"For Christ's sake!" he hissed, extending both hands toward her in a downward gesture meant to command quiet. Kate winced away from the hands, sat back quickly in her chair. Werner's face looked suddenly stricken. "Listen to me, Kate," he whispered. "I know you wouldn't want to hurt people who've never done anything bad to you. If your father were here, he'd say the same thing to you."

"My father?" Kate whispered, staring at him in confusion.

"Douglas Lundgren," he explained. "I know him slightly, you know. We used to play golf sometimes, years ago, when he came here on business."

"He played golf here?" Kate murmured, stunned now. "At the country club?"

"Yes, of course," he said, impatience coming back into his voice. "There's no other place in Woodard to play golf. In fact, when I was reading about the Cruzan woman's family in the paper last week, I remembered that her father used to work for Doug. And now that I'm thinking about it, I believe it was Doug who got the girl her job at the club—recommended her, I mean."

"That's a lie," Kate flared. "You're saying that now because you want me to lay off you, but you didn't tell me that when we talked at the country club on Tuesday. Why didn't you *remember* it then?"

"It was all a long time ago," Werner said, sitting back, but now the silver eyebrows were arched, the long body beginning to relax. "One can't remember everything at once." He seemed to see that Kate was faltering, sensed that he'd gained the advantage somehow.

She tried to think of a response, opened her mouth, closed it again.

Jack came through the swinging door between the kitchen and the dining room carrying two plates on which mounds of angel cake, strawberries, and whipped cream were piled. When he saw that Kate and Werner were alone together in the room, he paled, looked at Kate with a searching glance.

"Elizabeth is upstairs," Werner said smoothly. "Kate and I have been having a little visit."

Jack looked down at him, the desserts poised in front of the great man's face, and then back at Kate, his eyebrows lifting quizzically from behind his glasses.

"That's right," Kate said, her voice subdued. "Just a little visit."

# CHAPTER 28

"I don't believe him about his knowing Daddy," Kate was saying to Jack, sitting forward at the edge of the sofa, too full of nervous energy to relax. "I think he's improvising because he thinks he can get me to give up on trying to identify my natural father if he can make me suspect Daddy."

The moment Mrs. Kramer and the Werners had left, driving off in the Werners' gray BMW sedan, Jack had demanded to know what Werner had said to Kate. And she had quickly recounted the conversation.

"And he's plenty scared now that Kinowski has started in on him," Jack said musingly.

"That's very encouraging, don't you think?" Kate asked him eagerly. "I mean, that Kinowski is considering something else besides Max."

"Of course, it could just be a loose end Kinowski is tying up," Jack replied. He was sitting opposite Kate with a glass of wine in his hand. "After you told him about Werner being at the Holiday Inn, I mean. Maybe Kinowski buys the story about Werner's dolly and has decided to drop it. I still can't believe Tom admitted to you that he's got a little on the side."

"Well, he might think it's less risky than telling me the truth," Kate said, sitting back now with a sigh. "If I believe his

excuse for my running into him twice in Woodard, he's clear
of other possibilities, and if I can be persuaded to protect him
from his wife finding out, I might stop all questioning about
him. I bet he spent the whole meal thinking that up."

"Of course, it *could* be true," Jack said quietly. "It would
explain why he was so thrown by seeing you here tonight, especially after the visit he got from Kinowski. Scared you'd blab it
in front of Liz, about seeing him at the motel."

"I think he's scared about a lot more than that."

"And also, you don't *want* to believe what he said about
your dad," Jack said now, leaning forward to look at her more
intently. "If your father did get Terry her job at the country
club, even before she was pregnant, it doesn't look too good,
does it? If you put it together with what Lubinsky said about
him spending a lot of time with Terry, and if you remember
that your dad is on Ford's client list—"

"I know all that," Kate said hotly. "But what you have to
understand is that it's not possible that could have been Daddy
in my room last night."

Jack's eyebrows went up. "Do you mean you found out he
was home in White Bear Lake?" he asked. "You know that for
sure?"

Kate hadn't told Jack about this morning's conversation
with her mother; she was trying to minimize it in her own mind,
didn't want Jack to start analyzing it. "I talked to Mom," she
said now. "Daddy was with her when she went to sleep and he
was still asleep when she got up this morning."

"But can she be sure he was there the whole time?" Jack
asked, almost as if he'd sensed what was behind her careful
wording.

"She took a sleeping pill," Kate murmured.

"I see," Jack responded, and looked as if he might go on,
but then sat back and crossed his legs in an impatient gesture.

"What I meant," Kate said, a kind of desperation in her
voice now, "was that Daddy wouldn't try to kill me. He couldn't
hurt me, no matter what."

"Maybe," Jack said softly, "you just don't know how desperate he is. Desperation can drive people to things they would
never dream of otherwise."

Kate was silent for a while, considering.

"I'll tell you what," she said at last. "On Monday, I want to go with you to see that secretary in Ford's office—your friend's mother."

"Mrs. Jensen," he said, but his expression was dubious.

"Yes," Kate rushed on. "If Kinowski won't take up this lead, we'll do it ourselves. We'll both work on Mrs. Jensen to get her to tell us *what* business Werner had with that lawyer. And we'll ask what business my father had, too, whether it was more than just the property deals he had here in Woodard. If we explain to her that Ford might have been killed over it and that the police just don't see it yet, maybe she'll let out enough to give us the answers we need."

Jack didn't respond, just sat there swinging his right leg, his arms folded, his face in shadow now that he'd sat back in his chair. Finally, he sighed deeply and relaxed his arms.

"I don't think it'll do the least bit of good," he said quietly, "because I don't believe she'll talk to us like that, but all right. I give up. I'll take you to see her on Monday."

"Thank you," Kate said simply.

"You want some more wine?" he said in a tone suggesting that the other subject was now closed.

"No," Kate said, looking at the half-empty glass next to her elbow. "I'm already almost unconscious. What I should do is call my family and tell them I'm not at the motel—just in case they try to reach me. I was going to do it as soon as we got here, but then all of this stuff with Werner coming over pushed it right out of my mind."

"The phone's on that secretary desk in the dining room," Jack said, standing up now. "I'm going for some more wine for me."

It was Eric who answered the phone. "What's up?" he asked, concern immediately evident in his voice.

Kate told him about Bruce Maxwell's arrest and the removal of her police guard, declining comment when he expressed his conviction that it was "finally over." She also told him she'd checked out of the Holiday Inn and was staying at the Kramers' house.

"Well, that's good," Eric said. "None of us wanted to think of you being alone there."

"Can I talk to Mom for a minute?" Kate asked. All afternoon, she'd been thinking on and off about Sheila.

"She's in bed," Eric answered.

Kate glanced down at her watch, a frown forming between her eyes. "It's not even ten o'clock yet," she said.

"I know, but she's just done in. You haven't seen the strain and what it's done to her the past two weeks."

Kate felt dangerously close to tears. "She didn't take another pill, did she?" she asked, almost whispering, as if somebody might overhear.

"No, not tonight. They just knock her out and that's not the same as resting. She was so tired over dinner already and that's partly the result of last night's pill. I think she'll sleep for real tonight."

"Is Daddy with her?" So fresh was her recent conversation with Jack that Kate could hardly bring herself to ask about him.

"No, Dad's at the plant again," Eric said. "Once he knew I'd stay with Mom and that she was going to bed early, he decided to run down there."

"But it's Saturday," Kate murmured, her face stiffening in alarm that, once again, the whereabouts of Douglas Lundgren were uncertain.

"He thinks he's got the biggest problems narrowed down to one or two section foremen," Eric explained. "The sabotage stuff, in particular. That's been happening mostly on the weekend shifts. If he finds a foreman napping in the break room, or maybe even ducking out to meet some babe, he'll know how it's happening."

"But I don't know why he has to do this himself," Kate said, irritation creeping into her voice. "What does he pay his managers for, anyway?"

"You know Dad," Eric sighed. "He never believed in delegating much authority. He thinks that if he doesn't see to everything, it will all just slip away. It's that Depression mentality."

Jack came into the dining room now, carrying his wine, and he looked quizzical when he saw Kate's expression.

"Do you have the phone number for the plant?" Kate asked now, looking away from Jack.

"I could dig it out, I suppose," Eric responded after a little pause. "Why?"

"Just in case I might want to call him," Kate answered, but even she could hear how lame it sounded. "Maybe I just want to hear his voice before I go to bed, okay?"

"All right, all right," Eric said, reacting to the sharper tone of the last sentence. "Just give me a sec."

Kate looked at Jack now, signaled at a cylindrical box of pens and pencils next to the phone. He nodded, started across the room toward her. She was lifting a pen when Eric came back on the line.

"Here it is," he said and began to recite numbers.

"Hold it," Kate cried, then turned to Jack. "Is it all right if I jot a number on this?" she asked, pointing at a piece of paper in the corner of the desk. It looked like some sort of invoice for a delivery—she noticed Jack's scrawled signature across the bottom of it.

"Sure," Jack said. "Just turn it over."

"Go ahead," Kate said into the phone and then began to write as Eric spoke.

"Tell Mom I'll call her tomorrow," Kate said now, tapping the pen against her chin. "At one, like I told Dad."

"Okay, kiddo," Eric said. "Maybe now that the bad guy is on ice, you can tell her when you're coming home."

"Maybe," Kate said noncommittally, and then said good night to her brother.

"What's that all about?" Jack asked as Kate moved away from the phone, avoiding his glance. She crossed the room without answering.

"Daddy's gone off somewhere again," she said finally, too worn and too worried to fabricate anything. "He told Eric he was going to St. Paul to the factory, to spy on troublemakers."

"But you're afraid that might be a lie," Jack said, watching her intently. He leaned against the desk, looked down at the number she'd written. "And so you asked Eric for this number so you could check up on him," he said, lifting the piece of paper with his free hand.

"Maybe," she said. "I don't know what to think anymore, Jack. Dad doesn't seem to have a provable alibi for any of the times that bad things have happened here in Woodard. It doesn't look good that he keeps making excuses for not being in White Bear Lake, does it?"

"And you're thinking that if every excuse is connected to an incident here, maybe he's up to something tonight, too," Jack said, setting his wineglass down on the desk.

"I'll call St. Paul right now," Kate said, starting back toward him. "He'll come to the phone, and then I'll know that all this extra traveling he's been doing lately is genuine, that it's really related to a bad patch in the business." And she reached out for the number.

Jack put the piece of paper against his chest. "Think this over, Kate," he said. "Didn't you just tell me he claimed to be going to the plant to spy? If that's true, he wouldn't tell anybody there he was coming. So somebody answers the phone and says, 'Mr. Lundgren's not here,' and then you spend the rest of the night making yourself crazy about it, when maybe he *is* there all along."

Kate dropped her hand to her side. "I know you're right," she sighed. "And even if he came to the phone, it only means he's there *now*, not that he'll be there all night."

"Give it a rest," Jack said, putting the paper back down on the desk and picking up his wine again. "Try to put it all on hold for now. Monday is time enough to go back to playing detective. You've had a nasty series of shocks and, if you're not careful, you're going to just short out."

"I know you're right," she repeated stupidly, feeling the exhaustion even as he was talking about it. "I'm so sick of all this. Of being scared all the time and worried about my family. And mostly of feeling that it's all my fault. If I'd just let well enough alone, none of this would've happened."

"Cut that out," Jack said, and his voice fell somewhere between kindness and exasperation. "Even if everything you suspect is true, there was no way you could have known ahead of time that all of this would happen. Stop beating up on yourself."

He put his left arm around her shoulders gently, careful of her bruises, and led her out of the dining room. Back in the living room again, he took a seat next to her on the sofa instead of sitting down to face her, as he'd done earlier. Kate sank gratefully against his side, breathing the smell of his cologne. It felt so wonderful to have him next to her like this, a delightful combination of comfort and excitement.

"I'd like to be able to forget for a while," she said, turning her upper body into his, lifting her face up to him.

He looked thoughtful for a moment, his golden-brown eyes slightly hooded because he was looking down at her. Then he lowered his face and brought his mouth softly against hers. She could taste the wine on his breath. She moved closer, arched her back to press herself against him as he leaned over her, moved her left hand up his chest toward his shoulders and then his face. When he began to pull back, she caught his ear and pulled his face toward her again, reaching for his mouth with her own.

Under her forearm, she could feel the tension of his shoulders giving way, relaxing. He made a faint moaning sound and then gave himself to the kiss with a sudden force that parted her lips and made her conscious of the pain in her jaw. It was better when his mouth left her face and began to nuzzle her throat, her shoulder.

Kate longed for abandon now, had begun to feel the familiar rush of heat, the shortening of breath. She strained against him as his arms tightened against her back. But a sudden stabbing pain in her side surprised her, made her cry out. The pressure of Jack's embrace had come in contact with the bruised rib.

"What is it?" he gasped, sitting up and holding her away from himself.

"It's the damned bruise," Kate said, putting her hand down onto the pain. "Whoever tried to smother me last night was kneeling on me right here."

"Jesus, Kate, I'm sorry," Jack breathed. "I'm so sorry."

"It's not so bad," Kate said, eager to reassure him. "Nothing's broken. It's just a nasty bruise, and I'm pretty sore all over from fighting him off."

"Then this is not such a good idea right now," he said, sliding away from her. And she could see that the moment had passed. Now Jack's face registered only concern, almost a fear of hurting her further.

"I think you're probably right," she said softly, trailing her fingers along his jaw, feeling the rasp of whiskers. "Not right now, but I'd like to take a raincheck, if that's all right with you."

"Sure," he said, and he looked as if he might be blushing a little. "Plenty of time when you're healed."

"Plenty of time," Kate said, letting her hand trail down his arm before she put it back into her lap. "Maybe I'd better just go to bed. I didn't get much sleep last night and I think being beaten up must make you extra tired, because I feel like I've been scrubbing floors for a week."

Jack chuckled now, a deep sound at the back of his throat.

"Right," he said, "like you would know about scrubbing floors for a week."

"I used to do it at summer camp," Kate protested as he offered his hand to help her get up. "Honest. I helped scrub the dock every week."

"It's not quite the same," he laughed.

"Are you coming up to sing me to sleep?" she asked playfully, taking his arm.

"No, that's probably a dangerous plan," he said, his face serious now. "I'll just stay down here and finish my wine. That ought to help me get to sleep later." And he bent forward to plant a gentle kiss on her left cheek, the side that was less swollen.

When Kate stretched out between the floral sheets, she could feel every sore joint, every bruise. She'd swallowed two aspirins after changing into a nightshirt, and hoped they would begin to work soon. Now, when she closed her eyes, she kept seeing Jack's face in close-up: his eyes, the sprays of freckles on his cheeks, the full mouth. It was a nice way to fall asleep, she thought, and a distraction from a nagging feeling at the back of her mind, a sense that she'd overlooked something important in the day's events, missed some connection that she should have made. Was it something Kinowski had said this afternoon? Or maybe something this evening, something Werner had said or done? Something Eric had said on the phone? It drifted near the edge of her consciousness, annoying as the buzz of a mosquito in the dark.

But Kate was too exhausted to pursue the feeling, to do the mental sifting through the day's events that would be required to track down the nagging detail. Besides, she didn't want to think about it because that would mean thinking about Douglas Lundgren and whether he was really at the factory in St. Paul. It was much more pleasant to think about Jack Kramer, his strong arms, the tender skin behind his ear. She yawned, settled farther into the comfortable mattress, and drifted quickly into sleep—the deep sleep that comes when relief and the feeling of safety have replaced great terror.

# CHAPTER 29

He was approaching the back of the house now, careful to stay in the shadows of trees. It wouldn't do to be seen openly crossing a lawn. He paused to look at the two neighboring houses—all dark and closed up. Unlikely that anybody would be looking out back windows at two-thirty in the morning. At least there weren't many neighbors and the houses weren't close together. Still, better to be careful. He'd worn dark clothing, put the knit cap on again. His feet ached a little from walking in thin soles for more than an hour over the rough terrain of the development: He'd walked to the ravine, circled the edges of the vacant lots—thinking, planning. And it was chilly tonight, too; after that hot spell, Minnesota had reverted to its more typical summer weather.

But the aches he felt all over his body were more closely related to his exhaustion. He could no longer remember when he'd had more than two or three hours of sleep at a time. The worst part was having to pretend alertness and attention during the day, when all he wanted to do was to put his head down onto the nearest horizontal surface and go to sleep. But pretending was required of him; there were eyes watching his every move, measuring his energy, counting the very bites of food he ate. And those eyes were sharp, though loving. Perhaps it was loving that made eyes so sharp, he thought. To be so loved was a burden, an extra responsibility when he was already so overburdened that he felt himself sinking, as if the ground had turned liquid under his feet.

The bruises on his knuckles were starting to show, even though the thick gloves had given him some cushioning. Thinking about the bruises made him think about how he'd got them, and that brought on the waves of nausea again. If only she hadn't struggled so hard! When he had seen her there, sleeping with the silly mask over her lovely eyes, he'd thought it would be easy. He would smother her while she slept—it would be quick, painless. And somehow, in the alien costume he'd put on, he had felt anonymous. Even if she saw him, she might not recognize him. It would be easier to do it if he could think of himself as somebody else to her. Then he could leave the false evidence as he'd planned, steal away as quietly as he'd come, and it would all be over. Bruce Maxwell would go to prison for two murders and Robert Allan Ford's death would be declared a suicide. The nightmare would be over.

But she'd fought him, refusing to go quietly. It was just like her, he thought with a sudden flash of anger. He'd put himself at considerable risk to warn her off, hadn't he? Was it his fault that she refused to scare? Why did she have to be so goddamned stubborn! When she'd started to struggle under him in the bed, he'd panicked almost instantly. It was panic that had made him hit her, because what he meant to do was strangle her. If only she would be still, if only he could force her to lie still, not make any noise! It was almost as if his arms and hands had done that desperate punching on their own. And then that terrible panic when he himself was attacked! He'd been so careful, had double-checked in the late evening to make sure the room next to Kate's was empty, had reassured himself that sounds wouldn't carry to the next room after that.

Why couldn't she give up and leave Woodard? Even today, he'd hoped, was almost relieved that she was still alive, and began to believe that this was finally enough to make her run for home. Then it could still be all right. But if she was so determined to get herself killed, what could he do? And she was smart. If she kept at it, she was going to find out. He felt a perverse sense of pride that she was intelligent—good bloodlines, that. But it was dangerous, too, bound to bring him down.

Whenever he thought about the consequences of her finding out, he could think only of the effects it would have on him: ruin, humiliation, and, worst of all almost, the perception that the world would have of him. Nobody would believe that he'd never intended to kill anybody—not even Terry until she made him so angry. Everybody would think he was crazy. That would be worst of all.

Whatever he did now would have to be improvised, made up as he went along. And he was so worn out that his brain wasn't working smoothly. He was no longer even very interested in the monetary side of it—it seemed years ago that he'd considered that a good reason to manipulate and silence Teresa Cruzan. Now the only thing that mattered was not being caught. It enraged him that every crime seemed to require another crime to cover it up. How could this have happened to him? Everything was spinning out of control and he hated that feeling, the dizzying sense that he couldn't make anything do his bidding. He'd always hated carnival rides because they made him feel that way.

On his long walk around the development, only one plan had occurred to him—crude, iffy. But at least fairly simple. If Kate's body were found facedown in the stream tomorrow—a blow to the head that could have happened in a fall and then simple drowning—that could be seen as a regrettable accident. A young woman, distraught over the murder of her mother, perhaps still disoriented by the beating she had received at the murderer's hands, had wandered out into the night and, confused in unfamiliar terrain, had fallen into that ravine. Then Bruce Maxwell would go to prison. No great loss to anyone— a public service, really.

Now he stopped at the edge of the patio deck, looked up at the darkened windows. She was up there, safe inside. He knew his makeshift plan was stupid, bound to go awry as everything else had. But he was so tired that he couldn't think of anything else. There was almost no time left, no time to plan. He didn't want to think about what she might do even as early as tomorrow if he didn't stop her.

He had to sit down. Maybe he would think more clearly if he could rest. He grasped the railing of the wooden stairs leading to the deck, pulled himself up quietly. It was only when he was almost to the top that he saw the figure crouched at the other end of the deck, poised near the wide glass doors—some-body in dark clothes, elbows tipped out, head straining forward and alert. He almost collapsed from the shock, his hand frozen on the rough wood, his knees going suddenly rubbery.

After the initial jolt of adrenaline, the flight response kicked in. All of his brain was screaming, "Run! Get away, get away!" But now the man opposite him stood up straight, the face clearly visible, looking straight at him. It was too late. He could be identified now—no chance of escaping and then being able to claim he was somewhere else. With a groan that came from the depths of his body, he grasped the rail with both hands and launched himself up onto the deck. The impetus was enough to get his feet moving, too. He crossed the short space in three strides and threw himself onto the other man, who was not yet set to receive the charge.

The force of his forward motion carried him and the man he was now grasping into the edge of the sliding patio door. The glass cracked—he could hear it—but the door jumped its rails and fell inward without shattering. The other man had recovered slightly, turned his body so that his shoulder was braced for a second against the side of the door frame. He was able to push off, using the frame for leverage, and now his hands came up and closed around the cap, ripping it upward as both men, caught in a deadly and silent dance, tumbled over the threshold into the Kramers' dining room.

# CHAPTER 30

Kate swam up out of sleep, feeling a vague sense of alarm even before she opened her eyes. What was it? She had a dim memory of a pounding sound, intermittent but rhythmic. Nothing near to her. Distant, muffled, but nagging enough to arouse consciousness. When she finally opened her eyes, she experienced the shock common to people waking in unfamiliar surroundings—that gripping of fear and confusion. There was just enough light from the window for her to gradually make sense of the room, and then she remembered where she was.

She found herself listening, all of her body alert now. But there was a profound silence in the house, an absence of even distant traffic noises that was unfamiliar to a lifelong resident of suburbia. What had wakened her? Had the pounding she vaguely remembered been only some dream fragment? She sat up now, groaning as the movement roused a dull throbbing in all of her bruises. What time was it? She reached for her watch on the small table next to the bed, fumbled with the light switch on the lamp. The sudden burst of light caused the painful contracting of her pupils. After a few seconds, she could see the watch; it was two-forty. The middle of the night.

She swung her legs out of bed. She was stiff now—always worse the second day, people said. She padded into the hallway, walked to the open door of Jack's bedroom. His room was dark, but there was enough light coming from her own bedroom to show her that Jack's double bed was rumpled but empty. She stood for a moment, puzzled, listening. The house seemed almost preternaturally quiet, as if poised and holding its breath, as she was doing. Kate tiptoed down the hall to the head of the stairs.

"Jack," she called, but only a faint, breathy sound came out of her mouth. "Jack!" she cried, forcing more volume into her voice, jumping at the sound as it echoed in the stairwell.

There was no answer, no sound. Could it be that Jack was in the kitchen at the back of the house and couldn't hear her call? She began to creep down the stairs, moving slowly and hugging the wall. She could not have said why she felt a need to move with such stealth. Maybe it was the memory of the pounding that had awakened her. She considered calling for Jack again as she reached the bottom of the stairs, but changed her mind.

She leaned into the front hallway, listening. Now she thought she heard something—a faint scuffing sound coming from the direction of the dining room. She stepped across the hall and was about to enter the dining room when she heard a crash—the shivering *bang* that metal makes when it's struck hard. It was followed by another crash, even louder this time, more sustained. These noises were coming from directly in front of her, from the patio.

The sounds made Kate freeze, the adrenaline rush so intense as to produce momentary catatonia. Her eyes had adjusted to the gloom and she could see moving shapes now on the other side of the room. She saw a chair topple as if in slow motion, felt no surprise at the sound it made as it hit another chair and then the floor. And she heard other sounds, too— grunting and panting noises. All of this registered in seconds. When she was finally able to react, she began to turn, her leg muscles gathering themselves to run. The front door was behind her now and she had it clearly in mind, could almost see it already opened, with the path to escape leading away from it.

But in the split second before her gaze left the dining room, she caught the outlines of the grappling figures on the floor—

really one rolling mass rather than two distinguishable forms. She turned her head back to the room as if hypnotized. As she watched, the heaving mass rolled more toward the center of the room and she was able to see that one man was down and the other was crouched over him with his back to her. The man with his back on the floor was getting the worst of it at the moment, turning his head to dodge blows. When he jerked his face to the left, Kate could see that it was Jack—without his glasses and with his hair hanging onto his forehead, but clearly Jack.

The sight was enough to catapult her into action, to quash the flight impulse. She jumped into the dining room almost before she knew what she was doing. She remembered where the phone was, could see the outline of the secretary desk even though its chair had been hurled aside. Her path was littered with overturned chairs, but Kate managed to skirt one, step over another. When she got the phone in her hands, she didn't know for a second what to do with it—she'd gone for it on impulse, some idea of summoning help uppermost in her mind. But when she closed her grip on it, she froze for a second.

Then Jack groaned, turned his head and cried, "Kate!" a sound almost like a bark. Kate ran forward with the phone in both her hands, felt the cord tighten as it reached its full extension and then snap as she approached the crouching back of the man who was throttling Jack Kramer. She didn't swing the phone. She used the forward motion of her body and the sudden extension of her arms, straight out from her chest, to ram the phone into the back of the man's head.

He fell forward onto Jack like a bag of potatoes, stiffened, tried to rise, and then collapsed completely. Jack had to roll the man off his body in order to get free. One of the inert man's arms swung loosely over his body and fell on Kate's bare foot. She leaped away as if it had been a snake, dropped the phone.

Jack rolled over now, pulled himself to his knees, and stayed that way for a few seconds, rocking, drooping his head toward the carpet.

"Are you all right?" Kate managed to gasp.

"Give me a minute," he said in a strangled voice.

But Kate ran forward, skirting the body of the other man, and put her arms down onto Jack's shoulders. He lifted his head now, rocked back onto his haunches, and let her help him up. He leaned against her for a few seconds, gave his head a few shakes.

"The light," Kate murmured. "Where's the light switch?"

"Here," Jack answered, pointing ahead of himself at the short wall next to the archway that led into the hall.

They walked to it together, Kate still supporting him, and he threw the switch, bathing the room in sudden light, causing both of them instinctively to lift a free hand to shade offended eyes. Without a word, they turned in unison toward the fallen man, who was lying very still, curled into a shapeless lump with his head almost completely hidden from their line of sight.

They looked at each other now, and Kate had an impression that Jack's face was scraped and beginning to swell. He was wearing a navy blue knit shirt and the dark trousers he'd had on at dinner. Again, they didn't speak, but moved together toward the other side of the room, keeping well away from the dark bundle, until they were on the same side as the head. Finally they could look down at the face whose left side was pressed into the floor, at the thick gray hair, at the bright stain that was spreading like a halo around it in the pale carpet. Kate made a shuddering sound, a drawn out "ah-h-h," and now Jack had to support her, for the man on the floor was Douglas Lundgren.

"Who is that?" Jack said now, his own face furrowed in confusion.

"It's Daddy," Kate gasped. "It's my father. Oh, God. I think he's dead. I killed him."

"No, he's breathing," Jack said, leaning foward a little. "I can see his side moving."

"We have to get help," Kate said, pulling away from Jack's side and sinking to her knees on the carpet. "Get a doctor, an ambulance. He's hurt bad."

"Don't you know what this means?" Jack said above her. "He was sneaking around at the back of the house. When he saw me, he jumped me, smashed me into the door. And then he tried to kill me. Can't you figure out what he's doing here?"

"Don't talk about it!" Kate cried, her voice rising toward hysteria. "Just dial nine-one-one. Make everybody come, the police, the ambulance, I don't care. I think he's dying." And she stared into the beloved face, with its mouth agape and drooling now, the eyelids slightly parted as if he might wake up at any moment.

"The phone is broken," Jack said, his voicing sounding rather numb, almost nonchalant. "There's a phone in Mother's room."

"Go," Kate sobbed. "Go upstairs and call."

"What if he wakes up while I'm gone? He'll hurt you. He might kill you. I think that's what he came here to do."

"No, no, no." Kate was rocking and sobbing while she said it, the full horror beginning to settle into her mind now. All she wanted was to cradle the wounded head in her arms, but she knew Jack was right, knew what it must mean that her father was here in the middle of the night and had attacked her protector.

"Come here," Jack was saying now, pulling on her shoulders to raise her. "Stand at the bottom of the stairs where you can see him. I'll run up to make the call, and if he moves at all, you yell as loud as you can. That way I can come running. Maybe we should find you something to defend yourself with, just in case."

"No, no," Kate breathed now, but she did let herself be helped up. "I couldn't hit him again. I couldn't do it."

"Okay, okay," Jack said soothingly. "Then just stay at the bottom of the steps like I told you."

He had to back Kate out of the room because she was unable to take her eyes off the fallen man. She had an irrational terror that if she looked away, he would stop breathing, and when she looked back he would be dead. Jack sprinted up the stairs, two at a time.

Kate wrapped her arms around herself to stop the shaking—it was shock, of course, and she hadn't even noticed when the trembling had started. It was cold, too, she was sure of it. The night air was pouring straight through the opening where the patio door had been. She watched the inert form so intently that her eyes began to burn from not blinking. She found that she was willing Douglas Lundgren to move—not to get up, because that would have scared her, but to move an arm, to roll over onto his back: any sign that he wasn't near death. All her other feelings had numbed, and her mind had turned resolutely away from any thought of her father as a murderer.

Jack came trotting back down the stairs now. "They're on the way," he said, close to Kate's ear. "A few minutes. We have a few minutes now."

"What happened?" Kate asked, and she thought it was odd that her lips were so reluctant to move that the words were little more than a mumble.

"I woke up and couldn't get back to sleep," Jack said. "Wine does that to me sometimes. So I just decided to get up and read for a while. Before I could even get the lights on, I heard something outside, in the backyard. I just threw on some clothes as fast as I could and came down here in the dark. When I got to the patio doors, I saw a movement out there, a shape. I got down and opened the door enough to crawl out onto the deck. And then he came creeping up the steps from the lawn."

They were huddled together at the foot of the stairs, their shoulders touching.

"He saw me, and then he just charged while I was trying to stand up," Jack went on, as if she'd asked a question. "It's lucky that door didn't shatter or I could've got cut up during the struggle. Good safety glass. You know the rest, I guess. Boy, he's strong. I can't believe somebody that old could be so tough. He almost had me until you hit him."

Kate flinched at the last words, pulled away from Jack.

"You shouldn't stay here looking at him now," Jack said, putting an arm over her shoulders. "Let's wait outside for the police. There's no reason to keep watch now. He hasn't moved, has he?"

"No," Kate murmured, tightening her grip on her own elbows. "No, he hasn't."

"Come on," he said softly. "Come with me."

"I'm cold," she whispered. "It's cold."

"I can see you're shaking," he said. "I'll get something for you."

"Don't go," she gasped, catching hold of his arm as he moved. "Don't leave me again."

"Not upstairs," he said quietly. "Just to the hall closet. I've got some jackets there."

Kate stood swaying slightly while he crossed the hallway, opened the closet, and returned with a tan sports jacket.

"Here," he said, holding the coat open for her. "Put your arms inside. This is lightweight, but it warms up fast."

Kate loosened her arms and got into the jacket.

"Come on," Jack said. "I'll lead the way, so you don't have to look at him on the way by."

Kate was no longer able to formulate a coherent thought of her own, was willing to be led. As she trailed after Jack, she wrapped the jacket over her nightshirt, folding her arms tightly again. There was a sharp stabbing pain under her right arm, as if a needle had been jabbed through the sleeve into the flesh of her triceps, but she was so numbed with shock that she didn't cry out, only released her arms to relieve the pressure of the jacket sleeve.

With her left hand, she reached around to the place that hurt, felt something sharp on the outside of the sleeve. When she pulled on it, it stuck for only a second and then came away from the light wool. She brought her hand up under her eyes, turned it into the light. What she was holding was a wire that had once been a circle. It was broken now and bent, so that the two sharp ends pointed in opposite directions, but there was no mistaking what it was. It was the gold hoop from an earring.

# CHAPTER 31

Kate stood staring at the earring for a full five seconds before her mind could absorb the significance of what she was holding. Jack had turned by this time to look back at her.

"What is it?" he said, his voice puzzled.

Kate closed her hand over the wire, lowered it to her side. A fresh rush of adrenaline kicked her brain into gear.

"Nothing," she said, forcing her mouth to move.

"Come on, then," he said.

Kate turned her back on him, trying to compose her face. She found herself looking at the secretary desk, seeing the shiny surface where the phone had been, the same surface where Jack had put, facedown, the paper with the phone number scrawled on its back. That paper was gone now, and Kate suddenly realized what she'd been trying to think of before she fell asleep—the nagging detail at the back of her mind, like a mosquito that buzzed but wouldn't light. She'd noticed Jack's signature on the invoice, but there had been something above the signature—a date: July 14. If Friday was the thirteenth—and she realized now that she'd had that fact in her mind, had even been extra careful crossing streets on Friday—so, then, the fourteenth was Saturday. How could Jack have signed something when he'd spent Saturday in St. Cloud and arrived home only when he came from the motel with her? He'd told her he came straight to her without stopping at home. And no deliveries had been made while she was here.

"What's the matter?" Jack's voice was right next to her ear, and she whirled to face him, muffling a scream.

He was looking hard at her, squinting without his glasses, and she realized how lucky it was that he couldn't see her clearly. She turned from him again, bent forward. She mustn't let him get too close to her face because she was still too stunned to get her features under control. "I feel sick," she managed to whisper. "I'm afraid I might throw up. I have to get to the bathroom."

And she ran from the room in a crouch, made her wobbly legs move on the stairs. The only thought she was able to form was that she could lock herself in the bathroom until the police came. Only when she was inside the room did she realize that, of course, the police weren't coming. Jack hadn't called anybody. That was pretense, like everything else.

Now she felt she might really be sick. Her legs wouldn't hold her up anymore and she sank to her knees on the cold tiles. She lifted her hand and opened it. In the glaring overhead light, the crushed hoop winked from the trembling of her fingers. Jack Kramer's sleeve had accidentally torn this hoop from Teresa Cruzan's ear while he was strangling her. Forming the words in her mind like that brought Kate to the brink of sobs, but she choked them back, closed her hand again, and slipped the earring into the pocket of the jacket.

Realizations were tumbling over each other in her mind, and each one had a new power to shock her. It was not Thomas Werner who had followed her to the library—it was Jack. And he'd only pretended to hear someone in the parking lot that night after the play. He'd pretended everything. Of course, he'd never asked around about Douglas Lundgren—that was all improvised to make her stop asking questions. There was no Mrs. Jensen, no Ben Lubinsky. And she had confided in him, told him her every move! Even given him the hint about how to manipulate her when she let him know how afraid she was that Doug might be her natural father.

"Why?" she whispered, rocking back and forth on her knees. "Why, why, why?"

"Kate?" It was Jack's voice, right outside the bathroom door.

She clapped both hands over her mouth to stifle a scream.

"Are you all right in there, Kate?" Did his voice sound suspicious?

Kate straightened up, and something inside her straightened, too—some combination of rational thought and primitive cunning. She took her hands away from her mouth. "I'm a little better," she said, hoping that the shakiness in her voice would be interpreted as part of the physical sickness. "But I'd better stay here another minute just in case. You go back down to wait for the police. I have to get cleaned up. I'll be down when I can make it." And she pulled herself up by hanging on to the sink; her hand had almost stopped shaking when she reached out to turn on the tap.

"Okay," Jack said, his voice just barely audible above the running water. "Hurry up."

Now Kate's brain was racing. Two things were clear to her: She must get away from Jack, and she must get help for her father. The thought of Doug, motionless and bleeding into the carpet, the realization that *she* had done that to him, brought her to the brink of weeping again, but she fought against the impulse, focused on the task of escaping. The bathroom window was tiny, so she must begin by leaving this room. She turned off the tap, walked to the door, and put her ear against it to listen. Nothing. She switched off the light and carefully turned the knob. The click seemed loud to her, but she guessed Jack wouldn't be able to hear it downstairs. The door opened inward and she pulled it slowly toward herself, peeking around the edge into the darkened hallway. When the opening was big enough, she slipped through, her bare feet moving carefully.

Now what? She didn't dare to try for a downstairs door—the stairway and downstairs hallway were too exposed to view from either the living room or the dining room; in the symmetry typical of the Cape Cod style, the lower floor was bisected by the stairs, with one large room on either side. Perhaps the best thing would be to get to the upstairs phone—to dial 911 and summon the help she needed. Then she could try to escape through an upstairs window—drop to the ground below after hanging by her hands. Mrs. Kramer's room was at the front of the house, about eight feet down the hall from the bathroom, and the door was open as it had been when Kate went to bed. She hugged the wall, hoping there would be no creaking of the floorboards under the thick carpet. As she tiptoed along, she paused frequently to listen for any sounds of movement from downstairs. There were none.

At the threshold, Kate's right foot contacted the cold of the metal strip separating the hall carpet from the paler carpet of the bedroom. It was darker inside Mrs. Kramer's bedroom, but Kate could make out the bed and night table between the pale rectangles of the two windows. She crossed the room carefully, straining to see the objects on the cluttered surface of the night table. When she got there, she used her hands to inventory these objects: the small lamp, a box of tissues, a book, an eyeglass case. Nothing else. She had begun to turn away in confusion when the voice spoke from behind her, forcing a short scream from Kate's lips even as she whirled.

"The phone isn't in Mother's room, Kate. I had it moved to my room so she wouldn't be disturbed by late calls."

Jack stepped from behind the door and Kate could see his silhouette against the faint light from the hall. She was trapped and knew better than to try to bolt. After an initial buckling sensation in her knees, she managed to straighten up again, supporting herself with her hand against the headboard of the bed.

"How did you guess?" Jack asked; he wasn't moving toward her and his voice was quiet, conversational—as if he were asking her about the weather or the gas mileage on her car.

Kate was silent, instinctively determined not to tell him about the earring; that was evidence and it might still convict Jack Kramer—no matter what happened to her.

"Was it the invoice?" he said, taking a step toward her now. "Did you finally realize what you'd seen? I looked at it after you went to bed, saw the date. It was stupid of me to leave it out like that, but I was so tired." His voice was almost dreamy now. "You see, I thought I could hide out here for a while this morning because Mother would be gone all day. But the guy who delivers salt for the water softener just walked in on me. He delivers it at the side door, and it wasn't locked. I had to sign for it. I just didn't think what it might say to anybody who noticed it. Even Mother. Of course, I could always handle her."

Kate had stood her ground, stubbornly silent as Jack approached her. Now he took her arm gently, as if he were going to escort her onto a dance floor.

"Why?" she said finally. "I don't understand. Why would you kill Terry?"

"You have to be very quiet now," he said, lifting his right hand as if he were silencing a crowd. "I need to think and I'm so tired. I've been tired for days."

"My father needs help," Kate said as Jack began to drag her toward the door. She knew it was irrational to try to appeal to Jack's sense of mercy, but she couldn't stop herself, couldn't wholly believe in his perfidy.

"I want you to come downstairs now," Jack replied in that calm, singsong voice—as if he were coaxing a recalcitrant child. "Just be quiet and come along." And he was pulling her as he spoke, his fingers closing so tightly over her forearm that she was beginning to feel the pain.

The pain somehow made her believe: This man had strangled Terry and meant to kill her, too. Panic flooded her in a terrible rush and she screamed, a single piercing sound that made Jack jump and almost lose his grip. He spun around and swung at her, his fist grazing her left temple as she tried to twist away from him. The force of his intended blow carried him forward into her body, and she toppled backward. Her wrist came free and, as she hit the soft carpet, she rolled, bringing her knees up to protect her body. When she'd made a complete barrel roll, she came up onto her knees with the top of her head against the open door. Behind her, she heard the sounds of someone trying to get up off the bed, and she realized without looking that Jack's momentum must have made him stumble and fall there. She reached for the doorknob, pulled herself upright, and bolted through the doorway.

Kate raced for the top of the stairs, grasped the railing as she started down, jumping two steps at a time. Even in her panic, she was aware of the need for caution; she must not fall on the stairs, for then he would be on her. All she could hear was the sound of her own gasps. When she reached the landing midway down, she swung herself to the left, using the newel post as a lever, and cleared three steps before landing. She stumbled and almost fell, but the railing saved her. She could see the hallway just ahead, bathed in the light coming from the dining room. There was the door and, just beyond it, escape.

Just as her feet came in contact with the cold tiles of the hallway floor, something struck her in the back between her shoulder blades and sent her flying forward onto her knees. The air rushed out of her lungs in a loud gasp, and a viselike grip closed on her shoulders.

"Goddamn you!" She heard the snarling voice next to her right ear, felt the pressure of another body against her back, felt hands turning her and forcing her to rise.

Still on her knees, she began to sob, choking and gasping in turn.

"Get up," Jack was saying now. "Stand up or I'll kill you right here."

Kate went slack and still, her mind focused on the words *kill you*. She drew a ragged breath and then stood up, turned, and lifted her head to look at her assailant. She stared at him, noticing how blank and shallow his caramel-colored eyes seemed now that he wasn't looking through his glasses. He blinked twice under her gaze.

"I want you to come into the dining room now," he said, suddenly calm again.

"I'll go if you tell me why you did it," she gasped, still breathing hard, not letting herself think about the other why— why he might want her in the dining room. "Why did you kill Terry?"

"Because, you stupid little bitch," he said, and the tone of voice—singsong, almost pleasant—was a weird contrast to the words themselves, "your father and my father were the same man."

"That's a lie!" She said it instantly, loudly. But even as the words were echoing in her ears, she recognized their truth. In a flash, everything was clear.

"Then you're my brother," she murmured. "You're my brother, and you were going to make love to me tonight."

He laughed now, a sharp, barking sound, heavy with mockery. "Oh, that's rich," he said. "I'm about to kill you, and you're shocked because I was ready to screw you?"

He jerked her forward now, through the archway into the dining room. Kate planted her right heel in the thick carpet and spun around, dragging Jack with her, but he didn't let go of her arm. He stumbled a little, recovered, raised his left hand to strike her. He had his back to the room now. Kate looked past him suddenly, widened her eyes, and gasped.

"He's getting up," she screamed.

And Jack whirled, his grasp loosening. Kate shoved at him with all her strength and, already off balance, he fell backward, sitting down hard. Then Kate ran across the dining room, past her father's still-motionless body, and out the open door. She crossed the deck without feeling its surface under her feet and then jumped down the steps onto the lawn. She raced to her right, conscious of the grass only as a sensation of cold against her feet and legs. The nearest house lay behind a fence, and Kate could see as she got nearer that she wouldn't be able to climb it before Jack caught up with her. She veered sharply right, heading for the street. She could hear pounding footsteps behind her now, was afraid to look back.

When she got to the front of the darkened house, she turned a sharp left, crossing from the Kramer property to the neighbor's lawn. As she headed for the front door of that house, she had to pass the garage, whose wide doors were open. There was no car in the garage, and Kate realized with horror that there was probably no one at home. But it was too late to turn back; Jack must be right behind her. How long could she out-run him?

She cut left again, racing around the empty house and heading for a pair of houses she could see in the distance out-lined against the dark sky. In one of them, a lighted window beckoned. She began to run straight toward it. Within fifty feet, though, she found herself cut off by the slashing ravine where she and Jack had once taken a walk. Again she was forced to choose a left turn. The ground was more irregular here, rocky, and she was dimly aware of pain in her feet. Ahead of her now was the undeveloped part of Kramer Valley, clumps of pine trees, rugged slopes.

Kate was sure that she couldn't stay in front of Jack for very long, that she would have to find some cover. As she neared the pines, she stole a glance behind her and, sure enough, there was a dark figure in earnest pursuit, perhaps fifty feet behind her. Before she could look forward again, she found herself falling. A sudden sharp slope had intercepted her path. She hardly felt the impact with the ground, was rolling before she could take another breath. Her descent was fast, much faster than if she'd tried to run down that steep surface. As soon as she could feel herself slowing, she bent her knees to stop herself, scrambled up to her feet again.

The speed of her downhill trip had given her a bigger lead now—the dark shape behind her was slowing to make the backward-leaning descent on his feet. Now she sprinted uphill and toward the left until she reached the edge of the pines, where she crashed through the underbrush—thick with foliage from the wet spring. Now her legs as well as her feet were being torn at, raked. But still the pain wasn't making its full impact on her sensibilities. The wool jacket gave her arms some protection, and she used them to part the thick shrubs as she moved first right, then left, almost instinctively tacking in an effort to throw off her pursuer.

When she could see that she was approaching the outer edge of the grove on the other side, she searched in the dim light for a place to go to ground. A tightly packed circle of white birch trees was just to her right. High grass crowded against the base of the tree trunks. Kate made a jump for this cover, crouched low to the ground, and tucked her knees up near her ears.

At first all she could hear was the rushing of her own blood, the pounding of her heart. She was gasping air into her lungs, needed to do that for a few seconds at least before she was physically able to hold her breath to listen. But finally, she could make out the sounds of someone moving through the underbrush—not fast, and with pauses every now and then. The sounds were off to her right and seemed to be moving parallel to her hiding place—neither approaching nor re-treating. At one point the noises stopped altogether for what seemed like an eternity to Kate, but she didn't move. She knew this trick. Grandpa Larson had a hunting dog who would stand perfectly still until his quarry, lulled into confidence by the long silence, would break cover.

Sure enough, eventually she heard the crashing sounds again, swift and sharp, as if her pursuer were taking out his rage and frustration on the underbrush. Finally, she could hear that he'd reached the far edge of the trees, must now be consid-ering which way she might have gone if she'd made it through to the other side. She could hear a swishing sound now—someone moving in long grass—and it was moving away from her even as it gained speed. Jack had started to run again.

She stood up, moving carefully, trying to minimize any noise. She knew it was impossible now to keep moving in the direction of the development's other houses; Jack was between her and that goal. By picking her way carefully, she was able to retrace her path, to emerge from the trees at almost the same point she'd gone in. Ahead of her and to the left was a long upward slope of half-wild terrain that ended at the back of the Kramers' house. She'd completed about two thirds of a ragged oval; one third more and she would be back where she'd begun. And that seemed now like the most sensible goal. Her car was there. If she could get to it, she could go for help, for an ambulance, and if she hurried, she might still save her father's life. She took only a few seconds now to calculate a path that would leave her least exposed. It wasn't a straight path, but a curved one that broke first left and then right, a path marked by trees, shrubs, knolls large enough to hide behind if one were moving in a crouched position.

Now Kate began to run again, her breathing quickened as much by anxiety as by effort. At each new cover, she ducked down, paused, looked in all directions. The night was cloudy, quite dark, but she felt she would have noticed anything out there as big as a human being if it were moving. Seeing no movement, she would crouch and run again, each time thinking only of the next interim goal. Along the back edge of the Kramers' lot there was a ragged line of wild lilac bushes, more than ten feet high and very dense—obviously, someone had decided to leave them as a rustic marker of the property line. If she could reach these bushes, the rest of her approach to the house would be screened from view. The last pair of wild trees—gnarled beech trees, probably pretty old—was still some forty feet from the lilacs. Forty feet of flat, open space.

Kate stood here a long moment, surveying the terrain in all directions, straining her eyes for any sign of movement, turning her head slowly in an effort to catch any sound. Satisfied, she drew a big breath and ran, her feet pounding against the grass. Once inside the deep shadow of the lilac bushes, she cast a quick look around and trotted to an opening between the bushes, an opening that would let her into the backyard of the Kramer house. Just as she stepped through the opening, an arm shot out and a hand caught the collar of the jacket she was wearing.

Kate screamed, more from surprise than from terror, and

spun around. The jacket was too big for her and the spinning motion was enough to make it fall off her right arm. Just as she was registering Jack's face, inches from her own, it occurred to Kate to spin the other way, to just twist herself out of the coat altogether and leave him holding it. He was reaching his other hand toward her face as she began the turn, and then she was free, running again up the slight incline toward the patio deck. But she was less than halfway there when something heavy struck the back of her legs and pitched her facedown onto the grass. She tried to kick, but her legs were now held in a powerful grip. She could feel him climbing her body, pulling himself up on top of her. She clawed in the grass, tried to draw her knees up, but it was useless.

Finally he was covering her, his face against her ear, his hands and knees working together to turn her over onto her back. "I thought you'd try to come back here," he gasped, his own breathing as labored as hers. "You're smart, I'll give you that."

She tried to scream, but his left forearm was now against her throat and she could feel herself beginning to gag instead. He had her on her back now, had straddled her body with his knees against her sides. The right hand descended against her mouth and now he began to lean into the pressure of the arm against her windpipe. He rocked forward, his head bending down toward her face. Then Kate saw a dark shape loom up suddenly behind Jack's head, a shape that looked like a country church, the steeple rising straight above the simple square facade. It took her a second or two to realize that it was a human shape, someone lifting something long above his head. Then the steeple swept downward in a slashing motion from left to right and Kate heard a resounding thump.

Jack said, "Uh-h-h!" and fell sideways off her, his right leg straightening and coming to rest across her stomach.

She coughed, a choking cough, and rolled to her left to escape the leg. By the time she could sit up, hands were on her shoulders, a voice was murmuring near her face. "Katie. Katie, say something."

She turned her head, looked up. Douglas Lundgren was kneeling in the grass next to her, his face ghastly pale against the night sky, his eyes wide and staring. He rocked a little, sat down suddenly in the grass, pulling her toward him until her head was resting on his chest. She closed her hands against his jacket, buried her face in the familiar smell of his clothes.

"Daddy," she sobbed in a voice muffled by his shirt. "Oh, Daddy."

"My Katie girl," he whispered, bowing his head over hers. Exertion must have reopened his wound, for a small trickle of blood had come over his ear, and now it began to drop down onto her hair.

# CHAPTER 32

Kate was sitting in the guest chair of her father's hospital room. Her mother was sitting on the bed itself, near the top, where Doug was propped up on pillows. It was Tuesday morning and they were all waiting for a visit from the doctor, who would give the go-ahead for Doug to check out and go home to White Bear Lake. His concussion had been a serious one—he'd slept much of Monday—and the doctor had insisted on another night of monitoring. It had taken twenty stitches to close the wound across the back of his skull. But there was no fracture and no serious subdural swelling.

Kate was simply enjoying being in the same room with her parents, watching her mother fuss with the serving tray, listening to them talk. Eric, who had been in Woodard most of Sunday and Sunday night, had gone back to White Bear Lake and his job at the pool, so Kate had her parents all to herself. Her own wounds were mending fast: Bandages covered the worst cuts on her feet and ankles; the bruises around her eye were fading and her lower face had returned to its usual shape.

Jack Kramer was in a room one floor below, and a police guard was posted outside the door. His wound had been the most serious of all—a fractured skull—and he hadn't even regained consciousness until Monday morning. One of the first things Douglas Lundgren had told Kate while they sat on the front porch of the Kramers' house waiting for the police and ambulance to arrive was how he had come to rescue her from her half brother. Rocking and shaking, fighting to stay conscious by talking despite her efforts to shush him, he'd explained how he'd come to be in Woodard in the middle of the night.

He'd gone to the factory in St. Paul, learned what he needed to know by eleven P.M. Then he'd pointed his car north and driven without a stop to Woodard.

"I was worried about your mother," he explained. "About how she was taking all this. And I felt one of us should be near you, whether you wanted it or not. Maybe if I saw you and we talked it out, you would come to your senses. I tried once before to see you, at the funeral, but I didn't even get out of the car."

When he got to the Holiday Inn, he'd asked for a room near hers, not intending to wake her, only to be on the spot in the morning. When he learned that she'd checked out, he assumed she must have decided to go home, but he called White Bear Lake from the motel to be sure. Eric answered the phone, explained that Kate was staying with the Kramers.

"He said you called home," Doug explained, "that you asked for the phone number for the factory and said you might want to talk to me. And he said you sounded kind of funny about it. I was worried, of course, so I came looking for you. I thought at first I'd call, but then I figured, heck, if you're going to wake people up, you might as well do it in person. Besides, I wasn't having much luck just talking to you on the phone."

When he'd arrived at the Kramer house, he'd become alarmed when he saw no sign of her car. He rang the doorbell several times and, when there was no answer, pounded on the door for some time. Now he was getting desperate, wondering why he couldn't rouse anybody. He'd circled the house, climbed the stairs to the deck. Just as he was discovering that the patio door was slightly ajar, he heard a noise behind him, dropped into a crouch, and then saw a darkly clothed man wearing a dark knit cap charging at him. They struggled and then the lights went out.

Consciousness had come back slowly: He could hear voices, but he couldn't move; then he got his eyes open in time to see bare legs flashing past him, darker legs in apparent pursuit, but still he wasn't able to make his muscles work. When he finally managed to get up, he fought off repeated dizzy spells to make his way outside. He'd almost fallen in the dark over a stack of firewood, but that had provided him with a weapon—in fact, he carefully chose a long, sturdy log about five inches in diameter.

He'd spent some futile minutes searching the neighborhood, had returned to the Kramers' backyard in time to see one shadowy form tackling another shadowy form from behind. In a few steps he was able to see what was going on, knew he had one chance to act—dizzy as he was, he would be an easy opponent for a stronger assailant.

"So I sneaked up on him," he said, a ring of satisfaction in his voice, "and I put everything I had left into that swing." Then, typical of this thoughtful man, he gave his wounded head a little shake and added, "I hope he's not dead."

Now there was a tap on the door frame of the hospital room, and all three Lundgrens turned, expecting to see the doctor. But it was Lieutenant Erwin Kinowski who came into the room instead. Other policemen had taken Kate's and Doug's statements on Monday, so this was the first time Kate's parents were meeting the officer. Kate made the introduction, motioned Kinowski into her chair, and sat on the bed next to her mother.

"I had a busy day yesterday," Kinowski said, flipping open a notebook he'd taken from his shirt pocket.

"You've had a lot of busy days lately," Kate chuckled, surprised by a flash of affection for this serious, blocky little man.

"Boy, *I'll* say," he responded, smiling at her as if they were old comrades in arms. "But this one is just about wrapped up now. We'll get a formal statement from Kramer when he's better, but I *did* have a little chat with him yesterday."

"And what did he say?" Kate asked. She'd felt a wave of anger and disgust at the mention of the name.

"Oh, he denies everything," Kinowski said complacently, as if this were an insignificant detail. "Says he can't imagine why you're saying bad things about him; he caught your father here prowling around his house and there was a struggle after which you, Mr. Lundgren, bashed him on the head."

"Hah!" Doug snorted, and then winced because making the explosive sound had caused his head to throb. "He's the one who was prowling, and he jumped me."

"I know," Kinowski replied. "And what's so funny about

that is he didn't have to do it. He wouldn't have had to explain to anybody why he was taking a walk in his own backyard. He could've covered for a while longer if he hadn't lost his head. Just a mistake in judgment."

"Well, I suppose I didn't really expect him to confess," Kate said quietly.

"But don't you worry," Kinowski said cheerfully. "We're gonna get the goods on him. We've already confiscated his clothes—the jacket you were wearing, Miss Lundgren, and lots of other things, too. We'll make the fiber matches, and we got some of the hair you yanked out of his head on Friday night in your motel room. It's gonna make a nice package. So it won't be just your story against his."

"He told Katherine that his father was her natural father," Sheila said now, and Kate smiled at this use of her formal name to a man who was, to Sheila, a stranger. "Did he really commit all of that terrible violence just to keep that fact a secret?"

"Oh, no, no," Kinowski said, shaking his head vigorously. "There's much more to it than that. That's what I spent yesterday afternoon checking out. See, I *was* closing in on young Kramer. I was gonna look at Ford's files yesterday in any case. After it got real clear that he wasn't a suicide." He stole a glance at Kate, who just raised her eyebrows at him without making any comment. "Of course," Kinowski went on sheepishly, "if your dad hadn't showed up, that would've been too late."

All three Lundgrens reached out for each other: Sheila's hand on Kate's back, Doug's on her arm, Kate's hands on her parents' shoulders. They'd been doing that a lot lately, whenever there was some reminder of how close they'd come to losing each other.

"Tell us what you found out," Doug said, giving Kate's arm a pat.

"Well, I got my court order in a hurry," Kinowski said, shifting in the chair in his excitement over what he now had to tell. "Sure enough, Hank Kramer *was* one of Ford's clients— changed his will a few months before he died. And I got a look at that will."

Here Kinowski paused for dramatic effect. Kate looked at him steadily, hiding her exasperation. Finally Kinowski went on.

"Old Kramer had added a codicil saying that he had a

natural child whose whereabouts were unknown to him, but that the identity of the child's mother 'is known to my son, John.' Those are the exact words. Then the codicil goes on to say that he wishes to leave a parcel of land in St. Cloud to his natural daughter, if she is located within two years following his death. If she can't be located, it says, the property will pass to his only son, John. All remaining property is given to the widow."

Kate was stunned, struggling to absorb this. "I don't understand," she said finally. "If it's in the will, why didn't everybody know about it. Why didn't Mrs. Kramer know about it? You're not saying she was in on all of this."

"No, no, of course not," Kinowski said, getting up to pace. "In Minnesota, a will doesn't have to be probated right away. You can take up to three years to do that. Young Kramer convinced his mother he would handle all that legal stuff, that he'd already read the will and it was pretty ordinary. She told me that herself yesterday. Then he probably conned Ford into delaying probate because Mrs. Kramer was taking the death so hard and didn't need any more grief added to it. Told Ford *he* would look for the child, based on knowing the identity of the mother. Ford was pretty sick by that time—just let Jack handle it."

"And he thought he could keep it a secret that his father had an illegitimate daughter?" Kate asked, still incredulous.

"I think that's what he hoped, yes," Kinowski explained. "I'm only guessing, of course, but I think Hank didn't even tell the boy about Teresa Cruzan or about you until just after his first heart attack. And that was just a few months before he died."

"And Jack wouldn't have taken that news very well," Kate murmured. "I don't think he liked his father much, anyway."

"Well, whatever," Kinowski said with a shrug. "Old Hank died without knowing what he'd left you. Even Ford must have thought the land in St. Cloud was just a modest bequest."

"But I gather that it wasn't," Doug said, sitting up straight against the pillows.

"You got that right," Kinowski said, smiling. "I had some boys in the St. Cloud department digging around for me yesterday afternoon. They turned up a serious offer for that land from a consortium that's getting ready to locate a megamall in St. Cloud. You know, that's one of the fastest growing parts of the state."

"Odd," Kate said now. "When he was lying to me about going to St. Cloud on Friday, he said something about some land his father had bought there—he said it was just farmland once."

"That's right," Kinowski responded. "The consortium came to Kramer Development only two weeks after Henry Kramer died—September, that was, almost two years ago—so only Jack knew about the offer. He kept real quiet about it, as you can imagine. He even got the consortium to give him a few years to arrange the deal. They don't want to even break ground for the mall until 1993, but he assured them the land would be available when they needed it. Even signed a conditional purchase agreement."

"So, if I wasn't found by this fall, the land would be his," Kate murmured. "He was so close. No wonder he was desperate to keep Terry quiet about who my natural father was. I'm sure she never knew why he was so desperate. How could she? He wouldn't have told her something like that."

"No, of course not," Kinowski agreed. "He wanted the fewest number possible to know about it. I figure Terry must have contacted him sometime this winter or spring to get him to start making the support payments his father used to make. We checked the bank records, by the way, and that's another nice piece of concrete evidence. Regular cash withdrawals from his private account by Henry Kramer from 1970 until his death—didn't risk writing checks, of course. Jack just started making cash withdrawals in May."

"Then Terry *was* blackmailing my natural father," Kate said softly. She could feel a constriction like a pain in her chest.

"Well, I don't know that it was blackmail," Kinowski said soothingly, stopping in his excited pacing to look at Kate. "I suppose it was just a sort of arrangement they had. Hank Kramer seemed to want to stay in contact with her, to make things right. The meetings in Duluth suggest that he sort of stayed in love with her over all those years. And who knows? She might have had some sincere feelings for him, too. It's maybe not so cold-blooded as you think it was."

"But she never told him where I was," Kate mused. "Even

though she knew all along. He wouldn't have needed to ask Jack to look for me if she'd told him what she knew."

"I guess not," Kinowski said, resuming his pacing. "Maybe she was afraid he'd try to interfere in your life."

Kate sat silent for a moment, considering this possibility. She remembered what Tammy Travers had reported of Terry's words in the hospital: "I don't want him to support the kid. I don't think I want him to *know* the kid."

"But I guess Jack was willing to give Terry anything she wanted," Kinowski was saying, "just to keep her quiet. And, of course, he was waiting for Ford to die, because then there would be almost no attention given to the codicil when the will *was* finally probated. Everybody else in the firm would just assume Ford had conducted a search and failed to find the girl."

"And then he would get the land and be able to sell it," Kate said, leaning back against her mother's shoulder. "Nice and tidy. But I threw everything out of whack by showing up on Terry's doorstep."

"What I can't figure," Kinowski said with one of his frowns, "is why he took the risk of approaching you in the first place. Woulda been much safer to just stay away from you altogether."

"Oh, he never meant to approach me," Kate answered. "But Werner trapped him into meeting me at the library, and once that happened, I suppose he decided it might be wise to keep me under his eyes most of the time."

"What was the offer?" Doug asked. "For the land, I mean?"

"A shade under two million," Kinowski said. "It's a choice location now."

Doug whistled softly and sat back in the bed.

"That would've bought Jack the life he wanted, I suppose," Kate said softly. "It would've got him out of Woodard, let him go back to his music."

"It's yours now," Kinowski said, grinning at her. "Shouldn't be too hard to prove you *are* the heir. Werner will help there."

"Werner?" Kate asked, gape-mouthed. "What does he have to do with this?"

"I talked to him Saturday afternoon on my way home," Kinowski explained, blushing a little, "after you said he was hanging around the Holiday Inn, maybe outside your room. He told me he was meeting some girlfriend there, but he was scared, I could see, so I kept pushing, suggested that he might have been Teresa Cruzan's lover and your natural father. He told me that wasn't true, but he *did* have a pretty good idea who that man was. He said he'd seen an old friend of his with Terry when she was a kid working at the country club. But he said it wouldn't have anything to do with her death because that old friend was deceased himself. He wouldn't give me a name, said it was not relevant and it would just hurt innocent people."

"And you believed that, of course," Kate said, smiling at the irony. Kinowski had been right about Werner all along.

"Well, not completely," he replied, and the blush deepened. "I spent the whole damned night following him around. First to Kramer's house where I didn't realize *you* were holed up, and then to that dance, and finally to his house. That's where I was when the radio told me about your call."

"So we were *both* distracted by the wrong suspect," Kate said, glancing at her father. She realized that, of course, Kinowski had read her statement and now knew that *she* had been distracted by two wrong suspects.

"Well," Kinowski shrugged. "Right church, wrong pew. But now Werner can come forward to help you establish parentage."

"So," Kate sighed, "that's why he was always so mysterious and secretive around me. He thought he was protecting Hank Kramer—and Mrs. Kramer, too, of course. He never connected my search for my natural father with Terry's murder."

Now she remembered something Werner had said to her, and she turned to her father. "By the way, Dad. How did Terry get her job at the country club that summer?"

"I asked the chef if she could bus tables," Doug answered slowly. "I played golf there sometimes in those days, and Terry's father asked me if I knew of any work she could get, just for the summer. I guess, in retrospect, that wasn't such a good idea for her."

Sheila put her hand against the side of her husband's face. "You don't have anything to feel guilty about," she said. "If we wish that summer undone, we have to wish Kate out of existence. And we can't wish for that. No matter what, nobody can ask us to wish for that."

Kate blinked back her sudden tears before turning to Kinowski again. "Lieutenant," she said, "how do you think Jack Kramer planned to explain two more bodies in his house?"

"Oh, that's easy," Kinowski shrugged. "He was improvising, of course, confused about what to do right after you slugged your dad with the phone. But he must have had a few minutes to think while you went upstairs to the bathroom, and he saw it was a simple deal. He wanted to get you into the dining room so he could kill you there. He was hoping your dad would die, of course—maybe he would even help him along in that direction after killing you. Then he would just call us, say he'd heard a ruckus downstairs and surprised an intruder who'd just strangled you. Then, he'd say, he hit this killer with the phone—self-defense, of course—and called us from upstairs. He would have a lot of convincing bruises, too."

"And I suppose he thought he could convince you that *I* was Kate's biological father," Doug said, "and that I'd killed Terry to hide the fact. Then I was forced to kill Kate to cover the first murder."

"And I gave him the idea," Kate whispered.

"Never mind, honey," Doug said, touching her back gently. She'd finally told her parents yesterday of her suspicions about Doug, and all three of them had cried over it.

"It's done now," Doug went on. "We're all safe and that bastard is going to jail."

"Well, I gotta run," Kinowski said, moving toward the door. "I thought I'd catch you before you leave. You'll be called back for the trial, of course. Oh, I almost forgot. I was reading your statement and I saw that you made a little trip to Duluth, a trip I didn't know anything about, by the way. It seems you went to the motel and found out something about the car Terry's fella was driving." And he was beetling his brow at her in a mock-scolding expression.

"I'm sorry I didn't tell you about that," Kate said sheepishly.

"Well, never mind," Kinowski said with a grin. "This morning I asked around, found out Hank Kramer used to drive a vintage Mercedes. I guess that qualifies as a boxy foreign car. His wife sold it after he died because she doesn't drive. Another concrete detail. You see what I mean?"

"Lieutenant," Kate said, standing now herself. "You mentioned talking to Mrs. Kramer. How is she? I've been thinking about her, worrying about her."

"She's pretty upset," Kinowski answered. "Of course, she

doesn't believe for a second that her boy could've done these things. She says she doesn't know why you would say such things about him, when he was only trying to be kind to you."

"I see," Kate murmured. "I wondered if I should try to see her, but I guess that wouldn't be a good idea."

"Probably not," Kinowski sighed. "Don't take it personally. It's just mothers. That's how they are about their kids."

"I know," Kate answered softly, glancing at Sheila.

"You take care of yourself from here on," Kinowski said. "You hear me, kid?"

"I hear you, Lieutenant," Kate said, and smiled at the kindness she saw in his square features.

When Kinowski had gone, Sheila came up to Kate, embraced her briefly. "I'm proud of you," she said against Kate's hair, "for thinking of that poor woman and wanting to help."

Now Kate turned to her father, who was beaming at them from his bed. "Could you arrange to have the land given to Mrs. Kramer?" Kate asked him. "I don't want it. I don't want anything from him."

Doug was silent for a moment. "Maybe you shouldn't decide anything right now, Katie," he said finally. "Give it a few weeks. Maybe we can reach some fair settlement with her."

"I won't change my mind, Dad," Kate said firmly. "Terry knew Henry Kramer very well and she didn't want me to have anything to do with him. She even seems to have broken off with him for a while just about the time I was born. She told a childhood friend that she didn't even want him to know me. And I think her instinct was right. Look what became of the child he *did* raise. Besides, Mrs. Kramer needs to have *something* out of this mess, and I don't think she's very good at taking care of herself. I don't need that money. I've got the only inheritance I want."

The doctor's arrival stopped the conversation. He examined Doug briefly and pronounced him ready to leave the hospital.

"We'll just get Dad into his clothes and check out, then," Sheila said to Kate after the doctor had left. "Is there anything you need to do before we go home?"

"Just one thing," Kate answered. "It won't take very long. I'll be back in about twenty minutes or so."

*    *    *

The drive to Franklin Street took less than five minutes. Kate parked in the shade of the white birch tree, got out of her car, and stood looking at the house for a moment. Then she walked down the neighbor's driveway, past the hedge, and into the backyard.

The grass was overgrown, almost too long for a lawnmower now. Kate reminded herself that it hadn't been cut in more than two weeks. The rain had made everything lush, and the grass felt cool and damp against her scratched ankles as she walked across the yard to the flower bed on the other side. The bed was a real work of art, terraced up into three levels with lengths of railway ties bordering each section. At the back, against a weathered wooden fence, were the roses—red, yellow, peach, pink. Some of the blooms were huge, real prize-winners. In front of the roses were small beds of salvia, zinnias, the remains of early-blooming tulips. Near the front of the garden were the lower plants: petunias, snapdragons, marigolds, and a border of impatiens. The total effect of the garden was exhuberant, a riot of color, a harmony of shapes and aromas.

Kate shook her head slowly. What a bundle of contradictions Teresa Cruzan had been. Here was a living testament to her creativity and to her sad desire for respectability. Looking at this garden, Kate felt she understood what had moved Terry to turn first to Henry Kramer and then to Jack Kramer for money: She was somehow able to convince herself that taking money from a Kramer was "legit," while taking money from Max for hiding his stolen goods was sordid. A tidy house and a flower garden were *owed* her, somehow, after what she'd given up.

Kate understood that she would never know how Teresa Cruzan had really felt about Hank Kramer: Maybe she'd gone on loving him in some way, just as he'd remained attached to her; and maybe she'd only used him as a convenient sugar daddy while she took up with her young boyfriends. Even more deeply, Kate understood that she would never know how her birth mother had really felt about her: There were some clear indications that she'd thought carefully about what was best for the child she was giving up, that she hadn't given the baby up easily, that she'd held out bravely against Henry Kramer's efforts to find his daughter; but it was just as clear that Terry had been right when she said she wouldn't have made a very good mother. So her resolve to let someone else mother her child was one of the best and most courageous things she'd done in her crazy, mixed-up life.

Yet, here in this flower garden was the evidence of a buried love of order and beauty. Now Kate noticed a dark, triangular leaf poking through the impatiens. She dropped to her knees to look. A weed—deadly nightshade. She pulled at it vigorously and the snakelike root came up, dirt clinging to it and scattering over the delicate little blooms of the impatiens on either side of it. She threw the weed as far as she could over the fence. But near the ground like this, she could see other weeds now: in the petunias, twining around the base of the rosebushes. Chaos reasserting itself the moment the careful hands were stilled. There were far too many for Kate to remove on this brief visit. She sighed and stood up, looking around her for a moment longer.

Her gaze fell on one large rose near the left edge of the back terrace. It was peach-colored, but the edges of the petals were darker, almost coppery. It was swaying slightly at the end of a long stem, so heavy that it seemed the thin stalk could just barely support it. Kate moved quickly now, cupped the blossom in her left hand, feeling the cool satiny undersurface of the petals against her fingers, and slipped her right hand carefully between thorns to the stem. She caught it near the base of the bush, made a quick snapping motion, and came away with the rose in her grasp.

She held the blossom against her face for a second, inhaling the rich, heavy aroma as she turned to leave the yard. Just this one, she thought. She would take this one home.

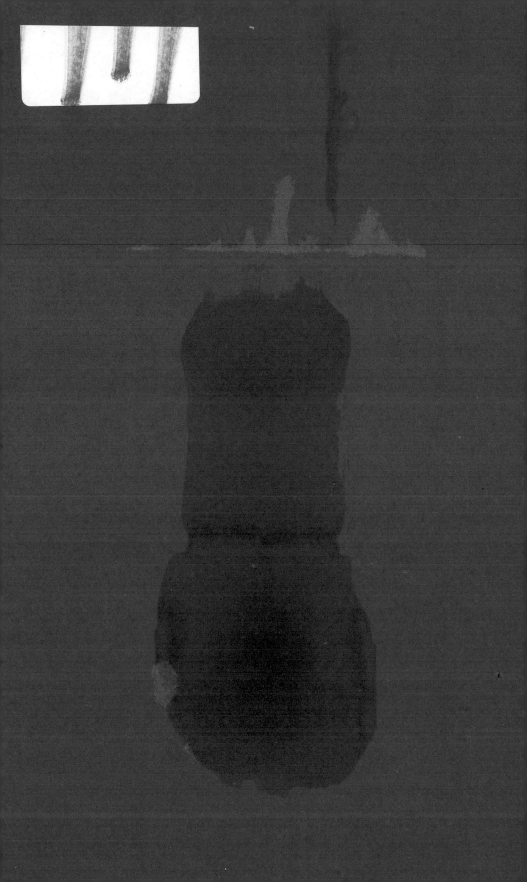